DETROIT PUBLIC LIBRARY
W9-BXE-134

GLAD RAGS

GLAD RAGS

BY
MACDONALD HARRIS

STORY LINE PRESS

1991

Second American Printing

Library of Congress Catalog Card Number:
90-52852

ISBN: 0-934257-34-5

Book design by Lysa McDowell

Published by Story Press, Inc.
d.b.a. Story Line Press
Three Oaks Farm
Brownsville, OR
97327-9718

At the age of fifty, Rilke went out in his garden to pluck a rose for a young girl. He pricked his finger on a thorn and died of blood poisoning. This book is dedicated to that girl.

In this May - December romance of contemporary Californians, a 58-year-old retired publisher falls in love with a harpsichord student less than half his age.

1.

Ben Gavilan was not a reckless man, or one ordinarily given to extravagant gestures; in all of his inclinations he was conservative and cautious. He dressed well in a subdued, rather old-fashioned way that used to be called Ivy League: tweed jackets with patches, flannel or khaki pants according to season, woolen neckties, Brooks Brothers shirts, and British walking shoes or Italian loafers. His only concession to flamboyance was that he liked to wear colorful socks—flamingo, magenta, puce, or orange—so that when you saw him coming in the distance he gave the impression of a pair of bright socks striding along by themselves and supporting an otherwise staid and conventional individual. The rest of his life, up to this point, was quite proper. His car, out of a desire not to be ostentatious, was a Mercedes but not a brand new one; and when he traveled he always went first class but stayed in rather old-fashioned, traditional, interesting hotels, which is why he was at Muir House in the

Sierras on this July weekend when the whole thing happened.

Leaving aside these accidentals, as Aristotle called them, features that are not permanently attached to a man but may be taken off like a pair of socks or added like a mustache, he was an educated man, well-read, intelligent, a graduate of a prestigious eastern university, independently wealthy, the publisher of a small press which was highly regarded although it had never made much money, still vigorous at fifty-eight but old enough to be wise in the ways of the world. He was the kind of a man who played Vivaldi on his car stereo, but he was not a musician. Divorced, but that wasn't his fault; everyone said he was easy to get along with. Attractive to women. (Young reader, do not imagine that you can't be at fifty-eight). He was keen, observant, discerning, one of those, as Henry James says, on whom nothing is lost. The idea occurs, in fact, that he was not too different from Lambert Strether, that incompetent Ambassador who ends up without the heroine and left out in the cold because he is too scrupulous. Up to that July weekend Ben had been a spectator of life rather than an active participant; in short the last person in the world you would expect to make a fool of himself by falling in love with a girl half his age.

2.

Muir House was built about a hundred years ago, in the late eighteen-eighties, in a valley at the top of a canyon on the western edge of the Sierras, about twenty miles from the flat farmland below. The valley was sculpted by glacial action and is surrounded by high polished granite cliffs; a small river winds through it, and the valley floor is covered with a thick forest of sequoias and redwoods. The altitude of the valley floor is nine thousand feet, enough to make it pleasantly cool in the summer, and to produce a heavy snowfall in the winter, but the proprietors of Muir House have never built a ski lift, feeling that this would attract the wrong kind of guests, vigorous young people in Porches with skis strapped to the top of their cars, who would probably drink too much in the evening.

The road up the canyon first passes through the small town of Muir, two miles from the hotel itself. As you continue on up the road it ends in a turnabout and a parking lot, and the hotel is partly visible through the trees, a fantastic rambling structure, a kind of Mad King Ludwig's Neuschwanstein recreated in shingles. Scattered in the forest around the hotel are a number of outbuildings and cabins, and Ben was staying in one of these cabins and not in the main building of the hotel.

When Muir House was built in the last century, there was only an unpaved road to it and everything had to be brought in by ox-team, including the stained-glass windows, the Chickering grand piano, and the French kitchen equipment. Nothing was spared to make it the showplace of the Sierras, a favorite resort of the wealthy from San Francisco and even from the East, from Boston and New York. It is still one of the best hotels in America; its dining room is internationally famous, recommended to tourists in guidebooks published in Europe. It is old-fashioned, of course, but it was precisely this sense of living in another century, of enjoying the opulent and reactionary ambiance of the Belle Epoque, that Ben liked about it.

In the summer season most of the employees of the hotel, including the dining room staff, are students who are combining a pleasant vacation with a summer job, and who live in a dormitory nearby in the forest.

3.

One of the customs at Muir House is that the guests share tables at breakfast. At Ben's table, the morning after his arrival, he met Henry Calendish, an editor of the University of California Press at Berkeley, with a specialty in European History. As soon as Henry learned that they were both involved in the world of publishing, he tacitly—without putting it into words, offering the idea simply through innuendo and implication—proposed an alliance of lonely middle-aged men. Ben wasn't lonely; he was used to staying in hotels alone. But he raised no objection. It was pleasant to have someone to talk to. Henry's conversation tended toward the obvious, but he was a friendly enough man, full of good will.

They spent a pleasant day together, hiking about the valley floor and afterwards sitting on a rock enjoying the wildflowers and the purling of the river under their feet. Henry made no comment on Ben's withered arm, which he disposed of by putting the hand in his pants pocket. He usually offered his left hand to people to shake, which sometimes caused a momentary embarrassment or confusion, but as a matter of fact he and Henry never shook hands, since they met at the breakfast table. Ben did catch him looking at the arm curiously now and then. Ben carried his lunch and his sweater in a light knapsack, which he was able to swing on with an adroit motion of his good arm, afterwards tucking the other hand into his pocket. He had learned to do almost everything that anyone else can to with two good arms, including driving a car, swimming, and even tennis when his opponent wasn't too skillful. Still, at his age walking had become his main form of exercise, and one he enjoyed very much. In the afternoon he and Henry walked down to the town of Muir to buy cigarettes for Henry and a bottle of Scotch for Ben, and then they came back at a leisurely pace along a path of pine needles at the side of the road.

A quarter of a mile or so from the hotel something happened to Ben, a kind of epiphany or premonition, like the aura that precedes the fit of the epileptic. It was mysterious, subtle, and pleasurable. It had something to do with odors, with a sudden perception of the mingled smells of the Sierras on a summer afternoon: the pines and redwoods, the warm sun on granite, the champagne-like tang of the river running over its stones. The sensation struck Ben with the force of a blow, as he and Henry came around a turn in the road. He told himself, *Something good is going to happen.* He felt extraordinarily happy. Of course he said nothing about this to Henry.

Dostoevsky, who was an epileptic himself, took a great interest in this aura that sometimes precedes the seizures of the disease. He, or his narrator, says in one place that "this feeling is so strong and sweet and for a few seconds of it one would give ten years of one's life, perhaps one's whole life." And Kirilov in *The Possessed* speaks of "seconds—they come five or six at a time—when you suddenly feel the presence of the eternal harmony again . . . man cannot endure it in his earthly aspect . . . there's something in it higher than love . . . I think man ought to give up having children—what's the use of children, what's the use of evolution when the goal has been attained?"

Thomas Mann is also highly interested in this subject, and he takes it up in his preface to a book called *Three Short Novels by Dostoevsky,* which is available only in

English; Mann never saw fit to publish this essay in German. He devotes a good part of his attention to the disease in both characters and author, and concludes, "In my opinion it is definitely rooted in the realm of the sexual, it is a wild and explosive manifestation of sex dynamics, a transfigured sexual act, a mystic dissipation."

So, perhaps, is a sneeze. It is preceded by a sensation that something pleasant, socially awkward but pleasant to the senses, is about to happen. Then the body goes out of control and expels something with a sudden violence. You are left feeling satisfied but a little embarrassed. Afterwards, there is a little fluid to be cleaned up with a handkerchief.

4.

Now it was eight o'clock and they were waiting for their table. The dining room was crowded. Ben and Henry sat in a row of leather chairs by the maitre's station, nursing their drinks from the bar. Ben had changed into an old soft tweed jacket and chinos, and Henry was wearing a corduroy jacket and a red bow tie, the proper uniform for a university press editor. Other people around them were standing. The maitre, in an immaculate white dinner jacket and a boutonniere, managed the crowd of people with aplomb, checking off the names one by one and hardly raising his voice when he called for a party.

Ben had his right hand tucked into his pocket as usual. He could light a match with it, or sign a credit card slip, but the arm wasn't strong enough to lift the glass. He was in excellent spirits, partly because he was looking forward to an excellent dinner, but partly also from the curious experience he had had on the path earlier in the afternoon. He was still in a placid state of contentment, knowing that he only had to wait and the *thing*, whatever it was, would surely happen without his lifting a finger to make it come. He remembered the sensation from the time when he was married — Erica was in the bathroom putting on her gown, while he lay on the bed with his hands behind his head, lazily watching the narrow band of light around the bathroom door.

5.

He looked down the shadowy cavern of the dining room at the glitter of linen, silver, and crystal on the tables, the bottles of wine glowing like rubies in the lamplight, the waitresses in their loose skirts with narrow black-and-white stripes, white stockings, and black shoes like ballet slippers.

He told Henry, "I like the people who work here. The students, I mean. They're far better than the staff in an ordinary hotel. They're more intelligent, for one thing. And more cheerful—they know they won't be doing this all their lives."

"I've always contended," said Henry, "that a good amateur is better at anything than a professional."

"Love for example."

"Ha!" said Henry. "Ha ha! That's right. It's called sex now, you know. I think you must be the last man in the world to call it love."

"Do you think it's an improvement that what used to be called love is now called sex?"

"No I don't."

"Neither do I." Ben felt a certain camaraderie between them. Up to now they hadn't discovered very much that they had in common. "I suppose I'm an old-fashioned sentimentalist. I don't care for a good many things that people do these days."

"Have you known a good many amateurs?" said Henry, smiling at him in a speculative and roguish way.

"Amateurs? Oh, I see what you mean. Well, quite a few in my time. Not so many recently." He hesitated and then asked him, "Are you married?"

In spite of their day together they had never exchanged this essential piece of information. "No," said Henry. "Never got around to it. Women are damned funny creatures. I can't say I understand them. I've never had much to do with them to tell the truth. I haven't had time. There's one in the Press office . . ." He sipped his drink and stopped dead. "And you?"

"I've been divorced for ten years."

"Ha! What should I offer? Commiserations or congratulations?"

"Neither. It was just a thing that happened."

"You know what they say about women. You can't get along with them and you can't get along without them. Well, I've been able to get along without them well enough."

"Good for you," said Ben. He too got along perfectly well without them for ten years, except for Ethel Track. Ethel was an old friend he saw now and then. He had known her from the time of his marriage. He didn't think he wanted to explain to Henry his very complicated and totally platonic relations with Ethel.

"I'm glad to have escaped. Vain, empty-headed, narcissistic creatures that they are," said Henry. "Just look back over history and see all the trouble that they've caused. I'm a historian and I know what I'm talking about. And what have they contributed? You'll say babies. Well, there ought to be a better way to do that. It isn't fashionable these days," he said sipping his drink, "to talk like this."

"No it isn't."

"How can you possibly take a sex seriously when their whole life is devoted to a narcissistic concern with their bodies? The amount of time they spend just fooling around with their hair. Splashing themselves with scent. Painting their faces. Putting on false eyelashes and false fingernails. Can you imagine a man doing that?"

"In some other culture, perhaps."

"That's it, they're another culture. They ought to be studied by anthropologists. Their strange customs. Their primitive mentalities. Their ways of mutilating their bodies. The mysterious rites they practice that are unknown in our culture."

"Mysterious rites?"

"I mean, shopping for example. Spending the whole afternoon going to malls with some other woman, not because they need anything but because they had something they could buy on impulse. Did you ever know a man who did that?"

"I can't say I have."

"All they think about is sex, but they won't give it away unless they get something in return. After all the talk about liberation, they still conceive of their bodies as a way to get ahead in the world. This woman in the Press office that I was telling you about. She's been my rival for years. She finally got the promotion I was in line for. And do you know how?"

"I can't imagine."

"Well, I won't go into details."

"I see."

The suave maitre, evidently a student himself, was at their elbow. "Your table is ready now, Mr. Calendish."

"Ah. Ah. Splendid."

6.

Henry had requested his favorite table, at the side of the room near the fireplace, where he could sit with his back to the wall and look out at the other diners. "I always have this table when I stay here," he said. "You might think it would delay things when you request a particular table. Actually it makes them respect you, and you get seated more quickly than you would otherwise."

Henry now turned his attention to his wine glass. He picked it up and looked into it as though it were a spyglass. Then he took his napkin and wiped the glass carefully inside and out, holding it up and looking into it again when he was done. After a moment of silence he did the same with his dinner plate, wiping it on both sides and inspecting it afterwards. Then it was the turn of the silverware. When he had polished the knife, the two forks, and the spoon he dropped the napkin on the floor.

"There are germs everywhere," he said. "This is an excellent dining room. Still you never can tell. It's never a good idea," he said, "to visit the kitchen in your favorite restaurant, no matter how much you trust it."

"I suspect you're right."

Ben was beginning to see that Henry Calendish was a typical cranky bachelor. Perhaps it was a mistake to get involved with him. Henry got out a slim paisley case and took a pair of Franklin glasses from it. He put these on with a precise gesture of his thumb and middle finger, as though he were measuring a very small fish. Ben put on his own reading glasses, which he used only when he had to; he thought they made him look older than he really was, or more studious. They both began studying the menu.

Ben was aware of a presence at his side, just beyond the edge of his peripheral vision. There was a faint pleasant odor. She said in her matter-of-fact voice,

"Good evening. I'm Cecilia and I'll be your waitress for the evening."

"Could you bring me another napkin?" said Henry.

She went off to another table and came back with a fresh napkin, which she set down by Henry's plate.

"Are you ready to order now?"

"H'mm. I th-i-ink we are," said Henry, still peering at the menu through his spectacles.

He ordered the most banal thing on the menu, the crab cocktail and the prime rib. Ben didn't get a very good look at the waitress at this time because he still had his eyes fixed on the menu. He was aware of someone standing by his side and a little behind him; he could catch a glimpse of black-and-white skirt at the corner of his eye. He considered the various items of seafood on the menu; he almost never ate red meat, because with his withered arm it was difficult for him to cut it and someone would have to do it for him. After a moment he ordered the Coquilles Saint-Jacque à la menthe and the Croustade de Homard au Whiskey. The wines, a California Chardonnay for him , a Merlot for Henry. At this point, as she was writing down the order on her pad, Ben looked up at the waitress for the first time and fell helplessly and hopelessly in love with her.

7.

"Why were you staring at the waitress?" asked Henry.

"Was I?"

"Looked like you'd seen a ghost."
"I didn't realize I was doing it."

8.

Like a man who had an accident and finds himself lying on the pavement with everything buzzing, Ben attempted to sort out his sensations. He knew his life was permanently changed from this moment, even if he never saw her again, and he was filled with a flood of euphoria. At the same time another part of him was appalled. A waitress, a student! He was twice her age. He attempted to pretend that it hadn't happened, to get his nerves in order and go on as he had before. This was impossible.

9.

She came back with the hors-d'oeuvres and served them without a word. Ben examined her covertly as she set the plates on the table. Taken apart from his extraordinary reaction to her, she seemed a quite ordinary young woman. He noticed the fine structure of her face, the fragile hands and wrists. The slightly full lips, which seemed too large for the rest of her face, were the only sign of sensuality in her features. She wore her hair in an unusual way, some of it loose and the rest of it gathered into two braids with flowers plaited into them, poppies he thought. This made her seem even younger than she was.

She opened the two bottles of wine. No sommelier at Muir House; the students did it all. Ben and Henry went through the wordless ritual of tasting them and nodded to her. She filled their glasses, then she folded up the corkscrew and put it into the pocket of her dress. In a moment she would go away. Ben was desperate to keep her standing at the table a little longer.

"I understand that most of you who work here are students."

"That's right."

"Where do you go to school?"

"At Berkeley."

"And what are you studying?" he went on, trying to speak in an even and matter-of-fact tone.

"Music."

"Music history?"

"No, performance. I'm a harpsichordist."

"That's an unusual instrument. I imagine not many people play it."

"There are four of us studying it in the department," she said simply. "There are other people playing dulcimers, sackbuts, and krumhorns."

"How very interesting. My friend Mr. Calendish is at Berkeley too. He's an editor of the University Press."

"Ah." After a pause she said, "Will there be anything else?"

"No."

"Enjoy your meal."

She was friendly, casual, and perfectly cool. She smiled and went away, and Ben was left with Henry again.

"Are you in the custom of striking up acquaintances with waitresses?"

"No. I don't know why I did it this time."

"It's not a good plan, I think. They respect you less. The best thing is to be polite and distant."

"I suspect you're right."

"And if you're going to reveal details of private life, I'd rather you revealed your own rather than mine."

"I'm sorry."

"It's not important. Still I don't like to go around wearing a badge with my job described on it."

They ate their hors-d'oeuvres in silence. Henry folded up his glasses and dug into his crab cocktail with a little fork. Ben picked away at his scallops with mint, sipping now and then at the wine. Like everyone newly in love he was acutely aware of every sensation, the crisp chill texture of the scallops, the delicate coulis of mint, the discreet tang of the wine.

"If you weren't such a level-headed chap," said Henry, "I would think you were struck with that girl."

"Struck?"

"Had a fancy for her."

"She's only a schoolgirl," said Ben. "You must be mad."

"Whatever you say," said Henry.

10.

In ten minutes she was back carrying the trays with the entrees. She set them on the stand, then she cleared away the dishes from the first course. Ben watched her do these things as though she were performing a magic trick and he had under pain of death to guess its secret. Her little finger trailed a little after the others, a minor negligence that had something aristocratic about it. Covertly he studied the creases at the side of her mouth as she set down his plate, holding it in a napkin, and removed the cover. In the lamplight her eyelash left a tiny shadow on her cheek. He noticed that her fingernails were not quite clean.

They exchanged a glance, and he imagined he detected a hint of understanding or complicity in her expression. Probably it was only a way she had. He turned his attention to the food before him. At the edge of the plate was a garnish of slivered vegetables and a tomato carved into a rose, and in the center was the lobster in its pastry shell. He set his fork into the pastry and it broke with a sound like crushed tissue paper. He lifted the fork to his mouth and savored the taste of the dish. The flesh of the lobster mingled with the crushed pastry; and the sauce with its hint of whiskey and some other flavoring, perhaps sage or coriander. Never since he was young had his senses been so keen. Lost in these sensations, he almost forgot why everything about him had this new and piercing vividness.

Henry was sawing away at his prime rib. "Your lobster all right?"

"Fine."

"Should have got that myself. I always have the roast beef. Want to trade a little?"

"No."

Henry looked at him oddly. "Are you feeling all right?"

"I'm feeling wonderful."

"Not a bad wine."

"Mine's excellent."

Henry sipped his Merlot, pursed his lips, and rolled it around in his mouth. He swallowed it and said, "I prefer California wines really. When I'm in California that is. When I'm in Europe I drink French wines. *Il faut toujours boire le vin du pays*, that's my policy."

"Oh, why don't you shut up."

"What?"

"You're rattling on about the wine. It's perfectly ordinary wine. And you swill it around in your mouth like that, it's disgusting. Your French is rotten too."

"There is something wrong with you. Did your dinner disagree with you?"

"I tell you I'm feeling fine. Stop chattering so."

"All right. I must say you're acting very queerly. You've probably drunk too much wine. You've finished the whole damn bottle."

"That's very likely it."

11.

As inconspicuously as he could, Ben looked over his shoulder to see if he could catch sight of her. He was behaving like a schoolboy. He felt like one too. He watched while Henry got out a cigarette and lighted it. Henry was the kind of a person who smoked between the courses of a meal. His cigarettes were oval Muratti Aristons in a hard cardboard box with a red stripe on it. Ordinarily Ben would have been interested in Henry as a queer specimen of mankind, a bit player in the amusing little drama of his weekend in the Sierras; now his mind was on other things. He calculated how long it would be until he saw her again. Probably five minutes, he told himself.

12.

She came back once during the meal to ask if everything was all right. They said it was. When the time came for dessert Ben still spoke only the necessary minimum to her; he remembered Henry's advice that you shouldn't strike up acquaintances with waitresses. Of course, she wasn't a waitress, she was the person he loved, but Henry didn't know this. It was a secret he fervently wished to conceal from him. When the two bills came, Ben signed for his but he didn't add a tip to the total; instead he left the cash for her on the tray. This way he could be sure she would get it and it wouldn't simply disappear into the accounts of the hotel. He calculated the size of the tip with care. It was too large, more than fifteen percent, but not large enough that it could be taken for a mistake. He planned exactly the impression he wanted to make: that of an affluent and well-dressed diner, friendly but not for the present making any personal overture, who left her a larger than ordinary tip in cash. He thought she would remember. On the bill he wrote, "Thanks for excellent service." Henry got out a pocket calculator and figured his tip to the penny, wrote it on the bill, and added up the sum. She took away the two trays without a word. Ben watched her go off down the room, the braids with their flowers swinging on her narrow back.

13.

In Ben's Hansel-and-Gretel cabin in the forest, there was a small living room with a fireplace at one end and a kitchenette at the other; beyond were the bedroom and the bath. He thought, *She is still in the dining room, only a hundred yards away. If she chose to, she could come here.* This thought made him giddy.

He had planned to read, have a drink from the Scotch he bought earlier in the afternoon, and go to bed. Instead he decided on impulse to build a fire in the fireplace. There was an ample supply of kindling and split pinewood. He soon had a fire burning briskly, snapping and sending up coils of gray smoke tinged with orange. The odor of burning firewood, a pungence he had forgotten since the camping days of his youth, filled the room. He raised his hands to his face to smell the pine he had handled. All his senses were intensified; every nerve stood erect and his blood stirred with a subdued excitement.

He poured his drink, a little larger than usual, and sat sipping it and looking into the fire. He was still a little bewildered by this thing that had happened to him. He had fallen in love at fifty-eight with a girl young enough to be his daughter. No, he calculated, it was far worse than that. If everybody in question started having children at eighteen, as some people do, he was old enough to be her grandfather. It was ludicrous. But his own feelings were unmistakable. There was no question now of pretending that he could go on with his life as he had before.

His chances of success, he knew, were tiny, considering his age, and considering that she no doubt had flocks of friends her own age who were interested in her. He was a realist and he knew the world, and he had never had any illusions about himself or his specialness in the universe. He was a clever persuasive person who had succeeded in most things he had tried in life; he was well educated, he dressed well, and women were attracted to him in spite of his withered arm, or perhaps because of it. He spent a great deal of time fending off unwanted advances from women his own age who found an affluent divorcé, with only a trace of gray in his hair, too tempting to resist. But this was different. In this he was asking for the laws of the universe to be suspended in his favor. He was asking for a miracle.

I have to have her, he told himself. I have to have her or my life from now on will have absolutely no meaning. I have to think of some subterfuge. Perhaps I could offer to sponsor her career as a musician if she would agree to move to Santa Barbara and live somewhere near me. No, that's insane. Think, man, think, he told himself. You're intelligent, you've been a success in the publishing world, and you're good at solving problems. Now here's a big one for you. There has got to be some way to arrange your life and hers so that you can see her every day, even if you're never allowed to touch her. The thought that he might not be allowed to touch her scared the hell out of him. He wanted to touch her. He thought about all the places he wanted to touch her and this almost made him faint. He took another sip of his drink.

Maybe, he thought, I could move to Berkeley and hire her as my assistant to do research for me. Research in what? It would have to be music, otherwise why would it be her that he had to hire? Of course, he really didn't know anything about music. And she was a harpsichordist not a music historian. Maybe he could persuade her to take an interest in music history. He took another sip of the Scotch, a long one this time.

14.

Young and beautiful women are more necessary to the old than to the young. To the young they are just people like themselves. For the old they are infinitely precious beings, talismans that can reawaken in them all the vigors and splendors of their own youth. Of course, there is a moral law that says this is indecent. This can be dismissed with contempt, in an age which has banished morality from sexual relations and declares that everything is good that feels good. A more serious objection is that young women have their own ideas about these matters and are free to dispose of themselves as they please. In the ordinary course of things, they don't give themselves to men twice their age. But this is wrong of them and shows a lack of open-mindedness. They really don't have enough experience of life to make such decisions; they are too valuable to be allowed to dispose of themselves so lightly. How often we see a pretty young woman in the company of some young man who is patently an idiot, vain, self-centered, untalented, brutish, having nothing in his favor except a pair of well-tended mustaches. It is against all justice that pretty women should be handed over to such empty-headed pups.

15.

Ben was still emotionally young, full of high thoughts, entitled to beauty, life, and happiness as much as anyone else. His age was his own business, and hers. If she should choose to ignore it then nobody else had the right to criticize. Growing old is part of the human condition. You could no more reproach a man for being fifty-eight than you could reproach him eventually for dying. He had not chosen his condition, that is, that he got older every year whether he wanted to or not, and it was one he shared with every mortal human being. If he found himself suddenly and improbably in love, he had the same right to this feeling as a younger person. It is the privilege of the lover to cast reason to the winds. All his life he had been a rational person who had behaved sensibly. Now he was not behaving sensibly; he was a feeling and desiring creature, a soul so fierce that it transcended body, an angel. A wicked angel perhaps, a dark angel in Cecilia's life, but even dark angels had their part in happiness. If she wanted a dark angel, if she chose to love a man of fifty-eight, then the Heavens had approved.

In his rational mind he knew that these were very strange arguments, with an element of the ridiculous in them. The ridiculous, not the immoral, was his true enemy; the world would find that he cut a foolish figure. But the foolishness of man is the wisdom of God. If he succeeded, then his foolishness would fall away and he would be more happy than he had ever imagined he could be. It is one of the qualities of being in love that it induces unrealistic expectations; in spite of all the odds he held out to himself the improbable hope that she would return his love, and in a part of his mind he believed this totally. He had to believe in it, or all this structure of happiness and bliss that he had erected in his mind would vanish. He believed in it with the faith of a religious believer, terrified of Judgement and knowing his own unworth. There were a lot of religious analogies. Ben was not religious and this copious welling-up in him of spiritual sentiments was the final proof that his feelings were genuine.

He poured himself a second drink, a thing he almost never did before going to bed, and sat with it for about an hour, staring at the images that played in the licking flame. Fire, he thought, was primitive man's equivalent of television, a mesmerizing light-source that people watch at night. If it didn't have any content neither did television. He preferred his own thoughts anyhow.

When the fire died down he put out the light and got into bed, pleasantly drunk. In the light of the embers still glowing in the next room, the bedroom was pink and wavering, a faery chamber. The dying fire snapped at intervals. After a while, when he had almost fallen asleep, he heard a faint sound as though of many spiders walking around on the shingles of the cabin above him; it increased gradually until it became a steady patter. To be in a safe dry place with the rain falling outside was a thing that had given him pleasure all his life. Now the sensation came to him with a keen acuteness, as though he were knowing it for the first time. He felt an extraordinary happiness. *The premonition on the path. This was what it meant*, he told himself. With the rain rustling on the roof, and the alcohol seeping through his veins, he fell asleep like a child.

16.

The next day was Sunday. He had planned to leave on Monday morning, but after breakfast he called at the desk and arranged to extend his stay indefinitely. Now he could plan his strategy with care, taking the necessary time for each step so that the whole thing would seem quite spontaneous or accidental, to Cecilia and to everyone else. If only he could get rid of that pest Henry Calendish. He successfully avoided him at breakfast by coming an hour earlier than usual. He spent the day visiting a nature museum in the town of Muir, renting a bicycle and touring around the valley floor, hiking to a waterfall and examining a sign explaining its geology, the usual banal tourist activities to tire him and give him an appetite for dinner. He kept a watch for Henry out of the corner of his eye but saw no sign of him. At four he swam in the pool at Muir House, then went back to his cabin, showered, and dressed with care. He sat in the bar drinking until seven.

Henry always ate dinner at the same time, eight o'clock. He was sure to avoid him if he went in an hour earlier. When he entered the dining room it was half empty, and most of the diners were older couples or families with children. The fashionable crowd came later.

He told the maitre, "I want the same table that Mr. Calendish and I had last night." He had to be in Cecilia's service area and he wasn't sure where it was. He knew that the table he and Henry had was in it.

The youthful maitre in his white dinner jacket was blasé and deferential. "Which one is that, Mr. Gavilan?"

"Next to the wall. The one just this side of the fireplace."

"That's a table for two, Mr. Gavilan."

"Yes I know. I don't think you have any tables for one."

"We usually put single parties at the small tables on the other side."

"Well, this time you can do it another way."

"Very well."

The maitre led him down the room. He was soon seated at the table. Now the problem was that Henry might come in earlier than usual and attempt to join him.

"Could you take that other chair away, please?"

"I beg your pardon?"

"The other chair. Take it away. Is there something wrong with your hearing?"

"Why, Mr. Gavilan?"

"Because it reminds me that I'm eating alone and I don't like it."

"Then Mr. Calendish won't be joining you?"

"No."

Let him think that he and Henry were a couple of old fairies and were having a quarrel. He could think whatever he wanted.

The second chair was taken away. Ben studied the menu, or pretended to. After five minutes or so he was aware of someone standing at his elbow.

"Good evening. I'm Cecilia and I'll ... Oh, hello." She smiled; she had recognized him.

He asked her advice on the hors-d'oeuvres; she recommended the pâté maison, but he said he didn't eat pork. Would she take him for Jewish? It didn't matter. He decided on the smoked salmon with dill. For the main dish, the seafood crepes, with a Chardonnay as before.

"You had seafood last night too."

"I don't eat red meat. I don't mind fish or poultry."

Had she noticed his withered arm? His real reason for not eating red meat, which had nothing to do with pork or being Jewish. She didn't seem to be staring at it, but she didn't seem to be avoiding it either; her eyes fell on all parts of him naturally.

"Where's your friend tonight?"

"He has leprosy. It was a sudden attack."

"Oh, I'm so sorry." She smiled. "He seemed like a nice man."

"He's a bore."

This light repartee was the sum of their conversation. She served the rest of the meal in silence, except for the ritual question in the middle as to whether everything was all right. Again he left her a tip in cash, slightly too large. He felt he was giving exactly the right impression. He was a man older than she, well-dressed, a person of culture, friendly, affluent, well-mannered and with a sense of humor, staying in the hotel by himself, and he was interested in her but only in a proper and gentlemanly way. This time as she gathered up the bill and the cash their eyes met and she seemed to show a trace of interest, or curiosity; something changed in her smile. She held his glance for a moment then turned away without speaking.

As he left the dining room he passed Henry waiting for

his table. It was about a quarter to eight. Ben smiled; Henry said nothing, but his face was as red as a tomato and he pursed his lips angrily.

17.

The next morning at breakfast, however, Henry caught him. He had guessed the secret of Ben's tactics and came a little earlier himself. He sat down at the table and flounced his arms around as he picked up the menu.

"You are a strange one, aren't you?"

"I am?"

"Last night I stood watching you for ten minutes as you finished your dinner. You were behaving very strangely."

"I don't know what you mean by that."

"First of all you came early and took my table, even though you knew it was the one I wanted. Then you went to pains to have the same waitress that we had the night before."

"Yes I did. She's a nice girl. An excellent waitress."

"You're making a fool of yourself."

"Well, I've done that before."

"And you betrayed a friendship."

"Oh really, Henry. We'd only known each other for one day."

"Still. There were things that were said. And things unsaid."

"I didn't notice them."

"You misled me, Ben."

"I did?"

"Of course you did."

"I don't know what you're talking about."

"I thought we had something in common."

"No doubt we do."

"You know what I mean."

"No I don't."

"I thought you would prefer me to—that girl."

"So you're gay?"

"Come now, Ben! You knew that."

"No, Henry. I didn't really know. Or perhaps I did know in a part of my mind, but I just didn't come to grips with it. I've never had the slightest attraction to other men. I don't feel that way at all. I'm sorry. That's just the way it is."

Henry, red-faced, said nothing. Ben looked around at the other guests in the dining room. The maitre, not the one who worked in the evening but another one, also a student, was just passing the table as they were having their discussion in elevated tones and quite probably overheard them.

18.

At four o'clock that afternoon Ben approached Muir House from the rear along a trail through the forest. He had been walking along the river upstream from the hotel, in a direction he hadn't been before. The first building that came into sight was the dormitory for the summer student workers. Beyond it the trail led into a triangular open space between the dormitory and the hotel, planted with ferns and young pines. It was very quiet; a light wind brushed in the trees. Over the sound of his footfall on the gravel he heard voices, and some instinct made him stop. Concealed by the pines, he had a view ahead through the branches. A few yards away, at the rear door of the hotel, Cecilia was talking to a bellman in a brown uniform embroidered in gold. He could see the two of them only imperfectly through the trees, but her voice was unmistakable.

He couldn't go ahead through the pines; he would have to go directly past the doorway where they were standing. And he couldn't retreat; if he came out into the open he would be clearly visible to them. He stayed where he was.

The male voice was so low it was only a murmur. Cecilia's higher voice carried better, and now and then he caught a word. *Silly. Nothing at all.* The male voice replied in a long complicated sentence with many phrases, stops, and turns; its tone was angry. Cecilia laughed. *He's sweet on me. It's perfectly natural. What do you care?*

The bellman's reply was inaudible. The voices ended and for a few moments there was no sound but the sighing of the wind in the trees. When Ben looked out from his hiding place the two figures were gone. He skirted past the rear entrance to the hotel, crossed the lawn to a footbridge over a creek, and went on down the path to his cabin.

19.

In the bathroom he switched on the light and stood looking at his reflection in the mirror, grimacing as though he were trying to dislodge a fly from his cheek and noticing the changes it made in his face. He had a funny sensation and he couldn't decide at first whether it was pleasant or not. He hadn't imagined that Cecilia would have noticed his feelings for her so quickly, or that the others in the hotel would have been aware of it too. Now it seemed they were all talking about it. Probably the maitre told the others about his request for a table, and his little quarrel with Henry at breakfast had been overheard. He was a little appalled at the turn events had taken. Something that existed, as he thought, only in his secret feelings had become public, a thing to be discussed by others, a thing that could be talked about in banal and silly slang: *He's sweet on me.*

He studied the slick blue reflection in the glass more carefully, examining its features one by one. His face was the same as always. It was square and tanned and had an engaging look to it. His hair was thinning but still dark except for a touch of gray at the temples. The light from the overhead fixture came at an angle that left dramatic theatrical shadows on his face. It was years since he had looked at himself carefully in a mirror, and he found the image more attractive than he expected. It could be the face of a fifty-year-old film star, the professor or scientist that the young girls fall in love with in a light entertaining comedy. All his doubts, his suspicions that the others were laughing at him, disappeared in a burst of confidence. He had made an important discovery, one he knew when he was younger but had forgotten, that being in love not only makes the person you love seem unnaturally beautiful but it makes you more beautiful too.

20.

That night when he went to dinner there was a contretemps. It was a little after seven, the same time as the night before. Since it was Monday and the weekend was over the room was only two-thirds full, and there was no one at the table by the fireplace. He told the maitre, "The same table, please." He pointed to it.

"I'm sorry, Mr. Calendish has reserved that table for tonight."

"But he comes at eight."

"He's asked us to reserve it every evening while he's here. Mr. Calendish is an old friend of Muir House. He's been coming here for years."

"So have I."

The maitre shrugged with a little smile. He was somewhat older than Cecilia, Ben noticed now. Perhaps he was not a student at all; certainly he was a very distinguished and suave personage.

Ben said, "Then I want another table near it."

"Near it?"

"Yes." After a pause he was forced to add, "In Cecilia's service area." He colored a little but stuck to his request.

After a silence the maitre said, "All right." Not his usual "Very well;" this was shorter and less deferential. He led Ben down the room and sat him at a table for four. This time Ben didn't ask for the extra chairs to be taken away. The maitre handed him the menu, bowed a little coldly, it seemed to him, and left without a word.

"Hello," said Cecilia. "Are you expecting three friends?"

"No. I'm expecting you. And here you are."

His interest in her had become a joke between them. He wondered if after all she had seen him through the pine branches and knew that he overheard her conversation with the bellman.

She had flowers plaited into her hair as usual, but these were a different kind; they looked like violets of some sort. Perhaps she gathered wildflowers in the forest to put into her hair; there wasn't a florist in town as far as he knew. He noticed for the first time a tiny mole on her cheek just at the edge of her mouth. It was the place where the ladies of the court of Versailles put beauty spots because Madame de Maintenon had a mole at that place. He found this detail so exciting that he could hardly contain himself.

With a steely effort at calm he ordered his two courses, selecting a Colombard this time instead of the Chardonnay. She wrote it down and went away, seeming exactly as she had before. A busboy came and removed the three place settings. Ben looked around the room; there was no sign of Henry and the table by the fireplace was still empty.

He ate his meal in silence, broken only by her stop at the table about halfway through to inquire whether everything was all right. Even this brief visit gave him an intense pleasure. She smiled in her cryptic way, a smile that meant nothing at all and was perhaps only mechanical, and went away.

He drank the whole bottle of wine and it seemed to have no effect on him. As he was pouring the last of it into his glass he turned and saw Henry Calendish being seated at his table by the maitre. He glanced at his watch; it was exactly eight. Henry sat down, shot his cuffs, got out his Franklin glasses, put them on, and began studying the menu. Then he put the menu down, took off the glasses, and stared at Ben across the room with an expression as blank as a fish.

Ben smiled cheerfully at him. He felt a little ashamed of the way he had behaved toward Henry. He was a decent enough fellow, and you couldn't object to a middle-aged bachelor developing a few odd habits. It was simply another way of saying that he was lonely. If he was in love as Ben was, Ben felt sorry for him. Never matter that his love was ludicrous. So was Ben's. However he didn't feel sorry enough for him to invite him to his table.

When Cecilia brought the bill at the end of the meal

she lingered a little to talk, although the room was filling up now and she must have had other things to do.

"Are you staying alone at Muir House?" she asked him.

"Yes."

"That can't be much fun."

"I'm used to it."

"You have an unusual name," she said.

He wondered if she had taken the trouble to find out his name from the maitre or the bellman. Then he realized she had seen his signature on the dinner check. "It's Spanish."

"Are you Spanish then?"

"No. I'm originally from New England. Now I live in Santa Barbara."

"Alone?"

"Yes."

They both fell silent at this, and then he said, "I imagine you have lots of friends here at the hotel."

"Friends?"

"The other students."

"Oh," she said, "not particularly. I've got to know one or two. Most of them don't interest me."

"So you don't socialize with them much?"

"No."

"What do you do on your days off?"

"Oh, various things. There are hikes you can take. I swim sometimes. Not here at the hotel; they don't allow that. I go to the public pool in town."

"Alone?"

She laughed at this. They were playing a game in which they were two lonely people. "Sometimes. Other times with a friend."

"I like hiking too. Can you recommend a good trail for me? Not too strenuous."

"There's Moon Lake. It's an easy hike. About an hour."

"When's your next day off?"

"Tomorrow as a matter of fact."

"Perhaps we could go to Moon Lake together."

She hesitated for an instant while his heart raced. Then she said, "All right. That would be nice."

"Where can we meet?"

"Oh, anywhere. At the rear of the hotel by the pool. The trail starts there."

"Shall we say eleven o'clock? We can take our lunch."

"All right."

He signed the check and added his usual tip in cash. When she took the tray she slipped the money into the pocket of her dress, he noticed. This casual and yet mercenary gesture excited him, as though she had touched him with her hand.

21.

Ben was out on the lawn behind the hotel a little before eleven. He was in khaki pants and a windbreaker and he had a knapsack with two box lunches in it, provided by the kitchen of the hotel. Cecilia appeared exactly at eleven. Perhaps she was punctual because for her too it was an important moment, the first step in their love (here his heart leaped like Wordsworth's when he saw the rainbow). She showed no signs of being in love. She was exactly as she had been in the dining room except that her costume was different; she was wearing corduroy shorts and an oversized white sweater with the sleeves pushed up on her arms, and she too had a light knapsack, evidently the book bag she used on the Berkeley campus. He had grown so used to seeing her in her waitress's uniform that this gave him an eerie feeling, as though she were someone else impersonating herself. She had done her hair in the usual way, in two braids with flowers in them. Today they were poppies.

"Hi," she said.

This youthful vocable reminded of him of their difference in ages. He said, "Hello."

"What's in the bag?"

"Our lunches. What's in yours?"

"You don't ask what's in a woman's bag. A book, a hairbrush, and a canteen."

"You won't need the canteen. There's wine in the lunch."

"Shall I go ahead? I know the way."

"All right."

She set off through a gap in the trees at the edge of the lawn, and he followed. The trail led over a sandy valley floor scattered with pine needles and on through the big redwoods and sequoias. She had turned up the corduroy shorts as far as they would go, showing her long legs with their translucent complexion. This made him feel warm and he tried to look at something else. It would have been better if he had gone ahead, he thought.

"It may rain," she called from ahead.

There were broken white clouds overhead, but to the west the clouds were darker, a heavy band of shadow. It was strange, the trail was deserted and there were no other people about. It was possibly because it was no longer a weekend; still it was July and the middle of the season. They had gone only about a half a mile up the trail when they encountered a pair of mule deer, a doe and a fawn. The fawn had only been born that spring; it was very small, hardly larger than a cat. It was spotted, and the doe was a clear gray with fringes of black. They were very elegant; they might have been a mother and child from a fashion magazine. They stepped delicately, printing the pine needles with their tiny hoofs. The doe's large ears erected in their direction like antennae and flopped down again. The two deer trotted in a wide circle around them, turning once to look back, then they disappeared into the trees at the other side of the clearing.

"Aren't they beautiful!"

"They're both females," he told her.

"Is that significant?"

"You never see the bucks on the valley floor. Either they don't come down out of the high country, or they're better at concealing themselves."

"Men are smarter than women," she said.

The trail began working its way up the mountain wall to the left. The valley narrowed to a steep canyon; above them was the lake that was their destination. The sun was gone now and the clouds overhead were darker. A drop of water spattered into the dust on the trail, and he felt another strike his face.

"Get out your bumbershoot," she called to him, her voice ringing cleanly in the silence of the canyon.

"I have a hood on my jacket. It's your beautiful sweater I'm worried about."

"It's Irish wool. It's been washed many times. A little rain won't hurt it."

The trail came out into a small clearing; beyond that it mounted up again through the rocks. As they started across the clearing something appeared on the trail ahead; at first he thought it was another deer, then he decided it was a dog. It was thin and long-legged, a rib-cage on four sticks, with a small sharp head and oversized eyes. It stopped and looked at them, scenting the air with its nose.

"I'll be darned. A coyote."

It was quite unafraid of them; it went on watching them for a few moments and then it trotted off the trail into the trees at the side. Twice he saw a moving patch of brown through the leaves, then a few yards behind them it came out onto the trail again. It stopped and turned its head and stared deliberately at them with a look of complicity in its manner. It said to Ben, *I don't judge what you're doing, so don't you judge what I'm doing.*

He told Cecilia, "He's coming down in the hope of getting that fawn. He's probably following its scent."

"Do you think he'll succeed?"

"He seems to know what he's doing."

"I hope he doesn't."

They had both assumed that the coyote with its quite mechanical rapacity was a male. There was no evidence for it; if he had genitals he concealed them cleverly. The last they saw of him he was headed with a brisk purpose down toward the valley floor.

22.

They sat down on a rock at the edge of the lake. The lake was not very large and it was crescent-shaped, thus its name. He had expected that there would be something lunar and mysterious about it. In the perfectly still air the water reflected the trees on the other side as in an old-fashioned romantic painting, a Boecklin. Here and there a dimple of rain appeared on the glossy surface.

"Cecilia—" He stopped. "Do you know, how odd, how grotesque and improbably, I don't even know your last name."

"I'm Cecilia Penn."

"Do you think you could manage to call me Ben?"

"It would be silly to call you Mr. Gavilan."

"I can hardly believe that I have got you here alone with me."

She said, "It does seem odd what's happened." But it was casually, without particular interest, as though they had met on a street corner by chance, or turned out to be second cousins. There were lupines growing at the edge of the lake, and she lazily picked some and set them one by one on the rock beside her. She undid the braids in her hair; the poppies were wilted and she threw them away. Then she began making new braids and plaiting the lupines into them. Something about the way she did this, the classic gesture of the lifted arms and the hands held behind the slightly inclined head, gave Ben a sensation as though he had been stabbed with a fine, very sharp stiletto.

"So you play the harpsichord?"

"Yes. I've been studying it since I was thirteen. I have one more year at Berkeley. Then perhaps I'll study more in Europe."

She was still braiding the flowers into her hair, and his attention was caught once again by her fingernails, which he had noticed the first night when she served him in the dining room. At the end of each one was a little shadow, a crescent of embedded dirt, an unexpected revelation of a childish bad habit, of something slovenly in her otherwise immaculate and self-assured person, a hint of the perverse.

"And after that?" he asked her.

"I don't know."

"Can you make your living as a harpsichordist?"

"There aren't many chances to play. But then there aren't many harpsichordists. Not good ones."

After a while, finishing with her braids, she inquired casually, "Do you like music?" It seemed to him that their whole future, the whole question of whether they were to have a future, hung poised on this question which she posed so lightly.

"Oh yes," he told her. "I'm a patron of the chamber music society in Santa Barbara. I don't go to every concert, but I go to quite a few."

"And do you play some instrument?"

"No. I'm a bad amateur pianist, but I wouldn't dream of letting you catch me at it."

Her eyes wondered for a second how he was able to play the piano, even badly, with his withered hand. Then she said, "And you're a publisher."

"I was until recently. I've sold the business now and I'm not doing anything in particular."

"You seem to have plenty of money."

"Why do you say that?"

"You stay at Muir House. You give large tips." She added, "And your car is a Mercedes."

"How do you know that?"

"I have a friend who works in reception. His name is Dave. He brought in the bags from your car when you arrived."

"I thought you said you didn't have any friends in the hotel."

"Oh, they're just summer friends," she said lightly. "They don't really count. In the fall I'll forget them."

Dave, of course, was the bellman whose conversation with Cecilia he had overheard. Ben almost decided to pursue this matter of Dave, then he thought better of it.

"Tell me about your friends in Berkeley."

"In Berkeley?"

"The other students."

"Oh, I don't know. They're perfectly ordinary people. Of course there is Stella." She began telling him about Stella so enthusiastically that he was seized with various totally unjustified suspicions, that she was a lesbian and Stella was her lover, that Stella was actually a code name for a male admirer, and so on. Ben was thoroughly bored with Stella and wished he hadn't asked her a leading question.

"And then there's Glover," she went on.

"You know, it *is* starting to rain."

The surface of the lake was spotted with raindrops now; they could no longer see the reflections of the trees on the other bank. He held out his hand to see how long it would be before a drop fell on it, a game he used to play as a child. She saw what he was doing and held out hers next to his, comparing his tanned muscular hand with her own, narrower and paler, with its dirty fingernails. He held out his left hand, of course; she her right.

23.

Inside the cave it was shadowy and cool, with an odor of pine needles. They sat down and took off their knapsacks. He had climbed hard coming up through the rockfall and he was panting a little. She too was breathing too hard to speak at first. She looked at him and laughed. The raindrops in her hair and on her sweater were like tiny pearls.

The cave was very small; there was barely room for the two of them. The rain pattered down outside. She was sitting so close to him that he could feel the thin bone of her hip through the shorts. Along with the scent of pine there was the odor of the wet wool sweater and her own scent, babyish and faintly musk-like.

"Let's see what's in the lunch."

He took the two boxes out of his knapsack and passed her one. There was a sandwich, a salad in a plastic container, fruit, and a miniature bottle of wine for each of them. Before she ate she took out her canteen and poured it over his held-out hands, then he did the same for her. This primitive but fastidious ritual was an idea that wouldn't have occurred to him. When he held out his hands to be washed the contrast between the left hand, strong and tanned, and its shriveled mate, which might have been the hand of a man of ninety or the victim of an Indian famine, was marked. Her eyes rested on the right hand only for an instant, then she looked away casually. It seemed to him that she colored, not as though she were embarrassed but as though she were excited. She said nothing. They dried their hands on their clothes.

"Where did you get the lunches?" she asked him.

"From the kitchen at the hotel."

"You've planned everything excellently."

"I always plan everything. Too carefully, I think."

"And what's going to happen next?"

"We're going to have our lunch, and then sit here talking until the rain stops."

"Did you plan that too?"

"No. That was nature intervening. In a fateful way."

He felt the snugness of being in a protected place when the rain is falling outside. It came down in gray streamers, rustling on the pine needles and running in rivulets down the trees. A tracery of black water worked its way down the rock at the entrance to the cave, but it didn't reach them.

"This sweater," she said, "stinks like an Irish fishwife when it's wet."

"You could take it off."

"I've got nothing on underneath it."

"You'd better not then."

They opened the small bottles of wine. There were plastic glasses; the hotel had thought of everything. He filled the glasses and they both drank. They were sitting so close together that he couldn't turn to look at her. He was aware of the odor of the damp sweater of of her hair, and the rain on the pine needles outside. Among these odors he tried to make out the scent of the lupines in her hair, then he remembered that wildflowers have no smell.

He felt the wine seeping into his chest, a sensation like the fine rustling of the rain in the forest outside. He threw down his wineglass, and after a while she did the same.

She said, "It's strange. Our being here together."

"Yes."

She turned and he felt the touch of her cool lips on his mouth. They fell over sideways onto the bed of pine needles.

24.

In the evening before dinner he walked the two miles down to the town of Muir to buy himself another bottle of Scotch. He had drunk the whole bottle in two nights, as unlikely as it seemed. You would that think being in love would make you happy, especially when it resulted in such brilliant successes as the one in the cave at Moon Lake, but instead it seemed to drive him to drink. Perhaps his happiness was so excruciating that the edge of it had to be tempered with drugs. He bought his whiskey, had an idiotic conversation with the store clerk in which he talked about the weather and the clerk responded with comments about baseball, and walked back to the hotel along the path beside the road.

There was a bellman on duty at the entrance. Ben started to go in, but the bellman stood in the doorway blocking him. He was a tall well-built young man in a brown-and-gold uniform, with a helmet of blond hair like a television cop.

"Mr. Gavilan, can I talk to you for a minute?"

"Me?"

"Yes, sir."

"All right."

"Not here," said the bellman gloomily.

Ben followed him in through the entrance to the hotel and down the corridor that led to the foyer.

"I'll bet you're Dave," said Ben.

"That's right."

"We can go in the bar if you like."

Instead Dave took him through a door past the kitchens and out the rear of the hotel. They stopped in an open place hidden from the hotel by a clump of trees, only a few feet from the spot where Ben had overheard Dave and Cecilia in their conversation.

"I can't go in the bar, Mr. Gavilan. Not in this uniform, and not even it I took it off. You forget that we're your domestics. Your servants. You can order us to do anything you want, and we have to do it."

He was perhaps twenty-five, with a red sunburned face and exaggeratedly blond hair and eyebrows. He had a little permanent crease of concern or thought in his forehead; this gave him a woeful air like a pedigreed bulldog.

"Should you be leaving your work like this?" Ben asked him.

"That's my business."

"What did you want to talk to me about?"

"It's about Cece."

"Who? Oh, Cecilia. I don't care for the nickname."

"What do you think you're doing, Mr. Gavilan? A man of your age. First you harass Cece in the dining room, and then you ask her for dates."

"Harass?"

"Call it anything you like."

"Did Cecilia tell you I harassed her?"

"We're not talking about what Cece told me. We're talking about what you're doing."

"I don't know what Cecilia told you. We went to Moon Lake today. We took our lunch and got caught in a rainstorm. She went voluntarily; no one forced her. I think she enjoyed herself."

"I don't blame you for being attracted to her. You feel protective toward her, don't you. You feel fatherly." Ben didn't contradict him. "Probably," he said, "you don't understand your own feelings. I'm ready to take you for what you are, a middle-aged sentimentalist. But when you take someone to a remote place where you'll be alone with her, and you take along a lunch with a sandwich, a salad, an apple, and a bottle of wine, it's pretty clear what you're up to."

"Your research is very thorough. You must have asked them at the kitchen. We didn't eat very much of the lunch."

"How old are you anyhow, Mr. Gavilan?"

"Thirty-seven."

"The hell you are. You're more like sixty. You're making a fool of yourself. If you don't understand your own feelings, they're clear enough to everybody else. You've had your time in the world. Now you ought to let the rest of us have our chance. Why don't you get back into your Mercedes and go back to Santa Barbara."

"I don't believe you know the first thing about my feelings for Cecilia. And you don't know what happened at the lake."

"What did happen?"

"It's really none of your business. Why are you bothering me with all this anyhow? Surely there are other people out front who want their baggage unloaded."

"Cece is a fine decent person and I won't have her trifled with."

"What an old-fashioned term."

"I know exactly what you're up to. Everyone in the hotel does."

"You're out of your mind, Dave. Pardon me if I don't know your last name. You're young and you've fallen in love, and this has made you slightly insane. You'll come to your senses after a while. I won't say anything about this to the hotel management. I'm not as obtuse a person as you imagine, and I'm not a monster. But I have some advice for you. If a girl wants to go out with you, that's fine. But women are people. They have minds and they can decide things for themselves. That's hard to see when you're in your state. I'm sorry if you're fond of Cecilia. As you say, she's a fine decent person. I want what is best for her, the same as you do. If I ever saw a sentimentalist it's you, imagining that I've captured Cecilia somehow and bundled her off to the lake and plied her with wine. It was only a very little bottle anyhow, eight ounces I believe. Didn't you find that out?"

"Damn you."

"Your attitude is very understandable," said Ben.

25.

Both Henry Calendish and Dave had gone out of their heads. They were sick with unrequited love. So thought Ben, looking into the mirror (a habit he had only recently acquired) in his cabin in the forest. And all over him. It was really quite flattering. It was good for his self-esteem. He hadn't felt so young in years. He was thirty-seven, just as he told Dave. He wouldn't tell a lie to so earnest and so unhappy a young man.

26.

At dinner that night the maitre stared at Ben in a peculiar way but led him down the room and seated him without a word. Evidently Henry had checked out because Ben was automatically given his table. He looked around for Cecilia; she was busy at the other end of the room. After a few minutes she came to the table getting out her order pad from the pocket of her dress. "Hello," he told her. "You're Cecilia and you'll be my waitress for this evening." She smiled, took his order, and served him exactly as she had before. Nothing in her manner suggested that there was anything special between them or that she knew him better than she did the other guests. He was a little perturbed by this easy skill of hers in dissimulating. Of course he was dissimulating too.

When he was finished with the dinner he put his usual large tip in cash on the tray and then sat waiting while she served the other guests, did something at the waiters' station at the end of the room, and stopped to talk to a friend. When she came back she took the tray in her usual way and slipped the money into her pocket. "Thank you," she said, "Mr. Gavilan."

27.

In the morning he left the cabin a little before ten and came to the desk in the foyer to pay his bill. He told the desk clerk, "The bags are in the cabin."

After a while he saw Dave coming down the path from the forest and across the footbridge, trundling ahead of him a cart with his bags and maneuvering it in through the door to the foyer. Neither of them said anything. Ben followed the brown-and-gold uniform down the corridor and out through the door to the front of the hotel. Cecilia was waiting by the curb with her own baggage. She was wearing the white Irish sweater and a pair of narrow tapering black pants. This time there were no flowers in her hair; she wore it loose with a turqouise clasp at one side.

Dave gave no sign that he had noticed her. He wheeled the cart with Ben's baggage to the curb and stopped.

"Your car?"

The parking lot was fifty yards away in the forest. Ordinarily the guests went to the lot for their cars and brought them to the door to have their baggage loaded. But suppose they were old or infirm or handicapped? Ben had a withered arm. He tossed Dave the keys, and Dave turned and went off to the parking lot with his bulldog frown.

Ben and Cecilia were left alone. He asked her, "Did you sleep well?"

"Perfectly."

"You told the hotel you were leaving?"

"Oh yes."

"What did they say?"

"Nothing. People quit all the time."

"You've had your breakfast?"

"I don't take much. Coffee and a roll."

"Isn't it strange we're talking banalities."

"What should we talk about?"

"I don't know. You act as though you've done this hundreds of times."

"You're funny."

Dave came wheeling down the narrow road with the Mercedes and parked it at the curb. Then the three of them went through an elaborate little ballet. Dave got out and left both front doors of the car open, then he went around to the back and opened the trunk. He began putting Ben's bags in the trunk, then Cecilia's. He was careful not to look at Cecilia, although he caught Ben's eye once and stared at him darkly. Cecilia got in on the passenger's side, leaving her door open. Ben waited until Dave had finished loading the bags, then he handed him a folded bill. Dave didn't thank him, but he didn't throw it in his face either; he took it and stuck it into the pocket of his uniform. Ben went around the car, got into the driver's seat, and shut the door.

Cecilia was still sitting in the car with her door open. When nothing happened she turned and looked at Dave. She was offhand and casual; he had an expression as though he was thinking of something a long distance away. Finally, without meeting her eye, he shut the door of the car for her.

Ben drove away. In the rear vision mirror he caught a glimpse of Dave standing by the baggage cart, following the car with his eyes. The car slipped softly down the winding road through the town of Muir—the liquor store, the lodge with its pool, the gas station, the garage—and out of it into the canyon that led down into the valley. When the last houses of the town were behind he sped up until the trees whistling by the window were only a blur.

Cecilia snuggled down sensuously into the leather upholstery of the Mercedes, then looked at him with a funny little smile. She said, "He's supposed to shut the car door. It's part of his job."

"Still it was mean of you to make him to it."

"Mean?" She laughed. "It was fun though."

"You do have a mean streak in you, don't you?"

"It was mean of you to make him go to the lot for the car."

"I gave him ten dollars for walking fifty yards." Their eyes met and they both laughed. She reached out and touched him affectionately, almost shyly.

Ben could hardly believe that he had her in the car with him. He felt a jump of joy in his chest and forced himself to keep his eyes on the road; it wouldn't do to have an accident when he was carrying something so precious and when he himself was in a state of bliss. He stole a look at her but he had no idea what she was thinking; she was as guileless and opaque as a child. He found that in the middle of his exultation he was still bothered by her malicious trick of making Dave shut the car door for her. He imagined some time in the future when, tiring of him, she would find little ways of hurting him with the same easy skill.

28.

Ben turned off the road into an archway with Spanish tiles on the top and bright red bougainvillea growing over it, the entrance to the Cantamar. To the right was the main building, also Spanish with tiles; across the lawn were the cottages. He drove around the circular drive and parked the car in the lot.

"Why are we stopping here?"

"This is where I live."

"In a hotel?"

"I have a cottage."

"A cottage?"

"It's a small house. The hotel people come and clean it every day. It's very convenient."

She looked around through the car windows at the tennis court, the cottages, and the Spanish-baroque palace of the main building with its blue tile decorations.

"Do you live here permanently?

"I have for several years. Since my divorce.

"When was that?"

"About ten years ago."

She got out of the car scenting the air like a beagle at the affluence of the place. He remembered that she identified him while she was still a waitress as someone who had money. Of course, he did everything he could to give her that impression.

He could have got somebody from the hotel to help with the baggage, but he decided not to, imagining Jack, the middle-aged bellman, examining Cecilia with his placid skepticism of a Molière servant. He had only one suitcase, a rather large one which he managed with his good hand; she got her own baggage out of the car and followed him. She didn't have much: a leather suitcase, a canvas duffel, and her knapsack which she carried slung over her shoulder. He led the way down the path with its many turnings, through a jungle of semi-tropical vegetation. At the cottage he unlocked the door and bumped through with his bag; she followed.

She seemed uncertain where to put her bags and set them down on the floor. Then she wandered around the small living room looking at things, while he watched her silently. There was a rosewood divan upholstered in green velvet, a low Chinese table, and two rosewood armchairs. One wall was covered with books in a white enameled bookcase, and there was a small spinet piano. The music open on the piano was an etude of Schumann, a finger exercise for beginners. If he had know she was coming he would have put it away. She made no comment on it. From the bookcase she idly pulled out a volume of Dürer engravings, a book on netsuke, and a biography of Lytton Strachey. Fitted neatly in among the books was a compact stereo with miniature speakers. On the wall over the bookcase was a Paul Klee engraving, *Two Men Meeting, Each Believing the Other to Be of Higher Rank*, numbered and signed by the artist, a more expensive work of art than Cecilia probably realized.

Turning away from these trinkets, she glanced into the bedroom, where the furniture was all antique: an old-fashioned four-poster in carved walnut, with a matching dresser, cheval glass, and twin nightstands. In the bathroom was a dressing table and a tabouret with green velvet upholstery. The small kitchenette, which she examined last, was modern.

"Is all this your furniture?"

"No. Everything belongs to the hotel except my books and stereo."

"Do you like living here?"

"Yes."

"Why?"

"It's small, but it's cosy and snug and I have everything I need within my hand's reach. It's like living on a yacht, in small space and yet in luxury."

She ran her fingers over the rosewood chair and seemed thoughtful.

He said, "Do you like it?"

"It's very nice. It's quite tiny though, isn't it? There's no room for my harpsichord."

"Do you have a harpsichord?"

"No. I need that too."

"Perhaps you can play the spinet until you get one."

"Not really."

He was excruciatingly anxious for her to like the cottage. He opened the shutters to show her the view of the town and the sea beyond. It was quite magnificent; the late afternoon sun hung over the water and made it sparkle with pinpoints of silver, and two dark islands lay along the horizon to the left. Far out to sea a ship crawled over the molten silver surface. She mused at this in her impenetrable way and then turned back to him, trailing her hand over the furniture.

"It's too early for dinner," he said. "What should we do? Go for a walk?"

"We did that yesterday."

"We did? Oh, the hike to Moon Lake." He found himself blushing.

"That should be enough exercise for a while," she said, "for a person your age."

"Whatever could we do then?"

She smiled like an older child at her dumb brother.

29.

Cecilia was taller than most girls, tall enough so that when she came up to Ben her chin rested on his collarbone. She was slender and willowy but gave the impression of strength, like a dancer. Her arms were long like a boy's and her elbows were a little knobby. Her hair was an unusual color, a kind of straw blond with hints of auburn, or russet, or flame, depending on the light. When it was undone it was long enough to reach to the top of her breasts. The hair seemed to cling together in strands, like that of a Botticelli Venus, or as though it had been lightly oiled. In their preliminaries for making love she was fond of this trick: she let the hair down evenly on all sides of her head until it covered her like a round tent, then she tilted her head slowly, slowly to one side. On the low side the hair clung to her face for a moment, then it abruptly fell away, revealing a single grave eye and an ear like a seashell. When she did this while naked she crossed her arms over her breasts, grasping her upper arms just below the shoulders. She had many of these playful modesties, all contrived no doubt. Another was that she always glanced at him and hesitated for a moment before removing the last garment. This trace of pudeur was pleasing. It occurred to Ben that there are some skills that throw their owner into a dubious light, as in the case of a man who shuffles cards too deftly, or a woman who is too quick about taking off her clothes.

The beauty spot on her face, which Ben noticed when he examined her in the dining room at Muir House, was brown with a reddish cast, the exact color of her hair. It was the size of a carpet tack, about three millimeters in diameter, and was just below her mouth and to one side. There was another one like it, a little larger, below her right breast. Except for this her body was flawless. It was the color of sherry, but it shaded off in different places to darker and lighter; in some places the finest dry cocktail sherry, in others a shadowy Amontillado. Her breasts were those of a fourteen-year-old, but a perfectly nubile one. Even though the symmetry seemed a little contrived, her nipples were the same color as her hair and birthmarks, brown with a tinge of russet. Her feet were large, and she often stood, especially when naked, with one foot turned out and its heel pressed into the instep of the other, like a ballerina or a fashion model. When walking around naked, she slunk elegantly in a way that kept her legs together, another fashion-model pose, or perhaps a genuine modesty or bashfulness.

The curious thing was that Cecilia was not really an exceptionally pretty girl. If you walked around any university campus, for example at Berkeley, you would see many like her. Some would be taller, some shorter, some would have fuller breasts or more fascinating eyes, but Cecilia would simply have disappeared into the others and be invisible among them. Unless, of course, you were in love with her, and then she would leap out from the others like a searchlight at night. She had a gawky quality; she was a little too tall and her feet were too large, her nose was a little larger than it might be also, and her lips were fleshy, as though she had been biting them to make them swell. If she were to be compared to an animal, it would have to be a giraffe. A young giraffe, still uncertain how to kick its long legs and arrange its neck. It was perhaps for this reason that she had developed her coy mannerisms, her fashion-model stance, her slinking, and her head-tilting trick that made the hair fall away from one eye: facsimiles of a grace which she didn't really possess.

Since Ben was in love, all of these things, charms and awkwardnesses, drove him out of his head with lust.

30.

Ben often dined at the Cantamar with guests, some of them women. They were usually not as young as Cecilia, but Charles, the dining room captain, hardly glanced at her. He led the way to Ben's favorite table on the terrace outside. The lights of the town winked intermittently through a screen of eucalyptus trees; beyond was the sea, now after sunset a black floor with two islands slumped on it like sleeping animals.

Cecilia sat down demurely and began examining the menu. From everything in her manner, it might have been the hundredth time she had sat at this table holding the menu with her little finger crooked and pondering it reflectively. Once again he noticed her easy skill at dissimulation. Twenty-four hours ago she was a waitress; now she had transformed herself effortlessly into a creature who had spent her life in luxury hotels like the Cantamar.

For starters, they agreed on the squab salad for Ben and a warm Chèvre salad with endive and pine nuts for her. She thought over the main dish for some time and settled finally on the most elaborate thing on the menu, the duckling with green peppercorns and raspberries. She spent money as though she was born to it, he thought. She probably learned this at Muir House. It occurred to him that if you set out to be a brilliant society fraud, being a waiter in an expensive restaurant would be a good preparation. You would know how to order food, you would know wines and perhaps languages, and you would have had plenty of opportunity to observe the manners and conversation of your betters. A Paris waiter from the Tour D'Argent could easily pass for a diplomat. As he thought of this he had an overpowering desire to take her to the Tour D'Argent.

"Do you eat here every night?"

"Usually. Sometimes I go to a restaurant in town, or I'm invited out to dinner. Of course," he said, "I don't always dine this well."

"Is there something special about tonight?"

"Yes. It's the first night of your Vita Nuova."

"My new life?"

"As a concert harpsichordist. I'm going to help you out in every way I can. If you need lessons or ... a harpsichord or whatever," he finished lamely. He had the feeling that this last would be very expensive.

"I'll be your protégée."

"Yes. My protégée. So far it doesn't seem so onerous, does it?"

"No," she said, "it's quite pleasant."

The entrees arrived, and along with them there was a light tapping on the canvas awning overhead, as though someone were dropping nuts on it. There was a scent of rain in the dust and on the dry leaves of the eucalyptus that sheltered the terrace.

The ever attentive Charles, glancing with professional hostility at the dark heavens, came up to the table and asked, "Mr. Gavilan, would you like to go inside?"

They seemed to be nicely sheltered by the awning, in danger only from random drops. He looked at Cecilia questioningly. She said, "It's all right here."

They went on with their dinner. The tapping increased until it was a steady rustle; the awning dripped and rivulets began running from it and falling into the shrubbery below. In the distance there was a rumble of thunder. Summer rain was very unusual in Santa Barbara; it never happened at all according to the Chamber of Commerce. The rain made Ben feel sexy; it reminded him of the cave at Moon Lake and everything that had happened there. Romanticizing recklessly, he appointed the rain the special custodian of his happiness, now and in the future. Just as Wagnerian heroes and heroines tripped onto the stage to the strains of their personal and private leitmotifs, so would the sound of rain falling always be the leitmotif of his love for Cecilia, of their love for each other. Sitting at the table listening to the rustle of the rain on the awning, he generated a whole poetry of rain, a metaphysics, a magic; it quickened the earth, breeding lilacs out of the dead land as Eliot says (it seemed that he, Ben, couldn't have feelings without referring them to something in literature and art), giving life to the buried seeds of the old year, sprouting lust in fifty-eight-year-old divorcés; how long would it be until they were back in the cottage? a half an hour, or at the most forty-five minutes. It would be the second time today, leaving yesterday out of it. He was evidently turning into some kind of sex maniac, a geriatric prodigy to be studied by specialists.

He told her, "I like the sound of rain."

Did this convey the whole and total tone of what he wished to say, reminding her of the idyll in the cave the day before, and asking her to agree too that the rain would be the leitmotif of their love? She only said, "Yes," in a matter-of-fact way, looking past him at the drops falling from the awning. He was left baffled by her sibylline calm and mystery, the mystery of the young as seen by the old, of woman as seen by man. He was entitled to hope, at least, that he was mysterious for her in a different way, but probably the hope was vain.

A gust of wind stirred the awning, it sagged, and a little splash hit the corner of the tablecloth. They both laughed. A waiter came running with a napkin and sponged away the water. When he went off carrying the damp napkin like a wounded bird Charles stopped him and said something in a low voice, pointing to the dripping awning and then to the two of them at the table. After a while the waiter came up and brought them Grand Marniers with their coffee. "Compliments of Mr. Charles." It wasn't clear whether he had done this because of the rain or because he had taken them for lovers. Cecilia only sipped a little of hers.

31.

They ran back to the cottage dodging the large warm drops and arrived at the door panting. Cecilia's wet sweater smelled exactly as it did the day before in the cave, and he strove to grasp the essence of the odor, in the hope of evoking the sensations of this scene again for aphrodisiac purposes. When he embraced her inside the door of the cottage she said, "You're sniffing me. You beastly creature."

She was very keen. He would have to be more careful about concealing things from her. "My mother," he told her, "a very proper Cambridge lady, said that workmen sweat, gentlemen perspire, and ladies glow."

"That's it, I'm glowing."

Her cheeks were pink and her face burned too, as though the drops of rain had set it on fire. There was a feeling of the festive, of the observance of some primitive rite, a midsummer festival or the burning of bonfires on hilltops. It called for an elixir or special potion; he wanted to be properly exalted during the celebration of this thing whatever it was. He went directly to the bookcase and got himself some Scotch, with some ice from the refrigerator. He was already feeling a pleasant buzz from the two wines at dinner and the Grand Marnier.

Observing him with an oblique look from across the room, she said, "Were you planning on going to bed with me?"

"Yes, I was."

"I don't care to have someone reeking of liquor clambering all over me."

"You don't?"

"No, why should I?"

"All right," he said. He sheepishly poured out the Scotch into the sink and put the bottle back into the bookcase. Then he didn't know what to do with himself; he always had a nightcap before going to bed.

"I'm going to curl up with a book," she said. She got the Lytton Scrachey biography out of the bookcase and settled into an armchair with it. He was sure she was teasing him. Resorting to the expedient recommended to schoolboys, he went into the bathroom and took a cold shower, turning the tap up high so that the sound drowned out the pattering of rain on the roof.

32.

"What happened to your arm, anyhow?"

"I was the last child in New England to get polio. It was a curious accident. My parents took very good care of me. The funny thing is, I don't remember whether I was vaccinated or not. Perhaps I wasn't; my mother in particular was rather absent-minded."

"What can you do with the arm?"

"The hand is strong enough. I can hold a pen with it and write, as long as I can get the arm into position. The feeling in the hand is just as sensitive as in the other hand, but the nerves in the arm are dead. It's an odd thing. I feel as though I'm carrying around somebody else's arm, and at the end of it is a hand that can somehow send messages to me."

"That was many years ago, when you were a child. You must be used to it now."

"I'm not, really. I'm always conscious of being different from other people. My body is specially made. I can't really know what other people feel, because my body's different from theirs."

"The rest of you except for the arm is the same."

"I can't really be sure of that either."

"I think I know what you mean," she said. "Although I don't feel that way myself. I feel like I'm just like everybody else."

"What do—" he groped for the right phrase. "How does it seem to you? I mean, do you mind my having a funny arm?"

"Oh, everybody's funny in one way or another. Since it's you, I like it. I wouldn't want it any different. If you didn't have a funny arm, you wouldn't be yourself."

"But to me, you're perfect," he told her.

She didn't admit to any of her putative flaws, her birthmark, her big feet, her fleshy lips. She only smiled as though she knew she wasn't perfect, but she appreciated his reasons for thinking so.

"My wife Erica was disgusted by the arm. I always had to make love to her from the other side, and with one hand."

For an answer she only took the withered hand and arranged it on her breast, as though she were applying some odd garment to herself, a half-brassiere. His suspicion was confirmed that she felt no repulsion for the arm, that instead she was excited by it; or perhaps she felt both of these things at once. The pencil-eraser in the center of the breast stiffened until he could feel it push his hand upward.

"You're lucky," she told him. "It could have been some other part of you."

"I don't know whether polio ever affects the penis. It probably could, though. It's full of nerves."

33.

In the morning he got up later than usual, about nine, and phoned room service for two breakfasts. When they came Cecilia was already dressed in her black pants and a turtleneck, but he was still in his pajamas. He met the Chicano waiter's eye resolutely. I must be careful not to leave him a larger tip on account of this, he told himself. Cecilia was as blasé as if they were married; she allowed the waiter to unfold her napkin and gazed past him out the window at the sea.

When the waiter was gone she applied jam to her croissant and turned her attention to Ben.

"What's that on your pajamas? Is it a duck?"

"No, it's an Eton crest. I bought them in England."

"Are you an Eton boy then?"

"I'm not a boy of any kind."

"I believe they're called old boys. All their lives."

"I suppose that's a fair description of me. You know, Cecilia, for your age you strike me as a very experienced lover."

"I do?"

"I mean. I'm not the first."

"No, you're not the first," she admitted, chewing the croissant.

"And is it something you want?"

"It?"

"It."

"Oh, that."

"Well, what do people your age call it?"

"Fucking."

"Spare us that. Is it something you want strongly?"

She ate the last of the croissant, tucking it daintily into her mouth with her finger. She waited until she was finished chewing before she spoke. Then she said, "Oh, it's all right when you have it. But I don't really miss it when I don't." After a pause she said, "I think men attach more importance to this than women." Another pause. "Some women do, they become obsessed with this thing, but that's a special situation. Such women are not normal."

"Are you normal?"

"I?" There was an even longer pause. Finally her answer was, "I just feel certain ways about certain things. I feel this way about this thing."

He couldn't get any more out of her on this subject. It was more difficult to understand what she was thinking than to kiss her, or to get her into bed. Yet we, the old, aren't mysterious for the young, he thought. (It was true that he was only fifty-eight, but he had fallen into the habit of thinking of the two of them in this neat dichotomy as young and old). Somehow they, the young, know all about us, and see through us and know exactly what we're like and what we're feeling, but they're a mystery to us. They live in another country, a foreign country where the old are not admitted. Even though we've been there, we've forgotten, or we're unable to recover the memory precisely *because* we've been there and you can only go there once.

He tried to remember what he felt when he was Cecilia's age; he could do this well enough, but it didn't help him to understand her now. And then he saw what the real difference was between the young and the old. It was that we desire them but they don't desire us. He left aside the question of whether this was true of him and Cecilia. It was true in general, and our vision is clouded by our desire; it's a veil through which we see them only imperfectly, in glimpses in which they are like works of art, beautiful but opaque. We can't know what's inside it. In the case of a work of art, there is nothing inside it, it's all outside. Perhaps that was true of Cecilia. Perhaps he was groping for something that was like paint on canvas, a clever illusion.

34.

Fragonard's picture *The Swan*. This is in the Wallace Collection in London. In a sylvan setting, watched over by a silent stone cupid, an old man is pulling a young girl on a swing. She is all in pink, and she seems flushed and excited. Her petticoats are showing. In the foreground, unnoticed by the old man who is intent on his job of pulling the swing back and forth with a rope, is a young man half concealed in the foliage. As the swing reaches its highest point, at the moment of the picture, he is in a position to see up the young girl's petticoats. He looks up at her amorous surprise. She has already kicked off one of her shoes to him, and the other is about to go, barely hanging from the toe.

35.

After breakfast Cecilia went out for a walk around the grounds of the hotel. She came back in twenty minutes for her bathing suit; she had found the pool. She put on the bathing suit in the bathroom, and came out wearing it and a pair of thong sandals and carrying a towel. The bottom half of the bathing suit consisted of a nylon triangle the size of a hand. The top part of it concealed very little; it hardly seemed worth the trouble of putting it on. She paused as she passed him as if modeling this garment in a salon.

"Won't you come?"

"No. I do sometimes in the afternoon before dinner."

"Bye."

He watched her go out the door, and caught another glimpse of her through the window. This view of her from the rear, with the creases on the bikini-bottom tacking back and forth as she walked, gave him a queer sensation; it turned her into just any girl, a random student seen on the beach, and it turned him into a middle-aged voyeur who liked to look at girls on the beach. She disappeared from sight around a turn in the path overhung with banana palms.

36.

Ben was in the bedroom of the cottage getting dressed. His clothes were neatly hung in the closet, with three sections for coats, shirts, and pants divided by pieces of colored cardboard; in the carved walnut dresser too everything was arranged carefully in the proper drawers—socks, underwear, handkerchiefs, and miscellaneous items. His neckties were hanging from a patent device on the inside of the closet door that held twelve of them, all he possessed. His six pairs of shoes were in a row on the closet floor, or rather on a special shelf about a foot off the floor, so they would be up out of the dust and easier to reach. Cecilia hadn't yet unpacked; her suitcase, duffel bag, and knapsack were against the bedroom wall, all three of them open and leaking clothes onto the floor. It was not clear where her clothes were going to go when she unpacked. Theoretically the cottage was intended for two—thus the double bed—but clothes are like an infinitely expandable substance, a gas, that fills any space available to it. At least his clothes were.

The clothes he wore in the Sierras were dirty and he threw them in the hamper. From the closet he selected a short-sleeved plaid shirt and a pair of khaki pants. From the dresser, the jockey undershorts, which were size thirty-four, the same size they were when he was a student Cecilia's age, and a pair of socks. The socks he selected were a bright fuschia, and they had the tiny figure of a polo player embroidered on each one. This figure was supposed to be worn on the outside of the ankle where it would show, so there were left and right socks and you had to put them on the correct feet. Everything else in the closet and the dresser might have belonged to the headmaster of a New England school, or a retired stockbroker in Connecticut. He contemplated the possibility that in spite of his conservative temperament he had always had this strain of the reckless, the flamboyant in him concealed under his pants cuffs; probably he could not have successfully carried out the capture of Cecilia if it had not been for the fact that he wore loud socks. It was possible too that the socks were his only concession to California. If he had been a New Englander in New England, wearing plain socks, he would never have had the nerve to make his overture to Cecilia. The clothes and the man, socks and soul, were one. In time we are penetrated by our masks. Just looking at the loud socks now in the drawer was enough to make him feel like Cecilia's lover.

The shoes he selected were Italian loafers with fringes on the flap at the top, whatever the thing is called.

37.

In the bathroom he found that when Cecilia put on her bikini she had simply dropped her clothes on the floor. There were the narrow black pants and the jersey, this second not quite clean, he could see now that she had it off. There was a small brown stain on the inside of the underpants. She had left the toothpaste tube out on the counter with the cap off, and there was a smear of green unguent in the washbowl. She had also used his hairbrush; there were strands of her reddish-blond hair in it.

Ben was a compulsively neat person. He kept the small cottage as though it were a yacht, as he told Cecilia, with a place for everything and everything in its place. His books were in alphabetical order and he had a card file for his records. The bathroom was cleaned by the hotel staff every day, and sometimes he took a hand towel himself and polished the chromium fittings until they shone like mirrors. His own clothes were always immaculate. Now the squalor she had left behind her threw him into such an elaborate paraxysm of desire that he could hardly contain himself.

38.

Ethel's number was busy at first. She had an active life and many other friends. He got her after about ten minutes.

"So you've been to Muir House."

"Yes."

"I thought you were coming back on Monday."

"As it happened I stayed over another day."

"You must have enjoyed yourself."

"I did."

She sighed. "I haven't been there for years. It's a heavenly place." She was clearly suggesting that he could have taken her along. He and Ethel had a curious friendship. After all the years they knew each other perfectly, but there were areas of conversation that were forbidden to them. For him she was only a friend, but she had always been a little in love with him. She had never married and worked as an art librarian for the university. She was a little younger than he was, about forty.

He said, "It is nice. I always enjoy going there. I stayed over a little longer because—"

"Are you going to the Voronoffs tonight?"

"Oh. Is it tonight?"

"Of course it is. Their Wednesdays."

"I didn't realize it was Wednesday. I must have lost track while I was staying at Muir House."

"You sound odd today, Ben. What's wrong with you? I'll be there with bells on. I observe the Voronoffs as though they themselves were one of Ilya's novels. You can't wait to find out what will happen next. Lately their marriage has been making splitting noises."

"It has for some time."

"Yes, but Betsy has been drinking more and telling everyone how much Ilya bores her. I have a great deal of sympathy for her. You know of course she admires you greatly."

"So do you. Why don't you speak for yourself, Ethel?"

"Ah. Now we're playing John Alden and Priscilla."

She seemed pleased, and he imagined her blushing at the other end of the line. He had never said anything like this to her before in his life. He was developing a new temperament, more reckless and more inclined to impulse. And more gallant to women. The question was whether it was a favor to Ethel to be gallant with her. It might only arouse false expectations.

But she, a woman of astute tact, didn't pursue it. They both left it in the air where it was, a joke. She went on about Betsy.

"She's really a charming person. I like her very much. She drinks too much of course, but it's not really her fault. I've always felt it was one of those marriages where the wife is cleverer than the husband. By the law of chance it ought to be true in half of all marriages, but we always assume for some reason that the husband is brighter. Betsy doesn't have a very easy time. You know, Ben, it wouldn't be very much trouble for you—"

"To what?"

"To be a little bit nicer to her."

"Ethel, are you suggesting that I have an affair with Betsy simply because she is more intelligent than Ilya and consequently bored?"

"Of course not. It's just that—"

"Just that I could be a little bit nicer to her."

"Exactly."

Ethel was a good friend of Betsy's and associated herself closely with her conjugal life; it was the only conjugal life that Ethel as a confirmed spinster was likely to have. This romance she had invented was only a part of her private drama about Betsy. He imagined himself taking Betsy to lunch, writing her clandestine notes, meeting her in obscure corners of the library, and then, of course, having her to dinner at the Cantamar with the cottage only a few steps away. Betsy, naturally, would give a daily account of all of it to her good friend Ethel. He suddenly remembered the reason why this was impossible in any case.

"I don't think Betsy would ever leave Ilya. He's too important a novelist and he has too much money. Listen, Ethel. I'm bringing somebody with me to the Voronoffs."

"Somebody?"

"Her name is Cecilia. She's a harpsichordist. I think you'll like her."

"This is something new. Why haven't we heard of her before?"

"I met her while I was staying at Muir House."

"And she's in Santa Barbara now?"

"Yes. I brought her down with me."

"I see."

"I wonder if you do."

"What *does* this mean, Ben?"

"It means," he said, "that I am coming to the Voronoffs and bringing someone named Cecilia who is a harpsichord player. I'm interested in her and perhaps I'll be paying her bills. It's an investment, Ethel. Not that I'll get any money out of it, but I'll have the satisfaction of helping out a talented person in her career."

"You can invest your money any way you please. Be careful how you invest your emotions."

"I've had them for a long time. I can handle them."

"It's because you've had them for a long time that I'm bothered."

"You're very keen, Ethel. Women's intuition I suppose."

"Women's intuition has gone out of fashion. According to the feminists it's an insult. When men say women have it they mean instead of brains."

"I don't know whether Cecilia has a brain, but she's very talented."

As he said this he realized that he had no idea whether it was true. She might be a rotten harpsichord player. He was amazed at how easily he had concocted this elaborate story about her, that she was his artistic protégée and he was helping her with her career. What a shabby hoax.

39.

Once again he could hardly believe he had her in the car with him. There was something ephemeral about her, about his love for her, about the whole thing; he felt that he might easily glance over at the other seat and find her vanished, as in some easy Hollywood trick in a movie about ghosts and phantoms. No, she was still there. He forced himself to take his eyes off her and turn them back onto the road. The most probable outcome of all this was that he would have a bad accident while gazing moonstruck at her sitting in the other seat of the car, picking at her hangnail.

"Who are the Voronoffs? Is it Ilya Voronoff the novelist?"

"That's right. They're old friends. For years they've held open house once a week. Their Wednesdays."

"Is he really Russian?"

"Oh yes. He left the Soviet Union at twenty. Betsy is English. He met her at Oxford. They were married in England and came to America when he finished his degree."

"I haven't read his books."

He was anxious for her not to read Ilya's books. If she liked them this might give her a penchant for Ilya, who was a very persuasive person. "Don't bother. He writes too much for anyone to read anyhow. He's made a lot of money out of it. He's already written an enormous trilogy about the October Revolution and the Civil War. Now he's working on another one about the Second World War. Books about the Nazis are always popular. Even though Ilya's an émigré he's very patriotic about Russia. He celebrates the Russian virtues and he's against western atheism and materialism."

"But you say he's made a lot of money."

"Oh, he's no fool."

He turned off the highway and wound along the road past the country club and the laguna. There was still a little light left in the sky, the land was dark, lights were coming on in the houses along the road. The sea was just ahead over the ridge; you could feel it in a cool briskness in the air. Cecilia was wearing the same black pants and oversized white sweater she wore the day before, and she had added a necklace of turquoise beads that came to her waist. She seemed to have very few clothes. He wasn't the kind to inspect her suitcase when she was gone, but there couldn't be very much in it and the canvas duffel bag. She still hadn't unpacked; she lived out of her baggage as though her stay in the cottage was only temporary.

On the hike to Moon Lake she had told him she couldn't take off the white sweater because she had nothing on under it. This stuck in his head, and every time she wore the sweater he was reminded of it. Perhaps it was a diabolical trick on her part. He didn't know if it was true that she had nothing under the sweater because she always dressed in the bathroom.

"You're looking nice," he told her. "I'm fond of that sweater."

"Oh, this old thing? It's what I always wear."

"Do you think clothes are important?"

He was trying to find out if she was one of those shopping women that Henry Calendish talked about, who spend all their time in malls with their friends. But she said, "Oh, they're very important. If people didn't wear them they wouldn't make love at all. Clothes are an aphrodisiac. People aren't very attractive with their clothes off." There was a silence, and then she added, Especially men."

This referred to him no doubt, and was probably just a joke. He chose to take it as a joke. He turned his attention back to his driving; there was Via Sonrisa, the Voronoffs' street. He swung right and then left on the curving lane and parked in front of the house. There were a half-dozen other cars in the lane. They were close enough to the sea now that they could hear the muffled grumbling of the surf.

They got out and on the sidewalk he took her hand. She said, "I'll bet you're wondering what these people will make of me." Ben gave her a smile and they went into the house.

40.

From the buffet table he caught sight of Ethel's long neck and ostrich-like elegance at the other end of the room. She was wearing a silver lamé dress that was too youthful for her, perhaps because he told her on the phone to speak for herself. She stared curiously at Cecilia but didn't come across the room to them now. Betsy Voronoff, in a long white satin gown, was clinging to Ben's arm in a possessive way while she chatted to Cecilia.

"Are you going to play for us a little later, dear?"

"Is there a harpsichord here?"

"I'm afraid not."

"I don't play the piano."

"Oh, how clever you are at repartee." Betsy was at her most characteristic tonight, with her Mayfair accent, her peacock-tuft hair, and her nervous laugh. The hired waiter passed them with a tray of drinks, and she stopped him and took a glass of vodka and ice. Then she turned back to Cecilia and fixed her in a long stare over the rim of her glass.

"Have you known Ben long?"

"No, not very long."

"I wonder what you have in common."

"An interest in music."

"Don't you have—someone else—you could have brought with you tonight?"

"Not especially."

"Do you live in Santa Barbara, my dear?"

"I do now. Until recently I lived in Oakland."

"Ben is so charming, isn't he?"

"Yes, he's very nice."

"And do the two of you make music together?" She tinkled her little laugh.

Cecilia glanced at Ben before she answered this one. Then she said demurely, "Not yet."

She was doing splendidly, Ben thought. She took some caviar on her plate and told Betsy, "Your house is beautiful."

"Ilya has no taste. He makes the money and leaves it to me to select the furnishings."

Cecilia, playing her part in this feminine duel, looked around the room with the cool glance of a furniture critic. Ben waited on pins and needles to see what she would say about it. There were sofas and chairs in white Danish leather, rosewood cabinets, Foujita aquarelles, and fragments from Etruscan tombs lying carelessly on tables. To match the Danish leather there were two white borzois, who lay indolently with their chins on the carpet, watching the guests out of their liquid eyes. Behind the buffet a glass cabinet held a collection of fossils, including some geodes the size of human heads which, when cut apart, revealed hollow interiors glittering with sharp violet and pink crystals.

What she said was, "Are you interested in fossils?"

"No, that's Ilya. They're really quite ghastly, aren't they? Like some kind of torture machine for tiny men. Here he is now."

Ilya came across the room toward them through the sea of white furniture. He was the kind of portly man who was quick and birdlike in his motions; he had agile feet and wore shiny black patent-leather shoes. He dressed as carefully as a girl, in a navy blazer with brass buttons, fitted at the waist in the Italian manner, and very narrow gray trousers. He slipped his arm around Betsy's waist and nuzzled her behind the ear. Then he stared at Cecilia.

"Ha. Um. I haven't been introduced." His accent was Oxford, carefully cultivated, with a trace of Russian to lend it interest.

Ben said, "Cecilia Penn. Ilya Voronoff."

"A new young face for our Wednesdays. How refreshing. We all get so tired of one another."

Cecilia allowed herself a moment to take him in, from the accent to the patent-leather shoes. Then she said, "I'm sure you don't. Everyone seems fascinating."

"I understand that you and Ben make music together," Ilya tittered, glancing around at the others.

"Your wife made the same joke. I really don't know what to say to it."

"Oh, stop calling me his wife. My name is Betsy."

"Well, what a charming thing you are. *I'd* love to make music with you."

Over the crowd at the end of the room Ben caught sight of the head of the Voronoffs' daughter Raymonde. Cecilia was a tall girl, but Raymonde was huge. She was six feet tall and perfectly formed, like a photograph of an ordinary woman that had been enlarged. Her hair was platinum with an orange streak in it, and she was wearing a pair of designer jeans and a denim jacket. She had pasted small tinsel stars to her cheeks, one red and one silver.

"Who is that?" whispered Cecilia, noticing her at the same instant.

"I'll introduce you."

41.

The crowd with Raymonde at the other end of the room, by the picture window looking out over the sea, also included Commander Pickering and his wife, Edgar and Jo-Nan Rolf, and Carolyn Wong. Carolyn's husband Arnold Schifter was away on a trip to the Far East. Carolyn was an astronomer at the University, and the Rolfs were in the import-export business. The formidable old lady who seemed to be dressed in flags was Estelle Galleon, a well-known philanthropist.

"I love your outfit," Cecilia told Raymonde.

The denim jacket was a striking garment. It was the ordinary thing you can buy in any shop, with flowers embroidered on the front and military brass buttons, but it was almost hidden under a collection of costume jewelry, clips, and pins: pearl insects, golden dragonflies, miniature knives and horns, a fake diamond clasp, a silver bird with monochrome enamel.

"I like to collect things," Raymonde explained.

"So does Ben." Betsy tinkled her silvery laugh.

"Oh, drop it, Betsy," said Ben.

"Am I missing some innuendoes?" said Raymonde.

"They're not suitable for an unmarried girl."

"Oh I see. You mean Ben and Cecilia. How nice." After a moment she asked her, "And what do you do? Aside from being Ben's friend."

"The harpsichord. I'm getting so tired of telling people. And what do you do?"

"I'm the curator of a museum."

"Fantastic. How do you get a job like that?"

"I studied art at the University."

"Is there someone at the University who teaches harpsichord?"

"Old Dominicus, I imagine. He teaches all kinds of funny instruments."

"I like your hair too. Is it hard to do?"

"Not if you took art at the University."

"I don't know anything about Santa Barbara. Are there shops and things?"

"Oh yes. Quite nice ones."

"Maybe we could go shopping sometime."

"Great. Do you like clothes?"

"I like yours."

Raymonde smiled like a pleased young lioness. "I have others. I'll show you. There's some stuff in the Museum that I can't wear. It would just fit you."

"In the Museum?"

"Sure."

"But I want to go shopping for clothes."

"We can do that too."

42.

Ted Pickering, who had been talking to Carolyn Wong, turned his head and noticed Cecilia for the first time. He brightened considerably. "Who is this sweet young thing?" he asked the company in general.

"Cecilia Penn. Commander Pickering."

Cecilia studied him for a moment as she had Ilya, and then she asked him, "What do you command?"

"I retired early because the damned Navy was too damned conservative for me."

"I expect a Navy would be."

"That was what I found out. This is my wife Snoozy."

"We haven't had anything to eat yet," said Snoozy. "I'm ravenous."

She led her husband away. Ethel swooped up, stretching out her long neck to Cecilia. "I know who you are. I want to talk to you, my dear. I understand you and Ben met at Muir House. It's such a nice place. Tell me all about it."

With some curiosity Ben watched this encounter between the two women in his life, a development that for some reason he had not foreseen when he first got involved with Cecilia. Of course, Ethel wasn't really a woman in his life. Ben was rather fond of her. It was odd how a strikingly attractive woman could look exactly like an ostrich: she had a long neck, a flat jaw, large exophthalmic eyes, and a fringe of hair like a crown. After an ostrich she resembled Katherine Hepburn, Edith Sitwell, Eleanor of Aquitaine; women who radiated a strange aviary effulgence something like a fluorescent light, cold and slightly tremoring.

Ethel and Cecilia chattered. Ben could no longer hear

what they were saying over the hum of conversation. He was almost cornered by Estelle Galleon, a bore who wanted to talk to him about halfway houses for convicts, but was rescued by Ilya, who pulled him away by the elbow.

43.

In the library Ilya got them drinks from the small built-in bar; serious drinks, not the vodka and blended whiskey available from the peripatetic waiter and the bar in the living room. They stood with their backs to the fire, an unnecessary comfort, since it was a mild July evening. However, it was an artificial fire, with plaster logs, and it didn't give off much heat.

Ben asked him, "How's the new trilogy?"

"It's going beautifully. I've finished the second volume now. I believe you're read the first?"

"Yes. *The Cauldron.*" Ben had speed-read part of it and glanced through the rest. It was a historical novel something in the manner of Tolstoy as imitated by Shokokhov and others. The hero Kostya fights bravely at the battle of Stalingrad, is wounded and sent to a provincial town as a governor, where he uncovers corruption in the local officials and falls in love with the daughter of a pre-Revolutionary aristocrat. He does nothing in particular to this lady, however, but discourse to her at length about the destiny of Russia and the need for resurrecting the Orthodox faith which can then be combined in some way with socialism.

"Your Kostya is a powerful character."

"Ah yes, dear old Konstantin Pavlovich. In the second volume he flees to the west and spends ten years in Paris at a country house in Hampshire, where he is befriended by a family of English aristocrats."

"More aristocrats."

"They're more interesting than other people, old fellow. This volume is called *Partibus Infidelis*."

"Do you think your readers will care for a book with a Latin title?"

"Oh dear yes, they'll love it. People are always intrigued by something they only half understand. I make it a point to include lots of phrases in French, and to refer frequently to Bakunin and Proudhon. At the end of this second volume Kostya becomes a writer and publishes a book on the Stalingrad campaign. The third volume—"

"This is excellent cognac."

"You may have noticed that I serve it from a decanter. I don't care to have people know what it is, because it would only make them unhappy, since they couldn't afford it. The third volume is to be called *The Prodigal*. Kostya wearies of the atheistic and materialistic west and goes back to Russia, secretly, disguised as a British journalist."

"Lots of opportunity for false passports, near escapes from arrest, and chances for Kostya to overhear conversations in Russian which people think he doesn't understand."

"Would you mind if I just arranged that tie of yours, old man?" He adjusted the knot with his short pale fingers. Probably he thought that Ben couldn't do a proper job of it with his bad hand. "You have excellent story sense, old fellow. You ought to be a novelist yourself. In one scene, which I've only planned and not written yet, he sits in a café and hears a group of writers in a provincial town discussing his novel. They praise it highly but misunderstand it. At the end of the scene, he goes to the group and asks for a light for his cigarette, in

English of course. While one of them is lighting the cigarette, he looks around at them meaningfully with a little smile. Then he leaves the café without another word."

"Your usual subtlety. You're a master at that sort of scene, Ilya."

"Shortly after this he's arrested. This is in the Krushchev period. There will be a long scene in which he is interrogated by the KGB, resembling the famous Grand Inquisitor scene in *The Brothers Karamazov.* The discourse is not at all political; instead it's philosophical and even metaphysical. He admits freely who he is. The inquisitors accept him as an intellectual equal and companion. At the end they embrace him in the Russian manner. Then he is sent off to a gulag, but he is happy there, preferring slavery in Russia to freedom in the materialistic west. He rediscovers the soul of his own country in talking to the common criminals who are his companions in the camp."

"That sounds like Dostoevsky's *Notes from the House of the Dead.*"

"No one will notice. People never read the classics. A few reviewers may, but they will only speak of profound Dostoevskian undertones. Believe me, my dear fellow, I know what I am talking about. I hope you won't mind my including you in the second volume which I've just finished."

"Me?"

"You know how novelists fictionalize things. No one will recognize you. You see, old fellow, in the house where Kostya is staying in Hampshire there is a house guest, a middle-aged British publisher. For years he's been in love with an art librarian. She's a guest in the house too."

"That sounds like Ethel," said Ben with a sigh.

"It's a novel, old fellow. It's fiction. The publisher is a foil for Kostya in their literary conversations. Kostya reproaches him for not doing anything about the art librarian. You see, my dear fellow, the way you behave in real life is far too passive for a character in a novel. You've known Ethel for years but you never do anything about her. In the third volume I'll have the publisher do something violent and bizarre. I had thought of a scene in which, driven by Kostya's taunts, he disrobes the art librarian on a walk in the country and she is stung to death by wasps."

"Ethel?"

"No, the character in the novel. Tell me a little about Cynthia, by the way."

"Who?"

"The child who came with you tonight."

"Oh, Cecilia. She's a harpsichordist. That is, she's a harpsichord student. I'm helping her in her career. I'll pay for her lessons, and perhaps I'll make it possible for her to study in Europe."

"You know, my dear fellow, you're hopelessly passive. You've never done anything about Ethel, and now you have this girl and you're not going to do anything about her either. You'll just pay her bills and stand on the sidelines while she becomes famous. In the end she'll marry somebody else."

"What do you think I ought to do?"

"Look here, my dear fellow. Why don't you let me take over and orchestrate the drama of your relations with her? I've always wanted to do that—to write a True Novel which would be acted out by real people. I would be in control and tell them what to do at each turning. I'm sure I can make it into a better story than you can."

"Very well, What should I do first?"
"On a walk in the country, you take off her clothes."
"But she'll be stung to death by wasps."
"I didn't mean that."

44.

Ben wandered around the house in the hope of finding Cecilia. Since she got into his car in front of Muir House on Tuesday, he had never been separated from her except for an hour when she went to the pool at the Cantamar. In the music room Ted Pickering was talking to Estelle Galleon. On the other side of the room a guitar and a flute were playing something baroque with a good deal of complicated counterpoint. Ilya and Betsy often offered live music to their Wednesday guests, although neither of them was particularly musical. The piece seemed vaguely familiar, and after a while he recognized it as a chaconne of Purcell transcribed for these two unlikely instruments. The flute was having trouble trying to cover the ground of a whole chamber orchestra. It would have been nicer if the Voronoffs had just put a good record on the stereo, but probably they felt that wouldn't cost enough.

They also offered marijuana to their guests, in a black-lacquer Russian box with a miniature love scene painted on it. Inside were the very best factory-made joints, Acapulco Golds. He had never taken any drug in his life except for an aspirin now and then, but as he told Cecilia, this was their Vita Nuova, a new life for both of them, so perhaps he had better sample a little of the youth culture in which people her age were said to move. He took one and looked around for a lighter.

There wasn't one of the top of the table and, with the joint hanging from his lips like Humphrey Bogart, he began opening the drawers. In the first one were playing cards and some sheet music. He opened the second one and found himself looking at a small gray automatic pistol lying on the green baize bottom of the drawer, like an exhibit in a museum. He knew even less about guns than he did about drugs, but he found the button to make the magazine pop out of the handle. It was full of small glowing jewels, copper at one end and lead at the other. He glanced at Pickering and Estelle but they were deep in their conversation. He started to put the magazine back in the gun and then, a thought striking him, he took out his handkerchief and carefully wiped it off to be sure his fingerprints weren't on it. He also wiped off the gun after he had put the magazine back in it. Then he shut the drawer and went on looking through the others until he found the lighter.

He lighted the joint and began inhaling it deeply, a thing he had heard you were supposed to do. He wasn't used to it and coughed a little but finally got three or four long drags of it down. Everything in the room began to float a little. He put the thing out in the ashtray. He had thought he would try it because it was something that Cecilia's generation did, but he was really too old to try new things. You would think that a generation who were so concerned about physical fitness would realize that drawing anything into your lungs isn't a very good idea, whether it's tobacco or marijuana. Probably it was all a part of their idea of living dangerously. The duo finished the Purcell and embarked into a Mozart divertimento, another piece intended for a full chamber orchestra. He nodded briefly to Pickering and Mrs. Galleon and left the room.

45.

Cecilia was not in the living room, she was not at the bar, and she was not in any of the bedrooms that had their doors open. He hardly felt he ought to try the others. He went outside onto a small terrace overlooking the sea, and thought he had found her, but it turned out to be Carolyn Wong. There was a shadowy figure at her side, murmuring something to her, but it stole away as he approached, carrying something flat and disk-shaped in its hand. He would not have had this strange vision if it had not been for his altered perceptions. A moment later, as the figure passed into the light of the house, he saw it was only the hired waiter who had been giving Carolyn another drink. She turned to him in the darkness; he could see little except a pale moon-shaped face and a shelf of dark hair over the brow.

"Hello, Ben."

"It's so dark I can't see you," he told her.

"The moon will rise in exactly one hour."

He laughed. "Can you be sure?"

"I have the motions of all the heavenly bodies in my head. That's Venus out there, glowing over the sea."

"I can't see very well because I've been smoking something. It looks like a picture by Van Gogh."

"The lens of your eye is just a little out of focus. There above it is Alpha Centauri, the nearest star. It's still quite a distance away."

"How far is it?"

She started to tell him, then changed her mind and took a sip of her drink, which was something tall with a straw in it. His eyes had adjusted now and he could see her better. She was in a long gray gown with a silvery sheen to it. Her oval Asian face was pale as marble and she had dark lashes like bird wings.

"You don't really want to know. The universe is so large that it makes you sick, metaphysically sick, even to think about it. Astronomers don't think about it very much. They deal with the numbers, but they are only numbers. If they tried to wrap their minds around what the numbers really mean, they would boggle and not be able to go on with their work."

The light on the terrace was curious. Now that he had been out of the house for five minutes or so he could see more, but there was a kind of unreality to the atmosphere. A glow seemed to rise from the surf below and hang around them, as though the particles of the air themselves were phosphorescent. He said, "It's frightening. At least it's frightening me a little."

"I hope so; that's what I intended."

"What's it all for? That stuff out there. The vastness of space, the emptiness of it."

"Oh, space isn't really empty if that's what's bothering you. It's full of little fuzzy things. No one is quite sure what they are. They used to call them ether back in the eighteenth century. Perhaps they were right. They don't know what to call them now so they just waffle around."

"Are they molecules, or larger?"

"Oh, they're much smaller than molecules. If you had one right in front of you in the laboratory you couldn't detect it."

"How do you know they're there?"

"For one thing light goes through space. Light can't travel through just nothing. It has to jump from one thing to another."

"I never knew that."

"It's the wave theory of light. There has to be something to wave. There's also a particle theory in which the little fuzzy things aren't necessary."

"Which is correct?"

"They both are, but not at the same time."

"People always say you're clever, but I didn't know you were clever in this way."

"What do you mean?"

He stumblingly began explaining that it was odd to have these disturbing complexities come from so pretty a woman. He had known for years that she was an astronomer and held a chair at the University, but she had never talked to him seriously about her profession before. She made astronomy sound much simpler than he had expected, and much queerer. Maybe this too was part of the effects of the joint he had smoked. He meant his remark as a compliment, but she counterattacked vigorously, without losing any of her aplomb.

"You seem to find some kind of limits in ways that women can be clever. Did it ever strike you that your ideas are terribly old-fashioned?"

"I didn't mean that."

"Then what did you mean?"

"I mean, I expected you'd know a lot of scientific facts. But you make it all sound like some kind of crazy poem."

"It is. It's even possible in fact—this is a theory that the most advanced people are discussing—that the universe is not a structure at all, it's just a vast metaphor."

"You can see all that through a telescope?"

'Not exactly. All you can see through a telescope is a lot of blobs of light of various shapes. It's up to the theoreticians to decide whether they're really there or only a metaphor."

She was really a very original woman. He had known her for years, but now he found himself taking a new interest in her, although he was not quite sure what this interest consisted of. Perhaps it was all a part of his Vita Nuova, the awakening of all kinds of things in him because of his love for Cecilia—an awareness of birds singing, flowers burgeoning, the rustle of rain on a roof, the discovery of little fuzzy things in outer space; he felt abruptly more alive, more perceptive and keen, aware of the complexity and beauty of a world that before he had very largely taken for granted. He knew very little about Carolyn's private life, except that she and Arnold Schifter lived together but had separate names.

"Carolyn, where is Arnold exactly?"

"At a peace conference in Tokyo, I believe. He's always jetting around the world to some place or other."

"Carolyn, are you and Arnold really married?"

"Oh," she said, "what earthly difference does that make in this day and age?"

46.

In the living room Betsy was in a cluster of people under the Foujita. When she saw him coming she left the group and made her way through the white furniture, past the couchant borzois, to the bar. Ben joined her, since she seemed to be signaling him.

She held out her glass to the barman and without a word he filled it with vodka and ice.

"What are you drinking?"

"I've been drinking cognac but I don't care for any more." He decided not to tell her about the joint. It was a bad mistake to have experimented with it. He felt almost normal now.

"Oh, be a sport," she told him. "If a lady drinks, it's impolite of a gentleman not to join her." She took the glass out of his hand and passed it to the barman.

"Betsy, have you seen Cecilia?"

"Yes, she's in the kitchen. Everyone's talking about the stock market in there. I can't imagine why she's interested. Don't go to her now. Stay with me here for a minute."

The barman gave him his drink and he left it on the bar untouched. "Ethel says that you and Ilya are making splitting noises."

"Yes, I told her to tell you that. It's not really true. It's just to get your attention. I get so bored with Ilya, it's a relief to talk to somebody else."

"Then why do you kiss him in public?"

"Oh, that's just the physical thing. After all one is human and one has needs. I kiss him in private too. But he's so boring to talk to. And he has irritating habits."

"Such as?"

"He insists on telling one about the novel he's writing. I have to listen to it by the hour. It's his only subject of conversation. When he eats soup he moves the spoon away from him in the bowl. He claims this is correct. He steals my scent and puts it on his wrists. And he cleans his ears with Q-tips."

Ben laughed. "We all have our little quirks. It seems to me that if you're going to be married you have to put up with such things."

"Oh, there's lots more. He wears satin pajamas with his monogram on them, and he smokes in bed. When we make love he puts the cigarette in the ashtray, and when we've finished he takes it up again. That will give you an idea how long it lasts. Ben, I tell you I get so bored that sometimes I could bite off iron bars."

"Why are you telling me all this, Betsy? I don't want to hear it. You ought to try a little harder to get along with Ilya. After all he's a brilliant man, a well-known novelist, and anyone so talented is bound to have his little peculiarities. You wouldn't be interested in him if he were just an ordinary person like all those faceless millions."

She shrugged. "I told you I had no intention of leaving him. His fame, his talent, his wealth. I know it all. Now tell me what you've been doing."

"Betsy, just because you tell me all the intimacies of your private life, don't imagine that I'm going to tell you all the intimacies of my private life."

She smiled. "I think it's grand about you and Cecilia. I don't believe for a minute that you're just helping her out in her musical career." She made once again her little tinkle of laughter. Ben remembered telling himself when he was still at Muir House that the ridiculous, not the immoral, would be the true enemy of his love for Cecilia. "But she's only a child, isn't she?" Betsy went on. "I can't imagine what the two of you find to talk about."

"She's a very intelligent person. We talk about all kinds of things."

She ignored this, in the way she had with facts she didn't care for. "Suppose we make a pact, Ben. I have boring old Ilya and you have this charming doll. That's our bed-life. But we have each other to talk to."

She took a sip of her drink, looking at him over the rim of the glass with a significant expression like a silent-movie vamp. This sort of flirtation was an old habit with Betsy; she did it with everybody, all the men, and even some women for all he knew. He had known her for a long time, and he had always managed, rather playfully, to skirt this side of her personality and escape unscathed. As a matter of fact she had given up long ago on him, writing him off as unattainable, reasonable and aloof, and not given to foolish impulsive gestures. Now he saw that the entry of Cecilia into his life, the fact that he had brought Cecilia to the Wednesday, had reawakened all of Betsy's latent instincts and sent something raging through her glands, or her mind, or wherever it was that her tremendous sexual ego was centered.

In her white satin gown, with her peacock-hair and the tiny shadows showing at the points of her breasts, she was a very attractive person tonight and she obviously knew it. He was suddenly aware of a great danger. Where Betsy had never been a threat to him before, except the kind of threat represented by mere gossip, now she became a woman who, if she had her way, could do him a terrible damage. If he made the wrong move, if he slipped and fell even a little, it could cause him to lose Cecilia. Even if the risk was small, it represented the loss of something so infinitely precious that the idea was frightening.

He told her, "We're talking right now."

"It's time," she said, "for one of our serious discourses."

"Do we have serious discourses?"

"If we don't, we should. You could take me to lunch sometime."

"You want to do everything in public, Betsy. You kiss Ilya in public and you want to talk to me in public. You flaunt your possessions."

"Oh, if I thought you would fly off the handle about it I wouldn't have mentioned it."

"And Cecilia is not a doll."

"What *do* you talk to her about?"

"Music."

47.

He found Cecilia in the kitchen as Betsy said. She was with a group of people including the Rolfs and Ilya. Whether they were talking about the stock market he couldn't tell; they stopped talking as he came up.

"What do you say we leave, Cecilia?"

"Oh, all right. I was enjoying myself though."

"Oh, ha ha. The impatient bridegroom."

"Shut up, Ilya."

"I don't blame you a bit, old fellow."

"It's not that at all, Ilya," said Edgar Rolf. "It's just that Ben knows young people should get lots of sleep."

"Of course, ha ha."

"It *is* midnight."

"Are you sure? We could ask Carolyn. She always knows what time it is."

"I was having quite a talk with Carolyn," said Ben. "She told me space is full of little fuzzy things."

"She was pulling your leg."

"She says that light is both particles and waves, but not both at the same time."

"Which is it tonight?"

"Particles, I believe. Come on, Cecilia."

"Goodbye. I so much enjoyed meeting you all."

"It was a pleasure. Please come again. Ha. ha."

"Goodnight, dear," said Jo-Nan."

48.

Outside they got in the car and drove in silence for some time. Ben felt good being alone with her after all the smoke and chatter and drinking of the party. Then he said, "What *were* you talking about to those people?"

"Snoozy Pickering was telling us about life as a Navy wife."

"Oh, fascinating."

"She has some good anecdotes. And the Rolfs are interesting. They're in the import business."

"I told you that."

"Maybe you did. I talked to them about harpsichords. They know all about them. Some of them are made in America but they're not very good. The best ones are made in England and France. The Rolfs have imported several for people."

He sensed the Rolfs invading the one territory of his strength, the help he could give her in her career. He said, "Never mind the Rolfs. We could go over and get one ourselves."

"That would be nice. The very best ones are made by a man named Walter Thorne in Sussex. Of course," she added, "we'd have to find another place to live, because there's no room for a harpsichord in the cottage."

"Are you bringing all this up because we're on our way home?"

"What?"

"I mean, first you want me to buy a harpsichord, and then you want me to buy a house to put it in. And you bring all this up just as we're going home to go to bed together. If I don't buy you the harpsichord and the house, maybe you'll have a headache."

"Oh Ben, how could you imagine such a thing."

"I've got a vivid imagination. I'm glad you had a good time at the Voronoffs because I was wretched. I kept looking all over the house for you and I couldn't find you."

"I was in the kitchen most of the time."

"Maybe we should go to England. If we stay here in

Santa Barbara we'll just be seeing that crowd all the time. I want to get you away from them."

"I rather enjoyed them."

"There's no one your age except Raymonde."

"Oh I don't mind that. I hardly ever notice a person's age."

Once again he was struck by the offhand mysteriousness of her way of talking. He couldn't decide whether this referred to him or whether she was just chatting. He decided to say nothing. When they got out of the car at the Cantamar she embraced him impulsively in the parking lot, even before they had started for the cottage. He could feel every detail of her body through the loose sweater. "Thanks so much for taking me, Ben. It was nice of you."

Standing there in the parking lot, it was only with difficulty that he could let her go. He could have gone on for hours exploring this sensation of their two bodies pressing together. The moon had come up now as Carolyn had predicted. They made their way together down the walk through the tropical landscaping. The giant Bird-of-Paradise outside the cottage, with its strange beaky flower, glowed in the milky light.

She said, "It would be so nice if you bought me a harpsichord."

49.

In the Mercedes which smelled of leather as the sun warmed its seats, Ben drove around the campus and found a parking place near the music building. Cecilia was still wearing the narrow black pants, which seemed almost as much a part of her as her legs, but instead of the white sweater she had on her blue sleeveless blouse. She had done her hair up in plaits again, leaving much of it loose and the two braids hanging in the middle of it. No flowers in them though. She had dressed in this way because she was going to play the harpsichord, which she couldn't do in the big white sweater and her hair over one eye.

They found the office of Professor Dominicus and Cecilia gave her name to the receptionist. After a while Dominicus, a tall bent man with a reddish beard, came out and looked at her with a frown.

"Hello, Cecilia. You can call me Egon. Who is this?"

"I'm Ben Gavilan. I'm a friend of Cecilia's."

"Do you have to come along?"

"Yes."

"Ordinarily we don't allow visitors at auditions."

"I'd like to be there."

Dominicus gave him a piercing look, taking in his well-cut clothes and his withered arm. "All right." He told Cecilia, "I can give you a half an hour. I have another appointment at ten. I hope you're not going to waste my time."

He led the way down the corridor, out through a breezeway, and into another part of the building. There he opened the door of a practice room and motioned both of them through it, rather impatiently. It contained a piano, a harpsichord, a table with a tape recorder on it, and one chair. A wire storage rack was piled with music, most of it dog-eared. Dominicus glanced at his watch. "Did you bring music?"

"Yes."

Dominicus sat down at the table, lighted a cigarette, and set it in the ashtray. Then he folded his hands on the table and stared at Cecilia intently. There was no place for Ben to sit so he remained standing. Cecilia took her place at the harpsichord and spread out her music.

The small room was insulated with acoustic tiles. It was so quiet that you could hear the soft crackling of Dominicus's cigarette. Cecilia set her fingers on the keys without depressing them. Ben had forgotten that harpsichords have two keyboards. The instrument seemed fragile and intricate at the same time. It looked as though it was difficult to play.

She played some Scarlatti and a piece or two from Rameau's suites. She seemed very good to Ben but he was no judge. Her fingers seemed to glide over the keys like white spiders instead of striking them as a pianist would. Forgetting that she was having an audition, he found himself moved by the intricacy and grace of the sonatas, the easy, almost negligent precision of the continuo in the left hand. Dominicus drew on his cigarette from time to time and watched her without expression. Gradually a haze of smoke filled the room; Cecilia gave a little cough. She had to slap at the music once to make it lie down and she missed a note. Dominicus sighed and glanced at his watch again. The thread of smoke from the ashtray rose slowly toward the ceiling. It was so still in the room that Ben could clearly make out the different colors of the blue and brown smoke mingled in it.

Cecilia finished the Scarlatti and started on the Rameau, this time making sure first that the music lay flat. The two pieces were sarabandes, the first slow, the second more lively. She played them with aplomb, turning the pages without missing a note. The second one ended in a little flurry of trills. She set her hands in her lap and turned to Dominicus.

He got up and took some music from the rack. "Try this."

Cecilia began sight-reading. It was something from Bach's *Well-Tempered Clavier* that sounded impossibly difficult. She made several mistakes and at one point stopped and started over. Dominicus's expression was exactly as it had been before. When she ended she was pink and there was a veil of perspiration on her upper lip.

Dominicus got up and crushed out his cigarette. For a long time he didn't speak. He sighed, took the Bach music, and put it back on the rack.

"Well," he said, "You're not so bad. I don't know who taught you fingering. You've got the principle all right but you haven't quite mastered it. I can take you in my senior class in the fall." He had a Viennese accent that made him sound lightly sinister, like Peter Lorre. He swallowed his r's—'pwinciple." He said, "Of course you'll have to apply for admission as a regular student in the University. That's between you and the registrar. I have nothing to do with it."

"Oh, I don't have to apply. I'm a student at Berkeley. I have the right to transfer to any campus I want."

"Oh, you're a Berkeley student. Well, that makes it much simpler. The quarter begins at the end of September. The senior class meets Tuesday-Thursday at four. In addition to the class you're expected to put in at least two hours every day in the practice room."

"That's fine. I don't have a harpsichord of my own yet."

Ben noted that "yet." He was planning to buy her one, but he hadn't expected her to jump to the conclusion so quickly.

Dominicus didn't invite them to accompany him back to his office. He said, "You can get to the parking lot right through here. Between now and September," he said, "I'll expect you to practice every day, Cecilia. You can use the practice room right here in the department."

"Thank you, Professor Dominicus."

"Egon."

He turned his back on them and walked away. In the car Ben told her, "That man seems to me a sadist."

"Oh, they're all like that."

"Who?"

"Everybody in music."

50.

They had lunch in Isla Vista at the Vision of Siam, a restaurant frequented by students; he thought she would like this. In the pond in front there were two old koi the size of cats; splotched gray tissue seemed to float from them and dissolve in the stagnant water. The wall at the side, which really belonged to the building next door, was covered with bright graffiti like neon signs. *Sorry, my karma just ran over your dogma.*

Cecilia smiled wanly. She said it was just like Berkeley. Whether it was a favorable or an unfavorable sign that it was just like Berkeley he didn't know; he desperately wanted her to like everything about Isla Vista and Santa Barbara in general. They went in and had their lunch: a single order of mee krob which they shared, and then the stuffed chicken wings for Ben and the mint salad with shrimp and ginger for her. For a while they were alone in the place. They were served by a moonfaced waiter who, in spite of the fact that it was midday and he was perspiring faintly, was wearing a black mess jacket like a steward on a ship. A pair of women came in, with long straight hair and layered clothing, and then a trio of students. There were only six tables and the restaurant was now half full.

They drank ice tea flavored with cardamon and honey, a cloying beverage that Ben rather liked. Cecilia set down her glass and wiped her lip with the back of her finger; she had apparently never learned to use a napkin properly. She said, "That is not a very good harpsichord."

"I don't imagine the musical instruments in schools ever are."

"No, they're not." She paused for another sip of tea, and then said, "Do you plan on going on living in the cottage indefinitely?"

Usually she was as mysterious to him as a Greek oracle, but now he could see every gear in her mind working, as though her skull were transparent. "I hadn't thought about it. Perhaps I might make some change."

"It's very tiny."

"Yes. I told you that when I first showed it to you. I like it precisely for that. It's neat and everything's close at hand. I like to keep my life simple. I don't like to own a lot of complicated things I don't really need. I like it in the cottage. I've lived there for ten years and it suits me and it fits my needs. Of course, now that—" he started to say, "now that I have you" and changed in mid-sentence —"Now that you're living there too, I might have to reconsider."

"That's what I think. We're going to need a bigger place."

Ben had known this conversation would come sooner or later, but he had imagined that he would be the one to suggest that they needed a bigger place, that he would confer the idea on her as a gift. Instead she was discussing it with him as though they were an old married couple.

"I might consider moving into a house. The trouble is, I don't like the idea of taking care of the yard, and doing all that housework. I don't imagine you're interested in doing it either."

"Not really. You can get people to do that for you. If you have the money."

He didn't tell her whether he had the money; she knew he did. He said, "It's something to think about. There's no point in rushing to a decision."

"The thing is," she said, "in the cottage there's—"

"There's no room for your harpsichord."

"Oh, Ben, you're so keen. You always know what I'm thinking." She smiled and sipped her tea again, eyeing him over the rim of the glass like an old Egyptian cat.

51.

Chekhov says that if there is a gun on the wall in the first act, it will surely be used before the end of the play. He probably got this idea from Ibsen, from whom he learned a lot about playwriting.

In Ibsen's *Wild Duck*, the gun is shown not in the first act but in the third. There is a shot offstage, and then Hjalmar comes on with a double-barreled pistol, with which he's been practising in the garret. He sets it on the bookcase and tells everybody, "One of the barrels is still loaded, remember that." His wife Gina, who is of humble origins, can't even pronounce pistol; she calls it a "pigstol." (Probably this bad joke is better in Norwegian). But she advises against keeping it around the house. She is depicted as a woman of good sense. In Act V, their little daughter Hedvig, mistaking herself for a wounded wild duck, shoots herself in the breast with it, in the same garret. We knew this was going to happen as soon as Hjalmar told us about the second bullet.

In *Hedda Gabler* it's a little more complicated but the

principle is the same. At the end of Act I (this is the play Chekhov was thinking of) we are shown a pair of dueling pistols which belonged to Hedda's father Colonel Gabler. In Act II Hedda fires playfully at her friend Judge Brack and misses him. But it's made clear in the action that she knows how to reload the things. At the end of Act II she gives one to Lövborg, the discouraged poet. She tells him, "Do it beautifully." Unfortunately he is too distracted to follow these instructions; he shoots himself in a whorehouse, and in the bowels. The audience thinks, Oh, oh, there's still that other pistol. Judge Brack, that old fox, knows where Lövborg got the first pistol, and attempts sexual blackmail on Hedda. In response, she goes into the next room and shoots herself in the temple. Judge Brack cries, "People don't do such things!" This seems like a good piece of dramatic criticism.

Chekhov's own *Seagull* is sometimes described as a parody of *The Wild Duck*. However, Chekhov is a good deal more subtle than Ibsen and the gun is not displayed to the audience so obviously. In Act II Trepleff, an unsuccessful writer, comes on stage carrying a gun and a dead seagull. He lays the seagull at the feet of Nina, who decides it must be a symbol of some sort, then he predicts that he is going to kill himself. Nobody pays much attention to him at this point, but in Act III he comes in with his head wrapped in a bandage from an unsuccessful attempt to shoot himself. Sooner or later, we know, he's going to learn how to work the thing. Sure enough, at the end of the play he kills himself with the gun in the next room. The people on stage take the sound for a bottle of ether bursting in Dr. Dorn's medicine cabinet. It doesn't seem so crass and contrived when you see the play well performed on stage; it seems like something that might happen.

It's an old axiom that Nature Copies Art. If this is true, then if a pistol appears on a wall, or in a drawer, in real life, than perhaps it too will be used before the end of the play. This is not because Art has any metaphysical influence on Nature, but simply because people model their lives on works of art they have seen and then perhaps forgotten entirely in their conscious minds. Of course, a gun on the wall is not just a decoration or a piece of bric-a-brac, like a Hummel figure or a piece of heather you brought back from Scotland. It's one of those machines that are useful for something; its intention is built into its design. It's good for only one thing. A gun on the wall, or in a drawer, is only the cold and concrete embodiment of the wish to destroy, whether its owner realizes it or not. He may wish to destroy some hypothetical invader of his home, or an elk, or the President of Zaire, or his wife's lover, or he may not have the least inkling what he wants to destroy. Yet this hidden impulse will surely work its way to the surface. At least in literature; but Nature copies Art.

Women do not, under natural conditions, own guns or take any interest in them. They almost never commit suicide with guns, in spite of Hedda's example. There are a number of theories as to why this is so. One is that it mars their looks; another is that they are afraid of loud noises.

52.

The office of the Turtle Press was on the second floor of a building on the hillside not far from the Cantamar, with a door opening onto an outside balcony, a very modest place. There was a sign on the front with the turtle logo, and some white enameled shutters which were now open. From the balcony Ben could see Peter through the window, bent over a manuscript he was marking. He stood lost in this innocent voyeurism for a minute or two; it seemed to him that in Peter he was looking at himself doing all the things he did at the Press for so many years, a younger Ben, starting the whole thing over, as innocent as a child and full of hopes and expectations. The poor bastard, he said silently, thinking more of himself at Peter's age than of Peter.

He pushed open the door and went in.

"Hello, Peter."

Peter looked up from his manuscript, made a final mark, and set the pen down. "Oh hi, Ben. You're back from your weekend."

"Yes."

"How was it?"

"Nice. Very restful."

"You went to the Sierras, didn't you?"

"Yes. Muir House. I've been going there for years."

Peter got up to make some coffee, a ritual when Ben visited the Press. He was genuinely fond of Peter. He was about thirty, Ben thought; he took his M.A. at the University about five years ago. Like Ben he was a New Englander. He dressed in an old corduroy jacket, a tattersall shirt, and khaki pants. He always gave the impression that he wasn't aware of his own good looks, which involved a lean movie-star face and glossy black hair which he pushed back constantly from his eyes. Ben made a mental note to keep him away from Cecilia as much as possible. He was the only man that young that Ben knew well.

The Press office consisted of a large room in front, where Peter was working on the manuscript, and a room behind which served as a storeroom and had desks for

Mrs. Partener, the accountant and business manager, and a student who worked part-time correcting proofs and filing. This part-time job had been Peter's before he bought the Press. In the front room were bookcases for the books the Press had published and a glass case full of California Indian artifacts, Peter's hobby. In the corner where it would catch the light from the window was a large ficus in a terracotta urn. The hotplate was also in the front, so Peter could offer coffee to his authors and other visitors without having to take them into the rather untidy back room.

"What are you working on?"

"It's a book on Joaquin Murieta. We're going to do it on good paper, with photos. It'll be rather expensive, I'm afraid."

"There are other books on that particular bandit."

"I know. This one was done by a woman in Sacramento who's spent her whole life studying Murieta. She's anxious to get it published. Maybe we shouldn't have taken it on."

"The fact that an author wants to get a book published," said Ben, "is not really a reason to publish it."

"I'm finding that out." Peter showed him some other recent books the Press had published. There was a nice short book on California archeology with color illustrations, a book of poems by a Santa Barbara high school teacher, and a humorous book on English usage by a man in Santa Monica who made his living as a proofreader. Ben got out his reading glasses and looked at the book of poems. Some of them were pretty good, as far as he could tell with a glance. The poor devil, it wouldn't get him out of his high school job, but it might do something for his ego.

"How are sales?"

"The archeology book is doing nicely. The others—" Peter sighed and pushed the hair out of his eyes. "You know how it is."

He was so good-looking that Ben could almost imagine what it would be like to be a homosexual: his fingers passing over Peter's lean cheekbones and tousling his mop of dark hair. He took the mug of coffee that Peter offered him and put some powdered creamer into it. If the Press did a little better, Peter could buy a small refrigerator and serve real cream with his coffee.

"Care for a Danish? Or a chocolate-chip cookie?"

"No thanks. It seems," he said, "that things are going along about as they did when I was running it. I wouldn't have published that Murieta book, but I made my own mistakes."

Peter picked up his own coffee mug and stirred the creamer into it, then set it down without drinking it. "I'm making some too. Sometimes when Mrs. Partener shows me the figures it scares me. You know, I have to pay a hell of a lot for my apartment. And you know what it is. It's down by the beach but it's nothing much. Everything is expensive in Santa Barbara. I have to pay Mrs. Partener three hundred a week. You can't get anybody for less. It's tough to get that kind of money out of a small press." He stopped and looked at Ben thoughtfully. "I don't know. How the devil did you manage to make it go?"

"Some years I put a little money in it."

"You mean you ran it at a loss?"

Ben nodded.

"Why didn't you tell me that when I bought it?"

"You didn't ask. People don't really go into this kind of business to make money."

"You have your money. I have to make a living out of

this. It's the apartment," he said, "that's really dragging me down. Seven hundred a month. I've thought of firing Mrs. Partener and doing the accounting myself, and moving into the back room. I don't know if it's allowed by the zoning. There's everything you need here, a toilet and a hotplate. There's no shower but there's the ocean. Without the apartment, and without Mrs. Partener's wages, I'd be making a small profit."

Ben looked through the open door into the back room where Mrs. Partener was working. Peter had spoken in a low voice but he still thought she might have heard. "I wouldn't do that," he said. "As soon as you start living in your office it's not a real business. People won't believe in it. Your authors would drift away. And you can't do the accounting. It's more technical than you think.

He glanced at his watch. "I have to—pick somebody up at the University at four." He decided not to mention Cecilia. "It's always nice talking to you. The archeology book is very nice. Congratulations."

"Why don't you drop in once a week or so and see what we're doing. I'd like your advice on things."

Ben noticed the plural first person—the publisher's "we"—even though it was really a one-man business. He had done the same when he owned the Press. "I'd like to. I don't have as much time as I used to. I have new interests in my life."

Peter didn't inquire what these were. He said, "I don't know if I'm going to make it, Ben." Ben walked slowly to the door without saying anything. Peter said, "You're still a partner. Suppose I asked you to put a little more money in it."

"I might be able to manage that. But the Press will never make a lot of money. I thought you realized that. It's very satisfying, but it's not the way to get rich. I could put a few thousand dollars more into it, but it might still go under.l You've got to face that reality. You could find something else to do, and the world could get along with one less small press."

"I've committed myself, Ben. I like running the Press. It's my life now."

"You've always had things your way. You came from a good family and you went to Groton and Dartmouth. You breezed through your M.A. at UCSC. You're good-looking and everybody likes you. Now you're finding out what life is like for everybody else. It's very tough and it doesn't care whether you're good-looking or you went to Dartmouth. It's dollars in and dollars out. If dollars in are less than dollars out, you go under."

Peter's good-looking young face was troubled; there was a furrow on the brow that Ben had never seen there before. Ben was suddenly conscious of his arm, the only real handicap of his own life. It made him feel superior to Peter in a way that was quite irrational. Peter said, "Ben, you've got to help me. You sold me this heap of garbage."

"Now, don't get emotional. You yourself said you liked the Press."

"I do. I love it. I don't want to lose it, Ben."

"Turn down the Murieta book. Ask Mrs. Partener if she'll take two-fifty. Fire the student."

"Oh, Ben. For God's sake."

53.

Because he arrived at the University a half an hour early he went to the library and looked up her name in the *Lives of the Saints*. Saint Cecilia was a noble lady of Rome who was martyred under Alexander Severus. Her festival is the twenty-second of November. There is a church in her honor in the Trastevere, built by Cardinal Sfrandrati in 1599. She was the patron saint of music and her way of praying was singing and playing her instrument. The *Lives* didn't say what instrument she played. Probably a harpsichord. He rather fancied this view of Cecilia as a martyred saint, sacrificed to his antique lust.

54.

When Ben and Cecilia got home there was a curious letter for him in the mail. There was no return address, and it was in a shabby envelope of the kind you buy in a drugstore. When he opened it there was a message consisting of letters of various sizes cut out of magazines and newspapers and pasted to a piece of cheap paper.

Crabbed age and youth cannot live together.

He felt the warm cheeks and discomfort at the pit of the stomach that anyone feels when he gets an anonymous letter, even when it's pure foolishness. It had to be one of the Voronoff set. After all they were the only ones who knew about his new life with Cecilia. But which one? Betsy herself? Mysterious Carolyn, whose motives about anything were never quite clear? Ilya, who in this way was manipulating him into performing a part in his novel, as he had threatened? They might all have their reasons. Maybe the three of them made it up, sitting around a table and cutting the letters out with scissors. It wasn't likely to be Ted Pickering; he himself was noted for his philandering with younger women. What was clear was that these people were discussing him among themselves and had attitudes toward his relations with Cecilia. A completely mad idea struck him: it was Ethel.

Cecilia took the letter from him and read it. Then she smiled and set it down.

"It's that idiot Dave."

"How do you know?"

She examined the postmark on the envelope, but it was smeared and illegible. "It's logical," she said. "He could have gotten your address from the hotel desk."

He had never told her about his argument with Dave, in which Dave told him that he had had his time in the world and he ought to let others have their chance.

He asked her, "Do you think it's true?"

"What?"

"What it says in the note."

She laughed. "What does crabbed mean?"

"Crabby."

"Then it doesn't apply to us."

"Dave had you, didn't he?"

"What do you mean?"

"He had you. There at Muir House. Probably in the student dormitory."

"What a funny way to put it." She was silent for a moment. then she said, "Well, what's wrong with that? It's perfectly natural. Everyone does such things."

He remembered that *perfectly natural* was what she had told Dave about his own infatuation for her, in the conversation he had overheard behind Muir House. She tended to repeat herself in diction, he noticed. Probably she had only a small stock of phrases which served for all purposes. He felt a little sick at what she had told him, although of course the naturalness of it, the obviousness, had already struck him in a part of his mind, a secret or hidden part he had not examined carefully before. They would have. Why not? She was on her vacation and wanted to have a good time. They were young. Dave was a good-looking young man. People didn't require a permanent commitment anymore before they did such things. There were lots of reasons. He examined the letter again, trying to decide whether he would have preferred it to come from Dave or Ethel. He really couldn't decide on this point. In any case he didn't intend to let the letter spoil his day, particularly his evening. He decided to do something special for Cecilia in order to make up for the fact that her former lover had accused him of senile impotence. Take her out to dinner, for example. He got out his address book and began looking up the phone number of the restaurant.

55.

The subject of old men and young women is a familiar one in the history of literature. It goes back as far as Ulysses in Homer's *Odyssey*, who loses his head first over Circe and then over Calypso when he should be getting back to his middle-aged wife and family in Ithaca. The Nausicaa episode in the *Odyssey* is ambiguous, but what happens essentially is that Ulysses exposes himself to a young girl so that she and her friends are embarrassed. In the classic Roman drama the character of Gerontion, the foolish old man, is a stock figure. He squanders his money, is easily tricked by others, and invariably falls in love with a young girl, with disastrous and comical results. He has an enormous vanity, particularly in matters of love, and has no idea how ridiculous he appears to others.

In Molière's *School for Wives*, the aged Arnolphe plans to marry his ward Agnès, whom he has raised from the age of four for this purpose. The moment she is nubile she falls in love with a younger man, Horace. Horace capers through the play courting her openly, and only Arnolphe doesn't notice what is going on. At one point

Agnès tells her guardian that Horace while caressing her took her—took her—she's afraid to say what it was. He'll be angry. For God's sake! Arnolphe is in a torment of suffering. Took her favorite ribbon, she says. A little later she tells him that she threw a brick at Horace, but omits to add that there was a billet-doux wrapped around it. In the end it turns out that Agnès is the long-lost daughter of a prince and engaged to Horace anyhow. The lovers are united and everyone has a hearty laugh at Arnolphe's expense.

In Rossini's opera *The Barber of Seville* the situation is much the same. Old Doctor Bartolo has a ward named Rosina whom he plans to marry. Aided by the clever Figaro, the young Count Almaviva makes the same kind of fool out of him that Horace makes out of Arnolphe. He invades Bartolo's house disguised as a poor student, a drunken soldier, and Rosina's singing master. The lovers exchange letters. Bartolo finds ink stains on Rosina's fingers, and a piece of her writing paper missing, and she tells him lies so facile that only a senile idiot could believe them. Rossini, or his librettist, doesn't bother with the lost-orphan trick; the agile Figaro takes advantage of the moment to get the lovers married by the same notary that Bartolo has hired for his own marriage to Rosina.

Even in the movies it's the foolish middle-aged professor who falls for the coed and makes an ass out of himself. It seems a curious theme. You'd think that in real life older people would be wise and the young ones foolish. They are, except in this particular matter. In sex it seems that you lose wisdom as you get older, so that when you reach your sixties you give the impression that you've forgotten everything you ever knew and are an absolute fool, at least compared to a twenty-year-old.

56.

The agent was a fortyish woman in a pantsuit, with peroxided hair and blue eyelids. She told them, "Call me Stacey." It wasn't clear whether it was her first name or her last name. They got out of her lemonade-colored Cadillac and stood in the drive looking at the house. It stood out sharply from the other houses on the street, all in the Spanish style; it was a large New England cottage in weathered gray shingles and white trim. There were gables in the roof and, opening from the bedroom upstairs, a typical New England widow's walk facing toward the sea. The detached garage was at one side.

As soon as Ben saw the house his heart leaped almost as it did when he first caught sight of Cecilia. He knew that this was the one he had to have, that *she* had to have it, that he had to buy it for her. In buying her this house he would be making her a gift of New England, of himself, of a bit of the East Coast transplanted to Santa Barbara, of a whole culture that was different from her own California culture that he couldn't hope to compete with. Living in this house with her, he would be on his own territory as an Easterner and cosmopolitan, offering her something that was as old as harpsichords and equally distinguished. It was true that it was fake, not a real New England house but an imitation. Never mind; he felt a joy in his heart as soon as he saw it. He attempted to conceal this emotion from Stacey, otherwise he would give away his hand and the house would cost him several thousand dollars more. He looked it over in silence, with a little buzzing sensation in his head.

"Three bedrooms, two baths, rebuilt kitchen, hardwood floors," said Stacey rapidly as though she reciting a litany. "Landscape lighting, a security system, and a fireplace."

The entry had double doors and a vestibule with a small shingled rooflet, exactly like a house in Massachusetts. Stacey unlocked the doors and they went in. The shutters were closed and it was shadowy and cool inside; they walked around through the rooms with their footsteps echoing on the bare hardwood floors. The kitchen was one of those with an island in the center and a counter over which you passed things to people in the dining area, as Stacey called it. It was not really a traditional New England kitchen, but probably it was more convenient. In fact, Ben began to see now that the inside of the house was thoroughly modern; it was like a yacht built to imitate an old-fashioned sailing ship. It was better this way; no worrying about rusted pipes, sagging floors, or dry rot. Another feature that was not authentically New England was the large circular window in the living room, five feet in diameter and divided into twelve radial panes like a clock. It faced toward the sea and it was slightly dusty now, so that the world outside penetrated through it blurred and with its outlines softened, like the background to a stage set. Act I: a living room on the coast of California.

They went upstairs and inspected the master bedroom, which had french doors opening out onto the widow's walk. He explained the widow's walk to Cecilia. "In New England houses, this was a place for the wife to walk back and forth to see if she could see the sails of her husband's ship on the horizon."

"Did the sea-captain ever come home?"

"No. Finally she married the doctor, who also held the mortgage on the house."

"I beg your pardon," said Stacey with her professional smile. "Do you know someone who lived here?"

"No. It was a house in a story."

They went back downstairs. "There is an intercom," said Stacey. "And here is the control panel for the security system."

Ben wasn't very interested in the security system. "Where's the mother-in-law annex you told me about?"

"The what?" Cecilia suppressed a laugh.

Stacey took them out the french doors into the garden at the rear. There were no palms or oleanders as there were at the other houses on the street. The trees were birches, maples, and sycamores, and the flowers were all annuals: phlox, petunias, pansies, and daisies. There was a small kidney-shaped pool with a screen of pussy willows around it so you could swim in it without suits if you wanted; Stacey communicated this possibility with tact. This, after the kitchen, was the only concession to the California way of life.

On the right side of the garden a covered breezeway led to a small house only a little larger than Ben's cottage at the Cantamar. It too was finished in weathered gray shingles. Stacey said, "This is in case you have an older relative or someone living with you. Or for guests. It's very convenient. This is the only house on my list that has one."

She unlocked the door and they went in. There was a living room, a bedroom, a small kitchen, and a bath. Like the main house it had hardwood floors. "This would be fine for Cecilia," said Ben. "She'll have her privacy here and there's room for her harpsichord."

"What *is* a harpsichord exactly?"

"It's like a piano," Cecilia told her, "but it's the kind they had in the eighteenth century."

"But this is the twentieth century."

"Yes, but you can still have them made in England. Bach," she said, "should properly be played on a harpsichord, not a piano."

"I see. How nice. I love old things."

"Cecilia and I are going to Europe for a month to buy one. We'll move into the house when we come back."

"Do you have very much furniture?"

"I don't have any at all. Perhaps you can take care of that while we're gone. Some nice replica antiques. We both like old things. I imagine you know a decorator? Most real estate agents do."

"Oh yes. But—"

"I'll open a credit line for you at my bank. You can draw on that while we're in Europe, then we'll settle the accounts after we get back."

Stacey stared at him. Still smiling, she proceeded cautiously as though she were dealing with a dangerous madman. "Is there anything else you'd like to see here? If not, we can go on and I can show you some others."

"I think this one will do."

"But it's the first one you've seen."

"It's a New England house. I never have cared for the Spanish style."

"Well of course Spanish is very popular in California. This house is unique in Montecito."

"That's what I like about it."

"They might take a little less than the figure I quoted you."

"All right. I'll leave that to you."

"I must say that . . ." Whatever it was, she decided that she didn't have to say it after all. "Well, you're very easy people to deal with."

"From what you told me, it's the only one with an annex."

"Yes, for Cecilia's—old piano. Is Cecilia your student?"

"She's not my student. She is a student."

"Are you a professor?"

"No. I'm a music lover."

"I see," said Stacey. Her skepticism was far from the raillery of the Voronoff set. She didn't ask him if he and Cecilia made music together. She simply didn't understand what the two of them were up to, so she said, "I see." It was much easier dealing with Stacey. All that really mattered to her was that she made the sale and got her commission.

Ben said, "Do you like the house, Cecilia?"

"I think it's lovely, but the walls won't do."

"The walls?"

The walls throughout the house were a light gray, somewhat dull with age, and it was the same in the annex. They were genuine plaster, as Ben could tell by tapping them with his knuckle. In most California houses the walls were plasterboard.

"If you buy the house," said Stacey, "you can do the walls any color you want."

"Yes, but we won't have time, you see," said Cecilia. "We'll be coming back from Europe and we'll want to move into the house right away. So you can take care of it, won't you, Stacey. These here in the living room ought to be a light blue. A robin's-egg blue, but not all the way up. There ought to be a picture-rail right about here." She indicated a place as high as she could reach on the wall. "A nice wallpaper above the rail, and the blue underneath it."

"I'm a realtor, not a contractor."

"The same decorator can do it who finds us the furniture."

"Are you going to hang pictures on the picture-rail?"

"Daumier prints. The decorator can find them too."

"This is a young lady who certainly knows exactly what she wants."

Ben said, "Is there anything else you want to change about the house?"

"Well, all of the walls, of course. Don't you think?"

Ben and Stacey followed her through the house while she indicated her ideas about the rest of the walls and the other details. The bedrooms were to be white, with the door-frames and trim left gray. The kitchen, off-white with mahogany cabinet doors. Those painted doors would have to go. They crossed the garden to the annex, where Cecilia gave her opinion that the walls here ought to be lemon yellow with white trim. No, primrose yellow.

"No picture rail?" asked Stacey with light sarcasm.

"No picture rail. This is where the harpsichord is going to go, so there needs to be a hanging light-fixture right here. But not one of those horrible Tiffany things. Something in pale yellow satin, to match the rest of the decor." She tried to make a cross on the floor with her foot, but it left no mark on the polished hardwood. "Have you got a pen?"

Stacey passed her a ballpoint, and Cecilia made a circle with an X and wrote "Hanging light" on the floor.

"Behind the harpsichord we could have a nice picture, so you could see it while you were playing. A Canaletto reproduction." She took the ballpoint and made another circle with an X in it on the wall, and wrote "Canaletto" next to it. "You do like Canaletto, don't you?" she asked Ben.

"Oh yes, Canaletto is very nice."

"It's eighteenth century, don't you see, so it's the same period as the harpsichord. We could have Sheraton furniture in here, or Louis XV."

"Sheraton and Louis XV," said Stacey. "What were the names of those pictures?"

"Canaletto and Daumier. I'll write Daumier on the wall too."

"I don't know if I can remember all this. Did you study decorating in college?"

"If you'd been listening to anything we've been saying," said Cecilia, "you'd know I'm a musician."

57.

Since Cecilia had now performed for him on the harpsichord, Ben showed her how he was able to play the piano with his withered arm, demonstrating on the small spinet in the cottage at the Cantamar. First he got the music out of the bench and put it on the stand. Then he sat down, picked up his right arm with his left, and placed the hand on the keyboard a little above middle C. His left hand was strong and he had a formidable bass. The right arm was not able to move its own hand along the keyboard, so the hand scuttled back and forth on its own like a crab. ("Crabbed age and youth," he thought). This meant that he couldn't make large leaps, at least with the right hand, but he could fling the hand three or four notes up and down the keyboard. His touch was not very good in the right hand because his wrist drooped.

He was a little ashamed of the simplicity of the music he set out on the stand. Some pieces from Schumann's *Album for the Young*, finger exercises for little girls; and then, a little more ambitious, Handel's *Alesford Piece* and a gigue by Couperin. Then he stopped and faced her, still sitting on the bench. There was a silence.

"Good on the warming up," she said. She meant the Schumann. "I like the Handel. Couperin is not really serious music. Couperin," she said, "is the Muzak of the eighteenth century."

58.

There is after all a kind of wisdom that I have and she doesn't. I can trade my wisdom of the world for her sex wisdom. Of course, part of my world wisdom comes from the fact that I had sex wisdom like her when I was young, and now I've lost it. But I can still remember it.

59.

The phone rang and it was Ethel Track. "I thought I'd call. I haven't heard from you for several days. What have you been doing?"

"I got an anonymous letter. At first I thought it was from you, but it turned out to be somebody else."

"Why would I send you an anonymous letter?"

"Perhaps you disapproved of something I was doing."

"Oh, we all disapprove of one another. That's no reason to send anonymous letters."

"You haven't asked me what the letter said."

"Perhaps something about crabbed age and youth."

"You did send it."

"Well, it's easy to guess. It's the obvious message for the situation."

"What have you been doing, Ethel, apart from sending me anonymous letters?"

"I had lunch with Betsy. She told me you had proposed to her."

"That I had what?"

"You told her that you had Cecilia and she had Ilya, so you didn't need anything more in that line. What you both needed was someone intelligent to talk to. So you proposed that you and she should meet every so often and talk."

"In public."

"What do you mean?"

"In restaurants and so on."

"I imagine that's what she had in mind."

"That is exactly correct," said Ben, "except that it was she who made the proposal to me, and not the other way around."

"Did you accept?

"Ethel!"

"Well, there's no fool like an old fool. I know that from my own experience."

"Please spare us your trite adages."

"She *is* a charming person. She has interesting ideas. She and I talked about Etruscan art at lunch. It's true she drinks too much."

"We all do."

"You didn't tell me what you've been doing."

"I bought a house. It has an annex for Cecilia's harpsichord."

"Oh, Ben."

"You told me it was all right to invest money, as long as I didn't invest my emotions."

"Tell me about your emotions. Are you investing them or just keeping them in the bank?"

"The experts say you should diversify."

"Ben, I hope you won't do anything foolish."

"Why?"

"What do you mean?"

"Why shouldn't I do anything foolish? When I look back, I've never regretted doing foolish things. I've regretted not doing them."

"I suppose I have too."

"Why don't you do something foolish then?"

"I can't think of anything foolish that an unmarried middle-aged librarian could do. Perhaps you could suggest something."

Ilya advised that the two of them should go for a walk in the country and he should take her clothes off. This seemed adequately foolish, but he decided not to mention it to her. "You could take up a guru cult, or color your hair orange," he suggested. They chatted about this and that, and Ethel reminded him that tomorrow was Wednesday. "Will we see you at the Voronoffs?"

"No, Cecilia and I are going to go to Oakland tomorrow and get her car. She left it at Muir House and a friend brought it to Oakland for her. We'll fly up in the morning and drive it back in the afternoon. It's a little Japanese car. We won't be home until midnight."

"I see. Well, I'll report to the others what you've been up to. I'll tell them about the house you bought."

"As I say, it has an annex at the side. Cecilia is going to live there with her harpsichord. I'll live in the main house."

"If you're in separate houses," she said, "how can you make music together?"

"Goodbye, Ethel."

He hung up and saw Cecilia watching him with a look of placid curiosity from the sofa. The cottage was too small for anyone to make a private telephone call.

"Do you really think Ethel sent you the letter and not Dave?"

"No. She's not capable of sending it. But she's capable of thinking it."

"Are you a little bit in love with her, Ben?"

"No."

"Were you at one time?"

"She's an old friend. I don't think you'd understand. You're not old enough to have old friends."

60.

At the Cantamar poolside, after her swim, Cecilia wore her towel wrapped around her like a long Tahitian skirt, a Gauguin effect. Drops glistened on her skin, each one a tiny magnifying glass. Her wet hair, heavy and straight, also lent her a Polynesian quality. Ben was almost dry now. He sat in a chaise lounge wearing his swimming trunks and a golf hat, watching her every movement out of the corner of his eye, a behavior that had become habitual with him now and occupied his every moment when he was with her. When he was not with her, he thought about her.

When the drinks came from the bar Cecilia sipped hers and set it down on the arm of her own chaise. While he watched entranced, she unwound the towel and dropped it carelessly on the flagstones, in the way she dropped her clothes on the bathroom floor, in the way she dropped all her clothes as soon as she took them off. Then she reached behind to untie her bikini top and slipped it off. The effect on Ben's nerves was like a flashbulb going off. The bikini top joined the towel on the flagstones. She lay face down on the chaise and sipped her drink through the straw. None of the other half-dozen guests at the poolside paid any attention to her.

A hummingbird shot by a yard from her head, but she didn't raise her eyes to look at it. He had already noticed that she was not observant, at least not in the way he was, aware of everything happening around him in the field of his vision. When she met people she looked indifferently into their eyes for a second or two and then turned away. She would never notice if his shoelaces were untied or if there was a grass stain on his knee, whereas he could have described every thread of her clothing, every mole of her person, from memory.

The tiny spot of violet and green flashed silently through the air again, just over their heads. This time, by turning to look at it and even getting up and sitting sideways on the chaise, he succeeded in getting her to notice it. She raised her head to look, lifting the edge of a white breast from the chaise, then lowered her chin to her hands again.

He told her, "It's funny. They're called hummingbirds, but they don't make any noise."

"It's an optical hum. A hum for the eye."

"I've read," he said, "that their perception of time is very different from ours. Their minds are so quick that they can't even perceive that a human being near them is in motion. To them it's like the movement of a glacier."

"Then why do they fly away when we try to approach them?"

"It's like a man who has built his cabin at the foot of a glacier. It doesn't move when he looks at it. But he says to himself, 'Last year that glacier was way up there. Now it's a lot closer. I think I'll move my cabin.'" This was his world wisdom; he was trying it out on her like a high school boy with a line. He enjoyed explaining things to her, he found. There was something fundamental about this that went beyond all feminism; men liked to explain things to women, and from all evidence women liked to have men explain things to them. They might be ironic about it in their secret minds, just as they were ironic about our often inept fumbling with their bodies, but they enjoyed both of them.

The hummingbird, zigzagging back and forth in the still air, found what he had been looking for, a bed of fuchsias at the side of the pool. Nervously vibrating sideways, he stuck his beak into several flowers before he found one with nectar in it. Then he twisted like a tiny screw, stabbing his needle into the flower with a rhythmic urgency.

"Do you think they are just tiny machines? Or do they have thoughts like us?"

"Pascal thought they were machines."

"Somebody must have made them. They're far too complicated to have made themselves. A watch implies a watchmaker."

"Of course." He smiled. "The argument from design. You learned that at Berkeley."

"Are you religious, Ben?"

"Not particularly. I think probably there's a watchmaker, but he may be just the law of physics, sitting on a cloud. And you?"

Instead of answering the question, she said, "My mother's a Unitarian."

"Pascal also said we should bet God whether there's a Heaven or not. If you bet no, and you're wrong, you lose Heaven. If you bet no and you're right, you gain enjoyment of the world. If you bet yes and you're right, you gain Heaven. If you bet yes and you're wrong, you lose a little of the world, but that's not important compared for a chance at Heaven. So bet yes, he said."

"He makes religion sound like a crap game."

"Even as a wager it's not worth it. If you give up even one particle of the pleasure the world offers for that false promise, then you've lost something precious and irreplaceable. You're giving up everything for a crude oriental fable."

"What if it's true? As Pascal says."

He found it a little unreal that he was explaining all this to a half-naked young woman in the sunshine in California. "There are hundreds of sects, all claiming exclusive salvation. Christian, Moslem, Hindu. Each one claims that only it can save you and all the others are wrong. It's not very likely that God has picked some small minority of people for salvation and condemned everybody else. And then there's the childishness of it. If you disobey I'll punish you, if you're good I'll give you ice cream. You ought to be good because it feels good being good. That and the Kantian Imperative."

"Behave," she recited dutifully, "as though your actions were to become a general rule for everybody."

"Exactly. We want to live in a world where people are decent, generous, and compassionate. We can't hope for that unless we are decent, generous, and compassionate ourselves. That's very simple. Compared to that, speculation about metaphysics is just a complicated hobby, harmless in itself, but rather pointless."

"Oh, I believe in some metaphysical things."

"You do?"

"I believe there's a silver cord that attaches our souls to our bodies when we're asleep. That's how we can wander through our dreams and find our way back to our bodies when we wake up. I believe we can communicate with the dead. Their spirits are all around us, and we only have to find a way to speak to them. I believe our bodies may have inhabited other souls in another existence. And I believe that each one of us has a karma that's inside us. Perhaps it came from our other existence, perhaps it's a part of the soul that doesn't change with it's reborn in different bodies. Anyhow, this karma is inside us and it tells us what to do in all circumstances, if we know how to listen to it. Listening to it is called meditation."

This Credo from Telegraph Avenue struck him strangely. He didn't know whether she really believed these things or whether they were only fashionable ideas that she wore, like the flowers in her braids.

"Do you meditate?"

"Oh, now and then."

"And did your karma tell you to take up with me?"

She thought about this for a while, rising on her elbow so that her breasts faced toward him, then she said, "Yes."

"I suppose it doesn't matter. You have your karma and I'll stick to Kant's Imperative. I imagine our actions will be much the same. It's often the way in systems of belief. Starting from different metaphysics, they end up with the same ethics."

"Like Buddha and Jesus." After discussing all these high matters, she said, "Let's go back to the cottage, shall we?"

"It's still an hour before lunch."

"That's it. We'll have just an hour before lunch."

61.

They were awakened from their drowsy half-slumber by the telephone. For some reason it was Cecilia that got up; he watched her naked body floating out into the light of the other room. She talked for some time, then she came back to the bed.

"That was Raymonde. She wants me to go shopping with her."

"Well, go ahead."

"She said she'd meet me at the mall. She explained to me where it is."

"Fine."

"The thing is, Ben, I can't exactly walk there. My Honda's in Oakland."

"Oh. Well, the keys to the Mercedes are in the bowl on the bookshelf."

"Okay. But you see Ben, I can't exactly go shopping."

"Why not? Just explain to me what it is that's bothering you."

"Well. . . If I went shopping with Raymonde I might want to buy something. Just some little trinket. It's no fun if you don't buy something at least."

"I see. You mean you don't have any money."

"Well, Muir House owes me a check, but it may be a while before they send it. And anyhow they'll send it to my mother's house in Oakland. I didn't have your address when I quit."

Still lying in bed, he reflected. He didn't have much cash himself at the moment; he ought to go to the bank. Anyhow he couldn't imagine giving her cash, especially after they had just been to bed together; it would be too crass. He could give her his credit card and possibly they might accept it, even though the signature wouldn't match. That wouldn't be a good idea either.

He didn't like to get out of bed naked in front of her, especially after what she had said about people being unattractive with their clothes off. She was now slinking around the room in her genital-concealing stance.

Finally he sat on the edge of the bed with the covers still over him and dressed in the way he remembered from the time when he was a boy in summer camp and shy about revealing his body. First he put on his shirt—their clothes were lying in a heap on the floor where they had both flung them a half an hour before. Then he sat with the shirt concealing him and pulled the underwear up under it, and then the pants. He stood up and tucked in the shirt. Shoes were not needed for the present.

"You can take my automatic teller machine card," he told her. "Do you know how to use it?"

"Oh yes."

"You have to have my PIN. My personal identification number. It's 887853. You just punch in the word Turtle, as in Turtle Press."

"Turtle. That's easy to remember."

He took the ATM card out of his wallet and gave it to her. "There's a machine in the mall. Raymonde will know where it is."

"Okay, thanks. Bye."

By this time she had put on her underwear, her tapered black pants, and the white wool sweater. She didn't do anything to her hair, which looked as though she had just been to bed with somebody.

"What about your lunch?"

"Raymonde and I will have something in the mall."

She left; he caught a glimpse of the Mercedes spinning rapidly out of the lot. With a twinge of melancholy wisdom, he remembered the words of Henry Calendish. *The mysterious rites they practice that are unknown in our culture. Spending the whole afternoon going to malls with some other woman, not because they need anything but because they might see something they could buy on impulse.* In a part of his mind he had not wanted to believe that women behaved this way, and in another part of his mind he had believed that they did but that Cecilia was exempt from the frailties of the rest of her sex. A third theory was that Cecilia in some way knew about Henry's remark and was just doing this to tease him.

It was the first time in years that he had been left without a car. He was a prisoner in the cottage until she came back. Of course, he could go for a long walk. He found a little left-over lentil soup in the refrigerator and had it for his lunch. It was too much trouble to heat it up for just one person, but it was quite good cold with a little yogurt in it. If Cecilia had stayed for lunch, he would have fixed her something more elaborate. He was a good cook and enjoyed fooling around in the tiny kitchen. In the times when they didn't go out for lunch and ate in the cottage, they had fallen into a pattern where he did the cooking and she set the table. This took her about thirty seconds: two plates, two tableware, two glasses, two paper napkins, and the salt and pepper. When she was done with this she watched him cook, as though it was something complicated like fixing a car that women couldn't do.

She came back from the mall after four hours with a pair of sunglasses thickly encrusted with fake gold, and enameled curlicues on the temples. They looked like a prop for a French farce, or something that mad King George III could wear.

"Just a joke," she said.

62.

Her defects. There were only two or three—the large feet, the slightly too full lips, and the mole on her cheek a little to the right of and below the mouth. And the knobby elbows like a boy's; he had forgotten that. These things made her more than a mere perfect wax figure, a department store mannikin. They lent flesh and blood to her, a sensual element that would have been lacking without them, solidify what would otherwise have been only an intangible angelic vision. Bacon: "There is no excellent beauty that hath not some strangeness in the proportion."

63.

From the Oakland airport they took a taxi to her mother's house. For some reason he couldn't think of it as Cecilia's house. He had known all along that she had her own private life, that she had friends, relatives, and interests of her own before she met him, but the idea that she had a mother was one he was not really prepared to come to terms with—the notion that she was somebody else's child, that another person had a claim on her affection and loyalty and the right to have an opinion about her actions.

"I don't know what you'll make of Babs," she said in the taxi. "She's a little—singular."

She was one of those women who call their mothers by their first names. He hadn't expected this but he didn't know what he had expected her to call her mother; certainly not Mom. He warily prepared himself to deal with this mother as an antagonist and perhaps a formidable one. The taxi stopped in front of a large two-story house on Rockwell Street in the hills overlooking the bay; Cecilia's Honda was parked on the street in front of the house.

Mrs. Penn was a woman in her fifties in a black Chinese tunic and black silk trousers. She wore her tinted chestnut hair, with black showing at the roots, in a chignon with a Chinese comb. Her voice was a menopausal baritone and she chain-smoked the entire time they were there. She said, "How do you do, Professor Gavilan," and removed a speck of tobacco from her lip. Then she offered her hand. The handshake lasted just a fraction of a second longer than was necessary; she smelled of tobacco and expensive scent.

"Where did you get the idea he was a professor?"

"You said he was bookish."

"I'm not bookish. I do like books."

"He's a publisher, Babs."

"It doesn't really matter what he is. I can see well enough what he is. Would you like something for lunch?"

"We had lunch on the plane."

It was about two o'clock. "Would you like some tea then? A drink?"

"I'd like some tea."

"I'll have coffee," said Cecilia.

Mrs. Penn said, "I'm going to have a drink myself."

"I'll have a drink too," said Ben.

If he expected to ingratiate himself with her in this way he was disappointed. She gave him the look that you give people who drink in the afternoon. She offered him a Scotch with ice and made herself a stiff vodka on the rocks with lemon. Cecilia went off to the kitchen to make herself some coffee. It was strange to Ben to think that this was her house and she had grown up in it, that she knew where everything was in it. In his own mind, she had been invented in the moment he first caught sight of her at Muir House, like Aphrodite springing from the sea.

Mrs. Penn said, "What *do* you publish?"

Ben sipped his drink while she gazed at him curiously. He said, "I've sold the business now. I'm no longer active in it. It was a small press in Santa Barbara."

"Then you're retired?"

"I've sold the business."

"How old are you anyhow?"

"I'm fifty-eight."

"You don't look it. I'm fifty-four and it's no circus. I think it's harder for a woman. Did Cece tell you about Harlan?"

"No."

"He was my husband. He died when Cece was ten. It was leukemia, in case you think he killed himself."

"I didn't think anything of the kind."

"People often do, for some reason. Perhaps it's something about me." She removed another speck of tobacco from her tongue. "I seem to project a temperament that people imagine would drive a spouse to suicide. As a matter of fact Harlan and I got along very well. The only thing we differed on was sex. I thought I was frigid. Actually my preference was for women. Unfortunately I didn't know that until too late, when I was in my forties. By that time no one was interested."

Ben wondered if she had been drinking before they came. She seemed perfectly sober. She removed a third speck of tobacco from her tongue and said, "So I spent fifteen years of my life locking my door against Harlan, when I could have been a happy lesbian."

"Why don't you smoke filters? Then the crumbs wouldn't get in your mouth."

"I like them stronger than that. It wasn't a picnic for Harlan either. Naturally it made me feel guilty as hell when he died. Why am I telling you all this? I live in this big house and I have no one to talk to. No one my age. You can't talk to young people about anything serious."

She examined her vodka to see how much was left. Evidently she only allowed herself one drink in the afternoon. It was still half full. Then she turned away abruptly and said, "What do you want, Robert?"

Someone else had entered the room. It was a boy about fifteen, in black pants and a neatly pressed white shirt. He had thick glasses that magnified his eyes, and his large hands hung awkwardly at the ends of his arms. He said, "The TV broke."

"You don't know how to adjust it, Robert. I've told you that before. You don't fool around with those knobs on the bottom. Just turn it on and select the channel."

"It's broke. It won't work."

"Broken."

"It's broken."

Cecilia came in with her coffee. She said smoothly, "Let's go back to your room, Robert. I'll fix the TV."

When they were gone Mrs. Penn said, "I had my second child at thirty-nine. It wasn't a good idea."

"Harlan forced the door?"

"No. It was my idea. Cece was fun when she was small, but when she got older she got—a little distant. As she is now. I thought I would have another one to have fun with for another ten years. The result was Robert."

He hadn't thought of Cecilia as being distant, but that was exactly what she was. There was always a little distance between them, in spite of her affection and intimacy. He decided that Mrs. Penn was not just an alcoholic rambler and he ought to listen to her more carefully.

"Does he go to school?"

"No. He can't do much of anything, Professor. He watches TV. Do you mind if I call you Professor? I know you're not, but I've started thinking of you that way and it's easier to go on."

"You can call me anything you want."

"He watches TV and he masturbates. I suppose he has a happy enough time. I wish I had things that I enjoyed as much. Alcohol," she said, "is a great consolation."

"But you allow yourself only one drink before dinner."

"How did you know that?"

"By observing you."

"You are keen. And none in the morning, of course. Every night after dinner I drink till I'm blotto. When I'm alone, of course. If there are other people I hold back. Usually I'm alone, except for Robert."

Ben felt he had to offer something to match her candor. He searched about in his thoughts and stumbled over the one thing he had not wanted to talk to her about. "What do you think about me and Cecilia?"

At this moment Cecilia came back into the room. Mrs. Penn went on exactly as though she weren't there. "I thought she might do this. Half the girls who go to Muir House in the summer end up having a romance with somebody. It's a matter of total indifference to me. She says you're just someone who's helping her in her music career and I don't care whether that's true or not. I've been around too long," she said, "to care who puts what part of himself in what part of somebody else's body."

"Oh Babs. Stop talking nonsense."

"There's not much harm you can do her after all," she said. "She's too smart to have children. She's seen what happened to me." Cecilia sipped her coffee, not trying anymore to make her mother stop talking. Mrs. Penn went on, "She'll do all right. Cece can take care of herself. I'm not worried about her. I'm worried about you."

"About me?"

"You're the one who might get hurt. What'll happen to you if it cracks up?"

"Why should it crack up?"

She didn't answer this. She said, "Cece will make something out of herself. A harpsichordist or something else. She's one of the invulnerable of the world. I saw that from the time she began to talk."

"And I'm not?"

"Neither of us is. You or I. Robert and Cece are invulnerable."

"Perhaps all children seem so to us."

She sipped her drink and set it down. "If you don't want any lunch I'll excuse myself. I have some things to do. Washing, and I have to take Robert to the optometrist."

"We'll be going," said Cecilia. She sipped the last of her coffee and set down the cup.

"The keys to your car are on the table. Dave is a very nice young man, by the way. Do you know him well?"

"Not very."

"It was Dave who drove the car down?" said Ben. This was the first he had heard of it.

"He's just a graduate student," Cecilia explained to her mother. "Somebody I met at Muir House."

It was curious, he thought, that Dave was still willing to drive her car down to Oakland after the way she treated him when they left the hotel. Maybe he was a masochist, or maybe he was really in love with her. He himself would lie down and let her put her foot on his neck if she requested it, so why should he feel superior to Dave?

"He stayed for a drink, and then I drove him to his place in Berkeley," said Mrs. Penn. "He told me Professor

Gavilan has a reputation for going around to resorts and picking up young girls."

To his surprise Cecilia took this very calmly. All she said was, "Babs. He's not a professor."

64.

In the car on the freeway going through San Jose, Cecilia said, "She and Robert are really married. They don't know it but they are. He needs her and she needs him. In a way, it's a very satisfactory arrangement."

"Why does she need him?"

"She needs someone to cook and keep house for. Someone who isn't a threat to her."

"You mean, someone who won't break down the bedroom door?"

"That's it. Robert will last her the rest of her life."

"If she prefers women to men, I would think she'd be closer to you."

"She'd like to embrace me," said Cecilia, "but she hasn't touched me since I was a child."

65.

There are some misconceptions about the nature of physical love. It was intended by our Creator for the purpose of procreation, but that doesn't mean that we're committed to this end. We're humans, we have free will, and we can take it and do what we will with it. What we have done is that we have made it into an art form, in the sense that it's a thing that is beautiful, that is an end in itself, and that has no other purpose. The French say that love is the poetry of the poor. It's true that a number of poor and ignorant people are quite good at it, much better than they could be at writing poetry, or painting in oils, but that doesn't mean that rich and educated people can't be good at it too. Poor people like to think we're not as good at it as they are, but that's just because they can't compete with us in poetry, or oil painting, and they want to think there's one area where they have the advantage over us. What they don't realize is that you are a lot better at it after having read Proust, or listened to the Liebestod from *Tristan and Isolde*, or made a careful study of the nudes of Poussin. It's much the same as the difference between square dancing and ballet. If you like square dancing you think that ballet is thin and effete; if you are a ballet dancer you think that square dancing is crude. Of course, ballet dancers can also do square dancing, but not the other way around. The central point is that love is an art form, one of our most popular, and one that can be enjoyed on many different levels. We need not be committed to the notion that its purpose is the continuation of the race.

66.

"Are you too smart to have children?"

"What do you mean?"

"That's what your mother said."

"Oh, I don't know." The question seemed to make her nervous. "Why do you ask?"

"I'm just interested in whether you're interested in having children. Not now perhaps, but later. It seems to be a very common female instinct."

"I don't know why you're asking. The answer is that I'm not. And by the way the notion that women have instincts is not fashionable these days." This was the same thing that Ethel told him. "If a woman wants to have babies, the feminists call her a maternalist. This means she's a throwback to the nuclear family, fixed gender roles, and all that obsolete stuff. I don't care all that much for babies and I don't coo when I see one. They're nasty little worms. They cry all the time and spit up milk, and stuff comes out their ends. I imagine you'd like to pin me down with one so I wouldn't wander around so much and you would know where I was."

"It's the farthest thing in the world from my mind."

"Keep them pregnant in the summer and barefoot in the winter."

Was this their first quarrel?

67.

In London they stayed in another one of Ben's favorite old-fashioned but distinguished hotels, the Russell in Russell Square. Cecilia had never been to England; in fact she had never been to Europe, although she spoke good French and was familiar with the geography of London from the novels of Iris Murdoch and Muriel Spark.

He was fond of the Russell in the way that a man might be of an old mistress, one who has lost her beauty but retains the elegance and aristocratic distinction of her youth. It gave him joy to catch sight of it through the trees when they came back from a walk around Bloomsbury: a palace of beige stone with a mansard roof and canopied statues on the facade, and its old-fashioned sign in white letters. He pointed to the Dutch gable high on the front where, in tiny letters, you could read the date 1898.

"You do love to explain things to me, don't you?"

"Yes, I'm a village explainer. I'm that old gaffer who wants to explain the whole village to you when you only want to look at a stone in the churchyard."

"Do you know, not only have I never been to London before, but I've never stayed in a hotel."

He could hardly believe this.

"Babs didn't like to travel. And before, when I was a child and Harlan was alive, they went off on trips and left me with the housekeeper."

Another one of his favorite rites in London was tea at Brown's in Albemarle Street, which dated from the same period as the Russell. Instead he took her to the Savoy in the Strand, with its white piano and its murals, where the atmosphere was Noel Coward instead of fin-de-siècle. He thought she might like this better. She looked around at the Nineteen-Twenties furniture and said, "All this is so passé. We did the Twenties back in the Sixties." In his efforts to stretch back over the years that separated them, he missed by at least a generation. It would be better if he offered himself simply as a Space Traveler, coming from Mars and not belonging to any particular time in history.

68.

It was a warm summer evening and the streets of London were thronging with young people. Ben felt that with all his alleged experience of the world he was wearing the wrong clothes, a seersucker suit with a tie. It labeled him as a middle-aged American as clearly as if he were carrying a sign. The only other person in a suit was a Japanese tourist walking along seriously carrying his third eye suspended from a leather strap around his neck. Cecilia was in her usual black pants and Irish sweater.

The other people in the streets were mainly in jeans and shirts, male and female, all of them with long hair so you could hardly tell them apart. Probably it didn't matter to them either; they just stuck something somewhere in the other person and it didn't make any difference. A couple went by in black leather with studs, then a girl with orange hair escorted by a boy in what looked like a waiter's uniform, a shabby old tuxedo with a jacket that left his dickey bare. It wasn't time for the older people to come out of the theatres yet, and all these youths were on the prowl. They drifted down the sidewalks like flocks of gazelles and forced Ben and Cecilia to walk in the street.

Covent Garden was full of people watching the buskers and eating cheap food they bought from the stands. There was a smell of fried potatoes and people were carrying around beer from the pub in Henrietta Street. They stopped to watch a mime, then a Jamaican couple who coaxed music out of jars and cigar boxes. Ben bought Cecilia a single red carnation from a hawker; it stood out like a flame against her sweater. He had an overwhelming urge to get her out of this crowd of young people. He had brought her to London to get her away from the Voronoff set, and now he wanted to take her back to the hotel to get her away from the Londoners. His impulse wasn't entirely carnal; he simply wanted to be alone with her. But it was still only ten-thirty. They made their way out of Covent Garden and into King Street, where it was quieter and there were only a few people walking along under the streetlamps toward Leicester Square.

In Leicester Square there were more crowds of young people. He pointed out the Empire with its garish neon front. At the turn of the century it was a music hall where Charlie Chaplin and a lot of other entertainers got their first start. Now it was a discotheque, the best place in London to meet someone of the opposite sex, or of the same sex, depending on taste. A young man in a gray tuxedo and a shirt with lace frills was at the door deciding who went in and who didn't, trying to get the right mix of sexes and keep out the troublemakers. Behind him was a black bouncer the size of a football linebacker. Nearby on the pavement were a couple of obvious hookers, with their two boyfriends, tough-looking blacks, watching from a little distance. Crowds of young people were milling around the door, waiting their turn to be passed or failed by the young man in frills.

Cecilia made a little moue of disgust. "Ugh. A flesh-market. Imagine going in there knowing you had to come out with someone else before one o'clock in the morning."

He didn't know whether to believe her or not. He had developed a great respect for her skill at simulation. Sometimes he had the impression that her emotions were ones that she chose, not ones that she felt. It didn't make any difference in the end, he told himself; it was the outsides of people you had to deal with, not what they were concealing on the inside. As long as she showed every sign of loving him... He took her hand and they went on out of the square toward Piccadilly.

He said, "Do you feel funny walking with me?"

"Funny?"

"There aren't any other couples like us."

"We're better looking than they are."

"I mean," he persisted bluntly, "our difference in age."

"No two people are exactly the same age."

"What do you think people will think of us?"

"They'll think I'm a chorus girl and you're my sugar daddy."

A little farther down the street she said, "Could we go to a pub?"

"A pub?"

"Yes. I've always heard about pubs and I want to see what they're like."

He found her one in Wardour Street. She had a pint of bitter, which she had read about in Iris Murdoch, and he a sherry. She hadn't realized the pint would be so big but she drank the whole thing. The other patrons looked at them with curiosity. It was obvious what they were thinking, and it was peculiar and a little annoying. They ought to admire him for having, at his age, captured such a young and attractive creature. On the contrary, their expressions seemed to suggest that there was something ludicrous in his position, something to be pointed out across the room and talked about behind their hands, something to be discussed afterwards and told to others as an interesting story, something odd or humorous they saw in a pub. His seersucker suit, her two braids fastened with rubber bands, and her oversized white sweater with nothing on beneath it.

69.

Watching Cecilia lick the flap of an envelope, sensuously, one half of it with one edge of her tongue, and the other half with the other edge. Imagining the taste of the flavored glue in her mouth, the crystalline saliva that flows to moisten the flap, the dangerous sharpness of the edge of the paper against her oversized soft lips. Her carnal fluency.

70.

The next day they went walking on the Thames near Richmond. At Twickenham, just beyond Eel Pie Island, there was a ferry and they crossed the river to the other bank. The ferry was a large rowboat piloted by a young man in jeans and a faded red tank-top. His shoulders glowed in the sunshine. Ben covertly keeping a watch on Cecilia as usual, saw her looking at them. As the ferryman rowed his pectorals strained against the tank-top; the black hair in his armpits was pearled with sweat, and he gave off a light odor of perspiration, not unpleasant. He was a perfect young man, a rustic Apollo. Ben would cheerfully have brained him with an oar and thrown it overboard. The fare was fifty pence and Ben gave him a pound. He remembered when he overtipped Dave at Muir House for bringing the car to the lot and putting the bags in it. This was a bad habit that he ought to get over.

71.

After they crossed the river they went on along the path on the right bank, past Ham House and the meadow with Richmond Hill behind it. A little way down the path another young man came toward them, a workman he seemed to be, in baggy tweed trousers, a white shirt, and a flat cloth cap. Just as they passed him he straddled his legs and, without looking at them, reached down and scratched his groin. Ben didn't know if she had noticed. She was silent for a while.

Then she said, "Why do they have to do that?"

"What?"

"Scratch themselves in public. It's disgusting. Don't they know it's not polite to touch yourself there?"

Ben said, "If you had your uterus and your ovaries hanging in little sacks on the outside of your body, you'd be interested in them too, and you'd always be feeling to see if they were still there."

She didn't seem impressed with this piece of insight.

72.

Richmond Park was vast, and they soon left everybody else behind. It was more like a French countryside than an English park. There were clumps of woods, patches of bracken, and marshy spots with reeds and willows. The grass in the meadow was being cropped by a herd of brown-and-beige deer, and they sat down under an oak to watch them. There was only one stag; the others were does and a couple of half-grown fawns. The stag had an imposing set of antlers that looked too heavy for him to bear, and a tuft of hair like a brush on his penis. He stared at them over the distance and tapped his hoof, ready to defend his clan.

She said, "Do you remember the deer we saw on the trail to Moon Lake?" When he didn't answer she said after a while, "I wonder if the coyote got that fawn."

He was confronted again with the question that dogged him like a tireless demon: what was she thinking? It was clear enough why the image of the two animals lingered in *his* mind. He was the coyote, she the fawn; but he couldn't tell whether it meant this to her. In everything she said there was a light subtext lingering just under the words, or so it seemed to him. It was all a Mona Lisa dialogue, mysterious, concealing some private amusement. He wondered if the time would come when she let him in on the joke.

"I think the coyote got the fawn," he said.

"You're a terrible pessimist."

"Yes. I've always been that way. It runs in my family."

"You never say anything at all about your family."

"It's no secret. You've never asked. The Gavilans have been in New England since before the Revolution. They're a part of an old Spanish aristocracy in Boston. Santayana the philosopher was one of them. I grew up in Cambridge in a big house on Beacon Street. My father was a successful physician who inherited money and made a lot more. My mother was an Aymes; she was artistic and painted china. We had a summer cottage on the Cape, a villa in Portofina, and all the amenities. I went to Tufts and studied English, tried my hand at writing poetry and found I wasn't much good at it, then when my father died I took the money and came to California. I ran a bookstore for a while and then I started up the Turtle Press." His life didn't sound like much when it was summed up like this.

She said, "You do look Spanish. My Hidalgo."

"I have the Gavilan eyes."

They were dark and Mediterranean, set in patches of shadow, with a wrinkle under each one that crossed to the cheekbone. Erica said that it made him look as though he was looking out of two caves. It occurred to him that he hadn't mentioned Erica in his miniature autobiography. Cecilia only knew that he had once had a wife. If she had inquired, he would have said, And I married a woman named Erica, but we didn't agree, so I divorced her, and luckily she married a film producer in Los Angeles so I don't have to pay alimony. As a matter of fact, Erica was also divorced from Casey Fedelman now. Perhaps she was married to somebody else; he had lost track of her.

He said, "And there was an unsuccessful marriage."

She hardly seemed interested. "And some other women."

He thought for a moment and then laughed. "Oh, you mean Ethel Track."

"And Betsy Voronoff. And probably some others that I don't know about."

He decided not to explain to her that he had never touched either of these women except for a playful kiss, and that the last woman he went to bed with before her was Erica, ten years ago.

"Does that bother you?"

"Bother me? Why on earth should it? You're obviously a man who knows something about these things. It's partly for that that I find you attractive."

She had never said before that she found him attractive. He felt himself being warmly manipulated by her and he had no objection. First she told him that he knew a great deal about women, then she said that she found this attractive. God knew whether either of these things was true.

73.

They lay for some time propped on their elbows in the grass, watching the deer. Guarded by the old stag, the does and fawns idled slowly away, grazing as they went. The stag, with a final toss of his antlers, turned and followed them.

"What are you thinking about?"

"I was wondering what I should do if I lost you."

"Oh, you won't," she said. But she said it lightly and playfully; it was part of a conventional repartee which could be borrowed from any movie.

"Do you know the story of Maria Callas and Meneghini?"

"Remind me."

"Meneghini was a Veronese businessman. He met Callas when she was an unknown American opera singer in Europe. He dropped everything else to devote himself to her career; he became her agent. His own family ostracized him. They were together for twelve years. Then when she became a world-famous diva she met somebody else and left him."

"It was Onassis."

"Yes. He had a lot of money. Even more than Meneghini."

"I wouldn't do that."

"I'm not talking about you and me. I'm talking about the way the world is. You can't do much about it. You can make promises in private, but they get broken when you take them out in the world among other people. We're not responsible for our affections. We're not responsible for them when they come, and we're not responsible for them when they go. You can't undertake not to behave with me at some time in the future like Callas with Meneghini. It's not in your power."

"Are you happy with me, Ben?"

"Right now I'm exquisitely happy. Make a note. Richmond Park, August twelfth, two o'clock in the afternoon."

74.

Locked in the bathroom at the Hotel Russell, he examined his naked reflection in the mirror and tried to decide which of the stories he told himself about him and Cecilia was the right one. A selfless lover advancing her career in music. A Menighini, a wealthy masochist.

(Not inconsistent with number one). A coyote stalking a fawn. A chorus girl and her sugar daddy. (Her version). He was convinced in some way that the secret to this pressing question lay in what he saw in the mirror. He peered at it intently out of his Spanish eyes. His body had the interesting complexity and delicacy of the old men in Leonardo da Vinci's sketches; there were sags, folds, textures, the liver-spots and blotches of age. A thin pelt of hair began on the chest, descended along the midline, and burst out like a dark flower at the groin. At his right side, which looked like the left in the mirror, his arm hung like a stick to which someone had attached an old glove, his almost normal hand. His hips, lean and hairless as a baby's, were marked with a fine reticulation of lines like a piece of paper that has been folded many times. There were semicircular folds under his breasts like a woman's. He was not overweight and there was almost no belly; when his body was hidden in his clothes nothing showed of these signs of age on it. But his head did stick up out of his clothing, and he stared at it with a kind of horrified disbelief. He still *felt* the same as he felt when he was a student at Tufts; he had the same emotions, the same desires and thoughts. But now he was evidently going to a costume party and someone had made him up as himself at fifty-eight, penciling in wrinkles, dusting the temples with gray powder, and deepening the cave-like shadows around the eyes. He was wearing a mask of himself as an old man. Attached to this dying animal, the cylindrical scrap of flesh at the groin was a pitiful parody, resembling an appliance he had bought at a sex shop to deceive a younger woman. It hung in his papery loins no larger than a man's thumb, shrunken by the chill of the bathroom.

She must never see this, he told himself.

When he went to bed at night he followed the procedure worked out in the cottage at the Cantamar, pulling on his pajama bottoms under his clothes like a boy at camp. When he bathed he went into the bathroom and came out in his dressing gown. He was as modest as a girl; it was she now, the girl, who had given up her genital-concealing slink and flounced around the hotel room in London as though she were a carefree nymph in the woods. She did mock ballet poses or stretched out on the bed with a rose in her hand like a fin-de-siècle nude. She made herself almost innocent in this disregard of her nakedness, a disregard which nevertheless invited him to regard it and be aroused. She was a fiend, a demon, one that he loved with a fierce and helpless tenderness. This was the fifth story: she was the temptress, he the victim.

75.

Having taken her to tea at the Savoy to please her, he now took her to tea at Brown's to please himself. She slipped as easily into the atmosphere of the old Edwardian hotel in Albermarle Street as she did into the Nineteen-Twenties chic of the Savoy; she was like a chameleon, adapting to any surroundings. A three-tiered tray came with tiny elegant sandwiches and cakes; the tea service was Wedgewood and sterling. There were only a few other people in the lounge, most of them middle-aged. Cecilia, looking like a child in the Land of the Ancient, had her teeth in a watercress sandwich, which she held with her little finger bent at an angle, when Ilya and Betsy appeared in the doorway.

Cecilia didn't notice; she set her sandwich delicately down on her plate and sipped her tea. The Voronoffs had not caught sight of them either. Still numb with surprise,

Ben watched the drama unfold to its inevitable scene of recognition. The frock-coated steward led the Voronoffs across the carpet, pointing with an outstretched hand to the table he had in mind for them. Betsy's mouth was working and the gestures of her hands indicated that she didn't care for that table and wanted another—she pointed—it was across the room next to the window—and at that moment Ilya turned and saw Ben and Cecilia. Pirouetting on his shiny shoes, he smiled broadly and spread his arms in greeting. He seemed not at all surprised, only pleased. Betsy turned to see what he was looking at. She *was* surprised. She gave a little screech, causing every head in the room to turn to her.

Ignoring the steward, they came over and sat in the chairs at the small table. Ben and Cecilia were sitting opposite them in a kind of sofa or love-seat in gray velvet.

Ilya smiled broadly and said, "On your honeymoon, are you?"

"As a matter of fact we're in England to buy a harpsichord for Cecilia. We're going down to Sussex next week to look at one."

"When you left Santa Barbara you didn't tell us you were going."

"We were fleeing from all of you."

"You *are* on your honeymoon," said Betsy. She had been drinking already, and when the waiter came she ordered a Beefeaters instead of tea. The waiter looked lugubrious and conferred with the steward. Brown's didn't approve of this deviation from custom. She was told the bar was not open, but she pointed out that it ought to be; it was after five. "I've got a ghastly cold. Booze is the only thing that will help." In fact her nostrils were red and damp and she dabbed at them now and then with a lace-trimmed handkerchief. Her Mayfair accent was on her side; they would never serve gin at tea-time for an American. The waiter appeared with her Beefeaters and tea and sandwiches for Ilya.

"Now explain *your* selves," said Ben.

Ilya and Betsy had a flat in Cadogan Place. He had come over to consult with his British publisher, and other things.

"And you know," he told them, "Carolyn is in Paris."

"What is she doing there?"

"I have no idea. Perhaps gazing at the stars from the Observatory. No doubt they look different from France."

"Have all of you people followed us over to Europe deliberately?"

"Of course not. You're a little paranoid, old fellow. There are quite a few of us in our little circle, and we all love to travel, so it's natural that a couple of us should be over here at any one time. Betsy darling, if you insist on drinking instead of having tea, please don't nibble at my little sandwiches. They're delicious. Isn't this a lovely place? It's my favorite room in all London. You remember, I was the one that first told you about it, old fellow."

This was true; Ben remembered that Ilya introduced him to the habit of tea at Brown's years ago. It was natural in that case, given that Ilya was in London at all, that they should meet here. Still the circumstances seemed a little mysterious and sinister to Ben. When you're in love, he knew, the world revolves around you and your beloved. Everyone took an inordinate interest in him and Cecilia, staring at them in pubs, showing them into their room at the Russell with elaborately blank expressions, and in the case of Ilya and Betsy, following them halfway around the world to see what they were doing on their honeymoon. He wanted to have

Cecilia for himself. When he stole her away from Muir House in his car, he hadn't counted on the fact that he would possess her among the billions of people on the surface of the earth, who would look at them with the piercing, indifferent, and yet curious eyes of strangers. Of course, Ilya and Betsy weren't strangers. This way lay madness. It was perfectly natural for Ilya and Betsy to be in London. They had a flat in Cadogan Square and he had come over to consult with his publisher.

"You know, Cecilia hasn't piped a word since we arrived," said Ilya.

"That's French, isn't it?" said clever Cecilia. "*Je n'ai pas pipé mot.* I've been busy eating all these things." She was putting jam on her scone. She was fastidious, a crumb-eater, and yet when she finished she licked the jam off her knife, while the three of them watched her. It was no more offensive than it would be in a child of six.

"You could cut off your tongue," said Ben.

"Then I'd be that Silent Woman that men so much desire."

"I believe," said Ilya, "that in the ballad she was silent because she was entirely lacking a head."

"That's the way they really want us, dear," Betsy told Cecilia.

"Don't start up the War of the Sexes, Betsy darling, because Ben and Cecilia are just newly in love. You can take up the subject again in a year's time."

"There won't be the slightest difference," said Cecilia.

Betsy dabbed at her nose and said, "You're very young, my dear."

Ben said "Shut up, Betsy." Now that he had got over his surprise at the appearance of Ilya and Betsy, he was angry at these people for spoiling what had been a very nice tea with Cecilia, and he didn't care for Betsy's condescending manner, her drinking, and a lot of other things.

Ilya said, "Why don't we stay together for dinner? I had thought about Walton's."

"Fine," said Ben. He calmed down a little, took a deep breath, and reminded himself that he was with Cecilia and he ought to be happy.

They finished their tea and Betsy had a second gin, brought by the waiter with a little more grace this time. Brown's had given in to Betsy. The other guests looked at them curiously. Ilya had been talking rather loudly, and Betsy had been making little chirps and screeches of enjoyment at the jokes. Ilya paid for everything with his Barclaycard, another indication to the staff that they were English and not American. They were shown out with bows and the flourishing of many napkins.

76.

Since it was too early to go to dinner, Ilya insisted on their going around to the Ritz bar, where they all drank for two hours; Cecilia sipped a little white wine. Betsy talked to Cecilia and Ben to Ilya. This bourgeois arrangement annoyed Ben, but after several drinks it didn't seem to matter so much.

Knowing that Ilya was really only happy when he was talking about his writing, he asked him, "Are you working here in London?"

"Oh yes. I always work four hours a day, old chap, no matter where I am. I've made an important change in the trilogy. You remember that in my second volume there's a middle-aged British publisher who's in love with an art librarian. His name is Mortimer and hers is Pensive Carwell. Well, I'm now in the third volume. I had thought of Pensive being stung to death by wasps during a love scene."

"You told me."

"Something violent and bizarre is needed. The readers are not interested in the banality of life as it really is. They have that every day. Still the wasps are really a cliché. I believe it's been done by Aldous Huxley."

"I don't remember that. In *Eyeless in Gaza* a dog falls out of an airplane onto people who are making love on a roof."

"That sort of thing. Well. I've thought of something better. In the third volume, *The Prodigal*, Kostya returns to Russia and leaves his friend Mortimer behind. What does Mortimer do but fall in love with an art student from the Slade. He forgets Pensive completely in his infatuation for this child. She's twenty and he's a man of fifty-five."

"Fifty-eight."

"Let's be reasonable, old man. If we make him too old nobody will believe it. The art student's name is Fenicia. He takes her out in the country and—"

"She's stung to death by wasps."

"No, he takes off her clothes, and removes his too, but in the course of the amours he becomes ill. A heart attack or something. I'm never too specific about the medical details. Fleeing for aid still unclothed, Fenicia stumbles into the arms of a handsome but tongue-tied farm hand. You can imagine the rest. A convenient barn, deep shadows at noon, the earthy smells of dung. Fenicia goes back to London and no one ever knows."

"And does Mortimer die?"

"Oh no. Not at this point. He goes back to London too, and the pressing problem now is, what is he to do about Fenicia?"

"Why doesn't he just go on with her as he did before?"

"Not a very good story, old man. The drama must advance, or the reader will go to sleep. Mortimer now realizes that he can't hope to keep Fenicia. The *manqué* Bower of Bliss in the country demonstrated that. He's too old and his heart isn't good enough."

Ben colored but said nothing. He had drunk too much to say what he wanted to say, and he was afraid of making a fool of himself in this bar full of well-dressed people.

"Well, old chap, what do you think I've invented at this point? Ha ha. Mortimer has an assistant in his publishing firm, a young man named Peter Bent."

"He couldn't be named Peter."

"You're right, he couldn't be named Peter. David Bent. A handsome lad, talented, intelligent, a Cambridge blue, attractive as hell. In short, a perfect Lothario. Well, thinks Mortimer, if I can't have Fenicia myself, the next best thing is to make David and Fenicia fall in love. He can manipulate this adroitly from the wings, as a kind of sexual Svengali. David and Fenicia are married, but Mortimer will always have Fenicia around him, because he and Peter, excuse me, David, are so closely associated in the publishing venture. He can even kiss her now and then in a fatherly way. The three of them can joke about this, he and Fenicia and David."

Ben reminded himself that the next time he was sober he should hit Ilya in the face, hard.

"Is that the end?"

"Oh no. Finish your drink, old chap. It's been sitting there in front of you for an hour."

"It's my fourth."

"It couldn't be. Anyhow, the three of them go on perfectly happily in this way for some time. They even share the same town house in London. So you see, this third volume has a wonderful system of appearing and disappearing characters, like a Balinese shadow-play. The novel is really about Kostya. But he goes back to Russia, and the interest shifts to Mortimer. Then gradually, without the reader noticing it, I move the balance point of the novel to Fenicia. After a while she leaves David and whirls off into the irridescent artistic world of Chelsea, attracting men like moths to a flame. Of course by this time Kostya is in a stalag. Kostya represents the Slavic soul; he understands suffering. Fenicia represents the soul of the West, given over the pleasure."

"Fenicia is the feminine form of Phoenix. The bird that arises from the ashes."

"Ah, you're clever, Mortimer old fellow."

77.

Dinner at Walton's was a three-hour affair, presided over by Ilya who smilingly selected the three wines and queried the waiters about sauces and coulis. Rubbing his hands, with a smirk at the others, he ordered a special kind of chutney that only Walton's had to go with his Jambon Persillé. They went through hors-d'oeuvres, fish, a main dish, and a salad. He said, "In honor of the new member of our little circle, Fenicia, ha ha! I mean Cecilia, we really must treat this as a gala occasion. La patisserie!" He made a gesture and the cart came up instantly. "And where's the cheese? Perhaps some of us would prefer to have cheese. Is there a Chèvre? Ah, there it is." He pointed to something on the cart that looked like a hockey puck. "It's a little rich for the ladies. Ben and I will have that, two old goats that we are."

"Speak for yourself."

"My dear fellow, I always speak for myself. That is why I am so eloquent and so cheerful."

Ilya and Ben had the Chèvre, Betsy a profiterole; Cecilia nibbled at a piece of Brie. Then they went upstairs to the lounge for coffee, except that Ilya ordered cognac for everybody. Ben had got past the point where he felt mellow from the drinks at the Ritz, and now he was feeling floaty and unreal. Perhaps if he went on drinking he would come out the other side. He drank the cognac and fixed his eyes across the low cocktail table at the image of Betsy, slightly blurred, no doubt because of the dim illumination.

At a certain point it occurred to him to wonder what had happened to Cecilia. There she was, at his side. If he turned his head he could see her clearly. He was filled with a sudden tug of affection for her and wanted to embrace her in front of everybody, but this would only induce one of Ilya's witticisms. Instead he felt for her hand, couldn't find it, and abandoned the search. He knew he was quite drunk now.

A dark discreet figure bent over Ilya with something on a tray. Without turning his head Ilya flung his Barclaycard onto it. Ben feebly groped with his one good hand for his wallet and couldn't find it. Probably it was in the other pocket. Ilya was saying, "In honor of Fenicia, we must do something quite special afterwards. I have in mind a certain pleasure dome, vulgar but amusing."

"Will you stop calling her Fenicia?"

"Oh, I mean Cecilia. I was thinking of another girl entirely."

"Ilya often calls me Nastasya," said Betsy. "She's a character is his first trilogy. He confuses life and art."

"It's nothing of the sort, darling. I don't confuse anything. Art is more real than life. With its tremendous solidity, its vigor, its bright coruscating colors, it breaks out of the confines of the book and floods over gray old life, permeating it and lending it the only reality it has. The characters in my novels are far more real to me than you three are, sitting here."

"You're drunk," said Betsy.

"That may be, we all are a little, but what I say is none the less true. Art is real, life is a dream."

"I've forgotten what happened to Nastasya in the novel," said Ben.

"She was eaten by wolves in the Pripet Marshes. The hero, whose name was Volodya, escaped but lost his hand trying to defend her."

"Ilya loves to kill his characters, but not those that he associates with himself."

"He sends them to stalags."

"Oh, they love that."

Would you like to be in a stalag, Ilya?" asked Cecilia. She had only touched her lips to the cognac; the glass was still full.

"Heavens no. Imagine the food."

"And they wouldn't take your Barclaycard," said Ben.

"You're not taking these things seriously, Mortimer old fellow. My theories of the novel. Art and reality."

"Neither are you."

"Well, it's different for me." He laughed merrily, rubbing his hands. The charge slip came and he signed it with a flourish like a Renaissance prince.

78.

The taxi drew up in front of the Empire in Leicester Square and they all got out, wavering a little to find themselves upright on the pavement. The facade with its gigantic red neon sign shimmered piercingly above them. The taxi disappeared without any money passing visibly between Ilya and the driver; perhaps he transferred it electronically as they do in banks. The usual crowd of people in bizarre clothing was milling in front of the entrance, but it made way for them as they approached. The young man in the frilly shirt examined them for a second with expression, then waved them through. They passed by the black bouncer and went down a corridor into a large room flickering with violet and magenta light.

The place was full of people, most of them dancing but a few sitting at tiny tables the size of dinner plates. The noise was deafening. It would have been hard for Ben to describe the music except that it was made with electronic instruments, and designed to excite young people at midnight and put them in a mating mood. By some miracle they found a table with three chairs and borrowed a fourth chair from another party. Ilya went off to the bar and came back with four gins on the rocks. Over the din of the music he recited in his fluty voice:

It was a miracle of rare device,
A sunny pleasure dome with caves of ice!

"Ilya dear, you know every cliché in English literature."

"And in several other literatures too. They became clichés because they are so beautiful."

The people were the same that Ben and Cecilia saw going in the place on their first night in London, some in outré costumes or with scarlet or green hair, some with their faces evidently tattooed by drunken Chinamen, some in ordinary clothes, but they were all young. For some reason, when Ilya was in charge of the party no one stared at them. They sat at their tiny table looking at the freaks and drinking gin. Cecilia left hers untouched. A little later, when the party at the next table went away to dance, she got up, went over to their table, and came back with a bottle of Perrier and a glass.

"You're an icy little minx," said Betsy.

It seemed to Ben that there was danger of a bad quarrel in public. He felt as though the four of them were going down a steep slope on a toboggan, with Ilya pretending to steer but not really paying attention. He, in his picture of it, was jammed into the toboggan between Betsy and Cecilia, vaguely stimulated by the whole thing. He drank his gin and to his surprise found there was another full glass in front of him. It was definitely another glass; the empty one was on the table beside it.

A singer, a mahogany-colored woman in a sparkly suit, boots, and white stockings, was trying to commit fellatio on a silver microphone. He couldn't tell from the sounds she made whether she was singing in English or Sanscrit. He looked at Cecilia to see what her reaction was and found she had disappeared from her chair. Turning his head, he caught sight of her being towed around the table by Ilya toward the dance floor.

He knew he was not dreaming but he was unable to get to his feet and interfere with these events, exactly as in a dream. He sipped his second gin. He grasped now that it was the one that had been Cecilia's; someone, either Betsy or Ilya, had slid it over to his side of the table.

Betsy said, "Don't they make a charming couple."

"I don't care for your sarcasms."

"Ilya needs a little relaxation. He's been working so hard these past few months."

"Oh shut up."

There were various ways of dancing. Ilya and Cecilia's way consisted of standing five feet apart on the floor, holding their fists in the air and weaving their waists. He wondered where in the world she had learned to do this. He finally grasped what he had not understood up to now, that she belonged to her own generation of twenty-year-olds and in some ways was no different from them. Other couples were simulating Charlestons or doing splits across each other's legs; the fists-in-the-air and weaving school, however, predominated. The music stopped for a moment and Ilya began chatting with the people around him on the floor. He took something from a flat case and passed it to a youth with lacquered hair; from the color of the tip Ben could see that it was one of his Acapulco Golds. Ilya took one for himself and they lighted them. They sucked them, staring at each other and smiling. When the music started up again Cecilia began dancing with the youth with lacquered hair; they joined their four hands, held them in the air, and wove their waists, staring at each other in the region of the groin. Ilya was dancing with a girl in violet tights and a miniskirt.

Ben, staring at the dancers, got up and held the edge of the table.

"Where are you going?"

He didn't answer, and Betsy got up too and linked her arm with his. Without speaking a word she led him out through the tables and down the corridor to the door. He was fascinated by the train of glittering slime under his nostrils, like something left by a snail. Outside, although he could still hear the music, the relative silence was like a flood of cool water. The huge neon sign over their heads turned the air a dark pink. Dimly beyond it, in the shadows, he could see the night life of Leicester Square, like an underexposed photo.

He found himself a taxi. Betsy was twined around him

and she felt warm and pleasant. He tried to remember what it was he left behind him at the place with the loud music and the lights. It was probably his wallet, but he couldn't feel for it with Betsy draped around his neck; he could no more resist her than a clam could resist an octopus. Anyhow she felt good. She was warm and solid as you might imagine a Rubens nude would be if it came to life. She still hadn't said a word. The diorama of London at night hummed by outside the glass. When the taxi got to Cadogan Place he got out and, still linked arm in arm with her, allowed himself to be led into the flat.

79.

When he got back to the hotel Cecilia was still up, sitting at the dressing table in her nightgown brushing her hair. He was almost sober now. He had a ghastly feeling of horror as though he had committed a crime and couldn't remember what it was; no, he knew perfectly well what it was.

"When did you get back?"

"About an hour ago."

"I'm sorry we got separated. I didn't know I would be so long. I should have come back sooner."

"You went to bed with Betsy, didn't you?"

"Yes."

"How was it?"

"Not much."

"I didn't think it would be."

"I'm sorry, Cecilia."

"Oh, it's all right," she said in her usual offhand voice, although it seemed to him a little strained now.

"What did you do?"

"I danced with some boys, then Ilya brought me back to the hotel."

"He didn't come up?"

"No."

"We seem to have a policy," he said, "of being absolutely frank with each other."

"So it seems."

"What do we do now?"

"Go on much as before, I imagine."

"You didn't mind?"

"Oh, I minded," she said patiently, "but there's not much to do about such things, and I'm not going to leave you on account of it."

"You know," he said, "Ethel told me to do this."

"Do what?"

"Have an affair with Betsy."

"Is that why you did it?"

"I don't know. Anyway it was a rotten idea. I can't imagine how I could act so foolish."

"Oh, I can. Anyone can act that foolish."

"You don't."

"Well I might. I've been lucky so far."

"You don't drink."

But even now she refused to agree with him and condemn his drinking. She said lightly, "We all have our little ways."

"What's your vice?"

"Moral superiority. Pride is a worse sin than fornication."

"Fornication feels pretty bad."

"Oh come to bed. You'll feel better in the morning."

80.

In the hotel in Cheltenham they had a big English breakfast—cereal, ham and sausage, eggs, mushrooms, toast, and broiled tomatoes—and then they set off for their walk in the Cotswolds. They had no baggage except for their knapsacks; they had left everything else in the hotel in London. They didn't have to be anywhere until the end of the week, when they had an appointment with the harpsichord maker in Arundel. At least he had got her away from other people for a while. The weather was bad, with a thin mist falling and a threat of rain, and he still had a hangover from his debauch of two nights before in London, but none of this bothered him much. He was with Cecilia and she had forgiven him. She hadn't exactly forgiven him, but she said she wasn't going to leave him on account of it. She might the next time. He would have to be careful. He could hardly believe that the thing with Betsy had happened, and he thought it wouldn't have happened at his age if his senses hadn't been awakened by Cecilia, so it was really a compliment to her. He didn't know how to explain this to her and decided not to try.

They climbed up a steep lane to Cleeve Common, a meadow on a windy plateau. On the way they passed a farmer in his truck, who leaned out the window and shouted, "Watch out for the crazies."

"Who?"

"The peace hippies. They're up on the Common. Stay clear of them."

These people had been in the newspapers lately; Ben remembered reading about them. They were vagabonds and cultists who tried to have a ritual of some kind at Stonehenge but were driven away by the police. No one could stop them from camping on the Common, which was public ground. They came upon their camp after a quarter of an hour of walking: a shabby collection of trucks, caravans, and old busses, with a mildewed old circus tent in the middle. Women in layered clothing stood in the falling mist watching them as they approached. A dog bayed.

"He said to stay clear of them," said Ben.

"Why? They're just people. Let's talk to them."

He followed her into the camp. The dog charged at them barking, and a woman in several sweaters, her hair in a bun, called it off.

"Hi," said Cecilia.

The woman only stared back. She didn't seem unfriendly.

"Who are you anyhow?"

Ben had a strong urge to pull her away. But the woman, after a pause, said, "We're Peace Folk. Some of us are Druids, others Born Again. We've got two witches. We're just people like anybody else."

"Imagine meeting a Druid," said Cecilia.

"I'm not one myself. I'm Born Again."

She was a very simple person. It was hard to tell whether this was because she was good or because she was simple-minded. She offered Ben and Cecilia a cup of tea, and they drank it out of unwashed mugs while a circle of people stood around sullenly watching them. The women were joined by some unshaven men in work clothes. They looked like rough characters, not very much like Druids or Born Agains.

They tried to pay the woman for the tea, but she wouldn't take anything. Cecilia persuaded her to accept a chocolate bar from her knapsack. Then they left the camp, trailed by the still barking dog.

"It was vile tea. I hope they haven't poisoned us." Still Ben was pleased with this little adventure. He wouldn't have done it if he hadn't been with Cecilia. They could tell this tale in Santa Barbara, the Druids they met in the Cotswolds.

81.

The next day the weather was worse; a fine rain fell all day. They had plastic ponchos but the rain came through the openings and their clothing was soon soaked. Ben remembered that in Santa Barbara it seemed to him that rain was the leitmotif of their love, that he felt good when it rained and that nothing could happen to the two of them when the rain was rustling on the roof. Now it was different; the rain was just rain and unpleasant. Perhaps it was because of his rotten behavior in London. They stopped early this day and found a room in a farmhouse. As soon as the door was locked they took off their sodden clothing and hung it on hooks on the wall. For the first time Ben was naked before Cecilia. They took turns rubbing each other with some coarse white towels until their bodies were pink, then they got into bed. Cecilia, laughing, teased him for being afraid of Druids. Her lean hard-limbed body was nothing at all like a Rubens nude. The rain rustled on the roof. Ben had never been so happy in his life. Tired from walking, they fell asleep in the odor of their wet clothes hanging on the wall and the cut hay in the fields outside.

82.

In the morning the sun was out and a few white clouds floated over the green hills to the west; the earth and the roofs of the houses steamed. Skirting the town of Broadway, they climbed up a steep hill to a tower, then followed along a ridge that ended in a patch of woods.

They had crossed the Cotswolds and come out on the other side; the rolling countryside of Oxfordshire stretched away to the east. They stopped at the edge of the woods to rest and look at the view.

It was August and the Cotswolds were full of people walking. Ben found that he had not really got Cecilia to himself as he had thought. They had passed a man and a pair of girls on the climb up to the tower, and now they could see a figure coming along the ridge toward the woods where they were resting. As it came closer they could see it was a young man in shorts and a red shirt. He seemed to be an experienced walker; he came steadily up the slope without stopping to rest, and his knapsack was faded from much use. He was wearing a pair of worn and dusty hiking boots with thick socks. His face was tan and he had a helmet of brown curly hair, long in the back.

He nodded in a friendly way and sat down a few feet away from them. After a moment Cecilia said, "Hi."

"Hello. I'm Clive."

"I'm Cecilia, and this is Ben." In the way of modern young people, they didn't bother with last names.

He said, "Rotten weather we're having."

"Isn't it."

"Better today though."

"I'm hoping," she said, "that our clothes will dry out today. They got soaked yesterday." She was wearing the shorts and Irish sweater she had worn on the hike in California. The damp sweater gave out a musty odor like a wet sheep. Her long brown legs were stretched out over a rock.

He looked at her for some time, ignoring Ben. Then he said, "Are you a student?"

"Yes."

"Where do you go to school?"

"In California."

"You're far from home then."

"And you?"

"Ekchully, the University of Kent."

"Oh, I was hoping you'd be Oxford or Cambridge."

He grinned and said, "We can't all be, you know. Some of us who aren't are very nice chaps."

Cecilia reached down and pulled a flower out of a cranny of the rock she was sitting on. She did it dreamily, without looking at her hand, as though she wasn't aware of what she was doing. She picked some more and piled them one by one in a little heap by her feet. Ben didn't know English wildflowers; they looked something like California lupines. She reached up and began making a braid behind her head, plaiting flowers into it as she worked. When she finished she reached into her pocket for a rubber band and put it on the end. then she began on the other braid.

Watching her stealthily, Ben saw something in her face, a thoughtful and yet absent-minded look, as though her mind were somewhere else. Perhaps she herself wasn't aware of what she was feeling, but he read it clearly. A kind of melancholy gathered in him, seeping into his chest like the memory of an old wound. *Child, child*, he thought, *blood of my veins, put the flowers in your hair for me*. None of the three of them said anything for a while. When she had finished the second braid and fastened it with the band she stood up.

"Ready to go?"

"All right."

With Cecilia in the lead they went on down the path in the grass. Clive followed a few paces behind them. He seemed to notice for the first time that one of Ben's arms was limp and he was carrying the hand in his pocket.

"Hurt your arm?"
"No."
Clive was evidently a well brought up young man and felt it was polite to keep up a conversation with people when you're thrown together with them, even when they're older than you. After they had gone a few more yards he said, "What do you do, Ben?"
"I'm a publisher."
"That's interesting. What do you publish?"
"Well, we're on a holiday now," said Ben. "I don't want to talk business."
"All right. Does Cecilia work for you?"
"No she doesn't."
"Are you her father or something?"
"Ben's just a friend," said Cecilia.
At the bottom of the hill they went through a kissing-gate, a kind of wooden escapement like that of a watch that allowed only one person to go through at a time and was impenetrable by cows. By this time Clive, the better walker, had passed Ben and was walking between him and Cecilia. Ben followed on behind the two heads, one with flowers in the braids, the other a curly mop. Clive and Cecilia chatted. She turned her head now and then to talk to him over her back. Ben fell behind a little and lost track of the conversation. When he exerted himself and caught up to them they were talking about her studies in California.
"Music? What kind of music?"
"Harpsichord."
"Oh wow, I can barely do Chopsticks on the piano."
"What are you studying at Kent?"
"Lit Crit."
"You should talk to Ben. He's the literary one."
"That so?" Clive didn't turn his head to look at Ben

behind them. The three of them went in Indian file along a hedge with a field of black-faced sheep on one side, over a stile, and down a slope to a brook. It was warm here in the shelter of the hill; the sun beat down and their damp clothing began to steam. In a silent agreement they sat down at the edge of the brook; Cecilia took off her shoes and socks and put her feet in the cold water. "Oh, that feels so good."

Ben and Clive did the same. Ben was bothered by a little soreness in his feet. The chill water didn't exactly make the pain go away, but his numbed feet simply ceased to exist. Cecilia's feet were bright pink under the rippling surface of the water, like two suave lobsters.

"What *kind* of Lit Crit?"

"Ekchully, American literature. I'm doing a thesis on Melville."

"Oh, fabulous."

"When I get my degree I'm hoping to do graduate work in America. Perhaps I could come to California."

"That would be super."

"I've already applied for a grant."

"Fantastic."

Ben was astounded to hear her falling into the clichéd lingo of her generation; when she was with him she always talked like an adult. After ten minutes of this kind of chatter Clive and Cecilia left him and went off barefoot down the brook, finding interesting pebbles and showing them to each other. When they were gone Ben looked at the six items of footgear lined up together on the grass. He took one of Clive's boots and examined it; it was worn and mudstained, and the head of a nail was showing in the sole. Picking at the nail with the blade of his Swiss Army knife, he found he could remove it easily. He unfolded another blade on the knife, a long thin one, and cut an opening through the nail-hole to the inner sole. Then, jamming the boot against a rock with his weak right hand and working with his left, he pushed the nail back into the sole and drove it in with another gadget on the knife intended for opening cans. He could now feel the prick of the nail with his finger on the inside of the boot. He put the boot back where it had been.

Clive and Cecilia came back laughing and chattering. When the three of them had put their shoes back on they set off over the fields, going through a kissing-gate now and then or climbing over a fence. After a half an hour Clive stopped and took his boot off. He looked inside, then he felt for the nail with his finger. He tried to pound it flat inside the boot with a small stone, unsuccessfully.

"You wouldn't have a penknife would you, Ben."

Ben said nothing.

Clive said, "I usually carry one, ekchully, but I didn't bring it this time."

"Put your handkerchief in the boot," said Cecilia.

He tried this but the point of the nail came through the handkerchief too. Putting the boot back on, he went on down the path limping. "Curse and Damn. It's always one's footgear that spoils a walk. I should have checked it before I set out." He wasn't able to walk so fast with his limp and Ben passed him without much difficulty. Now he was in the middle, with Cecilia in front of him and Clive behind.

After another hour of walking they came into Blockley, a scenic little village so perfect that it looked like something in a museum, and Ben treated them to lunch in a pub. There was a cobbler's shop in the village but it wouldn't be open until four. It was a quarter to two now.

"I'll have to linger till then," said Clive. "Hell and

Blast. Why don't you two hang around too, and then we can go on together."

"No, I don't think so," said Cecilia.

That night, in the inn where they stayed in Bourton-on-the-Water, Ben was collecting his soap and towel to go down the hall to the bath and Cecilia came up to him with a funny little smile and put her arms around his neck. She removed one hand and put it in his pocket, then the other hand in the other pocket; he felt her cool fingers slipping through his clothing. In the second pocket she found the Swiss Army knife and took it out.

She unfolded the big blade, no longer than her finger, and held the knife in the air. With a mock leer like a murderer she brought it down slowly until it pricked his chest. Then she handed him back the knife. He folded it up and went away to his bath.

83.

From the Cotswolds they went directly down to Sussex to look at the harpsichords. Ben had a rotten cold he caught from Betsy in London, but he was still feeling fairly cheerful after his encounter with Clive. In Arundel, a quiet country town clustered around the base of its castle, they inquired for Maltravers Street and were directed to a lane running along a hill at the top of the town. There was a handcarved gilded sign: *Walter Thorne, Instrument Maker.* The shop and display room were on the street floor and Thorne lived in the flat above.

Thorne was younger than Ben expected, in his mid-thirties perhaps. He was a narrow wiry man with ginger hair and a small goatee, and he was wearing a worn sweater with a hole in one elbow. He came out of the room in the back where two or three other people were working.

"Mr. Gavilan. And Miss Penn. So good of you to come all the way down from London."

"From the Cotswolds ekchully," said Cecilia. She had picked this up from Clive. Was it a joke? She probably did it just to tease him.

Thorne chattered with them about their walk in the Cotswolds and then showed them around the shop. He was a queer sort of salesman; he acted as though they were guests instead of customers. He hardly seemed to want to show them the harpsichords. There were three of them in the front; he had others in the back. There were also dulcimers and recorders, and a pair of lutes hanging on the wall. "We don't make the lutes here. They're made by a friend of mine in Lewes. They're quite beautifully made, don't you think?" He took one down from the wall and showed it to Ben, and in fact it was a miracle that this instrument like a large bulging pumpkin could be made by gluing strips of light and dark wood together. Throne gave the impression that he was distracting them from the harpsichords by calling their attention to the lute, which he had not even made himself.

Bored by the lutes, Cecilia sat down at one of the harpsichords and began playing it. It was something Ben didn't recognize, light and not very difficult, perhaps Couperin, the Muzak of the eighteenth century. Ben and Thorne listened until she had finished the short piece. Then Thorne said, "That one has a very nice tone, I think. It's a straightforward serviceable instrument. A nice one for a school. It isn't as elegant as some of the others."

The one Cecilia had played was perfectly plain, in a

light wood with a narrow strip of ebony let into it like a pencil-line. The other two were decorated, one in antique green and gilt, the other with a kind of pastoral frieze in the French manner, with pink nudes and cherubs. Cecilia played both of them, on one the Couperin again, on the other something from the *Goldberg Variations* which she stumbled over and gave up. "They're both nice. I don't care for the decorations. They're fakey."

"They're reproductions of eighteenth century instruments. This one is an exact copy of a Blanchet, made in Paris in 1740. You can have any sort of decoration you want; we can build instruments to order. It takes about a year."

"I don't think we want to wait for a year. Don't you have others?"

Thorne hesitated. Then he said, "I can show you one upstairs."

He led them through the door into the workroom at the rear. There were no finished harpsichords in sight in this room. A blond boy and an old man were clamping together something to glue it, and a young woman in a smock was painting decorations on a panel; there was a pleasant odor of glue and wood chips. From the workroom a stairway mounted up to Thorne's flat. They followed him up the stairs and into a large white room full of light.

Cecilia said, "What an ideal place to live."

Through the small diamond panes of the windows there was a view of the river with a glimpse of the castle at one side. There were two rooms and a kitchenette in the flat, but Thorne had installed his bed in the large square living room. The walls were white, and the bed was white enamel with a white bedspread. The floor was unfinished sanded pine, with plugs covering the nail-holes as on a ship. The only color in the room came from a small magenta rug at the foot of the bed and from a sofa with blue-green cushions. There was a green vase with dried rushes. The bed was a double one, Ben noted.

Cecilia ran her fingers over the sofa, then she went to the window and looked out at the view. Ben knew she was imagining herself living here. With Thorne; although perhaps her thoughts hadn't carried her that far yet. It was all perfectly natural; as soon as you saw a nice house or a flat you imagined yourself living in it. Ben compared the flat in his mind to the house he had bought for the two of them in Montecito, with its somber gray shingles, its birches, and its bare unfurnished rooms.

Thorne opened the door to the other room of the flat, at the front facing the river. "Here's the harpsichord."

He had converted the former bedroom to a music room; there were bookshelves, a record player, and a cabinet of records. To sit in there was a single white armchair. The harpsichord was next to the window where you could have a view of the river as you were playing it. It was finished in black lacquer with a frieze of twining yellow rosebuds, a kind of art nouveau effect, neither modern nor eighteenth century. Cecilia looked at it and something changed in her expression. Ben knew instantly that this was the harpsichord they had to have. Apart from its musical qualities, which he couldn't judge (he could see that Cecilia had fallen in love with it even before she had tried it), it would fit into the New England severity of the house in Montecito, and the rosebuds would add a touch of color.

"This is my own instrument. I might be willing to sell

it. But I'm afraid it would be a little more than the others downstairs."

He mentioned a figure. It seemed astronomical to Ben; at first he thought he had heard wrong. Cecilia said nothing; she looked at Ben with a little smile.

Thorne sat down and effortlessly, at quick tempo, ran through the piece from the *Goldberg Variations* that Cecilia had muffed. A certain kind of Englishman, precisely Walter Thorne's kind, was capable of this sort of malice. "Its tone is a little richer, a little more fruity, than the others." He might have been talking about wine. It was probably all nonsense, Ben thought, just as most talk about wine was. He didn't care for this man but he knew he was at his mercy; he was in love and Cecilia had to have that harpsichord. He knew this even before she had played it.

"What do you think, Cecilia?"

She sat down and tried it, this time sticking to the easier Couperin. "The action is nice." Her fingers flowed smoothly over the keys. "And a lovely tone. It's very mellow. It might be an old instrument." She shifted her right hand to the upper manual and launched into an allegretto passage. She was showing Thorne how well she could play when it wasn't Bach.

If Thorne was impressed he showed no sign. He said, "They cure with time. The wood melds together. This one is about ten years old."

"You play very well yourself."

"I began as a performer. I turned to making harpsichords when no one else could make one to suit me."

"You're not sorry to part with this one?" Cecilia asked him. "You say it belongs to you personally."

"Oh yes. But here in England we're used to Americans buying up our patrimony with their dollars."

He was still smiling in his subdued superior way. Ben, after a moment, said, "I think we'll take it if you're willing to sell it. We can't wait to have one built. We need it right away."

"Americans generally can't wait. It'll be there in six weeks or two months."

"Can you ship it by air?"

"That would cost about eight hundred pounds more."

"A trifle," said Ben, who didn't think it was a trifle, but they couldn't wait even two months for the harpsichord. It had to be there in the house when they came back from Europe.

Thorne converted the price into dollars and added the shipping, and Ben wrote him a check, while Thorne gazed curiously at his technique for doing this with his bad arm: first he tore out the check and laid it on the table, then with his left hand he arranged the right hand on the check. Once in place, the right hand had no trouble working the pen.

"You can get the V.A.T. back from the Inland Revenue once it's exported. I'll give you the certificate."

Ben wasn't sure he had the money in his checking account. He would have to wire his bank to make a transfer.

Thorne made out the export certificate and put the check into the drawer of the white-enameled table. "Why don't we go out and have a drink on this," he said.

Putting on a small flap cap like a workman's, he led them out of the shop to a wine bar in the High Street, which ran up from the river to the castle. Most of the people in the place were young, wearing sweaters and baggy trousers like Thorne himself. "Hello, Walter," said someone. They took a table and Thorne went to the bar and came back with three glasses of rosé. He had warmed up a little now and was almost amiable. "They say that rosé is the wine of amateurs. I'm an amateur about everything but harpsichords."

"It's very nice. What is it?"

"A Tavel '78," said Thorne shortly. With this he took back his amateurishness and established his authority about wine. He was a difficult character, very crochety for his age.

The other patrons watched with interest from across the room. They all knew Thorne, evidently. Ben could imagine what they were thinking. *There's Walter. And a customer. And a new girl that Walter's got.*

84.

Ben's favorite hotel in Paris was the Lutétia, on Boulevard Raspail not far from Saint-Germain-des-Près. This time he was a little more cautious about giving Cecilia a lecture on the subject; she could see for herself that it was a very fine old hotel, with a Proustian elegance that was only a little decadent; the plumbing was thoroughly modern. He refrained from telling her that Lutétia was the old Roman name for Paris. She would probably find that out for herself, or already knew it. They settled into the room and unpacked; Cecilia, who had worn a dress on the plane, changed into her narrow black pants and white sweater. It was true that she wore nothing under the sweater, he found now; he watched with a pungent interest as her narrow back, her two classic breasts, and her ribs that showed the concave arch of her stomach disappeared into it. She no longer went into the bathroom to change her clothes; he still did, except on occasions like that in the farmhouse in the Cotswolds when they were both soaking wet and rubbed each other with towels.

The room faced onto the boulevard and the traffic went by outside with a noise like a giant waterfall; it wasn't the quietest spot in Paris. But after a while Ben found that a part of what he took for the rhythmic thrum of traffic was actually something making a noise inside his head. He was also developing a bad cough.

"I don't think I'm very well," he told her.

"I like the hotel," she said. "It smells just like Paris."

"How could you possible know what Paris smells like if you've never been here?"

"We can imagine sights and sounds. Why not smells?"

"It's probably just the odor of coffee from the kitchen downstairs. Every French hotel smells like that."

"It's delicious. Why don't we go down and have some?"

It was about three; they hadn't had their lunch yet. "I think I'll skip lunch and just rest here in the room for an hour. You go on down. Take my credit card. Or you can charge it to the room."

"All right."

"And while you're gone, why don't you go out and see if you can buy me a fever thermometer."

"Oh. You said you weren't feeling well."

"It's just a cold."

"If it were just a cold you wouldn't need a fever thermometer. What's it called in French?"

"It's called a *thermomètre clinique*, just as it is in English."

"Well, you needn't be so snappish. I thought it might be called a *thermomètre à fièvre* or something."

"A *thermomètre clinique*. And don't look for a drugstore. They're called pharmacies."

"All right. Do you have any money?"

"I've got lots of money. Don't you remember, we bought francs at the airport."

"Well, can I have some?"

He threw her his wallet and she extracted a handful of polychrome French banknotes from it. "They *are* pretty."

"Bye," he told her listlessly.

"Maybe you'll cheer up," she said, "if you have a little nap."

85.

She was gone about an hour; he lay on the bed wide awake listening to the traffic and to the noise in his head, which was a hiss like escaping gas in little bursts to the rhythm of his pulse. He couldn't go to sleep because he had to cough every so often. There was also a fluttering sound in his ear like a soft bat-wing, no doubt a harmless spasm. When Cecilia came back she reported first of all that she had had an excellent omelette for lunch, with a glass of Beaujolais Nouveau. And some of that wonderful bread."

"You couldn't have Beaujolais Nouveau in August. You can only get it in November." He *was* cross, not with her perhaps, but he was cross about something.

"Well, the waiter said it was Beaujolais, and I had never had it before, so it was Nouveau. Here's the *thermomètre clinique*. You said there were no drugstores, but I got it at a place called Le Drug Store. It was very nice. They had everything."

She took it out of the package and shook it down expertly. "Here, stick it in your mouth. At least it'll have the merit of keeping you quiet for a few minutes. You don't seem to be able to say anything cheerful."

"Please don't be mad at me, Cecilia. I don't feel well."

"If you hadn't fucked Betsy," she said perfectly cheerfully, "you wouldn't have a cold."

"Can't you be a little more sympathetic? And I don't care for that language."

"Which is worse, to say it or to do it?"

He seemed to be dealing with a new Cecilia in Paris, more insouciant, more sure of herself, a little flippant and with scant respect for his finer sensibilities. He put the thermometer in his mouth and remained silent for a while as she recommended. When he took it out he tried to look at it but he didn't have his reading glasses. She took it from him and twirled it in her fingers.

"I don't understand these French degrees."

"Normal is thirty-seven, I think."

"What's thirty-nine?"

"It's two degrees above normal."

"That's not very much."

"No, but I think the French degrees are bigger than American degrees. There are only a hundred of them from freezing to boiling, whereas we have a hundred eighty."

"I don't see what that's got to do with it."

It occurred to him that the theory that women are incapable of mathematics quite probably had something to it. Whatever it was that he had, it was driving him into a peevish anti-feminism. He was not really able to cope with all of these things; he was capable only of the most rudimentary and oversimplified thoughts. The two French degrees of fever had turned him into the bad-tempered old man that he ought to be at his age, the person that everybody always complimented him on not being. Ben might be forty, everyone always said. Well, at the moment he didn't feel forty.

"Do you want me to get in bed with you?"

"You'd catch my cold."

"Betsy's cold," she said. "It might make me rich, intelligent, and beautiful like her."

"Oh please, Cecilia."

86.

At five o'clock he got up off the bed, went into the bathroom and washed his face in cold water, and felt a little better. His eyeballs were still hot and dry, however, and he had the impression that there was a thin veil of gauze between him and the world. He decided he was well enough to play the village explainer to Cecilia, at least for an hour or two; he took her to Saint-German-des-Près and they sat in the Café Bonaparte, watching people go by and looking at the dunce-cap of the old medieval church across the square.He had a rum with sugar and lemon, a medicinal mixture that he thought might make him feel a little better, and Cecilia had a Campari Soda.

"Is this the Saint-Germain where the Existentialists used to come?"

"Oh yes. Sartre. Simone de Beauvoir. Boris Vian. They didn't come here to the Bonaparte, though. They went to the Deux Magots up at the corner of the Boulevard. Nobody goes there now except tourists. They've raised the prices and the waiters will take your photo with your camera."

"Who comes to the Café Bonaparte?"

"Sophisticated Americans and their beautiful friends. Coyotes and fawns. Chorus girls and their sugar daddies."

This triggered some unconscious association and she

said, "You know, Ben, it was very nice of you to buy me the harpsichord." Or perhaps it was one of her jokes.

"It *was* nice of me. Also, now that you have me you don't have to work as a chorus girl anymore."

"You know, your drink smells exactly like the cough medicine that Babs used to give me when I had a cold."

"That's the idea."

"I think it had a lot of alcohol in it too. It used to make me drunk as an owl. I was about nine years old."

"Babs was a curious mother."

"She wasn't a mother. She was Babs."

"I like Babs. I conceived a considerable admiration for her, even in the short time I talked to her."

"She's an unfortunate case really. I feel sorry for her in a way. She needs someone like—" Here she seemed flustered and took a sip of her drink. "She needs someone to look after her. Not to look after her exactly but to be a companion in her old age."

"What were you going to say?"

"I don't know. Nothing."

"You were going to say that she needs someone like me."

"Oh Ben. For heaven's sake."

"She's not so old really. She's about my age."

"Will you drop it?"

"I could be a village explainer to her. I could explain Berkeley to her and take her to the coffee houses on Telegraph Avenue."

"You are cross today, aren't you? Why don't you drink your cough medicine. Oh look! It's Anny and Boss and Glover."

"Who are they?"

"Some kids from Berkeley." The three young Americans stopped and peered over the hedge of the terrasse, uncertain whether to come in; then they changed their minds and went on.

Cecilia got up from the table and ran out to the sidewalk to pursue them. After a while she came back leading them in a little procession; she introduced them to Ben while another waiter pushed two tables together to make room for them all. Anny was a small girl with a heart-shaped face and a lot of fuzzy blond hair; Boss was a pale slender boy in tight jeans, a levi jacket, and a black flat-topped cowboy hat. Glover, who lingered after the others and took his seat with an indolent leisure, was dressed entirely in black and had a three-day stubble of beard. He looked, not like a criminal exactly, but like an actor playing a criminal on TV. He sat down next to Cecilia and examined Ben through his silver sunglasses with a little smile.

None of them seemed to notice that Ben shook hands with his left hand, leaving the other one in his pocket. They were really quite cordial and friendly. Glover said, "It's really a pleasure to meet you, Ben. Any friend of Cece's. Where did the two of you meet?"

"At Muir House."

"Were you a waiter, Ben?"

"No, I was a guest."

"Did you have one of those neat cabins?" Anny asked him.

"Yes I did."

"That must have been a gas."

"It was very nice."

Glover said, "How did you like the cabin, Cece?"

"I never went near it. I was busy waiting on tables."

Anny said, "You're being bitchy again, Glover."

"Why, I'm not being the least kind of bitchy," said Glover in his reasonable voice. "I'm interested in Cece and anxious to find out anything I can about a friend of hers. What do you do for a living, Ben?"

"He's a retired publisher and a philanthropist," said Cecilia.

"Oh, why don't you let Ben speak for himself," Anny told her.

"It's all more or less true. I used to be a publisher but now I'm only a silent partner, and I've just bought Cecilia a harpsichord, so I guess that makes me a philanthropist."

"Oh, terrific," said Anny.

"Cece, what is a harpsichord exactly?" said Glover. Cecilia made a fist and struck him lightly on the shoulder; this was evidently an old joke between then.

"Cece is a terrific harpsichordist," said Anny. "She's going to be the Wanda Landowska of our generation."

Boss, speaking for the first time, said, "Cece is going to be the Cece Penn of our generation. Who is Wanda Landowska anyway?" His thin voice carried over the cafe terrasse. The other patrons were examining his cowboy costume; he colored and set the black hat at an angle over his eyes.

"I'll tell you what," offered Ben. "I'll buy you all a drink if you'll stop calling Cecilia Cece and call her Cecilia instead."

"Oh, okay," said Glover. "Let me try that out. See-seelya. Is that all right? Cecilia."

"That sounds *awfully* strange," said Anny.

"It's my name," said Cecilia. She seemed amused, unperturbed, and at home in all this raillery around her.

"What will you have?" Ben asked them.

"Beer."

"Beer."

"Absinthe," croaked Glover.

The waiter brought them three beers, and they sat there for a half an hour drinking them and talking about people they knew in Berkeley, the hangouts they always went to, and the quirks of professors in classes they'd taken. They all thought that old Hathcock in Victorian poetry was a riot; they quoted him reading poetry, accurately imitating his lisp. Occasionally Ben put in "That's Tennyson, of course" or "This Hathcock sounds like quite a character," but no one paid much attention to him; they nodded and then went on. He imagined that Professor Hathcock was probably about the same age as he was.

It was now seven o'clock, a warm humid Paris evening with a light blue smoke hanging in the air from the traffic, and they all decided they were hungry. On a light note of parody they rejected the Tour d'Argent (Ben had imagined taking Cecilia there) and the three-star Laperouse on the quay, and considered the Grenouille (too full of tourists) and a health food restaurant in Rue du Bac called Le Jardin that Anny wanted to go to, but Glover said this was "too sanitary." Boss had heard of a fish place in the Latin Quarter called Le Criée. Too expensive.

Glover said, "Where do you want to go, Humbert Humbert?"

"Oh, take it easy on Ben," said Cecilia. "Besides I'm not thirteen."

"Oh, I forgot, you were fourteen last month."

Ben was anxious to please these people and fall in with their jokes. "Cecilia *is* a nymphet. You're very shrewd. I feel exactly like the hero of Nabokov's novel. I do know of a nice restaurant near here called the Petite Chaise. If it's still there. It used to be in Rue de Grenelle."

"Oh, I saw it. White tableclothes."

That was out. Finally they decided to try a place in

Rue Monge that Glover had heard about from some French students. They went there on the Metro, although Ben would gladly have paid for a taxi. He still didn't feel very well.

87

It was an Algerian restaurant, so naturally everybody had couscous. The steamy greasy mixture of cereal with lumps of lamb and spices was too much for Ben and after a couple of bites he put his fork down. Glover, temporarily taking over the function of village explainer, demonstrated the Arab technique of taking the couscous from the platter with his fingers, which had crescent-shaped shadows under the nails just as Cecilia's did, but his were far darker. With this came some Pinot Noir, a wine for workmen, and sectors of hot pita bread. Ben nibbled at the bread and drank the sour red wine, as opaque as ink.

"This food is terrific," said Anny. "It's just what I needed."

"How do you like it, Humbert Humbert?"

"Oh, it's great. I'm not very hungry. Why don't you take some of mine, Cecilia."

"Humbert, excuse me, Ben, has a bad cold," said Cecilia.

Boss said, "*Voici l'anglais avec son sang-froid habituel.*"

"I beg your pardon?"

"That means, 'Here comes the Englishman with his usual bloody cold.'"

"Oh, for heaven's sake."

"What did we bring Boss along for anyhow? I hope you don't find him too puerile and banal, Humbert."

"Too banal and puerile."

"I like bad jokes," said Ben. "Especially bilingual ones." He told one about an Englishwoman who missed her train and ran after it crying, "*Je suis gauche derrière*." He was doing his best to be agreeable, and as puerile and banal as they were.

"Hey, I like that," said Boss. "Left behind. *Gauche derrière*."

"You would."

"You know, that's a nasty cough you've got there, Humbert."

"Violetta in the last act," said Cecilia.

"How did you catch your cold, Humbert?"

Ben looked at Cecilia. After a silence she said, "He climbed up a tree after a wet cat. It was while we were walking in the Cotswolds."

"How could the cat be wet if it was up a tree?"

"It was raining at the time."

"An *extraordinary* story," said Anny.

"I've eaten all these couscous but I'm still hungry hungry," said Glover. "Maybe we could have some dessert dessert."

They finished off with baklava. Nothing seemed to be costing enough; the whole dinner came to only a few francs apiece. They spurned Ben's credit card and all piled their French banknotes in a heap in the middle of the table. Ben tried to remember if there was a Paris like this when he was young; probably there was.

88.

From the restaurant they all walked across the Île Saint-Louis to the Marais, where there was some kind of a folk festival going on. It was in the Place Sainte-Catherine, a tiny square that Ben remembered perfectly now; the last time he was in Paris there was a good restaurant there, the Marais Sainte-Catherine, where you ate in a kind of crypt downstairs by candlelight. He imagined how the evening would have been different if he had gone there alone with Cecilia. Now there was a platform set up in the square to make a dance floor, and a band consisting of violin, trumpet, accordion, and drums was banging away. There were arc-lights throwing a sharp white glare onto the floor and leaving the rest of the square around it in darkness. Couples were dancing in the working-class French manner, swinging around with hooked elbows and then joining together to kick their legs from side to side. The music was tinny and cheerful. You couldn't hear the accordion when the trumpet was playing, but whenever the trumpet stopped the accordion could be heard straining reedily away at tunes like *Auprès de ma blonde*. After the Proustian Paris of the Lutétia, and the Left Bank student Paris of the restaurant in Rue Monge, this was a Paris of Toulouse-Lautrec. Cecilia danced with Glover and then with Boss. They all seemed to pick up this style of dancing by instinct, or already knew it in their bones. Anny then danced with Glover, and Cecilia found a French boy to dance with, a long-legged dandy with flexible limbs and a cap pulled down over his eyes, who had evidently been produced out of thin air by Ben's evocation of Toulouse-Lautrec. They all came back and sat at the table, including the boy in the cap, and were provided with sour red wine in paper cups.

Anny said, "Don't you want to dance, Humbert?"

"Ben has his *sang-froid*," said Cecilia.

"What? Oh, his bloody cold. Ha ha."

"I think this music is bitchin'," said Anny.

"Oh, stop talking like a Valley Girl. You're grown up now."

"Is all this happening or is it a French movie?"

They got up to dance again. Ben sat watching them for a while, then he got up and wandered out of the bright arc-lights to the edge of the square where it was cooler; he felt feverish and warm. When he circled around to the other side of the square he found the restaurant, just as he remembered it. He opened the door and looked in. There was a small entry or vestibule with a little desk for the patron, and at one side a miniature bar. Next to it was the brick spiral staircase that went down to the dining room in the crypt.

The *patron* in a black dinner jacket examined him with a careful smile. "You want, Monsieur?"

"Nothing. I was just looking. I've been here before."

"You know our restaurant?"

"Yes. As it happens, this evening I've already dined."

"Ah, you've already dined." The *patron* smiled again. "Perhaps I can offer you one of our cards."

"Thank you."

"On another occasion," he said, "you can call the number on the card to book a table. As it happens, this evening the restaurant is fully booked."

"I see."

Ben went on standing in the doorway for some time, blocking the way for other customers who might want to come in. It was difficult for him to focus his thoughts on this, however, because he was seeing everything, the entry, the spiral staircase, the bar, as though there were a dimple in the lens of his visual apparatus. It was not an unpleasant feeling, just odd, and it was interesting enough that it distracted him from his train of thought. He felt that he ought to explain to the *patron* why he went on standing in the entry of the restaurant instead of going back to the dance. Perhaps he should go into the tiny bar and have another rum with lemon and sugar. He told the patron, "*J'ai un sang-froid, vous savez.*"

89.

When they got back to the Lutétia it was after midnight and Ben didn't feel at all well. His cough was worse. His eyes didn't focus properly at any range, and he had the impression that he was about to throw up his couscous, a most unpleasant thought. Once was enough with that stuff. The one thing that would make him throw up was to put the thermometer in his mouth again, but he had to do it. He inserted it gingerly and held it under his tongue, tasting waves of Algerian grease mounting up his esophagus. He kept it in for the required three minutes and then took it out; of course he couldn't read it in his present condition even with six pairs of reading glasses, so Cecilia read it for him as she did before.

He had a fever of three French degrees. If you multiplied that by one point eight in your head, it came to about five and a half, and that added to ninety-eight point six was something like a hundred and four. He was sick all right. This figure, a purely mathematical concept, made him suddenly terrified when his symptoms hadn't. It was perfectly possible that twenty-four hours from now he might have a fever of a hundred and six, and forty-eight hours from now he might be dead. This was medically quite plausible and had happened to other people. It was an unreal thought, but all thoughts were unreal with the fever. He began rapidly making plans what to tell Cecilia about the plans for the funeral and so on.

Cecilia said, "I think we ought to get a doctor."

"Oh, that's not necessary. There's really nothing wrong with me."

"I'll call the hotel."

"We can wait until morning."

She went to the phone and began talking rapid French, in which he caught "*serieusement malade*" and "*soins medicals*." In only a few minutes the night manager himself came to the room. He lacked the elegance of the manager they had in the daytime; he was in rumpled pants, a vest, and a white shirt without a necktie.

"Monsieur doesn't feel well?"

Cecilia took over the negotiations. Ben didn't have to say anything at all. She said, "He is very sick. He has forty degrees and he needs a doctor."

For the first time the night manager noticed Ben's withered hand, which he was too weak to put into his pocket and just left dangling at the end of the arm.

"Does he possible have SIDA?"

"What's SIDA?"

Ben explained in a weak whisper that SIDA was AIDS in French.

"He doesn't have SIDA."

"Are you sure, Mademoiselle? Many Americans have it."

"He absolutely does not have SIDA. He needs medical attention, not some kind of moral lecture on his sexual behavior."

"I was not giving a moral lecture. I was inquiring whether he has SIDA."

"Do you have SIDA?"

"Mademoiselle, I believe—"

"Then mind your own damned business." (This in French was "*Foutez-mous la paix*.")

"There are no doctors available at this hour of the night. A doctor can be here by nine o'clock in the morning, or ten at the latest. It depends on how many other appointments he has. Of course, there will be a special charge for a visit to the hotel. Perhaps it would be better," he suggested, "if Monsieur went to the hospital."

"Can you recommend a hospital?"

"There are many good clinics. If you have a doctor, he can recommend a clinic. Otherwise there is the Hôtel-Dieu."

"Is the Hôtel-Dieu all right, Ben?"

"It's a public hospital. It's where the French poor go to die. I believe that ten thousand a year or so of them die there. It has the advantage of being free."

"And then there is the American Hospital," said the night manager.

"How about the American Hospital, Ben?"

"Excellent," Ben muttered. "It's in Neuilly and movie stars go there."

"I can call you a taxi," said the night manager.

In the end he *was* good for something; he called a taxi which came promptly, then he swathed Ben in a hotel blanket and provided a chair for him to sit on in the elevator. The three of them crossed the hotel foyer, Cecilia and the night manager supporting Ben who was still wrapped in the blanket. The night manager told him he could keep the blanket and return it later.

In the taxi Cecilia told the driver, "*L'Hôpital Américain, filez.*" Her French was getting much more vernacular and more fluent, thought Ben.

90.

Installed in a semi-private room—the other bed was empty, luckily—he was examined by a young woman doctor who was English, to judge by her accent; she sounded just like Betsy. She stuck her tongue depressor into his mouth while she shined a flashlight into it, and she asked him to breathe heavily and listened to his back with a stethoscope. She took his temperature with a clever device that had a dial on it like a speedometer instead of the usual thin red line. Then she folded everything up and put it away in her black case. "I'll have to do some tests, of course, but it's pretty obvious."

"What's obvious?"

"Oh, you have a fine case of pneumonia, all right. A classic case. They call it the Old Man's Friend."

"Because it takes him off so easily?"

"That's right."

"Am I going to die then?"

"Oh no. These days we can knock it out with penicillin. You'll have to stay here a few days of course. Get a nice rest. These things come from not taking care of a cold."

"The best thing," said Cecilia, "is not to get one in the first place."

The English doctor looked at her curiously. "Everybody gets colds."

"He went out of his way to get this one."

"Cecilia, please."

"And the worst of it is, as soon as I let him out of my sight he'll do the same thing again. He's incorrigible."

"Let's not bother Mr. Gavilan with the flaws in his character just now. He's a sick man. He needs lots of rest and a little loving care."

"Will I be needed here?"

"Oh no, my dear girl. You go back to your hotel. We'll take care of everything. You need your sleep too, or you'll be coming down with something."

"I'll stay a little while until he's settled in."

"Try not to excite him," said the English doctor.

When she was gone Cecilia said, "I'm glad you're not going to die, Ben. I do love you, you know."

"Did you say you love me?"

"Yes."

"You've never said that before."

"Well, there's never been any need to. You're always so cock-sure of yourself. Now you're sick and you need cheering up a bit."

"I wish you could crawl in bed with me but you'd probably catch my pneumonia."

"Yes. Besides there's probably some kind of rule against it. You know, I don't like that doctor."

"It's because she's a woman."

"And because she's English. Like Betsy."

"Ah." Ben was pleased by this. It was a more convincing evidence of her love than any mere statement could be; a good raging jealousy was an absolute proof. Perhaps he hadn't really done such a bad thing in going off with Betsy to her flat. No, that was going too far.

He told her, "And I love you too."

"Oh well, that's obvious from your behavior."

A nurse came in and gave him the first of the penicillin shots, an antipyretic for the fever, and an IV to make up for the lost fluid. She also inserted a plastic tube in his nose and connected it up to an oxygen machine, without asking him if he wanted this done. He resisted the suggestion that he ought to be fitted with a urethral catheter. "There are some things I can to for myself." The nurse only remarked, in French, that it was customary with older men. She set the urinal on the table beside the bed and went off to her other duties.

Cecilia stayed for another five minutes, then they

came to tell her that her taxi had come. As she left she said, "Please don't fool around with that English doctor, Ben."

Another one of her jokes.

91.

Cecilia came faithfully to see him once a day, always at the same time, around eleven o'clock in the morning. She liked to get up late and have a long leisurely breakfast at the Lutétia, she told him, and she had other things to do in the afternoon. He was sure she did. In fact he could even imagine what some of them were, and his imagination was assisted by his fever, which stayed high for a couple of days in spite of the antipyretic and the penicillin. In his slightly unreal state of mind he imagined her in the arms of Clive the English student, Walter Thorne the harpsichord maker, and hordes of other people who had somehow discovered her whereabouts and swarmed over to Paris from England and other countries to take advantage of his illness, including her Berkeley friends who went around dressed like cowboys or TV criminals. In this way she took revenge on him for that thing with Betsy in London. But she said she loved him, at least he thought she had, although perhaps that was only another hallucination brought on by the fever. There she was, coming in through the door in a new pair of jeans and a leather coat which according to her story she had bought at the Galeries Lafayette.

"They're very nice," he told her weakly from the bed. "Especially the coat; it looks expensive. Where did you get the money?"

"Oh, I don't need money. I have your credit card. Don't you remember?"

After he stopped to cough he said, "No, I don't. How

could you have my credit card? It's right here in my wallet, which is supposed to be in the top drawer of that dresser across the room."

"No, you gave it to me when we left the hotel to come here. I said what shall I do if I need money while you're in the hospital, and you said here take my credit card. You took it out of your wallet and handed it to me."

"Maybe I did." If he could imagine things that never happened at all, he could just as easily forget things that had happened. His feverish mind working on the past was like an incompetent poet trying to revise a bad poem, and making it worse.

Here was her own account of her activities. On the first day she went shopping and bought the jeans and the leather coat. That night she went to a harpsichord recital at the Concièrgerie. "It was Brigitte Haudebourg. What a stroke of luck that she was playing when I was in Paris. You've never heard of her perhaps, but she's one of the best in the world. The Concièrgerie is fantastic. It's an old palace on the banks of the Seine and you wander around through various dank corridors lit by candles until you come out in a kind of dungeon, and that's where the recital is. She played Dandrieu, you hardly ever hear that, and then some Bach and some Lully. Brigitte Haudebourg," she said, "is exactly what I want to be in five years. I want to be a professional harpsichordist and travel around the world and play in the Concièrgerie, and St. Johns Smith Square and the Purcell Room in London, and the Capitole in Toulouse. Of course, she won a gold medal at the Paris Conservatory. But I'm going to study in Europe too."

"Where did you hear about all these places?"

"Brigitte told me. They're all places she's played."

"You met her?"

"Oh yes, we met after the recital. She's very nice."

She seemed beside herself with excitement in describing this evening when he hadn't been with her. She said *That is what I want to be in five years* with greater fervor than she spoke of her love for him. Her love for him was only a tenderness; this was a passion. She dithered on for some time about her evening in the candlelit dungeon and the stirrings of artistic vocation it awakened in her. She said, "And do you know who went with me?"

Ben couldn't think. Or rather he could think but he kept his thoughts to himself.

"It was Carolyn Wong. She's been in Paris all the time we were here. I just ran into her by accident, when we were both standing in line for the tickets. She knows quite a bit about music."

"Yes, we both belong to the chamber music society in Santa Barbara. You say you ran into her by accident?"

"Yes, we were both standing in line—"

"Cecilia, there are seven million people in Paris. How likely do you think it is that you would run into Carolyn by accident?"

"Well, there are probably only a few hundred people who are interested in harpsichord music. That makes it more likely that we would meet."

"A little."

"Then we went to a place near there and had Choucroute Garnie. Carolyn told me some things about astronomy."

"I'll bet she did."

"Ben, did you know that every twenty-seven million years the sun goes berserk and the earth is thrown out of orbit? That's what happened to the dinosaurs; they all became extinct when the climate changed violently. There's a dark sun that circles around our own sun in an immense orbit that takes it far out into outer space. Every twenty-seven million years it comes looping in and destroys all life on earth. It's called the Nemesis Theory."

"When was the last time it happened?"

"About nineteen million years ago, Carolyn says."

"Well then, we still have about eight million years left."

"Yes, isn't it nice? We have plenty of time to do everything we want."

It was quite possible that she really believed this. He was beginning to see that she was a creature who lived for the day and had very little imagination for times before she existed, or after she would cease to exist. Whereas he was terrified at the notion that the world would someday end, and he knew it would.

92.

They had put a new patient into the second bed in Ben's room. He had been lucky so far to have the room to himself, but the luck couldn't last. There were all those seven million Parisians, and there wasn't room for them to die at the Hotel-Dieu. As a matter of fact the new patient wasn't a Parisian; he was a Rumanian dwarf who worked as a clown in the Cirque Médrano. As Ben understood it, the dwarf had some kind of pulmonary infection like his own, and he was being treated in the same way, with injections and a bottle of sugar-water hanging from a hatrack. He had an oxygen tube sticking out of his nose just like Ben's; it was even possible that they were both connected up to the same oxygen machine, sharing it like an odd kind of twins nursing from their mother, a nice thought. The dwarf spoke neither French nor English, which made things easier. He and

Ben simply smiled weakly at each other, and when they tired of this they experimented with grimaces, sticking their tongues out and horribly distorting their faces at each other like two six-year-olds. The dwarf was about the size of a six-year-old child and perhaps he was not a real dwarf at all, but a child who had been disguised as a dwarf and put into the other bed to spy on him. This idea was so insane that Ben decided he had better go to sleep for a while and rest his mind from these fantastic labors.

93.

The dwarf was actually Eugène Ionesco, whose photo was on the back of the book the hospital had given him to read. Ionesco in the picture was a little larger than the dwarf in the other bed, but he had the same wrinkled face and the same cheerful and slightly uncanny expression. This theory was enormously ingenious, because after a little more thought he remembered that Ionesco too was a Rumanian. And this predicament he was in, incarcerated in this hospital room and not being entirely sure of his identity or anyone else's, was right out of an Ionesco play. Ionesco was a hell of a lot better writer than Ilya, he thought. His world was grotesque, but it was a lot more like real life than anything in Ilya's novels.

94.

He was the middle of these thoughts when Carolyn Wong came in through the door. She looked at the dwarf—the six-year-old child—the Rumanian playwright —as though she had never seen one before but found him only moderately interesting. Then she turned to Ben and said, "This is a funny place to have your honeymoon."

"We left Santa Barbara to get away from all of you."

"So you told Ilya and Betsy."

"Carolyn, have you followed us over to Paris for some reason?"

"For some reason? What do you mean?"

"I mean, am I correctly paranoid in the sense that there really is a circle of people around Cecilia and me who are following us all over the world and talking about us behind our backs?"

"I don't think so. I *have* been talking about you behind your backs, if that's what you mean. Everybody does. I imagine you talk about me behind my back."

"That's not what I mean. Carolyn, what *are* you doing in Paris?"

"I'm here to have a good time and enjoy myself. Arnold is at a meeting in Geneva, and when the plane landed in Paris I got off, knowing that Geneva is a very boring town full of Swiss hotelkeepers and foreign diplomats. I'm staying at a little place in Montparnasse called the Hôtel de Londres, which has *confort moderne*, meaning that the bathroom is down the hall. I know a little restaurant in Rue Vavin where I can eat for ten francs, and last night I went to a recital at the Concièrgerie with a friend."

"I know who it was. Why are you so shifty about it? And why do you eat at a ten-franc restaurant, since you and Arnold have plenty of money?"

"There are many mysteries about this very complex life we are all involved in. I can't explain them all to you. How are you? Is there anything you need? What's this?" She picked up the Ionesco book and examined it. "That's very depressing. It's probably bad for your morale. I brought some other books for you."

She took them out of her bag and set them on the

table, a French paperback and two hardcover novels in English. "Sickness is mostly in the mind, you know. You ought to read something interesting and cheer up. We can make our minds do anything we want, just as we can with our bodies. Who knows what powers we have within us that are still untapped. We have five senses or so we think. But we may have ninety-five, or a hundred, and only be using five of them. We may have senses that enable us to hear messages from the stars, or know what's going on in other people's minds. Or we may have ways to tap into our pleasure centers and have experiences as nice as orgasms just by thinking about it."

"I'm sure that's true. I've had experiences as bad as being tortured by the Spanish Inquisition, just by thinking about it. Tell me something about astronomy, Carolyn. Not the Nemesis Theory. Something happy. The stars do twinkle down and watch over us, don't they?"

"They do twinkle. They're up there, so they twinkle down. Whether they watch over us is a matter that's still under study. Probably they do. I can tell you something that has turned up recently in radio-astronomy."

"Is this going to be a happy story, Carolyn?"

"Yes, I think so. It's curious enough that so far the radio-astronomers have kept it to themselves. I really shouldn't be telling you about it. You see, for years the radio-astronomers have been listening to space with their instruments, trying to find out if there's intelligent life out there and if they're sending us messages. They have thousands of hours of tapes, all of them random noise. But a few years ago they heard something different from a star in Casseopeia. Phase-coherent signals, they're called. Whoever it was out there, they had picked up weak radio signals from us, and they figured that the smartest way to let us know they were there and were listening to us was to send back the same thing. It turned out to be old Arthur Godfrey shows from the 1950's. The star they were coming from was fifteen light years away, so it took them that long to go out and come back."

"Carolyn, is this true?"

"It was never released to the press. I shouldn't have told you. Forget all about it. It's just something you thought of when you had a fever."

95.

After she was gone he put on his reading glasses and looked at the books she had brought. One of them was a novel by an author who seemed to have a very distorted outlook on life and believed that women were evil beings plotting our downfall. It didn't seem real somehow and he couldn't get into it. He set it aside and took up the next one; it was *Barnaby Rudge*. This kept him occupied the rest of the afternoon, the evening after supper, and part of the morning following. He got quite lost in the faded charm of Dolly Varden and her lover, and the account of the outrages committed by the London mob in the Gordon riots was thrilling. Now that was a good book. He had never before read a work of fiction while he had a fever and perhaps that had something to do with it; it lent a psychedelic cast to Dickens which he had never noticed before. He attempted to recommend it to the dwarf in the other bed by pointing to the book and grinning violently, but the dwarf only responded by grinning in the same way and pointing to the roll and jam in his breakfast which he was just finishing. Probably he was right; even simple good food was better than a work of fiction which only addled your thoughts and gave you a distorted sense of reality.

96.

Cecilia breezed into the room in her new leather coat and jeans, with a violet ribbon in her hair. This matter of her clothes was a puzzling one. She had very few clothes, at least in Santa Barbara, and he knew her wardrobe by heart: the white sweater, the corduroy shorts, the narrow black pants, an aqua dress with spaghetti straps, the turtleneck jersey, a sleeveless blouse, the exiguous bikini, and now in Paris the new leather coat and jeans. The clothes were all exactly the shape of Cecilia herself, and inside them was the mystery of her body, which remained mysterious even after the many times it had been revealed to him; it was a kind of constantly renewed virginity. Each time, even though he knew what was going to be inside the clothing, it surprised and delighted him, in the way we are surprised and delighted by the dawn of a new day even though we are familiar with dawns. However her new Paris clothes, the leather coat and the jeans, were a little unsettling. Inside them was a new Cecilia who had not yet been revealed to him, a body he did not know as he did her other bodies. Under normal circumstances he would quickly settle this matter; that is, he would disrobe this body to see if it was like the others or in what respects it was different. (Because, even though all the clothes were the shape of Cecilia's body, the body inside them was slightly different for each set of clothing, through the rule that the container influenced the thing contained; the white sweater was loose and the turtleneck tight, the bikini called attention to her hip-bones and the aqua dress to her breasts, and the memory of the clothes she had worn before disrobing always remained to distort lightly the perception of what had been inside them). But now he was in a hospital room with a Rumanian clown and he couldn't disrobe her to see how her body was different in the jeans and the leather coat, so perhaps someone else was doing it for him. For whom, or to what end, had she bought the new clothes?

She quickly settled this point by explaining that she came to the hospital with Glover on his motorcycle. What motorcycle? Well, it belonged to a French friend of Glover's, and it had the fashionable 75 on its license plate, indicating that the friend was a real Parisian and not some provincial student pretending to be one. (Cecilia was getting very knowledgeable about Paris). It was obvious that if you were going to go around riding on a motorcycle you had to have a leather coat, and if you were riding on a motorcycle in Paris it had to be a chic one.

"Is Glover outside waiting for you?"

"Yes."

"Why doesn't he come in?"

"He never goes inside hospitals. He has a phobia about death."

"He may have to go into one sooner or later."

"He knows that. That's why he has the phobia."

"If he has a phobia about death he ought to stop riding motorcycles."

"Oh, he's a very skilled motorcyclist."

He was probably skillful at other things too. "Do you wear a helmet?"

"Of course not."

In this concern for her safety he was behaving like a father and not like a lover; he decided to drop it. "I'm glad you're enjoying yourself a little while I'm in this stupid place."

"How are you feeling?"

"All right. I've been reading"—he couldn't remember

the title of the book by Dickens—"the book with"—he couldn't remember the name of the lady who had a lover.

Who's your roommate, she mouthed silently.

"It's all right. He doesn't speak English. He's a clown in the Cirque Médrano, although sometimes he pretends to be Eugène Ionesco."

"He couldn't be Ionesco. I saw Ionesco at the Coupole in Montparnasse. Somebody pointed him out to me. He was with his wife, and they were both wearing Astrakhan coats down to their ankles. He lives right there in Boulevard Montparnasse."

"Why don't you go to the Cirque Médrano and see if the clown is there too? He may be able to displace his body through astral projection."

"It's very likely," she said. "Many people can." He had forgotten that spiritualism was one of her hobbies.

"Where have you and Glover been going on the motorcycle?"

"Oh, everywhere. Do you know, Ben, that right at the end of this street that the hospital's on there's the Isle de la Grande Jatte. The one in the pointilliste painting by Seurat, you know, with the ladies with parasols and the gentlemen in their undershirts, and the little black dog. Glover and I went over there and pranced around, pretending to be made out of spots."

"I wish we could do some of these things together. Maybe we can when I get out of this damned place."

"We won't have time, I think. Today is Sunday and you're getting out of here tomorrow. We're flying back to California on Wednesday. I changed the plane tickets."

"You did?"

"Yes. Alice says you're well enough to travel now. You don't really have a fever anymore; it's just your imagination."

"Who is Alice?"

"Dr. Klein. The English doctor who's taking care of you. She's a very nice person really. She gave me a prescription for the Pill, because I ran out when we stayed over longer in Paris."

"Why do you need the Pill if I'm in the hospital?"

"You have to take it for the whole month, Ben," she said patiently. "Every month."

"I can't wait to get well."

"Neither can I. I mean, I too can't wait for you to get well. You know, I do love you, Ben, as I said previously, even though I only say so when you're sick. You'll have to forgive me." She went on to explain, looking around cautiously at the deaf-and-dumb clown in the other bed, that she was looking forward to returning to Santa Barbara and being in the new house with the harpsichord and with him. (In that order; he noticed that the harpsichord came first). Then she kissed him and left. He felt a great swell of desire for her, the first time he had noticed this sensation since he came to the hospital. He caught the dwarf's attention, and smiling and nodding pointed to his erection, which was clearly visible through the bedclothes. The dwarf smiled and nodded too and pointed to his own genitals to show that he did not have an erection. They were communicating perfectly, even without language.

97.

Outside in the courtyard he heard a rumble like thunder, which subsided into the burble of an idling motorcycle. After a moment the tone rose, settled, rose again, and then dwindled away gradually until it died out completely in the distance. He imagined Cecilia sitting snugly on the pillion with her arms around Glover from the rear in order to keep from falling off the motorcycle, the front of her body pressed against his back and the powerful black machine throbbing between her legs, the Paris streets going by as he swerved, banked skillfully, shifted gears with a deft twist of the hand, and adjusted the rising and falling note of the machinegun-like motor. At the river they stopped and dismounted with the stiff-legged gestures of all motorcyclists, she first and then he. He took off his gloves and slapped them down on the seat, then hung his helmet on the handlebar. (No, he didn't wear a helmet and neither did she, his mop of black hair flew in the wind with her reddish-blond mane as they shot down the avenues and boulevards.) Leaving the motorcycle, they crossed over to the island and joined the ladies and gentlemen in their Sunday best, *endimanchés* was the term in French, and the little dog. Glover in his black clothes and his three-day stubble, she in her leather coat and jeans, clothes he did not know, strolled on the island among the manniquins in their Edwardian costumes, he sauntering along with his thumbs in his back pockets, she holding a tiny parasol on a very long stick over her head, blurry, in dots, a pointillise vision.

98.

On the plane flying back Ben was still not feeling very strong and dozed much of the time. On the other side of Cecilia, in the third seat in the row, was a little boy who was traveling alone with a big red-white-and-blue card around his neck with his name and address. His father lived in Paris and his mother in Los Angeles. When Cecilia saw the boy squirming uncomfortably and quite embarrassed, she asked him if he would like to go to the bathroom. You would think the flight attendants would notice this and take care of it. The little boy said he would and the two of them went off toward the rear of the plane. When they came back they both sat down and there was silence for a while. Then the little boy said, "They don't have men and women on planes."

"What do you mean?"

"They don't have places for men and women."

"Oh." She laughed. "That's right. On the plane, we all go to the same bathroom. For some reason we don't mind."

She got along famously with this little boy. Earlier, she had told Ben that she didn't care for babies. Of course this little boy wasn't a baby; he was at least three. Still, the chameleon-like changes she could make in her attitudes, the way she could slip effortlessly from saying she believed in one thing to saying she believed just the opposite, were strange and a little chilling. At Muir House and in Santa Barbara she had said nothing about what she felt for him except that he was nice. In Paris, when he was in the hospital, she said she loved him. What would the next version of her feelings be?

99.

The decorator hired by Stacey had done everything exactly as promised; it was like a dream in which everything works by magic. The walls in the living room were robin's-egg blue, and there was a picture rail with some nice Daumier prints hanging from it. The kitchen was off-white with mahogany cabinet doors, and the bedrooms were white with gray trim. The furniture was mock antique, and not all bad. The walnut dining table was impressive, and there were some nice side chairs. The upholstery was a little garish, more like a hotel in Las Vegas than like Versailles, but you couldn't have perfection in everything, especially if you went off to Europe and left it to someone else to do. In the master bedroom was a four-poster with a damask canopy in royal blue and white, which stood out magnificently against the white walls, and the decorator, acting quite on his own, had put up some prints of Hogarth's *Marriage à la Mode*. He probably thought they were married.

In the annex, which Ben and Cecilia were already calling the Little House, the harpsichord had arrived from England. Stacey found a piano mover to unpack it, put on its legs, and polish out a few scratches and blemishes from its travels. It was the piano mover who suggested that a tuner be brought in to tune it; nobody else thought of this. The harpsichord, in its black lacquer with a frieze of rosebuds, sat under a hanging lamp of pale satin the same color as the painted flowers, and the walls of the room were primrose yellow. On the wall behind the harpsichord was the Caneletto, a reproduction of *A View of San Marco from the Isola San Giorgio*. Still in her traveling clothes, Cecilia sat down at the harpsichord and played something that sounded like a fragment of Couperin. She was always playing Couperin, even though when he played it on the piano she said it was the Muzak of the eighteenth century. Probably she played it when he was with her because it was so easy and she wouldn't make mistakes.

Even before they got home to the house in Montecito the question arose where they were going to sleep. At least it arose in Ben's mind, although perhaps not in Cecilia's.The Little House had its own bedroom, beautifully furnished like everything else, with a double bed and a matching bureau, twin bedstands, and a pair of chairs. On the wall was another reproduction, a large print of Monet's water lilies, this one in a walnut frame to match the furniture, with a forest-green matte. The furniture wasn't theirs and they hadn't chosen it, but it was very nice. It was as though they were living in a very superior hotel, in short like the Cantamar. It was understood that the Little House was Cecilia's to give her a place to practice the harpsichord in private, and it would have been logical for her to sleep there too. This gave Ben a chill around the heart to think of it, although of course he could always creep over to the Little House in his pajamas, or she could visit him in the master bedroom if she felt the impulse.

As it happened, when they came back from inspecting the Little House they both carried their bags from the hall into the master bedroom of the Big House without discussing it. She said,'You sleep on the left side, of course." Then she unpacked her bag and threw her nightgown onto the right side of the bed.

100.

As a matter of fact he still didn't feel that well. Just jet lag probably, although he also had a lingering cough and had the impression that he'd mislaid his energy somewhere; little things tired him. Alice Klein, the doctor at the American Hospital, said that once you have pneumonia you more or less have pneumonia for the rest of your life. The cocci are always there lurking in your body, and they make small places for themselves, tiny caves and dugouts in the lungs, where they can hide until the time to come out again and reproduce violently, whenever, for example, you get a little run down or do something unwise. It sounded as though Dr. Klein knew about Betsy, although this was unlikely. He also found a few gray hairs in his brush, which he had never noticed before, and he had developed a habit of groaning a little when he went down into a low chair, or came up out of it.

"Cough cough," said Cecilia. "It isn't the cough that carries you off, it's the coffin they carry you off in."

101.

Cecilia swam nude in the kidney-shaped pool, shielded by the pussy-willows that grew around it on the side facing the other houses. It was possible that some neighbor could penetrate the willows with a pair of powerful binoculars, but Cecilia wasn't worried. If a neighbor had binoculars, that was his problem, not hers. Ben wore his ordinary swim trunks, which he had had for many years. Cecilia was good at swimming below the surface; she could circle the pool several times this way without coming up for air. As he swam around the pool after her he had the impression that he was pursuing some elusive naiad, a water spirit or Undine, who would turn into a mortal woman if he could catch her in his grasp. Her long hair, green and transparent, streamed behind her in the greenish water. The water was the color of chlorine gas as it swirls around soldiers, stifling them and leaving them pale white flowers staring upward at the sky.

102.

For a long time he thought she didn't wear lipstick; now he found that she did but that it was the same color as her lips. This was a subtlety that totally baffled him.

Art that simulated the real world so exactly that it became invisible and *was* the real world. How many more things about her that seemed real were actually contrived, artificial, or illusory?

103.

"So you're back." Ethel's voice on the telephone was thin and distant, as though she herself were in London or Paris.

"Yes. We stayed a little longer in Paris because—something came up." He decided on impulse not to tell Ethel he was sick in Paris. As soon as he said this he knew it was a mistake, because Carolyn knew he was in the hospital and would tell everyone, including Ethel.

"Everyone missed you while you were gone."

"Glad to be back."

"How is Cecilia?"

"Just fine. We're in the house in Montecito, you know. You must come and see it."

"Oh, I've already seen it."

"You have?"

"Yes, I came around one day to take a look at it, and the decorator let me in. I told him I was a family friend. You could have consulted me, you know, Ben. After all I'm an art librarian. The Canaletto is quite nice, but the Monet is only a poster from the Metropolitan Museum. They cut off the print at the bottom and charged you for a real reproduction."

"It doesn't matter. I like the frame."

"Cecilia's bedroom is nice."

"Her bedroom?"

"Yes. In the little annex. The music house. What do you call it?"

"The Little House."

"She must be happy there."

"She is. Right now she's in there playing the harpsichord. I can hear it through the walls of the two houses."

"I think I can hear it faintly too. Ilya and Betsy are back too, you know. They got back last week. Ben, Betsy says that you and she had an affair in London."

Ben was silent for a moment. Then he said, "That is absolutely not true, Ethel. Betsy is a nymphomaniacal alcoholic and a mythomaniac. You know that."

"She could be all those things, and you could still have had an affair with her."

"What in the world do you mean by an affair anyhow?" Ben felt he should drop this subject right away, but he couldn't resist the temptation to find out what Ethel knew.

"Oh, I don't know. She just said you had an affair."

"Right under the noses of Ilya and Cecilia?"

"Men are clever at these things. Ben, Carolyn says you were sick in Paris."

"I was. I caught a cold in London, and it got worse in Paris. I'm fine now."

"I see." Ethel hung up a little after this, leaving the silence on the wire between them thrumming with surmise. She probably knew every damned thing, Ben thought, including how he had caught the cold. It was impossible to keep anything secret in this crowd of people.

104.

The fall term had started now, and Cecilia was gone away to her classes at the University, which consisted chiefly of Professor Dominicus' studio sessions, along with a trifle or two in art history and political science which she needed to finish her degree. With her gone the house in Montecito seemed very big and very empty. Ben, wandering through the rooms, fell into thought and remembered explaining to her by the pool at the Cantamar that Pascal says we should bet God on whether there's a heaven or not. If you bet yes, whether or not you win the bet you're still ahead, and you've got nothing to lose. It occurred to him now that he could apply this same wager to his love for Cecilia, to the question of whether she loved him or not. If he bet no and she didn't, he would only make himself unhappy. No, and she did, he would still make himself unhappy, and it would be unfair to her. If he bet yes, and she didn't, he would be happy for a short time and then unhappy. Better than nothing. If yes and she did, he would really be happy. He had to bet yes. It was about as accurate after all as pulling petals off a daisy. This piece of logic, which cheered him up a good deal, made him wonder if he shouldn't bet yes on Pascal's Godwager too. The whole mental process was getting flimsy and improbable. He had somehow talked himself into believing that because he loved Cecilia he was going to be ecstatically happy here on earth and then blissfully rewarded for all eternity after he died. It wasn't likely. Why should the universe go to so much trouble over him? On the other hand, it had flung Cecilia his way and made her behave, at least, as though she loved him. It was a perplex.

105.

Emulating Cecilia, he took off his clothes behind the screen of pussy-willows around the pool and slipped himself—all of him, the sags, folds, and liver-spots, the lean hairless hips, the jaded genitals, the hair touched with gray, and last his mind itself behind its lofty dolichocephalic brow—into the tepid water that was exactly the temperature of the blood, leaving only his nostrils exposed. He swam slowly around under the surface of the green mirror, his right arm trailing behind him like a rope overboard. Under the surface his bodily sensations disappeared, or merged with the greenish-blue chlorinated water around him, and his ego ceased to be something that stood out in the world and was noticeable by others and became simply What Is—this was called sensory deprivation by psychologists and was used in the treatment of certain mental ailments. He was alone with his thoughts, exactly as though he were disembodied, or had died and gone to Heaven, which was very much what it felt like. Nothing existed but his own bliss, his self-containment, his peace of soul. And when he came out of the water, as naked and invulnerable as Aphrodite on her shell, he would have waiting for him the most beautiful girl in the world, who loved him dearly and gave him everything he could dream for in bed, and all he had to do was cook her dinner for her, Chicken Birani with basmati rice and stir-fry it was going to be tonight, and around ten o'clock she would catch his eye in that funny, half-mocking, promising way, and then she would head off, dropping her clothes on the way, to the big four-poster bed with its blue-and-white sail, a magic boat which would carry them off to another age, the age of Couperin, Lully, Rameau, and that disgusting and tireless middle-aged rake Casanova. Ben had a very good time thinking of all this under the water of the pool, with his nose just showing above the surface. He could never have done this in the pool at the Cantamar; people would have stared. Perhaps the house was worth the money he paid for it, and it was a hell of a lot. Not to mention the decorator's bill, out of which Stacey took her cut—it was supposed to be six percent for real estate brokers, but she took a lot more, since he and Cecilia were such a pain in the ass about things. What good was it to submerge himself in lukewarm water to be alone with his thoughts if he only thought about money? He came to the surface puffing and breaching like a dolphin, pulled himself out onto the blue tiles, and dried himself with a large beach towel, trying not to look at those parts of him that indicated all too clearly that he was twice Cecilia's age plus the age of a highschool freshman.

106.

Wednesday evening at the Voronoffs. The usual people were there; Ben caught sight of Ethel's giraffe-like form and Edith Sitwell beauty at the other end of the room, but he didn't go to her yet. Or to Carolyn either. All these women, these Harpies, these middle-aged gossips and tattlers were the enemies of his love for Cecilia. Of course, Carolyn wasn't really middle-aged. She was a very attractive woman. Perhaps he should have an affair, as Ethel called it, with her too. He could find out once for all if the thing goes the other way, sideways, in Chinese women. It was an old Navy joke that Ted Pickering had told him. Ted hadn't been thinking about Carolyn when he said this, in fact she had been standing right next to him. He was rather obtuse in many was. Ben, who had had several drinks already, remembered that he couldn't have an affair with Carolyn or anybody else because he was in love with Cecilia.

Where was Cecilia anyhow? It was a large house with many nooks and corners in it, some of them poorly lighted. The two borzois were lying with their chins on the carpet, examining the guests as they passed but not moving. He nodded to Arnold Schifter, Carolyn's husband, in the library. Arnold was talking to Estelle Galleon, and Edgar and Jo-Nan Rolf were listening to them. At least he beat out the Rolfs and bought Cecilia's harpsichord himself instead of letting her get it through them. That cost a hell of a lot of money too, especially when you added in the air freight, but he would have paid six times as much to get that particular harpsichord.

The only place left was the balcony at the back of the house, a small terrace overlooking the sea. This was where he had had his conversation with Carolyn about the stars, the last time he had come to a Wednesday, before he and Cecilia went to Europe. It was where people often went to have a private conversation, since it was only dimly lit by the pink and green lights in the shrubbery below. There he found Cecilia. He stopped behind the door when he heard her voice outside on the terrace.

Ben had a private vice that he hadn't told Cecilia or anyone else about, and this was that he was fond of eavesdropping. He hadn't realized this himself until recently. The first time he was really aware of it was when he stopped and overheard Cecilia and Dave talking in the doorway at the back of Muir House. At first he had pretended it was only an accident, that he had stayed there listening to them because he couldn't go forward and he couldn't retreat; he was pinned down in his hiding place in the pine branches. Now he knew that he had been doing this all his life and pretending to himself each time that it was only an accident. It was not an accident now because he could easily turn away and go back into the house if he chose to.

He stood just inside the doorway listening, with his

drink held thoughtfully in his good hand, the left, at the level of his waist. He could hear every word because he was only about ten feet from them. The other voice was Ilya's, and he was explaining to Cecilia about his novel. He wrote quite a bit in London, and he had been working on it more since he got back. He had changed the part about the art student Fenicia. She was turning out to be a more interesting character than he expected, and he was going to give her a larger role in the novel. Also, Kostya was too good a character to leave languishing in a stalag. In the latest version he escapes from the stalag, with the aid of an old peasant who gives him a cold potato (this was borrowed from Tolstoy's *War and Peace*), and makes his way back to England. There he finds that his friend Mortimer has died just the day before.

"His heart never was very much good. The readers who know a little Latin will congratulate themselves on having anticipated this from his name, Flatter the little buggers, that's my scheme. Kostya goes to the funeral and meets Fenicia."

Ilya glanced at the doorway but evidently didn't see Ben.

"You see, the ghost of the dead man hangs between them. Such a situation is highly aphrodisiacal. Death enters in, because Mortimer's name means death, and this makes a Wagnerian shadow fall between Fenicia and Kostya. Eros and Thanatos. It isn't long before they are lovers, in an ethereal and extremely refined way. Of course they do the usual things too. I describe them only in poetic terms; my readers don't care for explicit sex. Pale blossoms opening, his desire for her like a white classic column, and so on."

"It's tough cookies on poor old Mortimer."

"Well, he's dead, you see. She learns a great deal about love from Kostya that she could never have learned from Mortimer, because of his Slavic soul. One morning they go together to lay flowers on Mortimer's grave in Highgate Cemetery. Afterwards they make love under the branches of an old cypress that hangs down to the ground. Have you been to Highgate Cemetery? It's a wonderful place, decadent and creepy. I've wanted for years to use it for a setting but I've never found the way."

"Shhh! There's Ben."

"Where?"

Ben turned away and went to the kitchen, where he found Ted and Snoozy Pickering and talked to them about his trip to Europe.

107.

Later, at the bar, he had a conversation with Betsy. He asked her, "Did you get over your cold in London?"

"Oh yes. It only lasted a couple of days."

"I got it too." He didn't bother to tell her that he had been in the hospital in Paris. Carolyn would surely tell her that, or Ethel. "Listen, Betsy, I want you to do a favor for me. There's someone I want you to ask to your Wednesdays. You need new faces. You always have the same gang."

"Who is it?"

"It's Peter Barstow."

"Oh, your young man at the Turtle Press."

This was the first step in a plan he had been thinking about for some time, although he couldn't have said when the idea first occurred to him. "He lives alone and doesn't have many friends. He's having a tough time of it at the Press. He needs cheering up."

"Young people," she said, "don't seem to mix in our circle very well."

"I suppose you mean Cecilia."

"Yes, and Raymonde too. I wish she'd go out somewhere with her friends on Wednesday nights."

"Raymonde is charming. I can see why you don't want to have her around."

She smiled tightly at this. "You know, Ben, I've never really cared for Peter Barstow."

"You probably made a pass at him once and he turned you down."

"Don't be crude. As a matter of fact that's more or less what happened. Under the circumstances, it wouldn't be very tactful to invite him here, would it?"

"You owe me one, Betsy."

"What do you mean?"

"Surely you haven't forgotten our deplorable behavior in London?"

"How could we have been so foolish." She sipped her drink with a trace of a smile.

"It was I who was foolish. You were quite deliberate, I think."

"We're all responsible for everything we do, Ben. All of us."

"Spare me your half-baked existentialism. It's left over from the time when we were both young. I'll tell you what, Betsy. If you'll do this thing for me, I'll take you out to lunch as you want."

She smiled for the third time, this time with a little satisfied crease of triumph, and set her glass down. "Do you have his phone number?"

108.

In the music room the flute and the guitar were playing something that sounded like a Bolero, but not the well-known one by Ravel. It seemed that baroque was old hat tonight and the modern was in. Ilya was standing alone by the piano, looking a little disembodied, as though he was out of place in his own home. Ben went directly to him and stood for a second or two before he spoke.

"I hear you've changed your novel."

Ilya stared balefully at him and didn't answer for a moment.

"I'm always revising, old man. It's a constant process. Art is difficult, have you heard that? It's a French proverb."

"Now it seems that in your latest version Kostya and Fenicia are having a love affair."

"Old man, if you will overhear private conversations, you will hear things you don't like."

"I'm sorry. I just happened to be in the doorway and I couldn't help hearing."

"You see, old fellow, reality consists of multiple truths. The things that I tell Cecilia in a private conversation, not intending to be overheard by anyone, are true, but they are not the same things that I'd tell you, which are also true."

"The manuscript of your novel is a physical fact. Either you've changed it or you haven't."

"I sometimes keep several versions until I've decided which one is best."

"What have you decided in this case? Is it true that you've killed off Mortimer?"

"Mortimer isn't you, old man. He's a character in fiction."

"In London you kept calling me Mortimer."

"That was just a joke."

"Is it true that Kostya comes back from Russia and goes to Mortimer's funeral?Is it true that he tells Fenicia he can teach her things about love because he has a Slavic soul? Is it true that he screws her on Mortimer's grave?"

"Don't be so crude, old man. So literal. I wouldn't dream of using such a word in my fiction."

"That's not the point. The point is, what do you mean by having this character who is obviously you have a love affair with Fenicia, who is obviously Cecilia? And then telling her about it?"

"Cecilia is interested in my work. She's a good listener."

"And you're a good talker."

"Well thank you, old man. One reason I've always liked you is that you are free from irony and everything you say is always warm and sincere."

Ilya was probably annoyed because he had guessed what happened between him and Betsy in London, Ben thought. This was the only good thing to come out of that dreadful event.

109.

In the library he joined the group including the Rolfs, Mrs. Galleon, and Arnold Schifter.

"We don't see much of you, Arnold," Ben told him. "You're always out of town."

"Oh yes. I'm just back from Tokyo."

"Tell us about it. Do you like Japan?"

"Oh, I don't see much of it. I fly over on a 747, I stay in

a western style hotel and I eat American food. I go to the conference and we talk in English about peace. And then I get back on the plane and come home."

"Then why go?"

"It's very important," said Mrs. Galleon. "Nothing could be more important than peace."

"Tell us about your trip, Ben."

"It was the usual thing. A little London, then a little Paris. Walked in the Cotswolds. Went down to Sussex to see somebody. I wasn't well in Paris. I didn't do much."

"You do look well now. I think that Ben stays young because he continually finds *new interests* in life," said Mrs. Galleon with heavy but cheerful irony.

Everybody smiled. So even she knew about it, the horrible hag.

"Were you by yourself?" persisted Arnold, *faux-naif.*

"No. I was with Cecilia."

"And you found a harpsichord, I understand," said Edgar. "I hope you didn't pay too much for it. Jo-Nan and I have our own connections and we could have got you one."

"A harpsichord?" repeated Mrs. Galleon, bewildered. "Oh, a harpsichord. Oh."

"And do the two of you—"

"Play the thing together. No we don't. Lay off of it, Jo-Nan."

"We're just having a little fun. That's what we come here for, isn't it?"

Edgar said, "Ben doesn't seem to find us much fun. He has to go Europe for fun."

"I had a lot of fun in Europe. I laid Betsy, hasn't anybody told you that yet?"

"You must be drunk, Ben."

110.

In the car going home he told Cecilia, "I'm going to have lunch with Betsy. I hope you don't mind."

"No, I don't mind."

"I have something important to talk to her about. I can't tell you what it is now. I'll tell you later. There's nothing personal. I mean, I have no personal interest in Betsy, believe it or not."

"I told you I don't mind."

"Maybe you could have lunch with Raymonde. Did you talk to her tonight?"

"Yes. She wants me to come and see her Museum. In fact she wants both of us to come."

"I've heard it's rather tacky. Full of old junk that nobody's interested in."

"She says there's a dead man in a cask of brandy."

"I can hardly believe that. The health authorities wouldn't allow it."

"Maybe it's all right if he's in brandy. I wonder if Betsy knows about it. She's interested in booze." This was a rather catty remark, the kind of bitchiness that the Voronoff set induced in people. It wasn't typical of Cecilia.

"You said you didn't mind if I had lunch with her."

"I don't, really." He had no way of telling whether she meant it. She was her usual self, placid and detached. He strongly suspected she was jealous of Betsy. She could hardly *not* be, considering what had happened. If she really loved him, that was. If she didn't love him, then she could be as indifferent about Betsy as she seemed to be. Ben thought that perhaps he ought to buy a book on how to understand women. However it would hardly do any good at his age; if he didn't understand them by this time he probably never would.

"I noticed you had a nice talk with Ilya."

"Yes. He was telling me about his novel," she said, looking him straight in the face to remind him that he had overheard the conversation, "and what's happening to the characters now. Mortimer dies. Kostya comes back from Russia. Kostya and Fenicia become friends."

"They make love on Mortimer's grave in Highgate Cemetery. I heard that too."

"This isn't much fun, is it Ben. It's going to lead to a quarrel. Let's quit."

"I don't care what you do with Ilya. You're free and you can do whatever you want."

"You know that's not true. If I did certain things I'd hurt you."

"I don't mind your talking to Ilya."

"After you interrupted us," she said, "he went on and told me that he'd like to write a True Novel. He's wanted to do this all his life. That is, it wouldn't be exactly a novel that he'd write. It would be a kind of charade that people around him would act out. Although they wouldn't really know they were acting, at least not all of them. He would orchestrate it and in some way influence people to play out the novel he has in his mind. They would be his characters, only they would be real people."

"What part would there be in it for you?"

"He called me Fenicia all through the conversation."

"What did you say?"

"I laughed in his face."

Could he believe her? He counted on his mental fingers the men who had already made him break out in a cold sweat when she showed some interest in them: the godlike ferryman on the Thames, Clive the English student, Peter Thorne the harpsichord-maker, Glover and his motorcycle. And now Ilya, the cleverest and most adept of all, with his dapper clothes, his fame as a novelist, and his wealth. But then, he told himself, she would hardly lose her head over a middle-aged man.

111.

He had lunch with Betsy on the terrace of the Cantamar, with its view through the eucalyptus trees to the sea. It was a rather odd sensation for him. He had lived at the Cantamar for many years, and he had only been away from it for a few weeks, most of that time in Europe. Now it was as though he had never left and as though he had never met Cecilia; the whole business of Cecilia might have been cobwebs, an unsubstantial dream which would vanish when he woke up in the morning. He was at the Cantamar having lunch with a woman friend. Only a few yards away was the cottage half-hidden by its oleanders and giant bird-of-paradise. It was a queer feeling, in fact incomprehensible, that he couldn't simply walk down the path and put his key in the door, that somebody else lived there now. Betsy was in a dark-blue sheath, perfectly simple, with a vee neck that showed her cleavage. Her stockings were sheer white and her shoes were blue stiletto pumps.

"Did you tell Cecilia you were having lunch with me?" she asked him.

"Of course. We have a policy that we tell each other everything."

"That's nonsense. Nobody can ever tell anyone everything about anything."

"We do it."

"There's a strong chance," she said, "that you're making a fool of yourself with this child."

"I can't help that."

"What do you see in her exactly? Why does she attract you?"

"I can't explain it. I don't really understand it myself. It's just that I feel that way and I did from the first moment I laid eyes on her."

"The way you describe it is awfully trite, Ben. You sound like a schoolgirl."

"I can't help that either. We're not responsible for our feelings. We're not responsible for whom we fall in love with. Please, no existentialism. I know we're all responsible for everything."

Betsy dabbed at her lemon sole and sipped from her vodka and ice. Ben had a bottle of Vouvray but she didn't care much for wine.

"You men," she said, "marry us when we're young, and then when we get a little worn out you cast us aside and find a younger woman. And when she wears out you find another young one, and you go on doing it as long as you can. But a woman can't do the same thing."

"You could try."

"No, it's not in the biology. It's not biologically sound. I read about it in a magazine. A man's sperm is renewed all the time. A spermatozoon is always young, so a man doesn't really age sexually. But a woman is born with all the ova she's ever going to have. As she gets older her genes can be damaged by radiation or chemicals."

"But you've just proved to me that what we do is right. That it's biologically sound for older men to fall in love with girls."

"What's right for biology may not be right for people. It's still terribly unfair for us. We have feelings. We don't enjoy being cast aside like an old shoe. I'm still the same as I always was, Ben. Inside I'm still twenty. But I've reproduced myself, and so from the biological point of view I'm obsolete."

"What are we talking about reproduction for anyhow? We know very well that you're not interested in me on account of reproduction, and I'm not interested in Cecilia on account of reproduction."

"But biology is reflected in the attractions people have on one another. Men are attracted to women by their beauty. When this is gone, men aren't interested anymore. But women's desire for men is more subtle, more complicated, not so crudely physical. They're attracted not only by looks but by character, by mind and intelligence, by a man's importance in the world. Some of the sexiest men are old and ugly. Jacques Cousteau. Picasso. Moshe Dayan." (Dayan was handicapped, he only had one eye, Ben thought. She really knew how to manipulate him). "An older man," she went on, "one who has an interesting mind, a body still in good shape, and some achievements in the world can always get young women. For a woman it doesn't work that way."

"It's not a system I invented. I don't feel I'm responsible for it. I'm in love and nothing else counts."

"You know, Ben, you're a much more romantic person than I thought. I mean, you have a much more romantic mind. I always thought of you as cool and rational. Now it seems you're a reckless sentimentalist."

"I used to be cool and rational. I've turned into a reckless sentimentalist. It feels wonderful, Betsy. I'd recommend it to you except that you've just explained to me that the situation is different for men and for women. Cecilia has made me young again. My outlook is different; I can see things freshly; I'm interested in new ideas and new experiences. In Paris I went around with Cecilia's friends, Berkeley students. They're different from us. I enjoyed being with them, even though they kidded me a lot about Cecilia. As a matter of fact, at your Wednesdays the Rolfs and Arnold kid me a lot about it. Even Mrs. Galleon does it. I knew when I began with Cecilia," he said, "that the world would find me ridiculous. I didn't choose it to be that way. I had no choice. I don't mind if people make fun of me. That is, I do mind but I can't do anything about it. It's as though I had a funny-looking nose. I can't change it; I can't change being in love any more than I could change a funny nose. There are things in life we don't have any control over. Being born and dying are two, a religious experience is another, and then there's falling in love. Of course, I could have fallen in love and chosen to do nothing about it. I could just have mooned around Cecilia for a couple of days, and then come back to Santa Barbara and never told anybody else about it. I didn't do that. Now I have her and I'm as happy as a child at Christmas."

"Children are happy on Christmas morning. In the afternoon, their toys are broken and they're tired and bored."

"I can't help that either."

"I fear for you, Ben."

"I'm not really a child at Christmas. I'm a grown man. I can take care of myself."

"You mean, if your toys break you won't cry?"

"First of all, I'm going to be careful not to break them."

"Toys are shabby and fragile."

"Cecilia isn't shabby and fragile. I love her and I'm happy."

"She may not be shabby, but she's fragile. Everybody's fragile. Every woman."

"You know, I do rather like you, Betsy. I don't trust you, but I like you. We ought to have lunch more often."

"That's what I told you. Don't you remember? You have Cecilia to go to bed with, and I have Ilya, but we have nobody to talk to. We should form an alliance. I don't trust you, and you don't trust me, but we can talk. I'm sorry about London, if you're sorry. I thought it was rather nice. But maybe it was a mistake. I can do foolish things too, you know. You don't have a monopoly on it. You see, it's just that I don't know what to do with my body. I'm so bored with Ilya that I could scream."

"Luckily I don't have a cottage here at the Cantamar anymore. Otherwise I might be tempted."

"Yes. That's too bad, isn't it?"

He imagined describing this lunch to Cecilia. As Betsy pointed out, you could never really tell anyone everything. He had told Cecilia he was going to lunch with Betsy because he had to talk to her about something important, but this wasn't quite true. It wasn't a lie exactly, but it was a rearrangement of the facts. He had already talked to Betsy about the important thing when he asked her to have Peter to her Wednesdays. To get her to do this he had to tell her he would take her to lunch. He just explained it to Cecilia the other way around. He wasn't really a liar, he told himself. An eavesdropper, a fornicator, all kinds of other things, but not a liar.

112.

Four o'clock. It would still be an hour before Cecilia came home. Of course, now that she had her car she drove herself and was free to go wherever she pleased. It was a radiant autumn day, sunny and mild, with a few fluffy clouds suspended over the sea, turning the offshore islands faintly green as though they were Tahiti and

Moorea. Ben went into the cool shady house and walked around in it, still draped in the beach towel like a Roman emperor. His penis dangled in the opening—poor pitiful scrap of flesh, it ought to have been turned out to pasture like an old racehorse by this time, that is, relegated to the status of something to pee through, and instead it was called upon to perform all the acrobatics of a second youth, as though it belonged to Glover the actor-criminal and motorcyclist, Clive the English student, or Walter Thorne with his sexy flat above the harpsichord shop in Arundel. He went to hang up the beach towel in the bathroom—there were two baths in the house, but they shared the one off the master bedroom—and found Cecilia's toothpaste with its cap off as usual, a tissue-paper kiss floating on the water in the toilet, and her underpants dropped on the floor. In this new house, which was larger and more work to keep clean—and no Cantamar staff to come in and do it every day—he had been converted from a bachelor with solitary habits into a diligent housewife. Cecilia never turned a hand in the kitchen, and she disliked housework. How he loved her. He capped the toothpaste, wiped the usual clot of green slime from the washbowl, and picked a few of her reddish-blond hairs from his brush, which she persisted in using even though she had one of her own. He put the underpants to his nose. They smelled like her, like a girl with flowers in her hair perspiring in a cave.

He dressed in slacks and a shirt, then he went into the living room and fixed himself a drink—even though she disapproved, he could sneak in one at least before she got home. He sat in a Hepplewhite armchair nursing a Scotch on the rocks and looking at this new house and its furniture—all fake, all sham, starting with the house itself and going on down to the furniture, the harpsichord which was really not an eighteenth century instrument but a replica, and the very pictures on the walls. Being fake was just a price you paid for living in California, probably, to pay for the excellent climate. The house was unreal; he could hardly believe that it belonged to him. It had been generated entirely by his money, and her will, but it still seemed strange to him. It was the strangeness of seeing things as though it were for the first time, and you didn't know what they were. Defamiliarization, the critics called it. His life had been defamiliarized by the entrance of this quite ordinary person into it, a Berkeley student, a would-be harpsichordist, a dropper of underpants on the bathroom floor.

The afternoon sun crawled slowly down the radial spokes of the big circular window facing the sea, a clock that marked off the hours, and the days—how many days since they came back from Paris? It was a month now and Cecilia had been going to her classes for two weeks. Everyone said that time passed more quickly as you got older, and by God it was true. She would finish her year at the University, she would take all her classes, then she would go to Europe to study for a year under a master harpsichordist—what would he do? Would he go with her or would he sit here in this chair watching the sun creep imperceptibly from pane to pane of the round window? Anyhow she would go and she would come back, and she would or would not become a professional harpsichordist, and he would gradually grow older, so that when she was thirty-two he would be sixty-eight, and when she was forty-two he would be seventy-eight, and so on. Ben had never been fond of numbers, and now he found them a horrifying and constant presence, like the pink toads that haunt the victim of delirium tremens. And in these years that were going to come, she would meet other people—at the University, on her year in Europe, in all kinds of ways, even at the Voronoffs. She was honest and frank and affectionate, she would do her best to be faithful to him, but in the end she wouldn't be able to help herself. He couldn't go on forever putting nails in the shoes of young men who were attracted to her. And he couldn't prevent her from breaking out into that particularly youthful gaiety, that slightly mocking insouciance, that playful flush of the cheeks, when she encountered somebody halfway decent-looking who was her own age. Betsy said that women were fragile, and this was what she meant. It was simply a law of nature. There was no way out of it or around it. It might not happen tomorrow or the next day, but it would happen sooner or later. This was as sure as his own mortality, and hers.

And suppose he could prevent this. Suppose he had some means of keeping her away from the world, a houri in a harem, a nun in a pornographic nunnery, is this what he really wanted, for her, and for him? In the end he would not be able to stand in the way of her happiness, her normal happiness. For all he knew, for God's sake, she might want to have children. She said she didn't, but she got along so well with that little boy on the plane. This thought was unthinkable but it was perfectly logical. Why was it unthinkable? Because it would interfere with the most terrific happiness of his life, a happiness he never asked for and never expected.

And, in a flash of wisdom set off perhaps by the sun creeping past a spoke of the clock-window and dazzling his eyes, he saw to the heart of the matter. Was what he felt for her love or lust? It was both, of course, it was a physical need, a thing of the body, but also a high spiritual thing, a selflessness, a willingness to sacrifice anything, even his own happiness, for her welfare. But what evidence did he have that he felt this second kind of love for her? Pretty damned little. He might wish to believe that he loved her in this way, he might have convinced himself in a part of his mind that it was so, but the way he behaved with her was that from time to time, as often as he could manage, he took her in his arms and inserted a part of his body into hers. No, that wasn't true, he argued with himself, he bought her a house, and a harpsichord, and a Canaletto reproduction, and he was going to pay for her musical education; wasn't that altruism? No, it was a hideous self-deception, either hideous or comical depending on how you looked at it. A dollar bill in one hand, he reached for her body with the other. He saw this now with a piercing clarity; the blinding sun struck his eyes and penetrated through them to the very center of his thoughts. He had been a person who was able to possess his soul in peace; now he was in a Dostoevskian turmoil and there was no peace. And to think that only a couple of hours ago he was telling Betsy how happy he was. Pascal's Wager was a sucker bet, and so was his betting that Cecilia was going to love him for the rest of his life, right up to the time when he became a shaky ninety-year-old and had to be fed with a spoon.

I fear for you, Ben.

In the afternoon their toys are broken and they're tired and bored.

Women are fragile.

I'm not a child at Christmas.

The sun had crawled over a whole pie-shaped pane now; an hour. He didn't have to do it tomorrow, he could do it at any time, but the longer he waited the more danger there was that she would fall into the arms of some Clive or Glover or Walter Thorne and be lost to him forever. This would happen anyhow sooner or later, but he had to hang on to a part of her, an arm or a leg or a piece of her soul, that would still be his or partly his. He had to convert her to some other kind of thing in his life, someone he could still love in that selfless way, the way of the spirit, even if he couldn't go on loving her in that animalesque way that was not very important after all (he told himself without much conviction.). The important thing was that she should not go out of his life, that he should be able to see her every day or almost, that she should smile at him, show her affection in small ways, show off her clothes to him, and share with him the intimacies of food, wine, and music. As for that thing between his legs, the one-time racehorse, he would put it out to pasture for good. (A sharp pain at the thought of this; God, this was all excruciating). He would be in the Little House with his books, his stereo, and his records. It would really be a very nice place to live; the vast majority of the world's population would think themselves very fortunate to live there. Everything would be at hand, it would be neat and compact, systematic, orderly; he would be able to have things the way he wanted them. It would be very much like the cottage at the Cantamar, very much like his cabin at Muir House; he would be alone in a small comfortable place with everything he needed, and close at hand would be a larger place with lights, conversation, music, human companionship, and good food, and all he had to do was step across a stretch of pleasant garden and he would be there. He couldn't go there whenever he wanted, of course, it wouldn't be his place, but it would be a place he could go to at times.

And Peter was himself, he thought. Peter would be another Ben, himself as a young man; a New Englander, educated, easy-going, intelligent, sensitive, human, the editor of the Turtle Press. It would be as though he himself, from a subsequent incarnation, were watching his younger self being happy with Cecilia.

113.

He heard the buzz of the Honda going into the garage, then the engine stopped and she came in carrying her books in a bag, the same knapsack she had taken on the hike to Moon Lake.

She said lightly, "Did you have fun with Betsy?"

"Yes. We had lunch until about two and then went our separate ways. She came in her own car."

"What kind of a car does she have?"

"A Jaguar. It's light green, the color of mint. We had a nice talk. She's really quite a sensible person when she doesn't drink too much. She only had two vodkas with the lunch. You know, afterwards I went around to see Peter Barlow at the Press." He hadn't done anything of the kind yet, but this was not really an untruth, just another one of his inverted sequences. He intended to do it soon. "He's quite an interesting person. He wants to meet you."

"Meet me? Why?"

"Oh, he's heard about you. All of your talents. He's quite interested in baroque music. He knows quite a bit about it."

"Oh?" She sat down on the sofa, set her book bag on the floor in front of her, and looked around in it until she found an emery board, and began filing away at a broken fingernail. "What's he like?"

"About thirty, I'd say. A New Englander. A little bit shy. A very nice person. I've always liked him. He's going to do great things with the Press. He's much better at it than I am. I think he's going to make it one of the outstanding small presses in the country. He showed me some of the books he's doing now. They're quite beautiful. He has good editorial sense and he has interesting ideas about bookmaking. You have to be something of an artist to design bindings and jackets. I never really was that. He lives by himself in a little place down at the beach."

"I guess," she said, "that you and Betsy couldn't have been up to very much hankypanky if you had lunch with her until two or so, and then went around to see this Peter person, and you're here now."

114.

It was a few days later that Ben and Cecilia paid their visit to the Pacific Maritime Museum, where Raymonde worked. It was on Telephone Road, a little north of the Voronoffs' house, a part of the beach that was not as fashionable as it was closer to town. The building was a former porcelain factory, built at the turn of the century by an imaginative capitalist named Torkelson who imagined he could make his fortune from a kaolin mine up a nearby canyon. The kaolin ended after a few tons were taken out, and the factory was abandoned. It had stood there empty until a few years ago when the Museum was installed in it.

The big brick building, with walls two feet thick pierced only by a few dusty windows, seemed even larger inside than it did from the street. The bare walls were supported by a complicated structure of iron beams and trusses that made it look like some kind of fantastic penetentiary, one of the imaginary jails in Piranesi's engravings. The ground floor was so vast that the Museum collection scattered around among the iron columns seemed sparse and thin. There was no one at the desk by the door, only a jar with a card on it saying, "Welcome to the Pacific Maritime Museum. Please put one dollar in the jar. Please do not touch the exhibits. Thank you."

As they were examining this Raymonde appeared with a smile from behind one of the dusty glass cabinets at the end of the room. She was wearing her demin jacket, the one covered with ornamental pins, brooches, and costume jewelry, and a pair of faded jeans. Her platinum hair with its orange streak was loose and flowing. She towered a head above Cecilia, and she was an inch taller than Ben.

"Hi. Oh, you brought Ben too. Super. Do you want to look at the stuff? Afterwards we can have a cup of tea."

"Okay. Do we have to put a dollar in the jar?"

"Oh no. You're my guests. It's just a lot of junk really. I don't know if you'd be interested."

"It looks fantastic. How did you get this job anyhow?"

"It was through Arnold Schifter. He's a trustee of the Museum. I've known him for years, from my folks' Wednesdays, and I also took a class from him at the University. When the Museum was set up they needed a curator, and he got me the job."

"Fabulous."

They trailed around after her through the dusty old building. The exhibits consisted for the most part of things washed up from the sea over a period of many years, some of them dating back to Spanish times. Until the Museum was installed in the old porcelain factory these things had been stored in a warehouse by the Coast Guard station. There were glass Japanese fishing-floats, odd puff-balls, a wheel-lock pistol salvaged from a Spanish wreck, and stuffed sea-creatures of various kinds. In one cabinet there was an antique obstetrical forceps and a bolt from the keel of a galleon.

She pointed out her favorites: a set of ivory toothpicks in a sandalwood box, a gold comb with a tiny cupid engraved on it, invisible except with a magnifying glass, and a small burnished mirror so old it seemed almost Roman. In a cabinet by itself was the corpse in the cask of brandy, a sailor who died in a far-off clime and was preserved in this way so he could be brought back and laid to rest among his loved ones. A small glass window had been cut in the cask to show the occupant, who was looking out with one eye open and the other closed, and a look of calm astonishment.

Ben turned away from this gelatinous and unsettling glance. He hadn't really believed there would be such a thing in the Museum. Raymonde said, "Here are my oriental dolls. I've been collecting them since I was a little girl. When I got the job here I brought them over and put them on display."

They filled a large glass case, and they were all uniform in size, with pale faces and almond eyes, and fat old mandarins. An Emperor dreaming probably of a butterfly; his eyes were closed and he was smiling voluptuously. A half-naked courtesan bent over a customer, who had his middle heaved up to her and was supported on his elbow. The courtesan and her customer were from Macao; they were for tourists and not real classic dolls. The visitors to the Museum could buy a postcard of them for a dollar. "But I prefer the Emperor dreaming of his butterfly," said Raymonde, opening the cabinet and fondling him for an instant before she put him away.

Ben was a little embarrassed by the courtesan and her

customer. He was sure that Cecilia knew about fellatio, but he didn't care to stand there with her looking at a couple of dolls doing it. He felt all at once puritanical and protective, wanting to shelter her from the vulgarities of the world, like Holden Caulfield trying to remove all the obscene graffiti from the city so his little sister wouldn't read them. This was silly; he couldn't do it anyhow and Cecilia was far too sophisticated to be bothered by such things. It was all a part of being in love, he imagined.

Raymonde had gone on to another display case. "Here's my cannonball," she told them. Ben and Cecilia stared through the glass at a rusty iron ball about the size of a grapefruit. "I found it on the beach. It's from the sixteenth century. The Spaniards probably fired it from their ship to impress the Indians."

"Why hadn't anybody else noticed the cannonball if it had been lying there since the sixteenth century?"

"It was buried in the sand. Tidal force made it work to the surface."

This didn't seem plausible to Ben. There were a good many things about the Museum that didn't seem to hang together. Maybe the whole thing was a hoax and Raymonde had bought the cannonball from a scrap-iron dealer.

115.

Someone else had entered the Museum; the light from the doorway was cut off for an instant. It was Arnold Schifter. When his eyes adjusted to the light he caught sight of Ben and Cecilia and stared at them with a look of annoyance. Then he ignored them and spoke directly to Raymonde.

"Why haven't I seen you lately?"

"I'm here every day."

"I came here yesterday and the place was wide open and you were nowhere in sight."

"I was probably upstairs. Or sometimes I go to the beach; it bores me hanging around here all day when no one comes."

"Why must I come here? Can't we meet somewhere else?"

"This is where I work. I've got a job, just like everybody else."

"I know, I'm the one that got it for you. How can you go to the beach when you're supposed to be here? Raymonde, we can't go on like this. You act as though I'm just nobody. Some student. Some boyfriend of yours. Someone who once asked you out for a date."

"Well, aren't you?"

Arnold turned to Ben. He was wearing a Harris tweed coat, a tattersall shirt, and flannel trousers; he was badly overdressed for a morning at the beach. He said, "Ben, who is this person with you?"

"Her name is Cecilia. She's a friend of mine."

"Well, why don't you beat it? And take Cecilia with you, I came here to talk to Raymonde." He turned to her and said, "You know damned well I'm not just some boyfriend. I'm Arnold Schifter."

"Oh, please don't recite your credentials. I know them by heart."

"I don't mean that I'm an important person. I mean that I'm supposed to be someone special for you."

"You are, Arnold. It's so nice when you come to the Museum. Why don't we all go upstairs and have a cup of coffee. Or tea; I fancy tea this morning. Elevenses they call it in England. I wish I could go to England. I've never been there."

116.

They all went upstairs, Ben trailing along last up an iron stairway. He thought they ought to have gone away as soon as Arnold came, but Cecilia seemed to want to stay. The upstairs room had evidently been used as some kind of storeroom for the porcelain factory. It was windowless, with a couple of bare light bulbs hanging from the ceiling. In the center of the room a wooden packing case was lying on its side to serve as a table, with smaller crates for chairs. Near it, on another crate, was an old-fashioned Victrola with a tulip-shaped horn and a crank to wind it up. On the other side of the room was a garment rack made out of pipe with a collection of dusty and faded costumes hanging from it.

While the three of them watched, Raymonde filled the teapot and set it on to boil, put a couple of tea-bags in the teapot, and set it by the hotplate.

She asked Arnold, "Where are you supposed to be now?"

"In Bangkok, I think. Or perhaps Manila."

"Won't your hosts miss you?"

"In the Orient they have no sense of time."

"Where have you left your baggage?"

"The usual place. The Dream Inn, near the airport. Listen, Raymonde, my car's outside and it's only ten minutes from here. My plane doesn't leave until evening."

"Arnold, how can you say that? You know I have to be here at the Museum."

"You told me that yesterday you went to the beach."

"We'd better go," Ben told Cecilia.

"Oh no, stay. Everybody sit down. The tea's just about ready." She set the tray with the teapot and some arrowroot biscuits on the improvised table. Arnold took out his handkerchief and dusted off the crate with it before he sat down.

117.

"These costumes were donated by a Hollywood studio," said Raymonde. "Don't ask me what they're doing in a maritime museum. Anyhow, they're a lot of fun."

There were a hundred or more of them on the rack: cowboy outfits, a British guards uniform, a long gown and a hat with feathers for a Gay Nineties music-hall singer, an old-fashioned tuxedo, and a Cleopatra outfit that consisted of nothing much but a gauze, skirt, a pair of brass cups, and a headband. This had once been worn by Theda Bara, according to Raymonde.

"Everybody pick one," she told them. "I'm going to put on the Edith Cavell costume. And here's yours, Arnold." She pulled down the British Guards uniform and took it off its hanger. To go with it there were high shoes with puttees and a peaked cap with a crimson band.

"Oh no. Not that bloody fascist uniform again. Raymonde—"

She went to him, put the cap on his head, and thrust the rest of the uniform into his arms. He was not quite as tall as she was, but he seemed tall because of his lean and wiry aristocratic look, with a long chin and a high intellectual forehead.

"Put it all on."

"Raymonde—"

She assumed a British accent from the movies. "A leftenant in the Grenadier Guards. Very tosh."

"This is childish," said Arnold. "I'm so tired of this."

"What do you want to wear, Ben and Cecilia?"

Ben and Cecilia exchanged glances. She smiled and began riffling through the costumes on the rack. He gave up and looked for one too; it was only a harmless game. She selected the Gay Nineties music-hall costume for herself and passed him a cowboy outfit. They began taking off their clothes; Arnold stood on one leg at a time to remove his trousers, then his shirt.

The Edith Cavell uniform was too small for Raymonde. Almost any costume would have been. She buttoned it with difficulty. It consisted of a long gray nurse's uniform with a white collar and cuffs and a Red Cross on the bodice, and a cap to match. There were white shoes to go with it, but they were too small to wear and she put her sandals back on. She piled up some wooden crates to make a grandstand for Ben and Cecilia. "Now you sit down. You're our audience."

118.

She faced Arnold in a dramatic pose, her head lifted high. "Leftenant, I've sheltered you in this porcelain factory while your wounds were healing, but you're well now. Sooner or later the Boches will find this place. You must get away immediately. I have friends who will help you. They'll lead through the enemy lines across the border into Switzerland. In two more weeks you'll be in England."

Cecilia laughed, with her hand over her mouth. She glanced at Ben but he stared straight ahead. He was embarrassed by the whole thing and wished they had left; he felt foolish in his cowboy outfit, which included huge leather chaps that flared out at the bottom.

Arnold said, "This is stupid, Raymonde."

"Nurse Cavell. You say, What about you."

"What about you?" he muttered.

"I must take my chances. There are more escaped prisoners who must be cared for. We have become good friends during these last three weeks, haven't we? In a perfectly proper way, of course. Now that you are leaving, let us have tea together for the last time."

She took him by the elbow and led him to the improvised table. They sat down on the crates and drank the tea.

"Now tell me. What will your life be back in England when you return?"

"What am I supposed to say?"

"Oh Arnold, don't be so dense. Improvise. Make something up. Your father is a wealthy landowner in Hertfordshire. You have two sisters."

"My father is a wealthy landowner in Hertfordshire. I have two sisters. One is named Eunice and the other Mavis. My mother is—dead I guess. Those people all seem strange to me. It's as though they don't exist. It's as though I'm making them all up, talking to you. Raymonde—"

"Who?"

"Nurse Cavell, listen to me." He glared at Ben and Cecilia and clenched his teeth. "All this is driving me insane. I wouldn't mind playing games with you if it eventuated in anything—"

"Eventuated? What a pompous word."

"Led to anything. I'm sorry, I've spent most of my life hanging around universities and I've learned to talk like that. If they led to anything, they might even be fun. But—"

"When you say universities you mean Cambridge I imagine."

"Oxford. Carolyn says—"

"Carolyn?"

"My wife. That is, I think she's my wife. She's Chinese. I mean, we call her La Chinoise, because she has beautiful almond eyes. Actually she comes from an old country family and we fell in love as children. She seems rather distant to me now here … in France."

"You haven't finished your tea, Leftenant. And the arrowroot biscuits. You'll need your strength when you're escaping through enemy lines."

"I used to eat these things when I was a child. They're awful."

"The tea is Earl Grey. We have only a little left. When that's gone, we'll have to drink coffee with chicory. Tell me more about your wife Carolyn, Leftenant."

"She has lovely almond eyes. She likes to—look at the stars. She knows a great deal about them."

"You're not very imaginative. And do you love her, Leftenant?"

"In a manner of speaking. She's become an old habit. It's you that I love …"

"Nurse Cavell."

"Nurse Cavell. Can't you understand, I'm mad about you. I think of you night and day. I can't sleep for thinking about you." He stared defiantly at Ben and Cecilia as though he hoped to make them disappear through a sheer act of will.

"But you still love Carolyn."

"Which Carolyn?"

"Your wife back in Hertfordshire."

"Yes I do. Perhaps that's hard for you to understand. When you get a little older, you'll find there are some very strange things about human nature. It's possible to love one human being in one realm of consciousness and another in another."

"Of course," said Cecilia. "If two, why not six or seven? We know what men are." She seemed to be enjoying the whole thing hugely.

"You keep out of this, Cecilia, if that's what your name is. What's a Gay Nineties music-hall queen doing behind the lines in France anyhow?"

"Or a cowboy," she said. "We're part of a traveling entertainment troupe, caught behind the lines when the enemy advanced."

Arnold ignored her. "Look, Raymonde—"

"Nurse Cavell."

"Nurse Cavell. I can't go on with this any longer." He pulled at the collar of the military tunic and the snap broke. "I'm stifling in this thing." He got up and came to her around the improvised table. She stood up too and they embraced briefly.

"Be careful, Leftenant. You'll pull the stitches in your wound. It's time for our farewell, I'm afraid. Soon my friends will be coming to lead you through the enemy lines to safety. And now, a last dance. You can remember me by that."

"Oh Raymonde, that goddam Victrola."

She went to it, wound it up, and put on a record. It was a slow fox-trot. They began dancing to a baby-doll voice with a band of saxophones and muted trumpets behind it. "You will think of me often, Leftenant," she whispered in his ear. "Oh, isn't this a nice song. In the arms of Carolyn, your Hertfordshire wife with almond eyes, you will imagine that you are still here with me hidden in this old porcelain factory, dancing our farewell dance. These weeks we've spent together have been unforgettable for both of us, Leftenant. Don't think I don't understand the unspoken messages that have passed between us. But what you ask me for I can't give you. I too dream of a long oblivious night of love, Leftenant. But I am not free to follow my own happiness. I must give myself to something else, Leftenant. To my country, and to all the other soldiers who are counting on me to succor their wounds and help them back to safety through the enemy lines. Sooner or later the Boches will arrest me, and I know full well what my fate will be at their hands. I am not afraid. I will live on in the memories of those for whom I have given my life, and that includes you, Leftenant. You will never forget me, and you will dream of me even in the arms of your wife Carolyn."

119.

In the car Ben said, "I didn't care for that man in the cask. I wish I hadn't seen it."

"Just think of it as a wax dummy. A Madame Tussaud thing."

"That's what's horrible about it."

"You know, Raymonde told me earlier how she found the cannonball. She found it in a trance."

"A trance?"

"Yes. She has them now and then. She said she was at the beach one day, on the bluff overlooking the cove, and something came over her. She felt queer and odd, as though her consciousness was coming out of her body. She found herself staring out to sea. There was a ship out there, silhouetted in the sun, with funny square sails. Down in the cove there were some Indians the color of mud, and they were holding sticks or weapons of some kind and looking out at the ship. Then the ship fired its cannon, and she saw the cannonball strike the beach not far from the Indians, sending up a shower of sand. They were frightened and ran away up a ravine into the chaparral. Then she fainted or something and when she came to she was lying on her back looking up into the sky. She got up and went down to the cove, and started digging in the sand with a piece of driftwood. She found the cannonball about two feet down, just where she had seen it in the trance."

"She made all that up."

"No, I don't think she did."

"Then she's crazy."

"She's not crazy just because she has trances. Many people do. Look at Carlos Castaneda."

"Oh, rot."

"People like you only believe in the material world. That way you miss half of what there is to see in the universe. More than half; maybe nine-tenths."

"Did it strike you," he asked her, "that Raymonde's Nurse Cavell teaparty is exactly like Ilya's True Novel? She makes up roles for everybody and makes them act them out."

"She's his daughter after all."

"But how does she have this power over people? How does Ilya?"

"I don't know. You wanted to leave. Why didn't you?"

"Because you wanted to stay. It was painful."

"Painful? I thought it was funny." He recognized again the strain of cruelty that surfaced in her now and then. He had noticed it first at Muir House, when she had forced Dave to shut the car door for her. She said, "It wouldn't have made any difference if we had gone away. They would still have done the same thing."

"How do you know?"

"Raymonde told me. They do it all the time."

"What have you told her about what we do?"

"Nothing, of course. Silly."

"Of course, you don't have such interesting stories to tell."

"Do you know what I think? She likes to collect dolls and Arnold's just a great big doll. She dresses him in costumes. Any girl would like to do that."

"Any girl would if she were ten years old. Not if she were grown up. Do you think the corpse in the cask is one of her dolls too?"

She laughed. "Maybe. I never thought of that."

"She's gone on stringing Arnold along this way for years. Do you think she's interested in sex at all?"

"She told me it makes her sick to think of it."

"You seem to go around with her a lot. You go shopping and so on. I don't see what you see in her."

"I really like her. She's an interesting person. She does some funny things, but she's harmless."

"She's perfectly harmless in herself, but she's bad for Arnold."

"Well, why doesn't he leave off then? He's got Carolyn. She's a very attractive woman."

"As he told all three of us, it's possible to love one person in one realm of consciousness and another in another. Arnold can't help himself. He's in love."

"You know," she said, "as I look around it's a queer thing. None of the women we know are in love and all the men are. Even Ilya. Ilya's in love with me."

"Oh, is he?" It struck him that she didn't mention she was in love herself, but perhaps that was just the grammatical form of the sentence. She said *the women we know.* That wouldn't include her. After a pause he said, "What about Ethel?"

"That's right. She's the exception. Ethel's in love with you."

"You don't really understand anything about that, Cecilia."

At this she only smiled.

120.

That afternoon Cecilia was gone to the University and Ben went around to see Peter Barstow again. From the balcony he caught sight of him through the open shutters, as usual. This time he wasn't working on a manuscript; he was sitting in his chair with his feet on the desk in front of him, looking out through the window. When Ben came in he smiled and got up.

"Hullo, Peter." They shook hands, a rather formal thing to do considering how well they knew each other, but they had always done it.

"How are you, Ben? It's been a long time since you were here."

"I've been away in Europe. And I've been busy with other things."

"Are you still living at the Cantamar? I tried to call you there the other day but I couldn't get you. The number was disconnected."

"No, I've moved." Peter still didn't know about Cecilia. He must have been the only person in town who didn't.

"It's nice to see you. Would you like the usual Danish?"

"What else have you got?"

"I think there's a donut around somewhere."

"Never mind, just a cup of coffee. What are you working on now?"

"I've finished the Joaquin Murieta book now. It'll be out in the spring. I'm reading a manuscript on folk art in the Central Valley. You know, people who make sculpture with a chain saw and so on. I can't decide whether to take it. It's an attractive book but it would cost a lot of money. It would have to have a lot of illustrations. So far the Press has lost money every month this year." He ran his fingers through his mop of dark hair; the fact that the Press was not doing very well seemed to make him look pale and wan, like Rodolfo in Puccini's *La Bohème*. He was far too good looking for a publisher, Ben thought; he should have been an actor.

"Have you thought any more about letting Mrs. Partener go?" Ben could see her through the half-open door to the storeroom at the rear; she had her glasses on the end of her nose and she was typing a letter. At the table beyond her the student assistant was wrapping a bundle of books, holding her finger on the string while she tried to tie the knot with the other hand. The knot slipped and she had to start over.

"Nope. I've decided you were right. I don't want to do that."

"You were complaining the last time I was here about how much your place at the beach costs. I think I may have found you another place to live. It would be a lot cheaper, and nicer."

"What kind of place?"

"I'll let you know later. I'm still working on it."

Ben sipped his coffee, which was pretty vile stuff; it had been sitting on the hotplate all morning. And the artificial creamer didn't do much to improve it. Peter didn't have his usual Danish, and he didn't touch his own coffee in the mug in front of him. A little permanent crease had formed in his forehead, which before had always been smooth and unblemished. He was no longer very young, thought Ben. He was about thirty.

After a silence, Peter said, "Betsy Voronoff called me up. She wants me to come to one of her Wednesdays, but I don't know if I'm interested."

"Oh, why don't you come, Peter? It's a rather queer bunch of people, but some of them are nice. Anyhow, there's someone there who wants to meet you."

"Who is it?"

"Cecilia Penn. You don't know her. She's someone who's just moved to Santa Barbara. A musician, a talented harpsichordist. She's heard about you and she'd like to visit the Press."

"Oh. I see." Peter didn't seem to pay much attention, but to be told that somebody is interested in you and wants to meet you is always irresistible. The idea was planted in Peter's mind now and he wouldn't forget it. It would come to the surface again the first time he met Cecilia. This little trick would work like a charm; Ben was sure of it.

Peter said, "I used to know Betsy at one time."

"So I understand."

"At that time she was going for anything in pants."

"Well, she's mellowed a great deal with age. They have a lot of money, you know."

"I know, I've been to the house. Do the Rolfs still come to the Wednesdays?"

"Yes. They're nice people."

"Probably I ought to go out more. I just work here all day long, and then I go home at night and listen to the stereo."

"You like baroque music, don't you? Things like Bach and Handel. Harpsichord music."

"I suppose. I'm interested in contemporary too. Poulenc, Philip Glass, John Cage. That sort of thing."

"Not the sort of thing you'd play on a harpsichord."

Peter let this pass. He didn't understand what Ben was driving at and his mind was on other things. He said, "Would you like to look at the folk art book?"

"Sure."

The manuscript was in a large cardboard box. Peter got it out on the table and spread it around. There were two authors, an art professor at U.C. Davis and a photographer. The photographs were color contacts the size of postage stamps; Ben looked at them through a magnifier.

"It could be a nice book. As you say, it would cost a lot of money. These photos are quite good. The more of them the better. Here's one you could use for a jacket." It was a sculpture made on a sewing machine, a stuffed figure that looked like a Henry Moore made out of scraps and patches of colored cloth, like a patchwork quilt. The colors leaped out vividly; the background of tree branches was out of focus and blurred. A nice photograph.

"You know what color photoengravings cost, Ben."

"Peter, the thing is that once in a while you have to have a little audacity. You could do a skimpy book out of this and it might do all right. But if you spend some real money on it, it has the possibility of being a very successful book. Don't tell me you don't have the money. If you want to do it, do it. Be a reckless sentimentalist. If you see something out there that seems crazy and unattainable, reach for it at least." He found himself swept away by his own rhetoric, and realized he was talking about himself and Cecilia and not about Peter and the Press at all. "You may fall flat, but if you succeed, there's happiness on the other side."

"Happiness? I don't know what you're talking about. I'm just trying to decide whether to publish this book."

"If the book is a success, you'll be happy."

121.

All true love stories end unhappily. Why is this? Love stories that end happily are only for children who are not old enough to fall in love yet, or for the very young who are still in love. They have to be told happy stories about love, that is lies, otherwise they might sheer off from falling in love and the human race would come to an end. As a matter of fact people who are in love don't read love stories very much; they're too busy with their own affairs.

It has been said that before Flaubert's *Madame Bovary* all novels ended with the marriage, and after *Madame Bovary* they begin with the marriage. This is a good definition of an honest novel, that is to say, one that tells the truth about life. The others are called romances.

122.

At the Voronoffs the guitar and flute had been replaced by a pianist who played George Gershwin show tunes. Ilya hummed along: *Bess you is my woman now.* It was autumn now and too cool to go out on the terrace overlooking the sea; the evening fog came in early.

In the living room Ben was standing in a circle of people, holding his drink in his good hand with the other hand tucked into his pocket. The group included the Rolfs, Snoozy Pickering, and Betsy. Ted Pickering was at the bar engaged in deep conversation with Carolyn Wong. Cecilia no longer wore her white sweater and black tapered pants to the Wednesdays. Now she had a new outfit, something she bought when she was out shopping with Raymonde: a pair of full-cut linen pants that seemed permanently wrinkled—this was something that young people were wearing right then—and a jacket of the same material. She had a turquoise scarf tied into her hair and a big turquoise pin on the jacket.

Ben said, "Cecilia, this is Peter Barstow. Peter, Cecilia."

"I've heard a lot about you."

"I've heard a lot about *you*," she said with a little laugh, as though there as something incredibly amusing about the fact that they should both be at the same party.

Peter was not comfortable in large gatherings, or even middle-sized ones. He too had dressed up for the occasion: a tweed jacket, flannels, and moccasin-seam loafers. Ben had never before seen him in a necktie. His dark hair fell over his eyes and he pushed it back with a gesture of unconscious male grace, corresponding to the grace of women brushing their hair. Betsy had given him a bourbon and water but he wasn't drinking it. The Gershwin tunes filtered to them from the next room.

Cecilia said, "So you run the Turtle Press. Ben's old press."

"Yes."

"That must be fascinating."

"It's a job."

"Tell me about some of the books you publish."

He started telling her about the book on Joaquin Murieta, and Ben slipped unobtrusively away from the group.

123.

At the bar he found Raymonde alone; Carolyn Wong and Ted Pickering were still immersed in their deep conversation at the other end.

"Where's Arnold tonight?"

"Arnold? I have no idea."

"I thought he was supposed to be in Bangkok. Or Manila," Ben said.

"It's very likely."

"I've always liked Arnold. He's very mysterious though. I don't know much about his private life. Apparently nobody does."

"What are you driving at? I don't follow you."

Raymonde was in her usual outfit, the faded jeans and the denim jacket covered with pins. He saw now at close range that the jacket and jeans were not very clean. A slightly musty odor came from her, not unpleasant, like the smell of a dog. As a concession to the fact that people dressed up in the evening she was wearing her small tinsel stars pasted to her cheeks, one silver and one red. He looked past her shoulder to the circle of people where Cecilia was still talking to Peter. Cecilia was smiling and a little color had come into her cheeks, but she was cool and composed as always. She was telling a story and at the same time illustrating it in pantomime; she made a gesture of taking off her shoe, then doing something to the imaginary shoe with some tool or other (here she laughed), then she put the imaginary shoe back on, then she limped, still standing in place. Ben realized she was telling the story of Clive the English student and the nail he put in his boot. Peter was smiling too, and he laughed when she limped and then threw up her hands to indicate that it was the end of the story. The Rolfs looked across the room at Ben, and Snoozy Pickering made a little moue of amused disapproval, as if to say, Oh that Ben.

"I suppose," he told Raymonde, "that I'm just carrying on the tradition of our Wednesdays. This is the way we're supposed to talk here." He was really only talking to Raymonde so that he could observe Cecilia from a distance, watching her every move, without seeming to interfere.

"The way we're supposed to talk? I don't understand."

"In innuendoes. Hints and coy references. We wittily slander people behind their backs. Everybody knows what everybody else is doing and we separate into little groups and talk about it."

"I certainly don't. I just say what I think. I don't know any innuendoes. In fact, I don't think I know what an innuendo is."

He dropped this and said, "Cecilia tells me you found the cannonball in a trance."

"What cannonball? Oh, the one in the Museum."

"Well, did you?"

"I wouldn't say that. I just *imagined* one day that a

Spanish ship might have sailed past the cove and fired a cannon to impress the Indians. Then I went down and dug on the beach, and sure enough, there was a cannonball buried in the sand."

"What did the Indians look like?"

"I didn't see any Indians. I just imagined them."

"I'll bet they were scared as hell when the cannonball struck the beach near them, eh? They must have hightailed it up into the brush."

"No doubt. I don't know for sure there were any Indians. Maybe the Spaniards just fired the cannon at the beach for target practice."

The others in the circle across the room had left now and Cecilia and Peter were talking alone. Cecilia was still making gestures, but he couldn't tell what the pantomime was now. Maybe it was the Ile de la Grande Jatte, or riding on a motorcycle with Glover. Peter stood quietly watching her and only speaking a word now and then. He was wearing a little smile, although he didn't know he had it on, and he sipped now and then from his glass. Cecilia seemed to have a Perrier and ice with a slice of lime in it. Ben tucked his right hand into his pocket, found his cognac on the bar, and drank half of it in one sip. He turned back to Raymonde. She seemed intent to convince him that she had not found the cannonball in a trance. Maybe trances were a thing that young people only discussed among themselves; she didn't trust his generation.

"You're older than Cecilia, aren't you? When did you get out of college?"

"Oh, a couple of years ago."

"And what do you want to do with your life?"

"People your age are always asking us what we want

to do with our life, as though it was a pocketful of money we have to spend. I'm quite happy just going on as I am, working in the Museum. I'm not interested in doing anything else."

"All your life?"

"Why not?"

"And you have your doll collection."

"I don't understand what you mean. Is that one of your innuendoes?

So she did know what an innuendo was after all.

124.

Driving home through the thin fog, they had the usual post mortem.

"Did you enjoy yourself?"

"Oh yes. It was a nice evening."

"They're nice people, really. If they don't drink too much."

"I saw you talking to Raymonde."

"Yes." He wondered if he should tell her that Raymonde denied she found the cannonball in a trance, but decided not to. One of the two of them was being untruthful, either Raymonde or Cecilia. There was no point in finding out which one it was. It was very likely Cecilia, he decided. She believed in channeling, disembodied spirits, and reincarnation. Of course, you could apply Hume's test for a miracle. Which would be more unbelievable, that Raymonde saw the Spanish ship in a trance, or that she just imagined for some reason that a Spanish ship might have fired its cannonball and then went straight to the beach and dug it up?

He asked her, "Who did you talk to?"

"Oh, various people. The Rolfs. Ilya. I didn't talk to

Ilya very long. I was afraid he would start telling me again about his True Novel and the part he wants me to play in it."

"What do you think about Peter?"

"He's very nice. I like him."

He stole a glance at her. She didn't realize he was watching her and she was looking out through the windshield with a funny little smile on her face, as though she were listening to distant music. She didn't know she was doing it; he would hardly have noticed it himself if he hadn't been looking for it. It was the first smile that seemed to come from inside herself and was not a part of the friendly easygoing mask she wore for the world. *It's working,* he told himself.

125.

There are various forms of mental discipline that you can use if you want to get over being in love with somebody. One is to imagine her as a child of eight, exactly as she is now but with her sex removed, so to speak, so that she becomes pre-nubile. Ben was perfectly normal and had never been attracted to eight-year-olds. He focussed his mind hard on this imaginary picture. Cecilia was in a frock with a pinafore, a pink bow in her hair, holding a doll. This didn't work because he suddenly grasped what it *would* be like to have a tendency to child-molesting.

Another way is to imagine her as her own brother. She is still the same general person but she is converted to the male sex. Usually if you perform this feat of imagination on a woman you can see that if she were a man she would be a quite ordinary person, and that she has only been transformed into something more by the illusion of your desire. You wouldn't be interested in her if she were the same person but a man. Ben tried this too, but it was even less successful. Although he wasn't a child-molester, it was possible that he had light homosexual tendencies. After all Henry Calendish was attracted to him, and he himself had thought, looking at Peter Barlow, that he was so attractive that it made you understand what a homosexual felt. The image slid rapidly into a scene in which he and Cecilia engaged in homoerotic practices.

The third is even worse. It's a thoroughly bad idea, although it might seem on the face of it that it would be effective. This is to do something to her that time is eventually going to do anyhow: convert her into an old woman, still with all her features and characteristics. Give her wrinkles, gray hair, a missing tooth or two, sagging breasts, in short a hag of eighty. This isn't too difficult to do if you have any imagination. It's like the picture in *Dorian Gray*, or the movie of it: as you watch the skin sags and wrinkles, the pustules of disease appear, the eyes dim, the smile turns to a senile grin. As Ben successfully did this, the thought occurred to him, *Now she's just like me*. He tried to forget this as quickly as possible.

The last one is a joke among high school boys, or it used to be when Ben was that age. It's a severe measure, to be used only in the most extreme cases. You visualize her sitting on the toilet, with all the corresponding images. When he did this, quite graphically, he found himself in the grip of such a complicated web of unclean desires that he felt like Laocoön trying to throw off the snakes. You wouldn't imagine what it suggested to him he might do. He was disgusted with himself.

126.

It was a couple of days later, a Friday afternoon. Cecilia had just come home from the University and was sitting cross-legged on the floor with her book bag by her side. Ben was on the sofa, nursing his usual afternoon drink.

"How are your classes going?"

"Oh, fine."

"Do you get along with Dominicus all right?"

"It isn't a question of getting along with Egon. It's a question of doing what he says and working very hard. If you do that, you get along with him all right."

"Do you think you're improving?"

"Improving?"

"I mean, is your harpsichord playing getting any better."

"Oh heavens yes. I'm advancing by leaps and bounds. Egon is even better than the teacher I had in Berkeley. I can't understand why he stays in an out-of-the-way place like Santa Barbara."

"Maybe he likes his students." He would like to know whether her relations with Dominicus were more than those of teacher and student.

"Egon doesn't like anybody. He doesn't even like music. He just knows how to do his job."

"I don't hear you practicing very much here at home."

"Oh I do. I practice a lot when you're not here. For some reason, I can't bring myself to play when I know you're listening, even though I know that I know a lot more about harpsichords than you do, and you're a rotten pianist. For some reason I need your esteem. Maybe it's because I don't get any esteem out of Egon and I need somebody's esteem. Oh, I do love you, Ben. I can't thank you enough for taking me to Europe and buying me the harpsichord and getting this house. It's just a wonderful place. Every time I sit down at the harpsichord and look at the Canaletto I feel good. And the kitchen is nice, and what a lovely big bed. I never thought I'd live in a house that had a pool. And one you can skinny-dip in." He had never heard her chatter on so much. "I find that I'm liking the furniture after all. At first I thought that turning it all over to that woman, what's her name, Stacey, was a bad idea. But whoever she found did a pretty good job after all. It's comfortable and it's elegant and I do like the Daumier prints. And the Hogarths in the bedroom." Without any transition, hardly interrupting her flow of speech, she said, "Do you know, Ben, we decided in London that we were going to have a policy of being utterly frank with each other."

"Yes."

"Well, Peter asked me to come and see him and I did. I stopped by on my way home from the campus."

"I see."

"He wanted to show me the Press office."

"Well, that's perfectly all right. Did you find it interesting?"

"Yes, very. Well no, not very, but Peter is—an. An interesting person."

"I've always liked him. I'm glad the two of you have met."

"You know, Ben. He also asked me to meet him in town for lunch. He said we didn't have a chance to talk about—my music and what I do. We spent all the time talking about the Press. It's at the—you know, the Captain's Landing, that seafood place down at the beach near where he lives." She hadn't met his glance while she was saying all this. Now she looked up at him.

"Why don't you go?"

"Maybe you could come too," she said in a queer faltering voice, as though it were a line she had decided in advance to speak.

"Oh, I don't think that would be a good idea."

127.

On Monday morning Ben phoned the art department and asked for Professor Dominicus. After a wait, a gruff voice came on the line and said, "Yes." It wasn't a question, simply an affirmative bark.

"How are you this morning, Professor Dominicus?"

"Who is this?"

"My name's not important. I just have a question. I understand that you recommend that your performance graduates go abroad for a year of private study after they get their degrees."

"Sometimes. If they're any good," he said in his slightly sinister Viennese accent, swallowing the r's.

"But is that really necessary? I mean, suppose a person didn't really want to go to Europe. Or suppose I know somebody who's studying under you and I don't really want her to go to Europe for a year. That's an awfully long time for her to be away."

"What instrument are you talking about?"

"The harpsichord."

"Then it's Cecilia. She's the only one who is any good. I don't know who the hell you are anyhow. You're probably the character who came with Cecilia the first time I auditioned her."

"Suppose an eminent European musician came to your campus as Artist in Residence for a year. Then Cecilia wouldn't have to go to Europe."

"I remember your name now. It's Gabilan."

"Gavilan."

"That's right. Mr. Gavilan. What eminent musician did you have in mind?"

"How about Brigitte Haudebourg?"

"She's just a performer. She doesn't give master classes."

"Who's the best harpsichord teacher in the world?"

"You'd have to be talking about Maurice Merleau in Grenoble. He's an excellent concert pianist who turned only in his forties to the harpsichord, and mastered it to the point where he was receiving world acclaim. His recordings of Bach's partitas are still the standard by which the others are measured. Then he injured his hand in an accident, so he became a teacher, one of the most distinguished in Europe."

"What about having him come over here for a year?"

"We have a fund for Artists in Residence, but we really can't afford Merleau."

"Maybe I could help out."

"Help out?"

"Maybe I could contribute to a fund to bring Merleau here."

There was a silence. Then Dominicus said, "Well, that might be possible."

"How much would it cost?"

Dominicus named a figure that was so large that it made something go cold in Ben's chest.

"My name must never come out."

"Don't worry. You're an anonymous donor."

"Tell you what. I'll come to your office and we'll talk it over."

"Don't come on Tuesday-Thursday afternoons. Cecilia is here then."

The two of them agreed perfectly. They had formed their little conspiracy after only a few sentences. Dominicus was not interested at all in what he and Cecilia did together; he was only interested in his job as a music teacher. Ben decided that he was someone he might be able to like after all.

128.

Ben got back from his interview with Dominicus about four o'clock. He parked the car in the garage next to Cecilia's Honda, shut the garage door, and entered the house with his key through the front door. The sliding glass door to the garden was open, but she wasn't at the pool as she usually was at this time in the afternoon. He looked in the kitchen to see if she was having a snack, but probably not because she had lunch in town. He knew she was home because her car was there. He was about to look through the rest of the house when she appeared in the doorway of the bedroom.

He said, "So you're here. I couldn't find you at first."

She didn't answer. She stood with her hand behind her on the doorframe, looking at him fixedly with an expression he had never seen before, an intensity that made her seem much older than she really was.

"What's the matter?"

She went on looking at him through two glistening pools that gradually obscured her vision, holding her mouth tight in an effort not to let her face wrinkle up. Then she turned slowly and went away into the bedroom. When he followed he saw that her eyes were welling over; crystal tracks formed and crept slowly down her cheeks. Except for that she seemed calm and still made no sound.

"Cecilia."

She wouldn't let him touch her. She drew away, went to the bed, and sat on it with her head turned away from him, then abruptly fell face down on the pillow. He watched her body shaking silently as though it was in the clutch of some strange seizure, as though her heart had gripped her body and was making it pulse to its beat.

She went on sobbing for some time. She still made almost no sound; it was as though she had resolved to control herself at least in this. For a while he watched her, then he went to the bed and sat down. He laid his hand softly on her back. She turned on her side and lifted her head from the pillow; her face was wet with tears. She still couldn't manage to speak.

"It's Peter, isn't it?"

She nodded.

"Cecilia, it's all right."

"Ben, we went to his. His—place. His apartment."

They were both silent again for a while. She was lying on her elbow, and he sat beside her on the bed. She had stopped sobbing now but she couldn't control the tears that welled out and slid silently down her cheeks.

"You didn't make any promises to me. You can't make promises about your feelings anyhow. I explained that to you in London."

"I don't know what to do."

"You mustn't think of me. You can't afford to base your whole life on sacrifice for somebody else. It's very noble, but it isn't the way to live in the real world. In the end it's our own happiness that we're responsible for, not the happiness of others."

"I didn't want this to happen. I didn't, Ben. I don't know why it did."

"You'll be happy. That's what I want. You don't know the first thing about love if you don't know that."

"I want you to be happy too."

"I'll be happy."

"He told me that he felt rotten about you too."

"It must have been a melancholy encounter. The two of you in his apartment sobbing together about me."

"It was wonderful. We said we'd always be honest with each other, didn't we? It was wonderful, Ben. I never knew I could feel this way. It was afterward that he said he felt rotten. I said I felt rotten too."

"He's a nice person. He's very attractive. I'm glad you've got him, Cecilia."

She tried to wipe her face with her hand and he handed her a box of tissues.

"Ben, who are you?"

"What?"

"Why have you come into my life this way? Why did it happen? Who are you?"

His withered hand had fallen out of his pocket and he tucked it back in. "I'm your personal guardian angel, Cecilia. The angel of your happiness."

"I don't deserve an angel. Ben, what's going to happen now?"

"Don't worry. It'll be all right. I know what's going to happen. You're going to be very happy and everything you want will come to you."

"I can't believe it."

"I'm older than you, Cecilia, and a lot smarter about a lot of things."

That night he didn't touch her. She slept on her side of the bed lying on her back with her arms at her sides, like a child-saint on a medieval tomb.

129.

Why do things happen? Some people believe that they happen because of Divine Providence; He makes everything work because He's Got the Whole World in His Hands. Ben didn't believe this. Or perhaps things happen simply by chance, just happen at random; there's no reason or explanation for them. He doesn't believe this either. The third explanation is that, in the case of some things, phenomena in the physical world, things happen because of the operation of the laws of physics. If you let an egg go it drops; if you drop a match in gasoline it burns. But in the case of other events, events that take place in the human soul, like a woman bursting into tears, there might be explanations like those in the world of physics, but they are much more complex and elusive and we can never really understand them fully, only make guesses. It all depends in the end whether you believe that people are simply made of atoms, or whether there's something called the soul. Ben's opinion was that probably men are made of atoms, but women have a soul.

130.

After ten minutes of driving Ben found the address at the end of Las Palmas Drive in Hope Ranch Park, on a bluff overlooking the sea. It was Christmas day, about six months after he first met Cecilia. Cecilia's car was already in the parking lot, along with a lot of others; he recognized the Voronoffs' Bentley and Ethel's old Plymouth Reliant. The place looked like something between a Mediterranean villa and a very modern hospital, with cypresses, rock gardens, and exotic cacti. There was even a pool, for some reason, and a Brancusi-like sculpture on the lawn. The half-dozen buildings enclosed a central patio paved with flagstones. At one end there was a square tower with a wrought-iron emblem on all four sides of it, a triangle with what appeared to be an eye in it.

In the patio he found a group that included Cecilia and Peter, the Rolfs, Arnold Schifter, and Raymonde. He got himself a stiff drink from the buffet, a thing he thought he needed and deserved on this occasion, and went to join them. Mrs. Galleon was drifting around like a lost soul in an enormous print dress and picture hat, and Carolyn Wong was talking to Ethel. There were other people he didn't recognize. The middle-aged woman in the caftan was Babs Penn, Cecilia's mother. He also caught sight of Dave, the bellman from Muir House. He was wandering around holding a drink and not talking to anyone. Probably nobody had introduced him.

Raymonde said, "Hi, Ben."

"What is this place exactly?"

"It's a church, silly."

"I've seen it from the road but I never knew what it was."

It was Raymonde who had found the church and made all the arrangements. She explained it to him. "It's called the Affirmation of Life Chapel. The denomination is called Religious Science. Except that it isn't a denomination. At least they say it isn't. It embraces all denominations."

Jo-Nan said, "Let's not get into theology, dear."

Cecilia said, "Raymonde found the church in a trance."

"Oh, I did not. Here's Ken."

Ken was a pleasant-looking young man with a round

face and carefully styled collar-length hair. He wore a tuxedo with a frilled shirt and a magenta bow tie. He embraced Raymonde, Cecilia, and Peter, and seemed capable of embracing Ben for all he knew. Ben kept a wary eye on him.

"Cecilia, dear, you're really charming," said Raymonde.

She really was. She was in a narrow sleeveless sheath that fell straight to her ankles without a belt. Whenever she turned and swung it clung to her waist in enticing wrinkles. It was another garment he didn't know, with an unknown Cecilia inside it. The others were all dressed informally. Ben, in a white linen jacket and dark trousers, felt very conventional. He should have worn something more striking, a cummerbund, or perhaps a dashiki. He tucked his right hand into his pocket and straightened out his tie with the other hand.

"Whenever you folks are ready," said Ken.

They all went into the largest of the buildings, the one with the square tower and the eye-in-the-triangle symbol. Inside there was no altar or anything of the sort. Ken took up a position at one end of the room and arranged Babs, Cecilia, Peter, and Ben in a row in front of him.

"I don't understand," said Ben. "Am I the best man or giving away the bride or what?"

"Oh, it doesn't matter. We just want the four of you standing up here."

The others sat down in folding chairs of the kind provided by chair rental companies, and the ceremony began.

Ken said, "In the name of the Affirmation, in the name of the Transcendent and the Immanent, in the name of Love, welcome, Brothers and Sisters. We are here to unite in matrimony our brother and sister, Peter and Cecilia. In the cycle of birth, life, and death, matrimony is one of the most sanctified of the Mysteries through which we pass on our journey toward the Infinite and our release from the burden of rebirth, which is called Nirvana. Peter and Cecilia have met in the world and have recognized their kinship of souls. All souls are but the expression of a single Soul, which is called Atman. We know that their bodies are drawn together too, and their minds. These things are good and we bless them. The body is the Temple of the Soul. Cecilia's body is a temple which Peter, the worshipper, enters in holiness. We bless this union and wish Peter and Cecilia joy of their bodies."

He stopped, as if to see if everyone agreed. Then he went on.

"Their minds too are joined in the most intimate of unions and have become one mind. Henceforth their minds are directed toward the pure and the beautiful, toward Love. In Peter's thoughts, Cecilia is holy, and Peter is holy in the thoughts of Cecilia. We will think of them in our thoughts, and wish them the happiness of the mind, in which gaiety is mingled with the solemnity of holy things. For the mirth of our children, Peter and Cecilia, is also part of the Infinite, along with the solemnity and the holiness of their love."

At this the two of them seemed really mirthful. They smiled at each other, and Cecilia made a little laugh. Perhaps it was some private joke that she and Peter had together.

Ken went on to souls.

"The union of their souls, which will last till infinity and has always been, is a mystery beyond the grasp of our terrestrial minds. But, if we cannot understand, we can bless and feel Love. The souls of Peter and Cecilia are in

Atman, the souls of Peter and Cecilia are Atman, and Atman is in them. We are happy for Peter and Cecilia in their bliss, which is only a foretaste of the bliss of Nirvana, which we shall all know when we are released from the cycle of rebirth. For all joy is in Love, Brothers and Sisters. If we love one another, if we love the Infinite in ourselves and in the world about us, then we shall prepare a place in the universe for the love of Peter and Cecilia. Let us then bless their love and wish them joy in it."

Ben inspected Ken a little more carefully. He seemed to be a perfectly ordinary person. Without the tuxedo and magenta tie he might have been a salesman or a stockbroker. The whole thing was crazy, yet to his surprise Ben couldn't find anything to object to in what Ken was saying about Atman, mirth, the union of minds, and bodies and temples. He still hadn't quite grasped what this was all about, that Cecilia was going to belong to Peter from now on and he himself wouldn't have her anymore. This idea caused him pain, but everything Ken said was so plausible and so beautiful that his petty pain seemed unimportant. What we must do, said Ken, was love the infinite in ourselves and in the universe, so we could prepare a place in the universe for the love of Peter and Cecilia. It was a good thing he had had a stiff drink in the patio before all this began; it made it easier to believe.

The rest of it was quite conventional. Do you Cecilia, and do you Peter, and so on. Ken said, "In the name of the Transcendent and the Immanent, in the name of the Mystery, in the name of the Most Holy, I pronounce you man and wife. And now Peter," he said, "embrace Cecilia, and in doing so lay your garlands at the door of the Temple. And now Cecilia, embrace Peter, and in doing so open the door to the worshipper who comes in holiness."

They embraced, and Ben saw there were tears standing in Cecilia's eyes. It was the second time he had observed this phenomenon in her, and both times were after she had met Peter. She may have been fond of him too, but he had not induced tears in her. When Peter let her go she wiped her eyes furtively with the back of her hand. There was no one to provide a tissue for her now, as he had in the bedroom of the house in Montecito. Who would look after her when he was no longer there to do it! Ben embraced Peter with one arm because his other hand was in his pocket, and Babs embraced Cecilia, a thing that according to Cecilia had never happened before in her whole life. It was a day of wonders and unprecedented things. A month ago, he would never have thought he would be standing here embracing Peter in front of a crowd of other people. Then in a flash of insight he realized what he was doing: he was forgiving Peter for what he did in his apartment with Cecilia, a thing that had made him feel rotten. And that was why Ted had put the four of them in a row, so that he could forgive Peter, and Babs could embrace Cecilia for the first time.

131.

The wedding feast, also arranged by Raymonde, consisted of margaritas, corn chips, and tacos. There was also some guacamole dip. Cecilia was hugged by various people. Peter shook a number of hands.

Ben found himself talking to Babs. "It seems a queer kind of a wedding," she said.

"Well, the young people arranged it all. We in the

older generation shouldn't interfere. When we were young we had our own ideas about things too."

"I wish you wouldn't talk that way. I'm not old and neither are you."

"I feel rather old today," said Ben.

"What happened with you and Cece?"

"Nothing. I was helping her with her musical career. She met Peter and they fell in love. Now they're getting married. I think that's wonderful."

"Oh, bullshit! Don't give me that. I've been around too long. I thought that you and I were going to be friends. I thought we could have a candid talk about what happened with you and Cecilia. The last time we met, in Oakland, I told you all that stuff about me and Harlan. And now you come out with this mealy-mouthed crap about how you're helping her with her career and you just love it that she's marrying this guy. You're a big disappointment to me, Professor." She went off to the buffet to refill her glass.

Someone had given Ben a margarita. The edge of the plastic glass was rimmed with salt. On top there was some white foam and underneath a thin whitish fluid that looked like whey. He got salt on his lips every time he took a sip, and this made him want to drink more. It wasn't long until the margarita was finished and someone gave him another one.

He followed around in a group including Peter, Cecilia, and the Rolfs to look at the grounds and the gardens. It was a clear winter day and there was a warm wind moving down to the sea from the mountains. Maybe this wind would be the leitmotif of Peter and Cecilia's love, like the hot wind that hurled Paolo and Francesca around clasped in each other's arms.

"Why is there a pool?" inquired Edgar.

"Perhaps," said Cecilia, "in case someone wants to be baptized by total immersion. They accommodate all requests here."

"Have a taco, anybody?" offered Raymonde, coming up with one in each hand. Cecilia took one and offered the other to Peter.

"No thanks."

"Mad with lust, he neither eats nor drinks," said Raymonde.

Ben took the taco, since nobody else wanted it. To do this he had to set his margarita on the flagstones so he could take it with his left hand. He was drinking too much anyhow; that was why he made a fool of himself with Babs Penn, a very sensible woman and a nice person.

"Can we expect a little Blessed Event in time?" asked Jo-Nan coyly. "Or don't young people believe in that anymore?"

Cecilia said, "Oh, we're going to fill up the backyard with children. Peter loves babies and so do I."

"I thought you were going to be a harpsichordist," said Jo-Nan in a malice typical of the Voronoff set. And she was one of the nicer ones.

"Oh, I'm going to do that too," said Cecilia, still blithe and mirthful.

This of course totally contradicted her earlier pronouncements on the subject of babies and what a disgusting nuisance they were. She really didn't have a mind, thought Ben. What she had instead of a mind adapted to every new situation like a chameleon. He felt a combination of tenderness and exasperation and realized for the first time what he was losing.

Dave the bellman had found someone to talk to, Ted Pickering. God knew what they were talking about. He had made no effort to speak to Cecilia. Babs Penn was over by the wall sulking with her drink. Ken joined their circle, smiling and holding his wrist in front of him in his hand. He didn't have a drink, but he took a taco when Raymonde brought him one. They chatted on for a while about Atman and Nirvana, about the meaning of the logo of the church, the triangle with the eye in it, and about the weather.

"It's a beautiful day. Happy is the bride that the sun shines on."

"It's this offshore wind that's warmed things up," said Ben. "It's caused by a high pressure system inland. The air is warmed as it passed over the desert," he heard himself going on, "and then it comes down out of the mountains onto the coast. It's called a santana."

"Ben is so useful to have around," said Cecilia. "If you ask him the least thing, he explains the universe and gives three examples."

They went on walking around the patio, admiring the cacti and the rock gardens. When they arrived at the entrance of the church again Ken left them. He said, "Have a happy trip, you two."

"Thanks, we're going to Hawaii."

"Well, I meant your initiation into wedded bliss."

"Oh," laughed Cecilia, "that's old stuff for Peter and me."

132.

In the hotel in Hawaii she stands naked in front of Peter and lets her hair fall down on all sides of her head, covering her face. She crosses her arms over her breasts, grasping her upper arms just below the shoulders. Her hair, blond with tints of auburn, clings together in strands like the hair of Botticelli's Venus. The posture of her arms clinging to the front of her body is also that of this famous painting. She tilts her head slowly, slowly to one side. On the low side the hair clings to her face for a while, then it falls away, revealing single grave eye and an ear as fine as a *Murex beaui*, a rare tropical shell. In the triangle formed by the fallen hair and the hair that still hangs over her face, her beauty spot glows like a dot of amber. Under the influence of the Hawaiian setting, her hips tilt this way and then the other way, as slowly as a clock, a hula in microscopic slow motion.

Ben imagined all this.

133.

On Wednesday evening, the Wednesday after Christmas, when Peter and Cecilia were still away in Hawaii, the pianist was back but instead of Gershwin it was Cole Porter and Rogers and Hart. The Voronoffs had evidently lost their interest in classical music, or perhaps they thought their guests had. Betsy, as far as he knew, was still a member of the board of the chamber music society. So was he, Ben, although neither of them had been to a meeting of the board for months. Perhaps it no longer existed. The two white borzois were lying on the carpet as usual, and there were jumbo prawn canapés at the bar.

Carolyn said, "You know, I've always been fond of you, Ben. Of course we all have. You're one of the regulars. You've been around for such a long time."

"I don't know whether I should take that as a compliment or not."

"Hamlet says we should bear those ills we have rather than fly to others we know not of. I imagine you've found that out."

"I didn't know you were a Shakespearian scholar."

"It's a well-known quotation."

"Then I'm an ill you put up with?"

"All other people are. They're all imperfect. We don't notice that at first sometimes."

She was wearing her long gray gown with a silvery cast to it again. It perfectly complemented her complexion, which was that of rare Chinese porcelain. With her dark lashes and her dark eyes, and the single brighter note of her pale-red lips, she resembled many things Chinese, a Chinese ink-drawing on pale rice-paper, and the pale lips were the signature done in red with a little stamp carved from stone.

"What is the ill that I flew to that I knew not?"

"Don't be so dense, Ben."

"I can assure you that I took nothing but joy from the whole encounter."

"What do you plan to do with your life now?"

"Do with my life? I'm going on exactly as I did before."

"You can never do that. Everything that happens to us changes us. At any given point, we're the sum of our experiences."

"You see, Carolyn, I'm basically a pessimist and that helps a lot. I never expect anything good to happen to me, so when it does it's a pleasant surprise. If something bad happens, it's about what I expected."

"If you don't expect good things, then they'll never happen."

"If you don't expect the worst, then you won't be prepared for the bad things when they happen."

"What if you're not prepared for the bad things?" she countered with a smile. "You're happy for a time at least."

"You're telling yourself a lie."

"There are all kinds of lies. There are things called white lies, and other lies that make people happy, or allow them to go on being happy. The lie of the cancer surgeon to the patient. The lie of the lover to the ugly woman. Suppose a wife isn't faithful to her husband. Where ignorance is bliss, it's folly to be wise. The husband is better off as long as he believes he's better off. The lie makes him believe he's happy, which is the same thing as being happy."

"Or a wife whose husband is unfaithful."

"Are you talking to me about Arnold and Raymonde?"

"Oh, Carolyn."

"I know all about that, if that's what's bothering you."

She was really a very wise woman, and very attractive. Ben imagined it would not be very difficult to get to know her better. Since she knew about Arnold and Raymonde, there would be nothing whatsoever wrong about it for either of them. The trouble was that he was still in love with Cecilia.

134.

"How's the novel going?"

"I don't want to talk about the novel, old fellow. I want you to tell me something. Was it from me that you got the idea of giving away Cecilia to Peter Barstow?"

Ben and Ilya were in the library, both of them holding a cognac. Ben's right hand was in the pocket of his flannel trousers, where it was concealed by a fold of his navy blue blazer. The blazer had gold buttons on it, and he really only wore it to kid Ted Pickering, who dropped out of the Navy because he had no chance of becoming an admiral. Ilya was wearing an identical blazer and gray flannel pants. They might have been tap-dancers, or twins in a comedy team, except that they lacked the straw hats.

Ben countered the question cautiously, "I don't follow you."

"At the Ritz bar in London, I told you that Moritmer realizes he's too old to hold Fenicia. Eventually she's going to fall to some younger man. So Mortimer arranges her to fall in love with his assistant in the publishing firm, a young man named David. This way he'll always have her around, and he can even kiss her now and then in a fatherly way. The three of them, Mortimer, David, and Fenicia, joke about this."

Ben said nothing.

"Eh? Nature copies art. The leaves of the climbing plant grow up beside the leaves carved in stone. That's from Proust."

"You're out of your mind. You know nothing whatsoever about the matter. I forbid you to talk in this way about Cecilia."

"We're talking about Fenicia. But you see, old man, I've changed all that. That whole business has been cut out of the novel. In the new version Mortimer dies and Kostya and Fenicia have a love affair."

"I know. I heard you telling Cecilia about it. They make love on Mortimer's grave. To my mind, the whole thing is in very poor taste and I forbid you to publish it."

"You listened to something you weren't supposed to hear. That's really caddish, old fellow."

"You're sore because you made some kind of proposition to Cecilia and she wasn't interested."

"Mortimer really is dead, you know, old man. And you are too. You're dead below the waist. That's why you had to give Cecilia away to Peter. And now they're in Hawaii, making love on your grave."

Ben remembered what it was in London he had promised himself he was going to do. He set his cognac down on the table and hit Ilya hard in the face, with his left hand. His other arm came up out of his pocket and dangled grotesquely; it gave him no help.

Ilya made a kind of a squeal, a high-pitched girlish "Oh!"

135.

"Did you really hit him, Ben? I didn't see it."

"I saw it," said Edgar Rolf. "Jo-Nan and I were standing on the other side of the room talking to Ted. He just walloped him with his good hand. I don't think it hurt Ilya very much."

"He gave out a bleat like a stuck pig," said Jo-Nan.

"Do we have to go over and over this?" said Ben. "It just happened. I wish it hadn't."

"Why did you do it?"

"Because I had too much to drink. We always do at these affairs."

They were all gathered around the bar: the Rolfs, Ted Pickering, Betsy, Raymonde, and Ben. Ilya was nowhere in sight; he was probably in the bathroom looking at his face. Carolyn was in the living room talking to Ethel and Snoozy Pickering. Arnold wasn't present; he was off on another trip to the Far East.

"What did he say that made you mad?"

"We were talking about Cecilia. He said a really dirty thing and I couldn't take it."

"What was it he said?"

"It's too dirty to repeat."

"I can't believe that of Ilya. He may do certain things, but his language is always perfectly correct."

"It wasn't the language."

"Where are Peter and Cecilia, anyhow, Ben?" asks Jo-Nan innocently. "I haven't heard anything about them."

"They're staying in a small hotel in Lahaina. They'll be back next week."

"And they're going to live in the Big House in Montecito? And you're going to live in the Little House?"

"That's right."

"H'mm."

Everybody smiled.

"You see," said Ben, "there are some misconceptions about me and Cecilia. My interest in her is purely selfless. I bought the house because the annex came with it. Cecilia had her harpsichord there, and she lived there. Now we've all just switched houses. I'll move into the Little House and she and Peter can have the Big House."

The others exchanged glances.

"You went to Europe with her," said Jo-Nan.

"They have twin beds now in most of the hotels in Europe."

This produced a round of laughter, and Ben joined in.

"Who are you kidding, Ben?"

"I'm not kidding anybody." This was an unreal conversation, Ben thought. They all knew he had been Cecilia's lover, and that it had been an excruciating blow for him to let her go. Now, as though the whole thing were a joke, they were discussing whether they should let him pretend that it was not so. Some were in favor of letting him pretend, others not. And why did he wish to pretend it was not so? In defense of Cecilia's honor, a very old-fashioned idea. He told them, "I'm very fond of Cecilia and I'm happy that she's married Peter. I'm interested in her musical career, and I'm going to go on helping her with it, just as I have from the beginning."

"Well, we have to believe Ben," said Ted Pickering. "There are a few altruists left in the world, and maybe he's one of them."

"Do you really imagine that an old duffer like me could lose his head over a girl her age? I'm not that foolish."

"We're all pretty foolish. It's no disgrace to be foolish."

"We drink too much," said Ben. "We've fallen into bad habits at these Wednesdays. We ought to come to our senses and behave like grown-up people instead of a bunch of high-school kids who've discovered alcohol for the first time."

"I think you're absolutely right, Ben," said Betsy a little unsteadily. "People do ghastly things when they drink too much. And not just at the Wednesdays. Ben himself, for example, in London—"

"Shut up, Betsy."

Everyone knew about this now too, but he didn't want her blurting it out in front of them all. To his surprise she did shut up. With a smile at the others, she turned wise and silent, as wise and silent as you could look when you'd had three or four vodkas on the rocks.

From somewhere in some other part of the house there was a pop like that of a champagne cork. Ted Pickering pricked up his ears, and a moment or two later he unobtrusively slipped away. The others went on talking.

"They must be having fun in Hawaii. To be young in a small hotel in Lahaina!" Jo-Nan just couldn't help needling Ben.

"We haven't been to Hawaii in years," said Edgar Rolf.

"Didn't we go there on our honeymoon, Jo-Nan? No, that was later. We went to Europe on our honeymoon. Paris, Munich, and Vienna. We made it into a buying trip too. Brought back a bunch of antiques and made a bundle out of them. That's what really launched us into the import business."

"How romantic."

"Erica and I went to Mexico on our honeymoon," said Ben. "Acapulco and Puerto Vallarta. I don't recommend it. We both got turista."

"Who? Oh, your first wife."

"I've only had one."

"George and and Chopin got turista when they were in Venice together. Or was that Alfred de Musset?"

"Anyhow, I don't recommend it for a honeymoon," said Ben.

Ted Pickering came back and took Ben and Edgar by the elbows. "Listen, guys, come over here, will you? Betsy and Raymonde and Jo-Nan, you stay away. I'm going to tell a very dirty joke and I don't want you to hear it."

"It must be awfully dirty if we haven't heard it."

Ted drew them away to a corner of the living room. He said, "Keep everybody out of the library. Especially Raymonde and Betsy. The fact is that Ilya has shot himself."

They went to the door and looked. As though gripped by an invisible muse, Edgar Rolf cried out involuntarily, "People don't do such things!"

Ilya was lying on the floor of the library near the table, in an extraordinarily awkward position, one leg crumpled sideways and his elbow bent under his chest. A piece of his skull in the back was missing and bright red paint had oozed from it and formed a pool under his head, glistening slickly. The small automatic pistol, as tiny as a toy, was still in his hand. Near him was the overturned cognac glass, as though he had held it in his hand until the last moment. Luckily the blood had covered the side of his face that was visible and you could not tell much about his expression.

136.

Ben had lost track of time but it was late at night now, halfway to morning. He drove home alone, opened the garage door with the little transmitter clipped to the sun visor of the car, and pulled the car in next to Cecilia's Honda, which was a little dusty since she'd been away for a week. At the bottom of the garage the headlights illuminated an old real estate sign left behind by Stacey, a folding lawn chair, and a stack of newspapers which he was saving to give to a recycling organization. He shut off the car and went into the Little House. It was very dark. There was no moon.

He felt wobbly and things seemed unreal. After all the police cars with flashing lights, the ambulance, the strangers pushing into the house to take pictures and carry in their ominous gurney, the endless repetitive questions, the wakeful and excited, numbed conversations of the witnesses in the street outside afterwards, he was very tired. He switched on the lights as he went from the living room to the tiny kitchenette, and automatically, without thinking what he was doing, fixed himself a drink. He was cold sober now and he hadn't drunk since midnight. But the idea of swallowing alcohol made him feel physically ill. He left the glass standing on the kitchen counter and went back to the toy-sized living room.

What to do? No chance of sleeping. He could knock

himself out with some powerful pill, but he had never believed in such things and there was nothing of the sort in the house. He put a tape into the stereo and started it up. Handel's *Music for the Royal Fireworks* filled the small room, and he sat down on the sofa with his withered arm resting on his leg and the other one next to it. The harpsichord had already been moved into the Big House, but they hadn't yet moved the Canaletto on the wall behind it. The gondolas drifted by on the grayish-green water, and a Dutch ship was becalmed in the middle distance; beyond it was the tacky Dogal palace, which looked like a movie house in Peoria. What was that ominous cloud hanging in the sky to the left? He had never noticed it before. Something was happening over there beyond the city, and Canaletto had put it into his painting, wondering if anyone would notice. It was a cloud of pestilence, a plague. Perhaps he, Ben, was the first one to make this discovery.

The music seemed boring and jangly. He shut off the stereo, stood thinking for a minute, looked for a key in the drawer of the desk, and went outside. It was midwinter and it would still be dark for three hours. To the west he could see the loom of the town over the hills, a band of frozen grayish light.

The Big House was only a black shape in the starlight. With some difficulty—he hadn't lived in this place very long—he made his way through the pitch-black garden and around the house to the front. There was a night light on inside, and the keyhole was illuminated by a tiny light above it. With the key, which he had kept after he moved into the Little House, he opened the door and let himself in.

When he switched on the lights he had an odd feeling of disorientation. Even though he knew that the furniture had been moved and all his things were now in the Little House, he had half expected everything to be as it was, his stereo and books in the living room and his clothes in the closet. The harpsichord with its yellow rosebuds was in the corner of the living room, with the Daumier prints on the wall behind it. The lid was shut and there was no music in sight; the harpsichord might have been merely a decoration, part of the fake-antique furniture of the room. There was no sign that anyone could open it and make music come out of it with her fingers. On the dining room table there was a vase of flowers, which had dropped brownish petals onto the polished walnut surface.

Still turning on lights, he went into the bedroom and tried to recall Cecilia as he knew her in this room. Her clothes were in the closet; the other side of the closet was empty. He found her tapered black pants, her oversized Irish sweater, the scarf she tied in her hair, the aqua dress with the spaghetti straps she wore in Paris. But she really wasn't there anymore. She was a ghost, and the bedroom was the room of strangers, a strange couple unknown to him. He was a burglar in a house where he didn't belong.

137.

Perhaps Ilya, in throes of composition (art is difficult), found that the inevitable course of his novel called for Kostya to commit suicide. He never mentioned such a scene, but books have a way of taking charge and going off on their own; the author doesn't always have control over them. What really interested Ilya at the end of his life was not the fiction itself but the possibility of writing a True Novel. He wanted to project his book into the world and manipulate people and make them do his will in real life, just as he did in fiction. The novelist is to his book as God is to the real world. Ilya was God in his book, and he believed he could be God in the real world too, that he could make the models for his fiction behave the way they did in the novel. But the book took charge and Kostya committed suicide. So Ilya had to do it too.

138.

Peter and Cecilia had been back from Hawaii for a month now. The Little House was the exact clone of the cottage at the Cantamar, and of the cabin near the main hotel where Ben stayed at Muir House. It was a small house where he lived alone, and nearby was a larger building with lights, people, life, and music. He could go there now and then, although it wasn't his permanent place and he didn't really belong there.

He had bought a small spinet piano similar to the one he had at the Cantamar; his books were in alphabetical order in the shelves with the various elements of the stereo equipment wedged around them, his records were catalogued, and the bedroom and kitchenette were in the same places in relation to the living room. The house was a little larger than the cottage at the Cantamar so he had some empty wall space. Perhaps he could get another bookcase, or a reproduction in a nice frame, one of Rembrandt's self-portraits, or a Vermeer with the light coming from the side and making interesting shadows. The Canaletto had been moved to the big house now, but he still had the Monet water lilies in the bedroom. He cooked his meals in the kitchenette, and one of these days he was going to have Cecilia and Peter over to dinner.

It was six o'clock now and it would be an hour before

he fixed his evening meal. He sat down at the spinet and got out a *Stuckchen* from Schumann's *Album for the Young*. These were only warm-ups, as Cecilia had said, but there were quite nice. They didn't have any leaps in the right hand so he could manage them. The *Stückchen* No. 5 was in C major so there were no sharps or flats. With his left hand he picked up his right hand and arranged it on the keyboard just above middle C. The right hand crawled back and forth on the white keys for practice, like an athlete warming up. He started off, following the fingering indicated to help the little girls. Most of the action was in the left hand; the right hand only played four notes per measure and went up and down like a rat wandering in a cage. He thoroughly enjoyed this *Stückchen* No. 5. He turned to the next one, No. 6, but it was a good deal more difficult. The right hand got stuck and had to be lifted up an octave by the left. He quit and put the music away.

139.

Betsy said, I told him he was a fool. I told him he had been a fatuous fool all his life and everyone knew it but him. He thought it over for twenty-four hours and then he went and did what he did. Ben hitting him in the face had nothing to do with it. It was because he was upset about what I said that he quarreled with Ben.

140.

In the weeks after Peter and Cecilia came back from Hawaii, the Turtle Press prospered. Since Peter lived rent-free in the house in Montecito, his money problems were solved. The Press got several books which were sure to be successful. A small press never makes big money, but at least one of these books would probably do quite well. It was the story of an old Indian shaman who was still around in Santa Barbara when the Americans took over California. He could see through walls and cure hysteria in women, and he predicted many wonderful things in the future, some of which actually came true. There were even a few primitive photographs of the shaman, taken in the Eighteen-Sixties at the end of his life.

141.

Do you know Kennedy, Ilya's doctor, said Edgar Rolf.

No, I don't think I do.

I know him a little. He and I belong to the same golf club. He couldn't say anything specific about Ilya, of course, but he did say something rather curious. He said, Maybe it's for the best. If an ordinary person said that, it might not mean anything. But if Ilya's doctor said it, it might mean that he knew something about Ilya that would explain what he did. Maybe Kennedy told Ilya some bad news. He knew that Ilya had something bad, like cancer of the colon, something that's not only terribly painful but disgusting and humiliating, and goes on for a year before it finally kills you. He might not have told Ilya that, but Ilya might have guessed it for himself. Ilya was very clever. He read everything, including medical books.

It's possible. Didn't they do an autopsy?

They have to in the case of a suicide. But all they have to do is state the cause of death. They don't have to mention that he had colon cancer as well.

142.

In his swimming trunks with an old polo shirt on over them, carrying a towel, Ben let himself out of the Little House and moved cautiously down along the hedge toward the pussy-willows that shielded the pool. He had heard splashing and laughter over there for some time. On the way he made a few coughs to indicate that he was coming and to avoid any danger of eavesdropping. When he came out through the willows he saw Cecilia going around the pool under water. Through the pale turquoise fluid he could clearly see that she was nude. Peter was pursuing her around the pool on the surface, trying to catch her and laughing. She popped to the surface in the shallow end of the pool, laughing too and pressing back her hair so that the water streamed in gushes from it. The water was only waist deep and her bare breasts were pointed toward Ben. They both turned to him, smiling only a little less, and Peter said, "Did you want something?"

"It's all right. It's nothing." He walked back to the Little House and got out J.L. Motley's *The Rise of the Dutch Republic*. It was a thick book and it would keep him occupied for quite a while.

143.

Carolyn said, I was talking to him about astronomy. I told him some things about infinite distances and the gradual cooling of the sun, and so on. It seemed to depress him. I wonder if it could have been because of that.

144.

Peter and Cecilia had invited Ben to dinner. There they were, in the large and well-equipped kitchen in the Big House, the two men sitting on blond-wood stools and watching Cecilia cut up things for stir-fry.

"What would you like, Ben? The drinks are there on the counter. *Faites comme chez vous.*"

They all laughed at this joke: just act as if the place were your own. Of course the house still belonged to him. He fixed himself a dry vermouth with ice and a twist. He was trying to cut down on the hard liquor. Cecilia had a little white wine and Peter a Scotch on the rocks, which was what Ben used to drink when he was drinking. Before he got married, Peter couldn't afford Scotch.

Cecilia was wearing her tapered black pants and oversized white sweater again. He wished she wouldn't do that. She had her hair up in braids but there were no flowers in them. It was a warm evening in the early spring, with a dry breeze coming down from the hills, Peter and Cecilia's leitmotif, in Ben's mind at least; he didn't know whether they knew about this. Peter said, "The shaman book has gone to the printer. It's going to be called *A California Wizard.* It could be as big as *Ishi*, which was also a book about Indians. That was published by the Cal Press, of course."

"Oh, don't talk shop," said Cecilia.

"Are you going to use lots of pictures?"

"Oh yes. They're the best thing about it. Those primitive old shots in high contrast all covered with splotches. They look like Matthew Brady."

"And they're black and white so they won't cost much."

"That's right."

"Oh, for heaven's sake," said Cecilia.

"How are you getting on, Cecilia? Are you learning anything from Egon?"

"I'm going to give my thesis concert in June. I hope you'll come."

"Of course. How could I not."

"Cecilia and I," said Peter, "can't tell you how grateful we are for the help you've given her."

"Put the things on the table, will you," she told Peter. She kissed him on the side of the mouth to induce him to do this.

"Good silver or ordinary?"

"The good, of course."

Peter set the table and then carried the things that Cecilia had cooked and put them on the table on some big blue tiles, which actually belonged to Ben. He had had them since he was married to Erica, and used them for years in the cottage at the Cantamar. The menu was curried lamb with rice and a vegetable stir-fry. The wine was all wrong but Peter and Cecilia didn't seem to notice. She had also put the wrong kind of almonds in the stir-fry; they ought to be slivered and not sliced.

"This is terrific, Cecilia," said Peter. "Where in the hell did you learn to cook like this?"

"Oh, from my mother. And from Ben."

This was a delicate subject and they passed on, leaving it behind. They never talked very much about the time when Cecilia was with Ben. The lamb was a little overcooked and mushy. Some people might not have noticed. Peter ate his with relish, and he took another helping of curry and rice. Cecilia ate delicately, cutting the fat off her lamb and setting it aside. She was still as thin as a model. Ben imagined her waist, her rib-cage, and her breasts inside the big white sweater.

"Do the two of you eat like this every night?"

"Oh, it's not always this terrific. But it's always good. Cecilia is a terrific cook."

It was hard to see how a man could be an editor of a publishing house and only use one adjective. He remembered that when he was with Cecilia he too picked up the vocabulary of her generation. In a minute, Peter would start saying super, or bitchin'. Cecilia didn't seem like a wife at all, except for her cooking. She still seemed a student, an intelligent and talented one, who talked a little more sensibly than the others. She and Peter behaved like two kids in love.

After dinner Cecilia played the harpsichord for the two of them. She was trying to master Dandrieu's *Premier livre de clavecin* for her thesis concert. It was the same thing she heard Brigitte Haudebourg play in Paris. It was very difficult and she had to stop now and then and start over, but her technical mastery was improving. He could see now that the Couperin and Scarlatti she played when he first met her were only for beginners. She finished off with one of the *Goldberg Variations*, which she now knew almost by heart. When she finished Peter said "Terrific" and Ben applauded by patting his left hand down onto his right which was outstretched on his leg.

"I ought to be going," he said. "I've got some reading to do. I'm in the middle of Motley's *Rise of the Dutch Republic*."

"Won't you stay for cognac?"

"No thanks." He wondered what happened to Ilya's excellent cognac. He always served it in a decanter, because he said that if people knew how much it cost it would make them unhappy. It was probably just ordinary Hennessy.

Peter and Cecilia went arm-in-arm to see him to the

door. "It's still early. What are *we* going to do tonight?" Peter asked her as though Ben weren't there.

"I don't see any reason to vary the usual routine."

"You don't want to go out to a movie?"

"Oh no. Good night, Ben," she called out to him as the door shut.

145.

The question is what a person who shoots himself in the head feels, or whether he feels anything at all. For example, does he hear the sound of a shot. It is possible that such a person remains conscious for as long as a second. If so, what he feels in that second doesn't even bear thinking about.

146.

It was the beginning of June now, only two weeks from her concert. The three of them had been swimming and now they were lying around the pool sipping wine coolers. Cecilia had her bikini on this time, since Ben was present. It didn't cover very much of her, but oh what a difference.

"What have you been doing, Cecilia?"

"I'm still working on that damned Dandrieu."

"She's getting a lot better," said Peter. "It's a terrific piece of music. You know, I'm really fond of baroque." Before he met Cecilia, he said he liked Philip Glass and John Cage.

"Cecilia, did you know that Maurice Merleau is coming to the University as Artist in Residence next year?"

"Yes. I heard it from Egon. How did you know? It's still supposed to be a secret."

"Ethel told me. She knows everything that's going on."

"He's the greatest. I think it's terrific that he's coming here."

"So now you can do your master classes right here at the University."

"In a way I'm disappointed. I'd like to spend a year in Europe. But this way I won't have to leave Peter. He couldn't go, of course, because he has to stay here and take care of the Press."

"That's right. You know, I wouldn't want you to go away either."

"I do love you, Ben."

Gathering up her towel to go into the house, she allowed him to give her a fatherly kiss. Peter looked on indulgently.

147.

Cecilia said, He wanted me to play a part in his True Novel. In this novel, he was Kostya and I was Fenicia. He wanted me to become his mistress and make love in a cemetery. He said he had a Slavic soul. I told him I wasn't interested. Then I married Peter, and went away to Hawaii. It was while we were gone that he did it.

148.

The phone rang and it was Ethel.

"Is this you in the Little House? I got the number from Peter. It seems they have your phone now and you have a new one."

"Hello. What's new, Ethel? I haven't talked to you for some time."

"I have some interesting news for you. You won't believe it. Carolyn Wong has been exposed as a fraud. She's not an astronomer after all; she's only the secretary of the Astronomy Department at the University. She got all those things she told us from the professors in the department. To think of all those years that she fooled us!"

"She certainly fooled me. She used to scare the hell out of me by talking about the Nemesis Theory and Arthur Godfrey shows coming from outer space."

"You know, she got that Arthur Godfrey thing out of a science fiction novel by Gregory Benford. It's called *Across the Sea of Suns*."

"I don't read science fiction."

"You ought to; you can learn a lot from it. The question arises whether Arnold knew that Carolyn was a fraud or whether he thought she was really an astronomer."

"I don't think Arnold has a very great interest in the details of Carolyn's life. He has other things on his mind."

"I know all about him and Raymonde, if that's what you're talking about. You know, Ben, I know everything."

"You're the sibyl of the Voronoff set. Of course, all those other things Carolyn told us about the stars may still be true. Just because she herself is a fraud that doesn't mean that everything she said is wrong."

"That's true, I never thought of that. I wish you hadn't pointed it out. I breathed a sigh of relief when I heard the news, thinking that we didn't have to be scared by all

those things. Now it seems it doesn't make any difference."

"According to the Nemesis Theory we have a long time yet, Ethel. Eight million years."

"I don't expect to see it. I haven't been feeling very spry lately."

149.

Ilya's new novel, the second volume of his trilogy, was published about a week before his death and received mixed reviews, some of them devastating. He showed no sign on the surface that this bothered him.

150.

Ben and Cecilia were having lunch at the Vision of Siam in Isla Vista. The old spotted koi were still swimming around in the pond outside, exactly as they were when he first came with her almost a year ago. They ordered the usual mee krob, stuffed chicken wings, and mint salad, along with cardamon-flavored tea. Cecilia seemed pensive and preoccupied; not pensive, exactly, but preoccupied.

"Peter doesn't mind your having lunch with me?"

"Oh no. After all you're an old friend of his. You've known him longer than you have me."

This seemed so obvious that he could hardly imagine why she was saying it. She must mean something else by it.

"Your concert was a great success."

"Yes, wasn't it."

"Everybody was there. Even old Egon cheered up and had a glass of sherry."

"He's a great teacher. But I think I've learned everything he has to teach me."

"Now you can look forward to a year of studying under Maurice Merleau."

"Yes." Her preoccupied look came back. It was really an abstract look, as though she were half-listening to distant voices and at the same times talking to him. "And there's something else too, Ben. You see, I'm pregnant."

He felt a little heavy place form in his chest. It was inevitable, he thought.

"What about your career? Your harpsichord? Studying with Marcel Merleau?"

"Nowadays they say you can Have It All."

"You've been reading those articles in magazines."

"I suppose I have. You know, when you're pregnant it affects your metabolism or something. I keep getting hot, then cold. Why did you ask me to wear this horrible white sweater and black pants? I'm getting so tired of this sweater. It's summer now and I'm sweltering inside it."

"You could take it off."

"I've got nothing on underneath it."

They both laughed.

"Anyhow," she said primly, "it wouldn't be suitable for a mother to appear half-naked in public."

"Unless she were suckling her babe. Are you going to suckle your babe, Cecilia?"

"I'm going to do everything to the babe that one does to babes. I'm going to wash it and feed it and clean the shit off of it and dress it up in clothes that I'll buy in very expensive shops."

"You told me once you didn't care for babies."

"Oh, your ideas change as you get older." (She was a year older now.) "Peter will make a terrific father," she went on, trampling blindly over the questions of whether he, Ben, would have made a terrific father. What she meant, of course, was that having a baby depended on who you had it with. She didn't realize what she was saying; she never had, in all the time he had known her. She was a staggering combination of the transparent and the enigmatic. You could see about an inch down into her as though she were glass, but then there was a mysterious core, black as night, shadowy and vague, that no one would even penetrate, not even Peter probably.

151.

After he had left her, in the car going back to his solitary existence in the Little House, he was plunged into thought, remembering every detail of their lunch together and particularly the way she talked now. *Super, cool, terrific, the greatest.* She had never talked this way when she was with him, even the first time they were together, on the hike to Moon Lake. She had instantly adopted his own language, the language of educated middle-agers. Then as soon as she married Peter she dropped this and went back to speaking naturally, in her own language. She was a linguistic chameleon, changing her speech effortlessly to fit that of the person she was with. And the lipstick that was the same color as her lips, her claim that she didn't like babies, her avowed lack of interest in clothes. The thought of her unconscious skill at dissimulating, the tissue of artifice she flung out around her so that you could not know what she really was, made him feel his old love for her like a knife-stab.

152.

The reasons for Ilya's suicide were ultimately mysterious. He had cancer of the colon, his reviews were bad,

Ben humiliated him in public by hitting him in the face, he made a play for Cecilia and she refused. It may just be that the novel of his own life didn't work out as he wanted to write it. Life is not a novel. There are no clear motivations, no clear motives, no clarity at all. There are only incidents, events, which we glimpse at the edges of our vision, and can't turn our heads quickly enough to see them clearly.

Life has no author unless you believe in God, and Ben did not.

153.

Ben and Arnold Schifter were walking on the beach, on the palm-lined stretch north of the Montecito bluffs. They had become quite good friends since Ilya died and since Carolyn's misfortune; they met once in a while for lunch or for a walk on the beach, as they were doing now. The reasons for this, Ben thought, were connected to Ilya's death. He realized now that Ilya was the best friend he had; this was a queer idea but it was true. And it was possible that Ilya was also the best friend that Arnold had. Now that Ilya was no more, they felt a gap in their lives and they filled it by seeing each other from time to time. They had more in common than either of them had previously thought. Ben had become familiar with all of Arnold's qualities: his long chin, his serious look, his habit of running his hand through his hair before he spoke.

They idled slowly along just at the edge of the water. The foam swept in in long sheets, and sometimes they had to skirt around it. Seagulls wheeled and cried overhead; there was a light breeze and the surf made a light crushing sound, so that the other noises, the voices of people on the beach and the cries of the gulls, came through it only as though through a filter. Two silly teenage girls passed them going the other way, very pretty, in bikinis. A little farther down the beach a woman about thirty was lying face down with her halter straps unfastened to tan her back. An attractive woman almost Ben's age came toward them, in a bikini with a light flowered wrapper over it, wearing a sun hat of the same material. They both turned their heads. She passed out of their field of vision to the rear.

"Lovely day," said Ben.

"Isn't it," said Arnold.

Some kind of unspoken communication passed between them. They exchanged glances, with a guilty look of complicity.

"They *are* pleasant to look at," said Ben. "And you know, no one can stop us from looking at them."

"No one. They can never pass such a law," said Arnold. "And isn't it glorious!" he went on eagerly as though a dam had burst. "We're damned lucky that we live in Santa Barbara so we can walk along here and see them wearing the stuff they wear on the beach. *They* think," he said, "that our obsession with them is dirty. At the very best they call it girl-watching, making a joke of it. But it's really an appreciation of the highest form of art. It isn't physical at all. It's purely speculative, appreciative, a tribute to beauty in its most pressing and essential form. Without this beauty there would be no human life and consciousness, no philosophy, no literature, no empires or cities."

"Do you think so?"

"Absolutely. All civilization is simply an expression of Goethe's formula: *Das Ewig-Weibliche zieht uns hinan.* The cultures that don't admire the beauty of women have no civilization. That's what drives us to do all these things, building cathedrals, composing symphonies, writing poems. Take art, classical art. Go into any museum, the Bargello or the Uffizi, and you'll see nothing but a paean to the Eternal Feminine. It may be sublimated into religion, or love of nature, or a fascination with the folds in clothing, but at the bottom it's just libido. That's why there are no great women painters. It's not their fault; they just don't admire female beauty as much as we do. Epstein was once asked what it took to make sculpture like his, and he said balls."

"Oh boy, don't tell that to the feminists."

"I'm telling it to you. Look, Ben, we can walk down the beach like this and it's like walking through the Grand Gallery at the Louvre. Each one is different and they're all pretty. God! it's wonderful. The whole world is a vast art museum where we can look at women."

Ben had to smile at the word museum. It was the second time Arnold had used it. "Do you see Raymonde much?"

"Yes, quite a bit. I'm hopelessly in love with her, you see."

"What do you do together?"

"Oh, I go to the Museum and we dance or do other things. Not *the* thing, but various things that she thinks up."

"Is that good enough for you?"

"No it isn't. But I'd rather have that little bit of her than nothing at all. At least no one else has her; I don't have to worry about that. Sometimes I think she hasn't got any sex-instincts at all, only ego-instincts. But she's so God-damned beautiful. The sheer size of her. It's overwhelming. It's more than a man can bear."

"Cecilia said you're part of her doll collection."

"That's right, I am."

“How did you get into this predicament anyhow? You met her at the Voronoffs, of course.”

“Not really. She must have been there at the Wednesdays when I first started going, but for some reason I never noticed her. At that time, of course, she was only a child. Then about two years ago she turned up in my class in International Relations at the University. The first thing I saw when I walked into the lecture hall was that platinum hair with the orange streak in it. She sat in the front row and crossed her legs; she was wearing a denim miniskirt. Of course, I was happily married to Carolyn. Anyhow, according to professional ethics I shouldn’t have anything to do with students. It wasn’t long until I was going out for coffee with her, and things went on from there. I had her only once, on my couch in the office during the noon hour. It wasn’t a success. I couldn’t do much, because she was so tremendous, and because I was afraid the secretary might come back from lunch at any time. Then shortly after that she graduated, and I got her the job at the Museum. I had to pull all kinds of strings to do it. I thought it would be a better place for us to meet. God, what a rotten idea that was. All this time, of course, I still loved Carolyn dearly. I still do.”

“Arnold, why do you do all these things? Putting on costumes. Dancing with her to the Victrola. Pretending you’re somebody else.”

“It’s the only way I can see her. I can touch her. I can see her take off her clothes and put on others. I can hold her in my arms. It’s not much but it’s all I have. Talk about erections. Ben, I have a collection that Masters and Johnson could put in a book.”

“You know, Arnold, you said it wasn’t physical, but it is physical.”

He sighed. "Yes, I know. I don't know why we say it isn't." They went on walking in silence for a while. Arnold dug into the sand with his toe and turned up a seashell. "Do you still see Cecilia a lot these days?"

"Yes, quite a lot."

"It's just like me and Raymonde."

"As you say," said Ben, "they can't stop us from looking at them."

"It isn't just Raymonde that bugs me," said Arnold. "It's all of them. Everything about them is so mysterious. Ordinary and yet mysterious. The way their eyes come in different colors. The way their bracelets clink. The colors they paint their fingernails. I'm very partial to pale pink myself, or silver. The posture they get into when they trim their toenails. Especially with no clothes on. They always trim their toenails with no clothes on, have you noticed that? How funny they are when they're asleep. How tiny their underwear is when they take it off. Those dresses they have where their waists are low, around the knees, and the others where their waists are high, just under their breasts. They can move their waists up and down as though they were something they owned. Those tiny shoes they can get into, and then walk around on two needles. The various lengths they wear their stockings. Just above the knee, or just below the knee, or ankle-socks, or clear up almost to the you-know-what. The way their hair swings when they turn. The way they lift their arms when they're combing their hair." Or braiding flowers into it, thought Ben. Arnold plunged on, a helpless victim of his litany. "The hollow under the foot. The way their hair shadows their neck. The veins inside the elbow. The hollow at the inside of their knees. Those two dimples on their back at either side, just above the bottom."

Ben felt that he could hardly match Arnold's experience. He had really only had two women in his life, Erica and Cecilia, and he had never once seen Erica trim her toenails or do anything else personal in front of him. Probably she had it done by a pedicurist. He tried to remember if he had ever seen Cecilia trim her toenails. Yes he had, and she had done it exactly as Arnold said, with her clothes off, sitting cross-legged on the bed. That night he had felt the clippings under him as he turned in the bed, and he had surreptitiously groped for them and slipped them into the pocket of his pajamas. He still had them, sealed in an envelope in his desk at the Little House. There was something primordial and satisfying in possessing in this way, in secret, a small part of the person he loved.

154.

He realized finally, now, what his encounter with Cecilia amounted to; it was simply his farewell to youth and beauty, a preliminary to his farewell to life itself. Because, before going off on the Ultimate Journey, you first have to leave your friends and their pleasant lighted rooms, their conversation, their pictures and their wine, and go to wait for some time in a gloomy railway station, among strangers and the smell of soot, or in an impersonal airport which is like something in a very modern play about Hell.

In time he would have to relinquish everything, as he had relinquished Cecilia. But not yet, not for a while. He still had his friends—some of them at least, one had gone—and he was in good health and emotionally young. He had Cecilia and Peter close at hand and satisfyingly dependent on him, just as he had planned. He couldn't hope to attract any more twenty-year-olds to himself, of course; that would be ludicrous (He was almost as anxious to avoid the ludicrous as he was to avoid pain). But he knew he was still attractive to women. This was proved by Betsy's behavior, for example, or Ethel's; or even by Carolyn in her silvery-gray gown telling him improbable fantasies in the starlight. He could still enjoy himself a great deal in his—in the time he had left. He refused even to think of the silly expression Golden Years.

He sat down with his drink (he had gone back to Scotch now) and reflected. There was all of his stuff, his books and stereo and records, and the engraving by Paul Klee. The tiny house seemed cramped to him now; it had been a mistake to live with Cecilia in the Big House even for a few months. He had lost his habit of austere monasticism. Happiness was a dangerous drug; once you had tried it you wanted more and more.

But you have your friends, he told himself.

Arnold. Arnold was nice, witty and ironic, a good conversationalist, a Victim of Love like himself. Steer away from Betsy. That way lay nothing but trouble; at least he was smart enough to know that. Ted Pickering and Snoozy—entertaining, slightly comic figures in a film. The Rolfs. Boring really. How many years he had gone on exchanging banal gossip with them, twitting them about their faults and being twitted by them, talking to them about the import-export business! Who else was there? He could have a romance with old Mrs. Galleon. She'd probably be tickled. It would liven up her Golden Years. She might put out more flags, chirp in more melodious tones, wear even more flamboyant and bizarre clothes. Ben Franklin had something about the advantages of making love to old women. Put a basket over their heads, he said, and you could hardly tell the difference. He smiled sardonically at his own joke. Too bad there wasn't anybody around to appreciate it.

Ethel. He had forgotten Ethel. She was really a good person, wise in her way and not without her own sort of originality, and she had been fond of him for years. He thought of her special aviary effulgence, her exophthalmic eyes, her melancholy wit, the silver lamé dress she went out and bought because he told her to speak for herself. As he sat thinking of how long he had known Ethel it almost made tears come into his eyes. One by one he reviewed the half-dozen items of her wardrobe; she had worn the same clothes for years. The old tweed skirt and jacket which she wore for walking. The navy blue suit and the rather mannish sort of shirt that went with it. A white dress with a black collar and a row of large black buttons down the front, which made her look like Punchinello in a comedy. And the silver lamé dress, which clung to her body and showed that she still had quite a respectable figure. He had always been partial to long sheaths that were beltless and clung loosely around the waist. At the end of this catalogue of Ethel's qualities he remembered her fringe of bristly hair like a crown, the tuft of an elegant zoo bird. He felt a stir of—what? Not desire exactly. Affection.

They could have lunch on the terrace at the Cantamar, or even at the Vision of Siam; she would think the funky little Thai restaurant was funny. They could go to Muir House for the weekend, or they could even go to Europe together. London. Paris. The French Riviera. Or Venice; Venice, he decided, was exactly the place for Ethel. She looked like something in a Venetian painting, a Bellini, with her long neck, her pop eyes, and her air of looking at you as though she knew she was somebody and didn't care what you thought. Her decadent elegance.

Once he thought about taking Ethel to Venice the whole thing began to crystallize. He was attracted by the absolute normality of going about the world with Ethel, staying in hotels with her, and taking her to restaurants; no one would notice them, and there would be no glances, ironic, arch, or disapproving. This kind of normality attracted him in the way a large warm sleepy double bed might, smelling of freshly washed linen. It would all be so restful. He would not have to worry about some Clive or Walter Thorne getting interested in her. He and Ethel, defying time and mortality, would flaunt their Glad Rags through all the capitals of Europe. They would be friends, companions, and co-conspirators in the battle of life, and he could even imagine folding her in his arms. He had a premonition that Ethel unclothed would lose none of her ostrich elegance, in fact it would even be enhanced; clothes, he knew now with a sudden conviction, were never intended for Ethel.

He owed a lot to Ethel for her patience over all the years. All those telephone calls. Her offer to select pictures for his house. She had good sense about art. What a waste the world had made of Ethel! To think of her spending all those years as an art librarian. Under other circumstances she might have been an Edith Sitwell, or Eleanor of Aquitaine, an odd-looking woman who commanded the attention of millions.

155.

Ethel lived in a small house surrounded by neatly kept flowers, in the hills up near the Mission. It was late on Sunday afternoon and she wouldn't be working at the library. Ben drove up the road and slowed down to identify the place; he had only been here once or twice and it was a long time ago. It was a little farther along, he thought. Finally he found it, a frame house painted white with green trim. At the next house a man was watering down his lawn with a hose. On the other side of the street the hills sloped away to a flat bench with the town on it, and beyond that was the sea. You could see the sea from just about anywhere in Santa Barbara.

As he started to park the car he saw that Betsy's mint-colored Jaguar was standing in the driveway. He hesitated, and almost decided to drive away and come back some other time. Instead he parked in front of the house, nodded to the man watering his lawn, and went down the driveway past the Jaguar. He proceeded cautiously; he could hear voices from the back yard.

At the end of the driveway, connecting the garage with the house, was a grape arbor with a small arched opening in it. At this time of year, in early summer, the vines were fully leafed out but the grapes were immature. He stopped at the arbor and looked through the screen of leaves into the back yard.

It was like looking into a theater set for a light comedy about life in small-town America. There was a small square of lawn, framed by the house on one side, the garage on another, and flowerbeds on the remaining two sides. Betsy and Ethel were lying face down looking at something black and colored on the grass. They were both wearing shorts, and their two behinds stuck up as people's do when they're lying face down on a hard surface. Betsy was facing away from him and her topknot was visible from the back, over the lightly bifurcated mound of her rear. They were only twenty feet away from Ben. Because of the way they were lying on the grass he couldn't see their faces, but he could clearly identify the two voices, Betsy's suave contralto with its English accent and Ethel's reedy bird-call. He was eavesdropping again, he realized. He had three choices. He could sneak away and go to his car, he could stand there behind the grape leaves spying on them, or he could burst in on them with a cheery greeting as though he had expected Betsy to be there all along.

He did the third. He walked around the arbor and said in an easy tone, "Hello, Betsy and Ethel."

"Why, look who it is!" shrieked Ethel.

They both rose up from their prone position and brushed the bits of grass off themselves. Betsy was wearing tan shorts and an orange tank top, but Ethel was not exactly wearing shorts as he had thought. She was wearing an extraordinary kind of sun suit that looked as though it were really designed for a child of fourteen; it had straps over the shoulders, a square neck with a middy-blouse flap over the back, and pleated short pants like an Australian soldier. It bared her bony throat almost to her breasts, and it showed her legs to a point halfway above the knee. He had never seen her legs before in all the years he had known her; they were sinewy and speckled with tan, as though they were made of soft cordoban leather.

The two women stared at him. As soon as he saw the two of them together he had an insight into the tribal solidarity of women that he had never had before. It was far stronger than he had dreamed; it transcended all culture and civilization, all races, all centuries, it even transcended the species itself. He knew now that he had never understood them, not even one of them. His power of understanding had been blinded by his desire, by the veil of mystery they cast over themselves, that each of them casts over the others, that all of them cast over their tribe like a circus tent, like a huge, silken, coruscating, apparently transparent but actually opaque circus tent. He would never know what was inside the tent, he told himself.

"Ben, you haven't been here for years," cried Ethel with what seemed to him a touch of embarrassment.

"I don't remember when it was." He said, "Hello, Betsy" again, an idiotic thing to say since he had already greeted her, but she got the point at once. "I was just leaving." Her face was pink and there were red marks on her legs from lying prone on the tough grass. "I'm sure Ethel will be delighted to talk to you." She tinkled her little laugh. "I'll just be in the way. It's late anyhow; I'm going out to dinner. I would just be *de trop*," she said again in a ringing affected voice. "Goodbye. About seven, Ethel."

Waving as she went, she vanished behind the grape arbor in the direction of her car.

Ethel smiled. She too had red marks on her legs from lying on the grass. On the lawn, just beyond the indentations left by their two bodies, there was an art portfolio with colored pictures strewn around it on the grass. They had evidently been looking at them drinking; there were two tall glasses on the lawn nearby, one tipped over and the other with a half-inch of pale fluid in it.

She followed the direction of his glance and flushed a little, it seemed to him. "Would you like a drink?"

"No thanks. I just came by on impulse, Ethel. I thought—"

"It's so nice to see you. We've been looking at some watercolors by D.H. Lawrence. They're originals, terribly valuable. I'm afraid they're not very nice." She shut the portfolio quickly, but not before he caught a glimpse on one picture of an out-of-focus penis emerging from fuzzy foliage.

"Ethel, where on earth did you get them?"

"They were sent from England for an exposition on campus. I'm not supposed to have them, of course. They're supposed to be locked in the vault over the weekend. I'll take them back tomorrow."

"Ethel, I just came by on impulse. I haven't seen you for a while, since the Wednesdays stopped. I thought you might be free for dinner."

"Dinner? When?"

"Tonight. It's about six now. We could have a drink—well, I said I didn't want a drink. We could talk for a while and then go out early, about seven."

"Tonight, as a matter of fact, I have an engagement for dinner. But—" she said. She seemed to hesitate.

"It doesn't matter. It could be any night. I just came by on impulse. Ethel, there's something I want to tell you."

"I can imagine what it is. The Rolfs are splitting up. Isn't that it?"

For some reason this horrified him. "Ethel, what are you saying? How do you know that?"

"Oh, I know it all right. They're splitting up as a couple, but they're staying together for business purposes. They're not getting along personally but they can't afford to keep two establishments. That's the way it is with so many people these days. To me it seems against human nature. How can they do such a thing? I mean go on living in the same house."

"It seems unnatural to me too. Ethel, I came by to tell you something else. We should see more of each other. Now that there are no more Wednesdays. I've been thinking of you lately and thinking about—how we should see more of each other," he finished lamely.

"Oh, I am fond of you, Ben. I often think about you too. You're perfectly right that we should see more of each other. And I have an idea about that too."

"We have so many interests in common. For example, you like Muir House. I can imagine us going there together some time."

"You mean overnight?"

"Of course."

The color sprang into her cheeks. "Why, Ben, I couldn't imagine doing such a thing. What in the world do you think I am? I'm an old maiden lady, Ben, and you're not exactly a spring chicken either."

"I'm sorry. I didn't mean anything improper. I just thought—"

"It's perfectly clear what you thought. It seems that you had an affair with Cecilia, and an affair with Betsy in London, and now you want to have an affair with me. Isn't that it?" She was still perfectly calm, although the color had not left her cheeks.

"We can talk about it at dinner."

"I told you I wasn't free for dinner. You evidently weren't listening. Betsy is coming back for me at seven. She's just gone home to change. And I'll have to change too."

"I've never seen you in an outfit like that. Ethel, what is your idea?"

"My idea?"

"Yes, when I said we ought to see more of each other you said you had an idea."

"Oh, I see. Well, Betsy says there won't be any more Wednesdays because it would be too sad, all the memories in the big house. So I've decided to have them here."

"Have them here?"

"Yes, in this little house. Won't that be fun? The same

people except not quite so many. Raymonde won't come of course. And I've never quite seen the point of Carolyn Wong and Arnold Schifter. Anyhow, as we know, Carolyn has turned out to be dishonest. And Arnold Schifter has a *very* strange relationship with that Voronoff girl."

"Raymonde."

"Yes, Raymonde. I think I don't call by her first name because it implies I know her better than I do."

"What about Peter and Cecilia?"

"No, no young people, I think. Just ourselves. Won't that be nice? We can all talk. You see, Ben, I do like to find out about what all kinds of people are doing, and then tell these things to other people. And I wouldn't be able to do that nearly as well if it weren't for Wednesdays, so I'll have to have the Wednesdays here. That's what I really do love, finding out about the hidden stories in people's lives. It's so fascinating and everyone has a story that's going on in his life but nobody knows it but him. Or her, as the case may be. That's my mission, you see. Finding the stories in people's lives."

"That's what Ilya did."

"No, he made up stories in his mind, and then tried to apply them to the people around him. They didn't fit and that's why he—did what he did."

"Are you free for dinner next Sunday, Ethel?"

"I don't think so. I don't think I'm—free at all. I don't know how to explain it, Ben, but that's how it is. And now I have to go and dress. It's so nice you came. I'm sorry you didn't have a drink. I am fond of you, Ben. I've always valued your friendship. It's been so precious to me. I want it to go on exactly as it is. And now I have a wonderful story about you, too, don't I? To tell to other people."

156.

You old fool, he told himself. He almost had to laugh. Ethel would tell everybody about this, as she threatened. There was a deep strain of malice in her that he had never suspected. She would start with Betsy, of course, and then it would spread to everybody in the Wednesday circle, from the Rolfs down to old Mrs. Galleon. They would bandy the story around for months and twit him about it. Even Cecilia and Peter would hear about it. It served him right for imagining a bright, or at least rose-colored, future for himself. He had betrayed his principles as a pessimist. He would never make that mistake again.

He was driving down from the Mission district along a winding road that would come out after a couple of miles on the coast highway. The car hardly made any noise because it was going downhill. In the distance the setting sun glinted on the sea like molten silver; it hurt his eyes. Just before he came to the highway he passed a couple walking along the road hand in hand. They looked like high school kids. As they dropped behind into the rear-vision mirror he remembered there were some sunglasses in the glove compartment and he reached for them, still rolling slowly down the road. To do this he had to lean far over and open the glove compartment with his left hand, while his right arm dangled and got in the way. He found the sunglasses, splayed them open with a trick of the one hand he had learned, and pushed them onto his face. The first thing he saw, through a glow like soft pink molasses, was a tree coming up slowly to the right fender. Before he could do anything the car lurched down on the right and the tree came to a stop against the window with a sickening metallic crunch, followed by a tinkle of glass.

Even though the car was moving slowly he lurched forward and struck his chest on the steering wheel. The sunglasses fell off and he was unable to find them. The glint of the sun on the sea was a pain like a knife.

He opened the door and got out. The car was tilted down into the ditch like a careened ship, and the young couple were loping up from behind, still hand in hand. It struck him how curious it was that they could run to assist somebody in an emergency and still exchange a caress, one of the mysteries of sex. In the hope of concealing the fact that he only had one good arm he got back in the car and tried to start it. He didn't have to do this because he found the engine was still running.

"Hi, sir, can we help?" asked the boy.

He was in swimming trunks and thong sandals. The girl was wearing a black bikini, a round straw hat with a black ribbon that hung down her back, and babyish Buster Brown sandals with straps. They both looked about sixteen.

"Oh, I'm all right," said Ben. The car had bounced off the tree after it hit it and the only problem now was that it was stuck in the ditch. He put it in gear and pushed down on the accelerator. The rear wheels raced and the rubber whined like a buzz-saw. The car struggled like a captive in bonds but remained in place. There was a smell of burning rubber and of hot oil from the engine.

The two kids were cheerful, intelligent, and sympathetic. He wondered whether he or anybody else had ever been that young.

"You have to rock it," said the boy. "Put the shift lever in low and race it, then slam it in reverse, then low, then reverse again."

"You do it," said Ben. He got out of the car and left the

door open. "While you're in there, see if you can find my sunglasses. They're down on the floorboard somewhere." He began planning already how he was going to keep this news from Ethel, that he had crashed his car into a tree while under the influence of emotional stress. The first thing was to get this boy to drive him home to his house in Montecito. He didn't feel up to doing it himself.

157.

"I'm Ben Gavilan," he said. They were rolling along the coast highway through town, past the big Moreton Bay fig with its transients sleeping in its gnarled roots, the hotels and restaurants along the beach, and the bird refuge with its palms and its ponds. The half-naked boy, in his trunks and rubber sandals, sat at the wheel of the Mercedes and slipped it through traffic as though it had been his car for years. He said, "I'm Mikey."

From the back seat the girl said, "I'm—"

"No, don't let her say it. She's going to say she's Kathleen. That's really square. Everybody calls her Kitten."

Ben said, "Her name was McGill, but she called herself Lil, but everyone knew her as Nancy."

"Hey, that's an old Beatles song."

"Yes, how in the world could you know that? It was written before you were born."

"Oh, the Beatles are cool. Everybody knows who the Beatles are. You don't have to be from the Sixties to like the Beatles. I've got, you know, the White Album? I mean, I borrowed it from a friend of mine."

"Let's not get started on music," said Ben. "You probably like rock. I think it's God-awful. I like chamber music myself. Harpsichord, for example," he forced himself to say, feeling a sharp pain in his vitals."

"Whatever turns you on," said Mikey. "The thing about music is, whatever kind you like you're not hurting anybody listening to it. Like if you were in the Army killing people."

"Exactly," said Ben. "Make a left up there by the real estate office."

"Montecito? Wow."

"Join the Army," said Kitten. "Travel to exotic foreign countries. Meet fascinating people with interesting customs. And kill them."

"That's cool," said Ben. He felt it really was cool; that is, eloquent, succinct, and truthful. It was good being with Mikey and Kitten and it was nice talking their language. It was easy; it had a vocabulary of only about twenty words.

"A classy neighborhood," said Mikey.

"Take a right on this street. It's the fourth on the left, the New England house."

"Is that what you call it?" said Kitten. "I thought it was called Victorian."

"No, it's a Cape Cod cottage. Just turn in there and leave the car in the drive."

Mikey brought the car sharply to a stop with a chirp of tires. Luckily the damaged fender and window were on the right, on the side away from the house, so Cecilia and Peter wouldn't see them immediately. Maybe he could get them fixed before they noticed it.

"Gee, a real old-fashioned house," said Mikey. "That's cool."

They all got out and examined the place, Ben too as though he were seeing it for the first time, through their eyes. "Wow, you've got a pool," said Mikey.

"Yes, would you like a swim?" Ben reconnoitered the

situation with a military swiftness. Peter and Cecilia didn't seem to be home. Peter's car was gone, and there was no sign of Cecilia at the pool where she would be at this time of the afternoon, unless she was practising, and he didn't hear the harpsichord.

"That would be terrific."

"You've got your suits on."

"Oh yeah, we were walking to the beach."

They pushed their way through the willows to the pool, and the two kids looked around again. Ben remembered Cecilia's astute appraisal of the Cantamar when he first brought her there from Muir House. Kitten, in exactly the same way, took in the money like a beagle sniffing, with her hand on top of her hat to hold it on. Her black bikini could have been fitted into a cigarette box. She said, "Who lives in that little place in the back?"

"Actually I do. I own the whole place, but the Big House is rented to a young couple who are away right now. We share the pool."

"A lot of people run down being rich," said Kitten. "I think it's terrific."

"Say, what happened to your arm anyhow, Mr. Gavilan?"

"It was polio. I was the last person in New England to get it. Maybe in the whole United States."

"I had an uncle who played polio, but he fell off the horse and hurt his head."

"Oh dry up, Kitten, your jokes are so stupid."

"I'll bet your uncle was sore," said Ben. "He should have gone to see Dr. Sulk."

"Oh, that's awful!" said Kitten. She groaned. "Well, if you really mean it about the pool?" She kicked off her sandals and took off the straw hat and set it on the patio table. Then she flung out all four limbs and crashed into the pool like a corpse thrown out of a window. She came up with her mop of blond hair soggy around her head, and Mikey jumped in beside her, narrowly missing her.

He shook his head to throw his wet hair out of his eyes. "Why don't you come in too, Mr. Gavilan?"

"I'll go in and put on my suit."

In the Little House he rummaged around in the drawer for his old swimming trunks, the ones he had worn in the pool at Muir House. It seemed like a long time ago. His ancient genitals, which seemed to him like some object found in a museum, disappeared into the blue trunks with their yellow stripe on each side and their drawstring. He put on his golf hat, then he went into the tiny kitchen to see what he could offer Mikey and Kitten to drink. There was his scotch of course, some beer, and some white wine in the refrigerator. He thought of these two kids, so fresh and innocent, so naive with their veneer of toughness and world-knowledge, especially Kitten. It would be easy to seduce them with a wine cooler and start them on a life of sin. Instead he began searching to see if he could find some Cokes, which he never drank but kept in the house for other people. He finally found three cans on the floor at the bottom of the cupboard, rusty and discolored, the aluminum tops gray with age. They were warm, of course. Somewhere he had some paper cups. He found them, put in some ice, poured the three Cokes into them, and set them on a tray. He looked around for some potato chips or something. There was a half-full bag of taco chips. They were stale but they probably wouldn't notice. He put the bowl of taco chips on the tray too and carried the whole thing out to the pool. He was a nervous as a girl giving her first party. He desperately wanted to please these two children and he had only inadequate resources to do it.

Mikey was out of the pool, sitting on the tiled edge splashing his feet in the water, and Kitten was still swimming around in a circle. Drawing up her legs like a frog, she swam a lap underwater. She emerged in front of Ben and wheezed out a mouthful of air, and then disappeared under the surface again. Through the glassy fluid her shadow flicked along the wall and turned the corner at the end.

Ben set his offering down at the side of the pool. "Oh gee, thanks, Mr. Gavilan, that's terrific. Hey Kitten, Cokes."

Ben took off his hat and sunglasses and flung himself into the water in the same way that Kitten had, except that only three of his limbs stuck out and the right arm hung limply. The tepid water struck him with a shock; he coiled into a ball, stretched out his limbs, and began swimming. He and Kitten circled the pool like two figures in a Swiss clock; first he passed Mikey, then it was Kitten's turn, then he came around again. Kitten looked over her shoulder and giggled. He couldn't catch her but at least he could keep up with her. Mikey gazed curiously at his one-armed two-legged flutter.

Ben swam in a kind of nirvana. He was conscious of the caress of the water slipping past his body, the splash of foam around his face, and of the warmth of the late afternoon sun filtering through the pussy willows. He was happy being with Mikey and Kitten. He felt a powerful affinity, a pull in the blood, for these two fellow creatures he had encountered accidentally on the road in the middle of a minor disaster. He avidly sucked their youth, and they gave it willingly, with a giggle, as though it were a bad joke, and bad jokes were fun. Was there something erotic in the attraction he felt for them? Absolutely not, and no funny remarks, he told himself. He was beyond all that now, all passion and all egotism left behind him, burned away in sorrow and humiliation. He had broken through into a new realm of the dispassionate, of a love free from lust or selfishness, of a common participation in humanity. He felt that this new land he had discovered was terrific and cool and far out and wonderful, and the discovery of it left him very calm. So this is what it is to be old, he thought. It was not bad.

He wondered if Ilya had written this too as he had written everything else. The power of Ilya's sorcery, the power of the art he commanded, transcended the petty ego he had flaunted when he was on earth. It was all in Ilya's book that he had met Cecilia, that he had stolen her and brought her home, that he had had his year of rapture with her, that incredible gift, and that he had given her to Peter with a wrench that made every nerve in his body cry out. Ethel was in the book too, and Betsy. His humiliating encounter with Ethel, and his car crashing into the trees. Maybe even the two kids, floating in Ilya's mind before he had time to write them down. He knew now why Ilya had removed himself from the scene, because the story he had written was coming to an end.

Ahead of him, through his water-blurred eyes, he saw Kitten pulling herself out of the pool and going straight for her Coke. She sat down next to Mikey, and the two of them, with a reflex as natural as snails, reached out for each other and held hands. Ben got out too and sat on the tiled edge of the pool next to them, panting.

"What do you call that stroke, Mr. Gavilan?"

"The polio waltz. I could go even faster if I didn't have to tow that second arm around."

Kitten put on her round straw hat and pushed it down; under it her eyes disappeared into a shadow like a cave. She said, "I think you're a terrific swimmer."

"I had a girlfriend who used to live here with me," he said. "We used to swim in the pool. She had two arms and she was a good swimmer. But I could always catch her."

"Was she, like, your age?"

"No, like your age."

They considered this, exchanging a glance; they were clumsy at concealing their thoughts.

"But that was some time ago," said Ben. "I'm a lot older now."

The two of them were still communing silently over the situation. Something had changed a little in the atmosphere, only slightly, but he could detect it. After a mute glance at Kitten, Mikey said, "This has been great, Mr. Gavilan. But we have to take off now. We're meeting some guys at the beach."

"Can I take you somewhere? Oh I forgot, my car is broken."

The three of them laughed in good-natured appreciation of the joke. Good will filled the air again, after the moment of awkwardness when he told them about Cecilia.

"You can hitch a ride with somebody on the highway," said Ben.

Kitten put on one of her Buster Brown sandals. "Where's my other shoe?"

Ben found it for her under the patio table. When he handed it to her he couldn't help saying, "It's so small. It's like a child's shoe."

"I could have it bronzed," she giggled.

In a moment of brilliant recall, Ben remembered

something he had in the drawer of his desk in the Little House. It was a tiny leather baby shoe exactly like Kitten's but in miniature, with a worn round toe and a strap. He didn't remember how it had come into his possession or why he had kept it for so many years. Evidently his parents had never thought enough of him to have it bronzed, or perhaps they planned to have it bronzed but never got around to it. He felt an odd pang of something like grief, not for himself but for the strangeness of life, in which tiny things grew large, felt emotions as complex as a god's, and then passed away leaving no trace. It was not entirely an unpleasant feeling. "You'd better go," he told them, "if your friends are waiting for you." He knew he would not ask them to come back; the notion that these two creatures so different from himself could become his friends was a delusion that he put from his mind like a trick of vice. The fact that they had passed through his life, that they had stayed for an hour, was in itself a grace. That they would pass out of his life again was nothing. The phantasm of youth he had been pursuing was real. He felt a gratitude to something, to the universe or to the God he didn't believe in, for these things that had happened to him, for his grief, for his love, for his story that he himself did not understand, but perhaps Ilya would have.